Promise of the Black Monks

Robert E. Hirsch

W & B Publishers
USA

Promise of the Black Monks © All rights reserved by
Robert E. Hirsch

W & B Publishers

For information:
W & B Publishers
9001 Ridge Hill Street
Kernersville, NC 27284

www.a-argusbooks.com

ISBN: 9781942981602

Book Cover designed by Melissa Carrigee

Printed in the United States of America

Dedication

The human heart, alone, leads humanity through the darkness; offering shelter, solace and hope against the storm of man's own wickedness. This book is dedicated to those courageous, enduring souls on this earth who have made it their life's labor through selfless service to assist, protect and elevate others. In particular, I dedicate this book to each and every public educator in America. These altruistic, persistent souls continue to march forward on behalf of this nation's children despite thankless financial reward, ceaseless political manipulation and interference, media distortion and public misperception. Their goals, despite obstacles thrown in their path, are to share their love of knowledge, offer hope, and provide opportunity for all children, regardless of race, socio-economic background, intellectual or physical ability.

Acknowledgement

I wish to acknowledge Dr. Charles Smith, my college history professor at Cameron College in Lawton, Oklahoma (1968-71). He developed in me, at a lost point in life, an appreciation and love for European history that endures to this day. Long since retired, he was a talented historian/storyteller who delved into the human foibles, egos, and misjudgments of those great characters who have driven the compass of human history through the ages. Charles, I thank you profusely for the impact you made on me and others without even realizing what you had accomplished. Thus, great teaching so quietly leaves its enduring mark.

Prologue

Peter the Hermit

Riding up and down the rows of crowded market stalls on his donkey, the wild-eyed little monk harangued all in his path. Bare-boot and wearing sack-cloth, his beard trailed to his waist and long, filthy hair tumbled in knots below his shoulders. Acquaintances swore he had not washed his feet or hair in years, claiming he refused all meat, fruit and bread—wine and fish comprising his only sustenance.

"Wash the Church clean, you damned sinners!" he shouted hoarsely. "Excommunicate bastard clerics who house concubines and have multiple wives! Imprison false priests stealing from your diocese, picking your pockets while preaching piety!"

Known first by a smattering of early adherents as Peter of Amiens, this little evangelist monk came to be called 'Peter the Hermit' as his reputation had spread. Increasingly, he was looked upon by believers as a divine light placed on earth by God Himself to lead the dispossessed toward salvation. But men of such unusual thread also draw detractors. Accordingly, the Hermit's rabid fervor for God coupled with his inviolable belief that God spoke to him directly made him known derisively in many quarters as 'Kuku Peter'.

On this particular day Kuku Peter was preaching in the Paris marketplace sprawling before the great Cathedral of Saint Étienne on the island splitting the Seine River known as Île de la Cité. With the fever of a man possessed, he was blistering Church corruption. But to many in the market, the Hermit was more of an oddity than an evangelist. Now in his second week there, he had been sleeping at night by the cathedral like some misplaced vagabond. But men of extreme belief are not easily daunted, so he cared not that he enjoyed greater success amongst the poor of smaller villages, and was now facing big-city apathy and ridicule. It but spurred him on.

Urging his donkey forward, he went to the section of the market that harbored vendors he loathed most—the relic sellers. His fiery eyes darting in their sockets with angry, circuitous motion, he pointed first at one vendor, then another, crying, "Shame! Profiting from the bones, hair and teeth of our holy saints! Tear down these stalls, you money whores! Repent for time is short! It's later than you think!"

The relic vendors ignored him until his attacks became so vociferous their tolerance dissolved—he was disrupting business. "Get the hell out, you imbecile!" they began shouting. "We'll beat your ass, you hairy moron!"

"You'll burn in Hell for that crooked coin!" the Hermit retorted. "God's watching you and marking it in his Book!"

As the Hermit hoped, his rant began to draw attention...and laughter. No matter—laughter drew larger crowds, and larger crowds drew more ears, which would precipitate into saving more souls.

Then, in the midst of his tirade, a blast of trumpets sounded from the Grand Pont Bridge.

Aha, they arrive, he thought, kicking his donkey in the flanks and making for the cathedral. As he left, the crowd shrugged, disappointed that their amusement had evaporated. Even those vendors who had cursed him realized that, with his departure, the crowds would disperse, because wherever he went, Kuku Peter commanded attention.

Those he came upon were simply unable to turn away; their numbers invariably multiplied as he launched into frenzied, charismatic preaching. And once within his grasp, it was impossible to break away from his frightening sermons so ceaselessly peppered with shouting, pacing and wild gyrations. Nonetheless, regardless of his spellbinding rhetorical genius and ability to mesmerize the poor, Peter the Hermit was roundly despised by the nobility. They ridiculed him bitterly because he demonized the excesses of aristocratic debauchery and greed. Worse yet, he brashly told noblemen to their faces that they would soon be burning in Hell for eternity. The high clergy of the Catholic Church also considered the strange, itinerant little preacher a vexation, feeling it dangerous that a man lacking ecclesiastical position might carry more sway with the poor masses than a bishop. Anomalies of such grain threatened the 'order of things'.

Peter had probably received some form of scholastic education, as evidenced by his sharp wit and ability to incite passionate, even hysterical responses as he preached. His incendiary flow of words had the same effect on listeners as 'sparks on bone-dry tinder'. It was also said he had spent some time as a soldier, which might explain how he would manage, in the future, to lead an army of 50,000 peasants armed with only forks and staffs on foot across the entire continent of Europe to battle Muslims in the First Holy Crusade. Indeed, to believers, everything he said seemed divine. Many even pulled threads from his tunic or plucked the hair from his donkey, treating these keepsakes as holy relics.

"I'm commanded by God to fish for men!" he proclaimed from the back of his donkey, tirelessly working one village after another. "I will lead you not to prosperity, but to holy salvation! God has told me this directly!"

That a man of such humble means and filthy appearance could muster such a following would seem improbable, yet the Hermit's following multiplied each year amongst the poor, the ignorant and the superstitious, of which there were many. By the year 1066 his primary passion was preaching church reform, for he was certain the Catholic Church was sinking into a morass of corruption and moral collapse. Interestingly, though they refuted him, the Benedictine monks were equally steeped in reforming the abuses of the Church at this same time.

Now, as Kuku Peter prodded his donkey toward the sound of trumpets nearing Saint Étienne, a new fire consumed him. Opportunity had arrived and lay just ahead. He planned to intercept two visiting church dignitaries who were in Paris to audit the parishes of the city. Today, they would be celebrating mass at Saint Etienne with the capital's high bishops and archbishops.

The Hermit's first target was the celebrated monk, Hugh of Semur, abbot of Cluny Monastery in southern France. Cluny was the hotbed of Benedictine reform. And Abbot Hugh was the most renowned cleric of the continent, eclipsing even Pope Alexander II. The second target was the young archdeacon of Rheims, a tall religious named Odo de Lagery who was one of the most revered clerics in all France.

"Here they come!" the Hermit shouted, frantically steering his donkey toward the cathedral steps.

Escorted by a contingent of royal guards, the two famous clerics were accompanied by an army of Parisian bishops adorned in their finest clerical garments and brocades while carrying bejeweled bishop crosiers. Standing apart, Hugh of Semur wore only the black, hooded robe of the Benedictines, and Odo de Lagery wore a simple archdeacon robe. Nonetheless, the two garnered far more adulation and applause than the other high clerics combined.

As the crowd parted to allow the religious train to advance, hundreds shouted the names of the two celebrated men, begging for blessings. Hugh of Semur and Odo de Lagery acknowledged them with waves and signage of the cross as the other bishops marched forward in silence, their expressions dour and grim. Odo and Hugh were smiling and interacting with the burgeoning crowd as it tightened around them, clamoring and reaching to touch their robes or their person. "Hail, Hugh of Semur!" the masses cried. "Hail, Odo de Lagery!"

Maneuvering through the mob, the royal guards formed two files before the cathedral entrance, facing each other stiffly with lances at the vertical. Two ushers stood before the cathedral, who as Hugh and Odo approached, opened its massive doors.

Shouting, the Hermit kicked his donkey in the flanks and blocked the entrance. "Stop! I've been waiting for your visit to Paris!" he shouted. "I've come to beg your help!"

Three guards broke ranks, knocking the Hermit from his mount, wrestling him to the ground beneath a flurry of fists and boots. Another guard grabbed the stotting donkey as it kicked and brayed with fury. In response, those in the crowd despising authority began to object. "Leave him alone! He's not harming anyone, you bastards!"

In the midst of this growing dissension, Odo de Lagery stepped forward, waving off the guards. "Hold there!" he shouted as his imposing shadow fell over them. "This man is a monk, it appears! Let him up."

Released, the Hermit stood, dusting himself indignantly. "Hands off, you piss ants!" he cried, pointing furiously at the guards who had bloodied his lip and nose. "Uniformed heathens! How dare you lay hands on a holy man? Can't you see that I'm *divine*?"

This generated guffaws from the crowd, even eliciting a wry smile from Odo de Lagery himself. "So then, Brother in Christ," said Odo, "what were you saying as you so dramatically made your entrance?"

Not expecting to be addressed with courtesy, the Hermit stepped back, swiping trickles of blood from his lip and chin. "I've come to seek your help," he said.

"Help?"

"Yes," the Hermit replied, keeping an eye to the agitated guards. "Your help against the Church."

"*Against the Church?*" echoed Odo, exchanging glances with Hugh of Semur.

"Aye," the Hermit replied, his eyes regaining their fire. "I've five times now petitioned Archbishop Moulin, right here in your very company, to ban the sale of relics in the market. But then, to my amazement, I learned that he himself takes a cut of the proceeds!"

"Oh?" said Odo, casting a glance at Archbishop Moulin.

The archbishop did not return Odo's look, but only glared at the Hermit with scorn.

"And those two standing right there, Bishops Montin and Bruyère," pointed the Hermit, "they keep a stable of flesh-pots not four blocks from here! I've been watching traffic going in and out of that whore-house for weeks now—to include priests of the diocese!"

Odo and Hugh exchanged another glance, their eyes drawing down to slits. "*True?*" asked Odo, addressing the two bishops the Hermit had identified.

Neither replied.

"There's more," said the Hermit. "I've come also to report Philippe, the King of France!"

Many in the crowd knew these accusations to be true and nodded with assent. But upon hearing this bold charge against the King, some issued gasps and backed away. Yet others twittered with snickering, thinking the accusation a jest.

"Did I just now hear you correctly?" asked Hugh, stepping closer, certain he had misunderstood; his hearing had begun to fail him a bit over the past year. "Did you say you wished to report the *King?*"

"Aye, I did," snapped the Hermit, setting his legs apart, crossing his arms. "He's selling religious office with impunity, for profit!" Casting a finger at the entourage of bishops and archbishops, he added, "Many in this illustrious company of fakers here purchased their bishoprics at exorbitant prices from King Philippe. And some of these imbeciles don't even speak Latin or know their prayers! Worse yet, these thieves then press parishioners mercilessly for alms day after day, only to fill their personal treasuries! Meanwhile, the King continues to auction off high Church office, piling up his own sinful hoard."

"This man is mad!" declared Archbishop Moulin, tapping his crosier angrily against the cobbled pavement.

"Aye, a loon!" proclaimed Bishop Bruyère. "And he's apparently taken a blow to the head at some point. Look at him—filthy as a field hog rooting in his own defecation."

"Oh, which is far better than shitting on the poor, as you do!" retorted the Hermit.

"Just smell him!" barked Bishop Montin, pinching his nose in mockery.

This prompted the guards to surge forward, as if by signal, and begin dragging the Hermit off. Kicking and screaming, he turned, shouting, "It's all true! Our clerics have sunken into depravity, and you're the only two men who can do anything about it! Step forward, Hugh of Semur, I implore you! Odo de Lagery, save our Church!"

Laughing, the two ushers motioned Odo and Hugh forward again, as behind them the bishops clucked with satisfaction, trading derogatory comments about the wild little man who had delayed them.

In the distance, the Hermit's fading voice could still be heard. "I'm not done here!" he wailed. "You'll hear more from me!"

Chapter One

The Beginning

T he Year 1066 was a year of destiny, a moment in
time that would alter the face of England and impact
Western Europe's political and social structure for
centuries to come. It began on January 4th with the death of
England's Saxon king, Edward the Confessor. Leaving no
heir, his passing opened the question of succession amongst
three separate claimants: Harold Godwinson the Saxon,
King Harald Hadrada of Norway, and Duke William, Bastard of Normandy. Losing no time, and wishing to keep
England under Saxon control, Harold Godwinson took the
throne only two days after King Edward's death, with the
support of England's representative body, the Witenage-
mot.

Haley's comet, seen as a celestial omen, reached per-
ihelion on March 20th, stirring a sense of dread and fore-
boding amongst both the superstitious and the spiritual. Exactly six months later, King Harald Hadrada of Norway invaded England, insistent that he was the rightful heir to
England's throne. His formidable Viking force was defeated by Harold Godwinson and the Saxons at Stamford
Bridge on September 25th. Even as this battle raged, William the Bastard of Normandy was preparing to launch his
own invasion of England. Three days following the Saxon
victory at Stamford Bridge, the Bastard crossed the Channel and landed his vast Norman army on England's shores

at Pevensey. Eighteen days later, his Norman force clashed with the Saxons in one of the bloodiest, most momentous struggles of Medieval history, the Battle of Hastings.

But as 1066 opened and the death of King Edward the Confessor was being announced throughout England, those in Normandy and France had no way of anticipating what lay ahead.

So it was in this ominous year that Lady Asta sat with her hand on her pregnant belly within a manor north of Saint-Germain-en-Laye, tucked between the French city of Paris and the border of Normandy. For her, war, invasion and bloodletting were as distant as the stars. She sat encircled by her corps of tutor nuns as they listened to her recite the Pater Noster in Latin, which was the only language in which this prayer was uttered. As the nuns nodded approvingly, Lady Asta then gave a brief recitation of the prayer's significance, first in Danish, then Saxon, German, and finally in Spanish. Just as she finished, her voice caught, as if upon a thorn, and she wilted on her stool.

"The baby comes!" cried Sister Angelina, eldest of the nuns, grasping Lady Asta with her right arm while with the left scattering the younger nuns like a flock of chickens. "Prepare the bedding!"

"Mielikki!" groaned Lady Asta, her eyes watering as the pang within her womb nearly took her to her feet despite Sister Angelina's steadying embrace. "I want Mielikki!" she wailed.

"No!" scolded the old nun. "Mielikki clings to her pagan past, Asta. Though she's been your nursemaid and keeper since birth, God will frown at her presence here as He bestows upon you this firstborn child!"

"Mielikki!" Asta cried, pushing the old nun away. "Where are you?"

Mielikki was in the hallway, having stationed herself there to avoid the nuns. Hearing her Lady's cry, she threw her knitting aside and burst into the room, shouldering Sister Angelina aside. Dragging Asta to the bed, Mielikki threw her on her back and flung the bottom of her tunic up over her waist. "Water and linen rags!" she barked, never looking up.

The nuns stood mute and motionless, their French sensibilities offended by this coarse middle-aged woman from the black forests of Finland; they despised her because of Lady Asta's dependence upon her. Despite Mielikki's recent conversion, the nuns knew she still practiced the black art associated with her Finnish ancestry, predicting the future by rolling bones, following the swirl of clouds or reading the flow of menstrual blood.

"Dammit!" cried Mielikki. "Did you hooded bitches not hear me?! Get the water and linen before she bleeds to death!"

The three younger nuns stood frozen, exchanging glances of fright until Sister Angelina gestured to obey. As they scattered, the old nun's own feet remained nailed to the floor as she glared with seething disapproval at Mielikki who was laboring over Lady Asta, whispering unintelligible bursts of Nordic into her ear.

Five hours later, the baby still had not come and Mielikki, like Asta, was bathed in sweat. Mielikki had delivered many infants over the years, but now sensed something was sorely amiss. She said nothing to reveal this suspicion, but in that secret backwater of dread where one ensconces private fears, she perceived that something extraordinarily tragic was transpiring before her, within Lady Asta's womb. *Asta will not survive this delivery*, she thought, pulling suddenly away from between Asta's writhing thighs…either that or the baby shall die…or we shall lose them both!

Asta's profuse bleeding was now soaking the entire breadth of the bedding; her screams so piercing that the youngest nun fled to a corner to wretch while another fell to her knees, weeping. Sister Angelina, whose tight-lipped scowl had never slackened, began to tremble as a cold finger touched her heart. *No human could hemorrhage such vast amounts of blood and survive.* "Oh, mercy, dear Savior," she whispered, slipping her fingers into her habit sleeve, extracting prayer beads as tears began to stream in rivulets down the crevices of her aged cheeks. "Do not take Asta, this gentle and beautiful angel, from our midst!"

Mielikki, refusing to abandon hope, resumed her position between Asta's thighs and was now forcing her fingers into Asta's womb, groping to locate the tiny features of the unborn infant within. "Asta! PUSH!" she cried. "P-U-S-H, Dear, for your very life!"

Watching as Mielikki's hands disappeared into Asta's flesh, Sister Angelina wailed with horror, "*My God, Mielikki, Asta is but a child of thirteen-years-of-age!* You're tearing the poor girl's insides apart!!"

Mielikki heard nothing as she had finally located the infant's head. Tightening her fingers, she grasped it and extricated it to the neck. As she did this, she suddenly witnessed the infant's startling grey eyes staring at her. Simultaneously, Asta's womb issued a gushing stream of dark blood filled with tiny pulsating lines of black flesh. Terrified, Mielikki drew back, releasing the infant's skull which was draped with dark afterbirth, looking much like a cloaked hood. This was a rare and terrible sign. Trembling, Mielikki stroked the wanton flesh and declared, "The Devil's Caul! Curse of ages! We must kill this child before it breathes life! Otherwise he will be the devil's vessel, haunted by spirits and caught between two worlds!"

Asta, so lost to the horrific agony of birthing the child, saw and heard none of this. But Sister Angelina, confronted by Mielikki's wild ravings, advanced toward the bed and knocked Mielikki from it. "We'll do no such thing you pagan whore!" she shouted. Then the old nun threw herself between Asta's legs, and seeing the infant's head emerged, grasped it, pulling with every muscle her frail old frame could summon.

Seconds later, the infant's torso broke free. Shuddering as it gulped air with the urgency of a beached fish, the infant's face twisted into a root and issued a string of terrified bleats, announcing its arrival upon the earth.

Sister Angelina prepared a clean knife to remove the membrane. Placing a small incision in the membrane across the nostrils so the child could breathe, she carefully unlooped the bulk of it from behind the ears. Next she gingerly peeled back the hideous murk from the skin and gently rubbed the fresh skin with a soft linen cloth. Satisfied, she held the infant high. "It's a boy!" she exclaimed, displaying his shriveled penis.

Asta heard this, but could scarcely make out the features of her newborn son. She was so spent she could barely feel the pulse of her own depleted heart. "Yes," she mumbled in a willowy, disjointed voice, "God is merciful and has spared us both. I shall name him…Tristan."

The other nuns, seeing the newborn and hearing his cries, swarmed the bed, encircling Asta and the baby. But Mielikki, having gathered herself from the floor and retreated to a distant divan, refused to come near. She sat there mute, shaking as though her body had fallen victim to seizures. Her eyes were no longer following Asta and the newborn, nor was she even any longer in that same chamber with Asta and the nuns, but in the nether world, pursuing shadowy necromancy and superstitions engrained into her Nordic clan over generations of isolation in the distant, forgotten reaches of frozen Finland.

Ah, but 'the Devil's Caul', she thought. *Those strange, aberrant black lines of pulsating blood and flesh that accompanied this child's entrance into light…what twisted trail of tragedy and disaster do they prophesize?*

"Nay," she said aloud, her eyes rolling back in their sockets until nothing showed but the whites, "twas not God's mercy that spared this child, but some other intent!"

Chapter Two

Seven Years Later: Abandoned in the Year 1073

Dawn's light had not yet risen when Lady Asta leaned against the carved stone arch of the window before continuing to speak to her son. She toyed a moment with the tapestry covering the opening to shut out the spring wind.

From his seat on the hearth, the seven-year-old boy surveyed his mother as one surveys the subtle details of a Greek master's finest sculpture. He had learned early that men dissolved in her presence, like the trembling mouse frozen in the serpent's thrall.

Her long flowing hair was thick and fair, more pallid even than the icy Nordic moon. This tumble of argentine tresses cascaded gracefully to her waist like rich clusters of harvested flax. When she turned at certain angles in the light of the horn-lantern, spontaneous specks of shimmering silver seemed to gleam like constellations of tiny distant stars backlighting the galaxies. He lost himself there for a moment, then quickly reverted his attention to her eyes to avoid the inevitable reprimand she would lodge his way for losing focus. The striking gray clarity of her eyes was glacial, nearly startling, and he did not wish to incur their disapproval. They haughtily announced her Danish ancestry with a finality that was unquestionable; a resolve that could not be shaken. Her son, too, had these same eyes.

"Tristan, you do remember your father, Lord Roger de Saint-Germain?" she asked.

The boy thought a moment. "Not well, Mother."

"I suppose not, you've only seen him four times in your life." She fingered the tapestry then, running her fingernail through the gardens delicately woven into the lush fabric. "Il est mort," she said without expression. "He was executed one month ago…beheaded in the square of Rouen with ten of his vassals for violating the law of Liege Homage. You do know what that is, n'est-ce pas, Tristan?"

"Yes, Mother, the oath of fealty," the boy said, sitting erect. "All vassal-lords in France must pledge allegiance to King Philippe, and those in Normandy to Duke William the Bastard, who is now also King of England since defeating King Harold at Hastings." This precise response was delivered crisply, reflecting academic recitation rather than conversation.

Asta raised a single eyebrow, nodding with deliberation—her signal that her son had adequately retained the information fed to him by his teacher-nuns. "I have spared you this information about your father until now because I have been trying to…sort things out. He, this past year, conspired with King Philippe and Count Robert the Frisian of Flanders against the Bastard of Normandy. The King of France, though he himself devised this conspiracy against the Bastard, turned around and sanctioned your father's execution, claiming it was indeed a violation of the treaty between the French and the Normans. Moreover, he denied any knowledge of the plot. So Roger de Saint-Germain's thirst for power, in the end, circled around to engineer his own downfall, and, subsequently, *ours*. We are ruined, must be gone from this manor by tomorrow. To further disguise his own deceptions and smooth the road with Normandy, King Philippe has confiscated our lands as a play of good faith to the Bastard even though your father was French and his estate stands in France, not Normandy. Our property has now been forfeited to Lord Letellier.

The boy's brows drew together. "The same Lord Letellier whose life they say Father saved during the Battle of Hastings?"

"Yes, the same. Letellier and your father were among the French who reinforced the Bastard's Norman invasion of England, lured by promises of land and plunder. They were friends, yet Letellier is among those who betrayed your father, so let his name burn in your memory." Here she moved beyond the tapestry and stared a moment into the horn-lantern. "Tonight you will sleep in a place you do not know, on your way to a new home. It is important that you watch over little Guillaume."

"Yes, Mother," the boy said, a spot of flush appearing high on his cheekbones. How children sense the arrival of the momentous before its pronouncement has always been a mystery, but young Tristan felt tugging at him that inner twinge that foreshadowed an upheaval more sinister even than the loss of property and position. He braced himself, anticipating the hammer's dreadful fall as Asta continued.

"But your father's brother, Lord Desmond DuLac, is…interceding. Seven years after Hastings, the Bastard finally issued your uncle his promised reward, an earldom and a rebellious Saxon's estate in England. Such is war. The Saxons lost their country, the Bastard stole a crown, and your uncle has become wealthy beyond his abilities. Though rumors circulate that Desmond DuLac may have been complicit in your father's betrayal, he has now returned from England and asked my hand in marriage. I have accepted. Furthermore—"

"B-but, you have never *approved* of Uncle Desmond," Tristan stammered, confounded.

"A fine choice of words, Tristan," Asta sighed. "What you mean is that I *despise* Desmond DuLac. I do, but no more so than I did your father. I now despise life also, but you see that I choose to live, because Dieu le veut,

God wills it. I will be leaving with Desmond DuLac for his estates in England this afternoon. We intend—"

"W-will Guillaume and I not be going with you, Mother?" the boy said with controlled urgency, his fingers knotting themselves together in his lap.

"Do not interrupt, Tristan," said Asta in that frigid, flat tone common among her people, the Danes, even in times of eminent turmoil. "No, you and Guillaume will not be going. Your uncle refuses you. He and your father hated each other. Desmond champions the Bastard, and Roger tried to unseat the Bastard. Born of the same womb, their mutual greed led them on disparate paths. Such is the way of men. But I am a woman, and though I live at the mercy of men, I will not now wallow in the mud amongst hard scrabbling peasants, nor am I willing to live in the filth of the townspeople. Therefore, I must remarry well, and quickly. But know, Tristan, I will also not allow a lost, miserable existence for you and Guillaume. Consequently, I have—"

"B-but what—"

"Tristan, if you interrupt just once more, I will send you from this room without the courtesy of an explanation on this, our final day together."

Tristan stared at her, unable to absorb these particular words. "Our final day?"

Turning, she stared at him sternly. "Tristan, you are beginning to give the appearance of the unnerved. I have taught you to listen, to weigh and measure thoughtfully before speaking, to not give away your position, ever."

Tristan closed his eyes, collecting himself, even though his heart was no longer thumping in his chest, but racing down the tortuous trail of supposition like some frightened rabbit. "Yes, Mother," he said dutifully.

"You may be confused at this moment," she continued, "but understand that none of this is my fault. I assign full blame for this travesty to the foolishness of men. They fight over the scraps of the earth, lust over the women of others, spoil and pillage all before them, and forget God until time for ceremony or the arrival of their own death. My hope is that you and Guillaume do not follow their ignorant course, which is why I have taught you since birth to read, to write, to speak Spanish, Italian, Latin, German and my own tongue of the Danish. I never want you to forget the Nordic tradition, or that you were born of high Danish blood. Forget your father's damnable French blood! It was neither your fault nor mine."

"Yes, Mother."

"If not for the political ruin of my father, you and Guillaume would be future high lords, and I, perhaps, a duchess. I was until last month at least a lady, but the men around me have altered the compass. It is a bitter medicine. My husband was too greedy to sit still, and my father too pure to withstand the machinations of intrigue."

"You have never spoken of your father," said Tristan, his curiosity pricked.

"Guntar the Mace," replied Asta, slipping into a reminiscent vein. "He was a lifelong brother-in-arms to the Bastard, carrying his standard and serving as his war counselor. But your grandfather was honest and spoke right, always. And William the Bastard, because he was birthed in France and calls himself a Norman, forgot his Danish roots. In his fog, he surrounded himself with the French, and even now thinks himself to be a refined Frenchman. Oh, but I learned well from my father's downfall; all brought on by clever French criminals in the high court of William of Normandy."

"But what caused your father's fall, Mother?"

"Generations ago, the Danes who settled here abandoned their culture and adopted the life of the French. The Bastard is no more Danish now than is the King of France. As Duke of Normandy, he thought it wise for the Normans to marry the French, to seal treaties and quell revolt. He one day announced my marriage to a Frenchman, your father, Roger de Saint-Germain. My father strongly opposed it because I was only twelve and Roger was forty. But the French manipulated Guntar's defense of me, his daughter, into a violation of fealty, and convinced the Bastard it was treason. My father was beheaded for the future of peace. So much for the Bastard's loyalty. For men, loyalty fades when plunder comes into view."

Tristan thought a moment, as a light broke over his brow. "So," he said, "my father opposed the Bastard and lost his life, and your father supported the Bastard, yet lost his life just the same?"

Asta looked at her son, nodding, as she lifted a single eyebrow. "Yes, you see the absurdity of this analogy, which is why I have taught you since birth not to parade your feelings or expose your position to others. It only invites treachery and the loss of advantage. Your younger brother, Guillaume, is not quite so clever. I will no longer be there to direct him, so I now leave this to you. You are more analytical, like me, and Guillaume, poor little soul, is more trusting, like my father." Then she softened a moment. "Does that not please you just a bit, Tristan, that you are strong like me?"

A slight smile began to creep up a corner of the boy's mouth, but he threw it into check. "Of course, Mother."

"Good boy," Asta said, content that Tristan's response indicated a resolve not to be entrapped by flattery, even if it flowed from the tongue of his own mother. "Tomorrow morning, you and Guillaume will depart. I have hired an oxman who is returning south to Burgundy. Orla and others of my Danish Guard will accompany you to the monastery of Cluny. It will be your new home."

The boy slumped, wishing to object. In the end, he humbly nodded. "Surely we are not to be monks, are we, Mother?"

Hearing this, Asta's frigid eyes grew intense, an action that Tristan interpreted as a faltering. Her expression suddenly seemed to reveal some secret inner journey that was creating in her great hardship at that instant. Then the look disappeared as quickly as it had come, which confirmed to Tristan that he really knew nothing whatsoever of his mother.

"There are but two paths to choose for the promising young men of this world, the cross or the sword. I send you to Cluny to continue the learning I have bred into you since the day you could first speak. We live in a dark time of ignorance and violence, and the monastery is the only place to acquire a high education. There are only two ways out of blackness, Tristan, through learning and through God. At Cluny, you will have both. This, then, is what I leave to you and Guillaume—the promise of the Black Monks."

As Asta fixed an unblinking stare at her son, a funereal silence fell between them. It was a sensitive and trembling moment, rooted in the knowledge that two people of blood who loved and adored each other would be parting, not knowing when or whether they might ever see each other again. Although neither Asta's nor Tristan's expression changed, each was in their own heart swimming against a devastating tide of despair. He looked at her longingly, with dog-like devotion. She moved closer to the hearth where he sat, looking down upon him with adoration. She attempted to smile, but the smile did not set. After a moment, a slight flush began to color her face as her lip trembled the smallest bit.

Tristan examined this occurrence with curious eyes, unwilling to believe that this strong, beautiful woman who had brought him into the world and spent every waking moment preparing and training him, was soon to vanish from his existence. Hurt, he wished he could, just once, pierce that impenetrable wall behind which she entombed herself. Mutely, with desperation, he searched her eyes with one final sweep of anticipation, hoping that in a moment of weakness she might change her mind about everything, leaving their life intact. But the search was fruitless, so he sagged, dispirited, as a sudden and profound loneliness invaded his soul, one that would never, until his final days, dissipate.

"I will miss you, Mother," he said quietly, remaining motionless at the hearth, fiercely fighting back tears even as they began to well up and slowly stream down his cheek-bones.

"Indeed, Tristan" said Asta, her face strained, "I will surely miss you also." She turned then, walking out of the room, leaving him sobbing quietly.

Chapter Three:

1073: Odo de Lagery and Hugh of Semur

Odo de Lagery was born of high nobility at Chatillons-sur-Marne in the province of Champagne in 1042. To the fury of his father, Odo abandoned his noble roots as a young man and turned to God, being appointed canon in the important diocese of Rheims. Shortly thereafter, he became archdeacon of Rheims, serving as an ordained cleric appointed by the Bishop of Rheims. His commission was administration of the entire diocese, which included over-seeing finances, collections, construction, recruitment and policy.

Wishing to devote himself yet even more to God, Odo left this position and joined the Benedictine order. At age twenty-eight he relocated to the Cluny Monastery in Burgundy in 1070 to join Hugh of Semur who was serving there as abbot. Hugh was twenty years senior to Odo, and had come from the wealthiest noble stock of Burgundy. Like Odo's father, Hugh's father was displeased at Hugh taking up the cross rather than upholding family heraldry. This common bond between Odo and Hugh did much to cement their intimate, lifelong relationship. As well, it provided both men a profound understanding of the mentality of the wealthy and powerful, which would help them both navigate the treacherous waters of international intrigue and politics in which they operated throughout their brilliant careers.

When Odo arrived, Hugh capitalized on Odo's talents as a logistician by appointing him 'claustral prior' of the sprawling Cluny operation. Odo's duties included overseeing thousands of acres of farmlands, running a massive infirmary to treat the poor and ailing, and managing a thriving pilgrimage trade supported by the Abbey of Cluny; the largest, most majestic cathedral of Western Europe, producing a thriving source of revenue and attracting tens of thousands of generous visitors each year.

Cluny monastery was considered a center of light by the people of Europe in an age of darkness, and was deeply steeped in a rigorous daily ritual of prayer by all 200 monks in residence. It was also the acknowledged epicenter for those wishing to achieve the highest education that could be attained in Western Europe. Seats for this selective education were restricted to Benedictine novices and monks, and the fortunate sons of high ranking French nobility.

Having just completed his third year as claustral prior, Odo was completing the annual audit of Cluny with Abbot Hugh.

"Oh, but fortunate we are that you came our direction," said Hugh. "You have greatly enhanced our treasury, enabling us to send money and resources south to fight the Moors in Spain, amongst other important political projects."

"God's work, not mine," replied Odo. "But tell, how goes the Reconquista in Spain against the Muslims?"

"Like the tide I suppose, in and out. By tiny increments, our Spanish knights are regaining lost territory from the heathens. We are doing far better against Islam than our Greek Orthodox brothers of the Byzantine Empire to the east. Since losing the Battle of Manzikert two years ago, they have ceded the entirety of Asia Minor now to the Turks." Shaking his head, Hugh sighed. "Such turbulent times, these. So much bloodletting in every quarter of the continent."

"Ah, fortis fortuna adiuvat," quipped Odo. "Fortune favors the brave. And there is no shortage of bravery on this earth, because there is no shortage of greed. Thus, the bloodletting. Everyone wishes to own everything now—the Muslims, the Normans, the Germans. But a ray of hope, I spent time with the visiting Benedictines from Engand last week and they claim the Saxon rebellions in England have finally ended."

"Oh, but at such a dreadful cost, Odo! Since defeating the Saxons at Hastings, the Bastard has ruthlessly outlawed the Saxon language and imposed Norman law. In the north of England where the rebellions were the most heated, he declared the 'Harrying of the North', which was his excuse to raze and burn. Norman Christians slaughtering Saxon Christians. And don't be fooled, rebellion still simmers there. And, what happened in England has now taken root in Germany."

"Still no chance of peace between King Heinrich and the German Saxon princes?"

"No, the bloodletting has resumed."

"Well, let us pray for the Saxon princes then, for King Heinrich is no friend of the Vatican," said Odo. "He continues to usurp Church authority by selling high Church office to the highest bidder, just like our own King Philippe. Parishioners then end up with unqualified, incompetent clerics, which throws mud on the Church. The Vatican needs to make a stronger stand against these kings and their investiture practices, I say."

Hugh smiled skeptically. "Pope Alexander is powerless to do anything about either Heinrich or Philippe, so the abuses will continue."

"Powerless, Hugh, or lacks the will?"

"Oh, but you cut to the bone, eh?" Hugh chortled. "Alexander is old and frail. Perhaps the next pope will have a stronger constitution." He scratched his head then and added, "You know, what we need is someone with your mind and diplomacy, and Peter the Hermit's audacity."

"Peter the Hermit?" exclaimed Odo. "Surely not!"

"No, not Peter the Hermit himself, just someone with his *audacity*."

"Hugh, since meeting him seven years ago on the steps of Saint Étienne, I have had the misfortune of encountering him on other occasions. A crack-pot! It's a miracle he has thus far avoided being lynched."

"Ah, poor fellow," said Hugh, crossing himself. "He simply refuses to collar that sharp tongue of his! But enough about the Hermit. How was your trip to Rouen?"

"Interesting, I suppose, but tragic, too."

"Oh?"

"I witnessed a series of the Bastard's executions while there. I also happened to meet one of the unfortunate widows, a certain Lady Asta de Saint-Germain. Her husband was beheaded for treason. Fascinating woman, though, striking in appearance, as well as in spirit. By the way, I agreed to take her sons in at Cluny to be educated."

"But treason translates into confiscation of titles, land and property. Surely this woman now lacks all means of affording the education of her sons here."

"No," replied Odo, a strange light entering his eyes, "she assured me adequate alms will be provided. Not revealing the details of his confidential conversation with the woman, he added, "I'm looking forward to meeting the boys, the older one in particular. She told me he is an intellectual wonder at only seven."

"Ho," sniped Hugh, "doting mothers always laud the fruit of their womb!" He grinned a bit then. "Surely you did not swallow that bait, eh?"

"I know how mothers are. Mine was the same. Yet, I believe this woman for some reason. But then, we shall see." Standing, he moved to the door. "It's nearly time for evening prayer and the novices will be waiting on me. Are you still leaving for Italy in the morning?"

"Yes, Lord Franzio is expecting a shipment of our wine and wishes to make another major contribution to our treasury."

"Ah, then enjoy the mountains, Hugh, and be safe." Odo smiled.

Making his way to chapel, Odo could not help but think of the look of Lady Asta's clear grey eyes at the moment the ax had fallen across the neck of her husband. They had been cold, showing no emotion. But an hour later, as she spoke of her sons, a single tear streamed down each of her cheeks, as though representing each of the sons she was about to surrender. Still, after witnessing her glacial expression during the beheading of her husband, Odo would have thought she lacked all feeling for anyone.

Chapter Four

The Road

E h alors, venez, hop aboard, you two boys," called
the oxman. "It's late afternoon already and we've
yet to part!" Lifting his young passengers onto the
seat, he then signaled to the five horsemen sitting astride
their mounts.

They were five of forty Danes who had been assigned
to protect Lady Asta since birth by her father, Guntar the
Mace. Heavily armed, sword and dagger at the belt, ax and
hammer at the saddle, their loyalty to her was unshakeable.
After delivering her sons to Burgundy, they would be rejoining her and the other members of her Guard in England.
Their continued service to Asta was most displeasing to her
new husband, Desmond DuLac, but Asta's stand on this
issue had been unmovable. "They are my blood and family,
and the last men left in this life that I trust," she had told
him coldly. "You have sent my sons from me, but should
you send my Guard and their families away, there will be
no marriage."

These men were fair skinned, far larger in girth and
stature than the French, and carried that brutish appearance
common to Nordic warriors. Their ancestors, Danish Vikings, had settled into France as payment of Danegeld generations earlier, becoming known as 'Normans' after the
French name for the province they now inhabited, la
Normandie. This had been established by agreement in 911

when King Charles the Simple of France had granted territory around Rouen to Hrolf the Dane in exchange for keeping other Vikings from attacking France.

These Danes, adept at embracing the cultures that existed in the lands they conquered or acquired, soon adopted
the language and ways of the French and eventually established a rising French aristocracy of their own. Nonetheless, there still existed among these Normans a tiny but
stubborn minority who, despite generations of settlement,
had rejected both the Norman tag and French culture. This
tiny pocket of hold-outs still referred to themselves as
Danes rather than Normans, and still honored traditions of
the old culture, including paganism.

Asta's private Danish Guard was composed entirely
of such men. They rejected the long tunics and short-
cropped hair of the Normans, still preferring long hair and
beards. Although they spoke French in public, they spoke
Danish amongst themselves. Also, as if to further demonstrate their disdain for the French-leaning Normans, they
continued to wear the woolen trousers, furs, and horn-
adorned helmets of Vikings in lieu of chain-mail armor and
mitered helmets of the French, which had also now been
adopted by Normans. More critically, since the execution
of Guntar the Mace, their patriarch, their simmering resentment against both William the Bastard's Normans and
the French had not abated a single measure.

The captain of Asta's Guard was Orla, a red-haired
giant whom Asta had nicknamed 'the Ox' as a child because his thick, reddish-brown hair resembled that of the
family oxen. Prior to this, he was known as Orla Bloodaxe
because of his deft handling of the broadax. Unlike southern Europeans whose names generally described a place of
origin or vocation, the Danes had a penchant for nicknames
describing physical attributes or behavior. Orla's face was
buried beneath a bushy forest of now reddish-grey whiskers
that concealed all but his huge blue eyes. He possessed unusually thick, muscled neck and arm flesh, and whenever

he spoke, it was as though heralding startling news to the world. Then, too, he was often swept away by his own laughter.

Riding beside Orla was his brother, Ivar Crowbones. Ivar bore great resemblance to Orla, and the two were at times mistaken for twins even though Ivar was four years younger. His nickname name derived from the tiny leather pouch he carried about his neck containing the desiccated bones of a raven. When Ivar was quite young, he had spent a great deal of time with his Finnish grandmother who practiced sorcery and read bird bones to predict the future. Ivar adopted her craft. By the time he reached adolescence, he had demonstrated a respectable ability to anticipate the future flow of events.

The three horsemen riding behind the caravan were cousins. First, there was Halfdan StraightLimbs, so called because of his unusually tall and lanky stature. When standing erect, his long arms terminated fell well below his knees, which cut a rather comical picture to onlookers. Halfdan was sensitive about this, and had a temper which would quickly become unhinged when people gawked or pointed. Those who knew him well, therefore, acted as though nothing was out of the ordinary with StraightLimbs. To his friends and behind his back, he was also referred to as Halfdan Thinskin.

The middle rider was Sigurd Fairhair. Possessing flowing, golden locks that fell to his waist, he had an extreme weakness for the women, and they for him. He was formal by Danish standards, adopting through observation the dignified public behavior of the more refined French. After consuming several goblets of barley-mead, this behavior was quickly forsaken and he could not help but revert to a boasting oaf spilling forth with comical jokes and bawdy tales of self aggrandizement.

The last rider was Guthroth the Quiet. Mistakenly assumed to be born of low intelligence due to a cumbersome speech impediment, he was actually far more perceptive and clever than most. Nonetheless, he had developed early the habit of not speaking except when absolutely necessary. More accurately, his father who had become the constant butt of jokes because of his son's stuttering, which was misinterpreted as empty-headednesss, beat him into silence. This, in the end, seemed to work well for both—Guthroth's father had no desire to listen to Guthroth's stuttering, so Guthroth had little desire to speak.

Had Tristan and Guillaume not grown up surrounded by Orla and the other Danes, they would have been terrified by these men, as was the oxman. But the Danes were family to the two boys, and had taught them to ride horses, catch fish by hand, snare birds and tend after livestock. Tristan in particular, being the older, knew he was going to miss them dearly upon their impending departure to England to join his mother. So he was in no hurry, then, to reach Burgundy.

Early evening was spent traveling south out of the Saint-Germain family territory which was located eight miles northeast of the actual town of Saint-Germain-en-Laye, founded in 1020 when King Robert the Pious established a convent there. Surveying each field, patch of forest and cluster of peasant dwellings as they traveled, Tristan found it difficult to fathom that these lands no longer belonged to his mother, Asta. Due to Lord Roger de Saint-Germain's constant absences, it had always been Asta who managed the farms, the woodlands and the peasants, with help from the Danes. For them, these recent years, their sole existence had centered around protecting and assisting Asta and her sons. Fortunately, they had not been engaged in the political schemes of Asta's husband. More precisely, they had loathed his very existence.

At dusk, crossing out of the Saint-Germain family lands, they came upon an oncoming procession of Lord Letellier's contingent, laden with his possessions, headed to the vacated Saint-Germain family manor. As with most roads twisting through the scattered farmlands and massive thickets of the region, passage was narrow, scarcely the breadth of a single wagon. The road itself was worn smooth and adequately maintained, but the shoulders were pitted, creased with troughs and obstructed with boulders.

Orla assessed the lumbering bounty of carts, live-stock, laborers and troops as the two cavalcades halted, each blocking the other. Each held there expecting the other to yield, but movement came from neither side. Finally, a French captain galloped forward impatiently. Deliberately bridling his mount into Orla's horse, he wrenched the reins back so hard the animal almost fell back upon its haunches, causing Orla's mount to panic. Orla's horse raised up, brayed with fright, then dropped its hooves to the ground, stamping with contention.

Orla angrily jerked his own reins, forcing his horse's face to slam into the torso of the Frenchman, nearly knock-ing him from his saddle.

"Ho there, jackass!" cried the Frenchman. Then, knowing his master's name would carry weight, he crowed, "I demand that you stand aside, in the name of Lord Letellier! We're moving his affairs into the manor of Roger de Saint-Germain, which has recently been awarded to Lord Letellier by Philippe, King of France." At this, the man spurred his horse so that it danced a bit, moving its hindquarters from side to side as performing in a parade.

Orla leaned over and spat. "You can tell your Lord Letellier to kiss the cavernous black crack of my Danish ass, you little French bastard!" he snorted. "We're the con-tingent of Lady Asta. We do not yield!"

At these words, the oxman put his hand to his fore-head. *This is not going to end well, then I'll be cast in with these damned Danish hold-overs by my fellow Frenchmen.*

The French captain shifted uncomfortably in his sad-dle. "Danes, Normans, I don't give a damn! You're all one and the same now," he barked. "By royal decree, Lord Letellier now owns this land, therefore this road is now his.

Yield, I say! Besides, you are but a small company and can easily move aside!"

Orla spat again, this time onto the Frenchman's boot. "Letellier stole this land through French treachery, you mean to say!" He then, from the saddle, lifted one cheek of his rump toward the Frenchman and flatulated. "I send Letellier the noxious gases of my ass!"

Moving toward the front of the wagon, Tristan and Guillaume peeked out from behind the oxman's shoulders. "Are they going to fight?" whispered Guillaume, his large gray eyes floating from man to man.

"Hush!" said Tristan, trying to anticipate the future direction of the Frenchman's nerve.

Simultaneously, several other Frenchmen spurred their horses forward to support their captain. This prompted StraightLimbs, Fairhair and Guthroth the Quiet, who had been situated behind the wagon, to advance. Convening at Orla's side, StraightLimbs growled something in Danish, pulling his sword. Fairhair and Guthroth the Quiet reached for their hammers, also exchanging words in Danish. Crowbones, meanwhile, shook his head at the French captain and smirked.

The Frenchman understood clearly. Still, he decided to initiate a final gambit at saving the road. "You're well outnumbered. You can't win, so what's your point here?"

"My point," Orla sneered, "is that we have just lost our manor and been reduced to homeless vagabonds. Perhaps our recent misfortune at the hands of Letellier, prince of Judas goats, has ended our lust for life. But you, Frenchman, do you really wish to piss away your life defending Letellier's name on a dusty road leading to an ill-begotten manor? Oh, Letellier may well raise a cup in your honor for defending his road, but will forget you ever existed by the time he sets his cup back down! Ay, my friends and I may well end being casualties today, but you, my fine little peacock, will be the first to be slain on this god-damned road."

The Frenchman glanced at his men, thinking superior numbers might bolster his own courage, but they appeared feeble and lacking in enthusiasm. "W-well spoken," the French captain stammered, bowing with deference. "You and I are but little men that matter none to the masters. We yield." Turning, he signaled for his train to move aside.

The oxman sighed, wiping perspiration from his brow with a long swipe of his sleeve before flicking the reins to urge his oxen forward. Tristan, settling in next to the driver, watched the opposing caravan as it moved cart by cart, horse by horse, off the road. As the small Danish troupe passed through their midst like the prow of a Viking warship cutting the waters ahead into frothing halves, Tristan stared curiously into the eyes of each Frenchman they passed, attempting to imagine their thoughts. *Contempt*, he decided, *but also fear*.

Chapter Five

The Ox Speaks

D ue to the late start and time lost as Letellier's heav-
ily-laden caravan had pulled off the road, the
Danes made little progress that first afternoon.
They were also slowed by the oxen-driven wagon which
creaked along the inordinately crooked path at a snail's
pace. Since the Saint-Germain manor was located a good
eight miles north of the town of Saint-Germain-en-Laye
itself, as darkness descended over the forest that evening,
the travelers stopped a mile short of there.

The oxman had hoped to spend the night at the Benedictine monastery in town, but the Danes refused. Although
King Harald Bluetooth of Denmark had sanctioned Christianity a century earlier within his domain, his conversion
created great dissension and rebellion, some of which still
existed among isolated Danish clans who refused the new
religion. Orla and the Danish Guard were among those who
remained distrustful of the Roman Church. This had been a
source of contention with the devout Lady Asta, but she
was absent so they decided amongst themselves to avoid
monasteries altogether until arriving at their destination of
Cluny.

After setting a fire and laying out a sparse assortment
of smoked meats and herring for the company, the oxman
chose to sleep beneath the wagon rather than by the fire
amongst the Danes, who still incurred in him a certain level

of terror. Tristan and Guillaume fixed pallets inside the wagon while the others settled beside the fire, wrapping themselves in their woolen mantles. Sleep came quickly for Guillaume, but Tristan remained restless. Peeking out of the wagon, he spotted Orla and Crowbones poking at and staring into the fire.

He was about to slip from the wagon to join them when the brush just beyond camp rustled furtively, and the sound of footfalls emerged. Quickly finding their feet, Orla and Crowbones poised ax and sword at the ready.

"Who goes there!" shouted Orla.

Silence ensued.

Then the shadowy form of an old woman leaning on-to a cane entered the meager circle of light afforded by the fire. She wore a ragged black tunic, and her head and shoulders were covered with a long black shawl. "Tis only me, Orla," the woman rasped. "Duxia de Falaise."

Orla dropped his weapon to his side, gawking at the woman, dumbfounded. "Mielikki?" he said, exchanging glances with Crowbones who appeared equally surprised.

"You know I no longer go by Mielikki, you great oaf," the woman responded, "not since Lady Asta exiled me from the—"

"Ho there, bitch," interrupted Crowbones, "come no closer."

"Ja," added Orla, "get away from this camp!" Pointing to the wagon where Tristan now sat clandestinely peeking from within, he said, "The boy is in that wagon there, sleeping."

"The *boy*?" the woman said, wilting a measure. "Tristan?"

"Ja, and Asta instructed us to kill you on sight should you ever approach him again," warned Orla, raising his ax.

"I merely seek something to eat," the old woman said, looking to the ground with defeat. "Since being forced from Asta's household, I wander the roads and woodlands just trying to survive. It's a beggar's life, and dangerous for an old woman. But surely you wouldn't kill me, Orla, simply because I beg for food, huh? Besides, had I known the boy was here, I wouldn't have come near. Despite what I did years ago, I no longer mean him any ill…"

As Tristan listened from the wagon, he grew confused by these words, also by Orla's and Crowbones' harsh reaction to the old hag.

Next he heard Orla say, "No food from us, bitch. And if you don't leave, yes, we'll end your misery here and now!"

At this the woman leaned against her came and shifted her weight to one leg. "Very well," she said, her weary eyes dropping with discouragement, "I'll leave, but to think we were once like family, huh?" Turning, she limped away, disappearing back into darkness.

Unable to suppress his curiosity, Tristan bolted from the wagon and joined Orla's side, pointing into the brush. "Who was *that*?"

Orla looked over the boy's shoulder and saw Crowbones shaking his head with a nod. Say nothing, the nod said.

"Nobody you need to be concerned with," Orla grunted.

"But could we not give her something to eat at least?" Tristan queried. "She looks frail from hunger…and she said something about being part of the family, did she not?"

"Ha! No family of ours!" Orla snorted.

"B-but she—"

Orla flagged his palm. "No more about the woman."

Tristan sighed, taking a seat beside the fire. Wrapping his arms about his knees, he said, "I keep thinking about this monastery Guillaume and I are being sent to, and cannot sleep. I have no wish to be a monk, but now fear being forced into it. Can I stay at the fire a while?"

"Sure," replied Orla, knowing that young Tristan's separation from his mother was an excruciating ordeal for the seven-year-old, although he had said nothing about it all day.

Setting their weapons aside, Orla and Crowbones resumed their seats at the fire as Tristan poked at it thoughtfully with Orla's stick.

After a few moments of silence, Tristan looked up. "Lord Ox" he said, "I am glad Mother chose you, Lord Crowbones and the others to take me and Guillaume to Cluny."

The two men nodded, slipping into that snicker of the tickled. They had always found it amusing that Tristan prefaced their nickname of Ox and Crowbones with the formality of the title 'Lord'. It was something Asta had insisted her sons do as a sign of respect for their protectors.

"Ja, me, too," Crowbones said.

Orla nodded in agreement, studying the boy a moment. "Tis a hard time on you and Mighty Mite, and I'm glad to share it with you." Mighty Mite was the name the Danes had given Guillaume because, from birth, the boy displayed a naked lack of fear. Then Orla patted Tristan, who all the Danes had simply tagged since birth as 'Boy', on the knee. "Don't be angry at your mother, Boy. It's a good thing she does here."

"*A good thing?*" Tristan shrugged.

"Ja," said Crowbones, "she's sending you two to the Black Monks to be educated and brought up like proper young lads. Be glad you're not going to England, which is wild and full of untamed Celts and Scotts running about with their blue-painted faces, not to mention angry Saxons. Burgundy is the safest place in all Europe, and ending up a priest or monk isn't such a bad thing. They live a good life you know, not scrapping about for food or land like the rest of us."

"Still," said Tristan, "I have no wish to be a cleric." Then he shook his head ruefully. "And I am not deceived. Mother sends us away because my uncle, Desmond DuLac, *refuses* us. She abandons us to be married to a rich man."

Hearing this, Orla bit his lip. "Is that what you believe, Boy?"

"It is true, Lord Ox."

Seeing that the boy was wounded, Orla rubbed at his beard. He knew this separation of mother and sons was more complex than appearances allowed, but Asta had given strict instructions that there was to be absolutely no discussion with the boys about her marriage to Desmond DuLac. Taking a different tack, Orla said, "You know, Boy, it's possible she was going to send you to the Black Monks anyway."

"Huh?" said Tristan.

"Ja, even before your father's demise, she intended for you two to receive the highest education in the world, which could only happen at Cluny under the Black Monks, you know. Many great nobles and holy men got their start there, learning under the Benedictines. But upon your father's disgrace, her plans fell to ruin. A Cluny education is reserved only for the children of honored nobility, and is very costly."

"But if that is so, how is it that Guillaume and I are still going there?"

"As only Asta could do," interjected Crowbones, "she's regathered the pieces somehow. That's all we need to know. Be happy you're going to be educated! Leave it at that!"

Feeling chastised, Tristan looked over to Orla, seeing himself and the fire reflected in Orla's great blue eyes. "Still," he whispered, "she abandons me and Guillaume." He welled up a little then, wondering where she might be at this very moment, whether she might be thinking of him just as he was thinking of her. "And I miss her so much my heart aches," he added, feeling his throat begin to lump.

Orla reached over to comfort him. "Two things you should know here, lad. First, even as Guntar's nuns drilled the Roman faith into her skull along with the refinements of France, she remained true to the Danes, still does to this

day. But she wants you and the Mite to be French, because
like it or not, France is your future. And secondly, following
her own upbringing, she surrounded you boys with her
nuns to educate you. But, you've reached the limits of their
womanly capacity, which is where the Black Monks enter
the picture. Understand?"

Swiping his cheek, Tristan grabbed at the stick again
and poked at the fire. "I hope she doesn't forget me," he
said, his face turning more ashen.

Orla observed this with a degree of sadness, realizing
that despite Tristan's unusual intellect for one so young, the
heartbreak of losing his mother was crushing him. Deciding
it best to change the mood, Orla raised a brow at
Crowbones, winking. "Of course, Boy, there's something
you haven't been told yet, something you need to know before we reach Cluny."

Tristan looked up. "Oh?"

"We're taking you to Cluny as instructed," Orla continued, taking on a worried look, "but the Black Monks
don't just accept every lad that shows up at their door, you
know."

Tristan sat erect. "Huh?" he said, sensing the onset of
some unanticipated complication.

"Ja, you must pass their big oral examination," said
Orla, closing an eye, nodding across the fire at Crowbones
again. "And if you fail, you can't go to England as you
know, nor can you return to Saint-Germain-en-Laye." Here
Orla stopped and gazed up at the night sky.

"Wh-what would happen then?" asked Tristan, urgency filling his face. I have never had a big examination,
only my recitals to Mother and the nuns."

Orla dropped his eyes and they settled on Tristan sol-
emnly. "Well, the Black Monks are far more learned than
the nuns, so their questions will be very difficult, I'd suppose. But then, you're such a clever lad, Tristan, you'll do
fine."

"Ja, ja," agreed Crowbones, nodding vigorously. "He'll do well. But it's little Guillaume whose neck is in the noose, not Boy's." Here Crowbones shook his head, looking away.

"What do you mean, Lord Crowbones?" Tristan said, his apprehension escalating.

But it was Orla who answered. "Guillaume's not nearly as smart as you, Boy. If he fails the big examination, which he probably will, then *that's that*. He's done for!"

A hammer blow to the head could not have rattled Tristan more than these words. "Done for?" said Tristan, his mouth falling ajar. "But what do you mean by—"

"Enough!" snapped Orla, satisfied that they had taken Tristan's mind from Asta. "It's late now, Boy, so go crawl back in your wagon and get some sleep. We've a long day tomorrow."

Though he had no desire to leave the fire, especially at this point, Tristan obeyed. Standing, he shook the dirt from his trousers and crawled into the wagon.

After he left, Orla looked over at his brother and shook his head. "Imagine that," he whispered, "Mielikki wandering about in the woods at night like some lost beast. Still, she should have never tried to drown Boy when he was three. He'd be dead had Guthroth not happened along just as she was holding Boy's head under water. All that damned jabber of hers about the 'Devil's caul' and him being a curse to mankind. Such horseshit! Yeah, ever since Asta gave birth to Tristan, it seems the old bitch's lost her mind, eh?"

"It's the ice and wind of Finland's far reaches," nodded Orla. "Lost and alone so far north in such isolation, many of those people go mad with age, just like our Finnish grandmother."

Chapter Six

The Foreigners

That next morning Orla and Crowbones led the group along the Seine River and cut southwest towards Paris. After working their way through several patches of farmland, they entered a deep forest where the road began to take tortuous curves around stands of majestic oaks. As they rounded one of these turns, they fell upon a retinue of four tiny box-wagons moving with obvious urgency down the road. Spying Orla and the Danes, pandemonium broke out within the approaching group as those on foot, screaming in foreign tongues, broke for the brush. Those riding the wagons jumped from their perches and also began to flee.

The oxman determined that the oncoming caravan was advancing as if in flight; that those scattering for the woods were bruised and bloody. He had only once before during his travels encountered such a scene, and the memory of that disaster alarmed him. "Trouble ahead!" he shouted. "Bandits! Turn about!"

"No," Orla commanded. "We'll wait and hold the road."

StraightLimbs and Fairhair spurred their horses alongside Orla and Crowbones while Guthroth the Quiet remained in place as rear guard.

"What is it?" asked StraightLimbs.

Tristan and Guillaume, startled by the sudden commotion, hung onto the oxman's shoulders and peered around his head. "What's coming?" asked Guillaume, excited by the arising activity.

"Hush!" said Tristan, pulling his brother back. "Get behind me!"

The Danes sat motionless, hammer and ax at the ready, as a minute passed, then another. Nothing came; not a sound to be heard but the fading flight of the panic-stricken travelers fleeing through the brush.

Dismounting, Orla stepped toward the abandoned wagons. "It's *us*," he said. "They're running from us."

"Ja, I think you're right," assented Crowbones, also dismounting and peering into the vacated wagons one by one with Orla. "Odd clothing," he said. Then, as he glanced into the last wagon, he caught movement beneath a blanket. Motioning to Orla and raising his ax, he jerked the cover back.

A naked young woman drew back in terror. Screaming, she clawed her way away from Crowbones with one arm while holding an infant to her exposed breast with the other. Her face was battered and she was bleeding at the mouth.

"*Misericordia!*" she wailed. "Por favor, ten misericordia de nosotros!"

Tristan, hearing the woman's cries, shouted, "I understand her! It's Spanish! Back away, Lord Crowbones, you are frightening her!"

Crowbones looked at Orla, then at the woman. "Very well, then, Boy. Come here, don't just stand about like a damned Frenchman!"

Tristan cupped his mouth and shouted loudly into the woods. "Oye, esta bien!" He repeated himself twice more and jumped from the wagon, moving next to Orla. Gazing inside the wagon, he spoke several words to the woman, who had by now covered herself with a blanket.

Soon a look of relief washed over the woman's face. Climbing out of the wagon with infant in arm, her torso scantly covered by the small blanket, she shouted into the woods. "¡Eh, regresen a los vagones! ¡Esta bien!"

Several of the travelers returned nervously to the wagons where Tristan exchanged words with them, and they grew calmer.

"Lord Ox," said Tristan, "perhaps you and Lord Crowbones might stand over by the oxman and our wagon. It seems your close presence is still frightening these poor people. I will find out what happened to them."

Orla motioned for Crowbones to join him back at their own wagon with the other Danes as Tristan spent several minutes huddled with the travelers, who numbered eighteen in all. They were dark-skinned, most were women and older men. It was the young woman with the infant who provided most of the information. She indicated that the four younger men who were bandaged and bloodied had all been bludgeoned, barely escaping with lives. But it was the story of their missing children that was most distressing.

Rejoining the Danes, Tristan said, "These people left Spain two months ago, fleeing from the Muslim civil wars and incursions against the Christian kings, Sancho of Aragon and Alfonso of Castile. They now seek refuge here in France, hoping to settle further north, far away from the Muslims."

Orla nodded. "I see. But why did they run at seeing us? We're not Muslims."

"And why are they wounded so badly?" asked Crowbones.

"Earlier this morning as they approached the river," replied Tristan, "they were set upon by a band of pirates, pillaged and beaten, and their children were taken. But a strange thing, they say the pirates were dressed just like *you*, like Vikings."

"*Vikings?*" echoed Fairhair and StraightLimbs in unison.

"Vikings?" repeated Crowbones. "Raiding along the Seine in France?"

"No," said Orla, shaking his head. "They're mistaken. The old treaties forbid it. And the Bastard forbids it. All Viking raids along the Seine ceased ages ago."

"I trust they are not lying," said Tristan. "Seeing you on the road, they thought the same Vikings had circled back to kill them. And the woman there, she says the Viking ship lies anchored in the river bend just down the road."

"Indeed?" said Crowbones, looking at his brother, then over to the other Danes. As he did this, a silent communion appeared to pass amongst the five men. It was a strange, disjointed mix of umbrage and anticipation. Moments later Crowbones' expression darkened and he said, "Ja, perhaps we best 'visit them'?"

"J-ja," whispered Guthroth the Quiet as the tiniest trace of a smile appeared from nowhere, but did not set well on his lips.

This pricked Tristan's attention, because Guthroth rarely offered a reply unless directly prompted. Furthermore, Tristan noticed that a change of mood had suddenly also struck StraightLimbs and Fairhair. Seeing this, Tristan tugged at Orla's arm. "Lord Ox, when you meet these men, perhaps you could ask them to return the foreigners' children?"

Orla brushed Tristan aside and mounted his horse. "No, Boy, that is none of our affair."

"But—"

"No," said Orla, "now get in the wagon and leave things be. My task is to get you to Cluny, not to save the world."

Chapter Seven

The Norsemen

Moving briskly, Orla led the others down the road as it turned back along the Seine. Just ahead he detected a bend in the river, where he spotted the out-of-place mast of a small vessel poking straight up beyond the crooked limbs of river oaks. "Wait here," he said to the others, dismounting.

Pulling his ax, he quietly wormed his way through the low foliage until, finally, he heard voices drifting through the brush. Men were speaking Norwegian, a language Orla understood. Crouching, he moved closer, melding into a heavy growth of ferns, parting them.

The ship's sail had been stowed to disguise the vessel as it anchored along the bank. The vessel itself was small, unlike the larger Viking longships used for oceanic travel, nor was it broad-beamed like the traditional Viking knorr, a trading ship with enough space to carry freight and livestock. This ship was built for speed and secrecy. It was a raider, as used by small, clandestine Scandinavian war bands. Its prow was carved and hued into a dragon's head, as was the custom for Nordic warships and raiders. Danish Vikings turned Norman had long since ceased placing the dragon head on their ships because the symbol frightened the native French and had proven to have a negative impact on Norman commerce.

Counting the men moving about the campsite and voices coming from aboard the ship, Orla surmised there were about fourteen men altogether. He saw no signs of children anywhere, but guessed they were hog-tied aboard the ship. Unsure whether to trust these men or not, he thought to first return for Crowbones and the others. Then, as he had a passable command of Norwegian, he determined he would, instead, make a bold move. Looping his ax to his belt, he stood. "Ho, there!" he shouted. "You Norsemen! Welcome to my woods!"

The men scattered, grasping weapons and yelling warnings to each other.

Orla reared his head back and laughed. "Ja, you Norwegians, bolting like mice! Calm down, it's only me, Orla Bloodaxe, a Dane from Normandy! Raising his hand in friendship, he motioned the raiders forward. "Good to see some men from the Northland again! I mean you no ill. My friends and I are simply moving through, just as you are! Come, I've French wine in my wagon!"

The men exchanged glances, peering through the woods for enemies. There were none. Finally, a large man sheathed his sword and walked toward Orla. "Ja," he said, "a Dane, eh? What the shit are you doing here in these woods?"

"As I said, just moving through, on our way south to deliver two lads to a monastery."

The large man sized up Orla, who was even larger than himself, deciding he intended no harm, and appeared to be, as declared, a fellow Scandinavian. Gesturing, he instructed his men to stand down. "I am Frode Longsword. I'm the captain here," he said to Orla, raising his hand in greeting. Then he pointed to the young man standing beside him. "And this handsome dog here is my son, Alf, but we call him WolfPaw."

The young man pointed to a birthmark on his left cheek. "Because of this mark on my face," he smiled, "it's the identical size and shape of a wolf's paw-print."

"Aye, I see that," remarked Orla.

"Hail, then, Orla Bloodaxe," the young man said. Good to meet you. But then, you say you're taking two boys to a monastery?"

"Ja, to Cluny in the south," Orla said, raising his hand to acknowledge Frode's son. "We're from Normandy, but most recently lived in French territory near Saint-Germain-en-Laye. It's too long a story to go into, but I'm happy to meet you both!"

WolfPaw raised his hand in return. "Then you're Norman?" he asked.

Orla shrugged. "Not willingly. We are by way of politics, I suppose, but we remain Danes at heart."

"As I can see," said Frode, casting a glance at his son. "WolfPaw, no need to ask so many questions. You can plainly see that this man is Nordic like us."

WolfPaw nodded. "Ja, Father."

It is a strange fact that when those who share common geography or culture, however thready, encounter each other far from home in a strange land, an immediate bond arises. This peculiarity began to work on the leader of the Norse party. He and Orla exchanged news of Normandy, Denmark and Norway, then engaged in small talk for a few minutes more. With Frode's consent, Orla then called into the woods for the oxman and the other Danes.

By evening, the Danes and Norsemen appeared to have developed an extremely amicable relationship. During the course of conversation, Frode shared that a caravan of hapless travelers had inadvertently come upon their camp that morning; that his men had pillaged the wagons. They had also seized the women and ravaged them all. Then they beat the men for jest. When this rampage was over, Frode had then decided he would take the five children and sell them."

"The Moors like foreign children," chortled Frode, "for their slave markets and the harems of the Muslim lords. Funny thing, little boys bring as much coin as girls and women."

Orla nodded, issuing a puzzled look. "You know, I'm a bit surprised you didn't take the women along with the children. They'd bring a good price also, huh?"

Frode shook his head. "The women would be too much trouble. They'd resist and clamor throughout the journey. Worse yet, they'd distract my crew who'd wish to spend their time poking them rather than tending to business. My voyage is strictly for booty, not for manly pleasures. Besides, women are a curse aboard vessels, you know that!"

"Ja, I understand," said Orla.

The conversation then turned to sailing, and Orla was quick to comment on the sheer audacity of the Norwegians. "It's amazing," Orla said jokingly, "that you've made it this far already."

"We travel by night and anchor by day," Frode replied. "We came down the Seine after slipping through Normandy. We know better than to anger William the Bastard. We know about the bargain struck by his ancestors with the French, so we slipped through Normandy until reaching France, sailing only at night. Paris is just downstream, so we'll turn about and sneak back through Normandy for the Atlantic, then down to Spain. We figured you Normans wouldn't mind us taking from the French. After all, you Danes now calling yourself Normans took from them in exchange for keeping other Vikings out, didn't you?"

Although Frode had clearly expressed to Orla how and why this land exchange involving Normandy had occurred between the French and the Danes, it somehow appeared that the actual operational concept of this agreement made generations before entirely escaped Frode. Otherwise, he would have never dared to cross Norman territory to raid France. In any case, Orla and the Danes made light of it all, sharing ale and wine with their new friends.

This newfound camaraderie offended Tristan, who refused to engage in any exchanges with the Norsemen because of the captive children in the boat—so he sat there glumly watching from the oxman's seat while Guillaume fell asleep within the wagon. The oxman, more uneasy than ever upon meeting yet more Vikings, chose to sleep in the woods well away from the campsite. *It'll be good to finally get back to civilization and well away from all these damned savages*, he thought, churning about restlessly on the ground.

As the hour grew later, the merriment around the fire heightened, and Tristan's quiet resentment turned nearly to rage. How could these good men he had known and revered his entire life consort with these wicked, child-napping raiders of the North?

As Tristan looked on, Fairhair appeared to be utterly intoxicated; had begun mimicking female responses to his past amorous conquests, which made him an immediate favorite among the drunken Norsemen. StraightLimbs and Crowbones were having a large time also, as was Orla, who appeared to be reveling in companionship with the Norsemen. Although Guthroth the Quiet was not speaking, as usual, even he was bursting into occasional fits of laughter at Fairhair's comical interpretations. And all this while, Tristan fretted over the five children being held captive within the boat. Finally, he made the sign of the cross, said a short prayer for the children, and decided that he should go to sleep rather than stomach any further the unacceptable merriment unfolding before his eyes.

At that precise moment, Orla stood and raised his drinking-horn to the fire. "To King Olaf, the good and wise ruler of Norway!" he shouted. "And to Frode Longsword, to his son, WolfPaw, and to all these brave Norsemen who dared traverse Normandy to raid the French despite Hrolf's Code of years gone by!"

Frode raised his cup and tried to stand with Orla, but in his drunkenness, stumbled. Laughing, he placed both palms flat on the ground behind him, looking up at Orla, grinning. That is when Orla swiftly pulled his ax from his belt and brought it down in one mighty sweep, cleaving Frode's fore-skull clean in two. The Norse captain's head fell open like two halves of a cleanly lopped apple. Next, as if a signal had passed, the other Danes unsheathed axes and hammers and fell upon the other Norsemen. Fairhair, shedding all trace of his previously feigned drunken stupor, brought his hammer to bear on the two Norwegians seated before him, splattering their heads like eggs hurled against rock. Simultaneously, Orla dropped his ax and slipped a dagger through the neck of the man standing beside him, then attacked another Norseman standing back from the fire just as he reached for his sword, becoming aware of what was happening.

Crowbones and StraightLimbs, as Orla had begun his toast, had casually moved toward the three men standing guard by the ship. The instant Orla dropped his ax into Frode's skull, they attacked the unsuspecting guards with axes, felling all three within seconds. Aboard the boat, three other men were guarding the children, and by now the bloody actions of the Danes had begun to register in their heads. From their position in the boat, they began to curse, staving off Crowbones and StraightLimbs as they attempted to climb aboard.

Guthroth the Quiet had, moments before Orla's toast, accompanied two other Norsemen into the brush to urinate. As the two oblivious Norwegians laughed, holding each other up in their struggle to stand upright and urinate, Guthroth came from behind and silently stuck a dagger in one's spine while hacking the other's neck with his broadax. He then moved around the ship's stern, entered the water and emerged over the vessel's port beam, attacking the three guards who were fighting off Crowbones and StraightLimbs from behind. All three were soon dead.

"Done here!" cried Orla from the fire. "Brother! Are you done?"

"Done here!" Crowbones shouted back.

"Done here!" cried Fairhair. "But the young one ran off into the brush!"

"Chase him down, dammit!" screamed Crowbones, alarmed. "The young one is Frode's son! Don't let him escape!"

"No, don't bother, we'll never catch him in the dark," Orla answered. "Hey, Guthroth! Are you done up there?"

Guthroth gave a nod that he was indeed done, then moved toward the five children huddled at the ship's stern. They had witnessed the fighting aboard the ship, and though they had been terrified of the Norsemen, they seemed even more so of Guthroth as he stood there holding his bloody ax. Seeing this, he dropped the weapon and released them one by one.

Tristan had witnessed the entire massacre in utter disbelief, and now sat frozen to the oxman's seat. The only blood he had ever witnessed before was during the annual slaughter of the hogs and sheep at the manor, and even then the helpless, bleating cries of those poor animals coming under the butcher's blade had disturbed him to the point of revulsion. But now human blood was everywhere, effusing from the dead men's wounds, pooling in scarlet swirls, mixing with the earth.

Horrified, Tristan fell to trembling. It had all happened so quickly and unexpectedly. One moment Orla was laughing and raising his horn in toast, the next he and the Danes were slaughtering helpless, drunken men in a savage blood-fest of ax and hammer. Feeling ill, Tristan collapsed in a fit of retching

Orla saw this and moved toward the wagon. He picked Tristan from the seat and leaned him over the ground, shaking him to rid him of the vomit. "There, Boy, get it all out," he said.

Tristan stood. But dizzy with illness and confusion, his legs gave way again. Orla picked him up and carried him to the fire. Then, reaching down, Orla began dragging the corpses slumped near the fire away from it. Finally, he took a seat next to Tristan. "Sorry I am that you had to see all this, Boy, but the children are free now. Isn't that what you wanted?"

Tristan raised his eyes, but said nothing.

Orla continued. "These men violated Hrolf's Code. No Vikings of any origin are allowed to plunder France. These men had to die. They violated the Treaty of Saint Clair which has stood defended by our people for generations now. These men knew well that they were breaking our sacred code. They took a terrible risk, and have been justly rewarded, Boy."

Tristan stared blankly into Orla's eyes. "B-but these men, I saw you laughing and talking..." he mumbled. "You made them y-your friends. You—"

"These men stood to destroy everything our Danish ancestors gained. There would be no explaining the presence of these raiders, nor our letting them by. It was our duty."

Tears began to stream down Tristan's cheeks as he heaved uncontrollably. "B-but they were all l-laughing, and singing. Y-you... "

Orla shook his head. "Surely you don't suppose that I and the others enjoyed this butchery, do you? May the gods forgive us. These men were fathers and husbands just like me, and now their families will never know their fate, whether they're alive or lost or whether they'll ever return. And not knowing is worse than death itself. Indeed, how many nights do you think their wives and children will stand there, waiting at the edge of the fjords thinking that their fathers and their husbands might yet return? I'm sick over what I've done to their families, but there was no choice!"

"But... " Tristan wept, "y-you slaughtered them like dumb animals. You—"

"Ja, it had to be like that. When the numbers are against you, you must turn to trickery. Would you rather that I and Crowbones were dead in their place?"

Tristan gave a tiny shrug. "N-no, but—"

"All right then, gather your wits, and never forget this night. There are hard lessons to carry away from all this, but some you'd best remember in the days ahead."

Tristan stood, giving a glance at the pile of blood-soaked corpses lying nearby, human beings who just minutes before had been living, breathing and laughing. Making the sign of the cross, he uttered something in Latin which Orla did not understand.

"Good lad," said Orla, patting Tristan on the shoulder. "And don't forget what these men did to those foreign travelers. Just as you miss your mother now, how do you think these children would've felt, lost far from family, in bondage? Now gather up these children and we'll take them back to their clan. And be glad, Boy, that little Mite is still asleep and didn't see all of this bloodletting."

Chapter Eight

The Gypsy Tale

Orla called the Danes to the fire and pointed to the corpses. "Strip the bodies and dump them in the river," he said to Crowbones and StraightLimbs. "Toss the weapons and helmets in the river, too, but burn the clothes. Fairhair, you and Guthroth torch the ship and push it off. We'll want no trace of it left here. If we hurry we can find the foreigners down the road and deliver their children."

Nodding, the men set quickly about their tasks. The oxman, who had been awakened by the screaming and fury of the massacre, hid behind the wagon, still recovering from shock. "My God and Savior," he whispered in a fit of prayerfulness, "if you allow me to make Burgundy alive, I'll offer double alms for the rest of my life!"

Tristan gathered the children and explained that the Danes were taking them back to their families, which caused an outbreak of tearful joy. He then crammed them into the wagon with Guillaume while the men broke camp. As he spoke, the gaze of one particular girl, several years older than himself, seemed transfixed upon him. Though she said nothing, her large dark eyes stared at every motion he made, as in wonder.

"Come along, we must hurry," Tristan prodded, noticing that she perfectly resembled the young woman with the infant the Danes had discovered in the wagon.

Within the half hour, the troupe was ambling down the road. The full April moon sat heavy over the oaks, lighting both the road ahead and the surrounding country-side, easing their travel through the night. As they moved forward, they left in their wake a towering blaze that lapped at the charring ruins of what once was a plunder-ship from Norway. Two hours later Orla and the oxman detected a campfire ahead.

"Tristan," Orla called, "you and the children unload. I think it best if you walk them in and approach the camp so as not to frighten everyone again. Tell them the Norse are dead."

Tristan complied, and as he and the children entered camp, they found only two men awake, standing guard by the fire. At seeing the children, they ran toward them, grasping them with emotion. "Ay Dios mio! Dios mio!" both men cried, as the eldest motioned for the younger to wake up the others. "Rapido, despierta a los otros!" he shouted, pointing at the wagons.

Within moments others climbed from their wagons and the entire camp broke into a wild chorus of weeping, shouting and embracing. Orla and the Danes heard this clamor from the distance, and looked at each other, nod-ding. "We've done a good thing for these people, I sup-pose," said Orla, his tone flat.

"Ja, but such a shame about the Norwegians," replied Crowbones. "I liked them, actually, didn't you?"

"Aye, very much so. Especially their captain, Frode."

"Yet," said Crowbones, "I worry about his son escap-ing into the woods. We should've chased him down." He paused, shaking his head. "No, then we would've had to kill him just as we did the others. I know we had to do it. But still, I don't much like the way it was done, Orla."

"Stop thinking too much. Let it be, Ivar. As for the escaped son, if he ever makes it back home he can serve as a warning to the other Norse to respect Hrolf's Code. But let's go, sounds like Boy has cleared the way."

Suspecting that the foreigners might still be fearful of them, the Danes were surprised to be mobbed by men and women surrounding their horses, pulling them from their mounts to embrace them. "Vamos a celebrar!" they shouted as men re-stoked the meager fire and women made food appear from nowhere.

"They want us to stay," Tristan said to Orla. "They want to thank you."

"I can see that, Boy."

As they all gathered about the fire eating and drinking, it was the young woman they found in the wagon with the infant who spoke. Her name was Nuri, and it was her smooth, caramel skin that struck Tristan first. As she began to talk, Tristan studied her thick raven hair and large, dark, almond eyes. *She is so beautiful*, he thought, with that innocent admiration that strikes young boys before comprehending lust.

The flickering firelight enhanced Nuri's beauty yet more, casting mystical shadows against the delicate features of her face and the warmth of her full smile. As she spoke, her heart was swollen to bursting. One of the children the Danes retrieved was her other daughter, Mala, a beautiful girl of ten; the same girl who had earlier stared so intently at Tristan as they prepared to leave the Viking camp. Now she sat there quietly listening to her mother, but her full attention was still fixed, as before, on Tristan. Though he was younger than her, she had never encountered a boy such as this—so forthright, so intelligent. He seemed an oddity to her, and he fascinated her.

This did not go unnoticed by Tristan. The only girls he had ever encountered before were a handful of the Danish Guards' daughters, to whom he had never paid an ounce of heed. But this girl, Mala, struck a different chord. She was so utterly different. Perhaps it was the smooth darkness of her skin, or the firelight's dancing reflection in her anthracite eyes that were identical to those of her beautiful mother. Nonetheless, as Tristan sat there, he fell into a bit of a trance. Hypnotized by both mother and daughter, his eyes gravitated from one to the other, then back again.

"Nearly seventy years ago," Nuri began, speaking directly to Tristan so he could translate to the Danes, "our clan left northwest India, fleeing from the Muslim invasions led by the violent Mahmud Ghazni. This devil of a man and his soldiers came through the passes of Afghanistan and butchered all before them, making mountains out of Hindu skulls. They plundered Hindu temples, burned villages, defiled the dead and sold the women and children into slavery. Our people, the Romani, fled India and made their way to the Middle East where they settled for a short while."

"The Middle East?" asked Tristan. "But is that not the homeland of the Muslims?"

"Si, but there was more tolerance in the Middle East among the established Muslims than among the invaders who pushed into India. But soon civil war broke out and the radicals came to power there also, so the Romani began to flee again. A few, my people, moved into North Africa. But the infighting followed them there also, so they pushed up into Spain amongst the Muslim Berbers of Granada where I and my daughters were born and raised. The Romani lived there in safety and harmony for decades, but the violent Abbadide Mohammedan dynasty of Seville began to rise and push against the Berbers of Granada, and also north against the Christian kings. The Christian, Fernando El Magno of Castille and Leon, has defeated them and they pay him tribute now, but we suspect that the Abbadides will be back. They won't be content until they one day take over the entire world by fire and sword."

"So," said Tristan, "the Romani are Christians?"

"Yes, since fleeing Africa generations ago."

Tristan conveyed Nuri's story to the Danes.

"These damned Muslims," said StraightLimbs, shaking his head. Sounds like they enjoy killing each other as much as killing others, eh?"

"Ha, no more so than we Europeans, or the Christians!" laughed Fairhair.

Orla pulled at his beard thoughtfully. "These people have no home—they're a bit like us now."

"Ja," said Crowbones. "Our people left Denmark for Scotland and England, then into France and Normandy where they lost their language and Danish customs, yet now our own small clan is on the road again."

"Our home is Lady Asta now," interjected Fairhair. "Where she goes, we go."

"J-j-ja," said Guthroth the Quiet in a low voice, as talking to himself, "our h-home is Lady Asta."

At this unanticipated comment from Guthroth, the other Danes looked up, surprised. "Damn you, Guthroth!" shouted Orla. "If you keep jabbering so much on this trip, I'll have no ears by the time we reach Burgundy!"

Guthroth slid silently back from the fire, embarrassed, as Orla and the other Danes broke into laughter. The foreigners, observing this outbreak of hilarity amongst the Danes, broke into laughter also, although they had no earthly idea what it was that had so tickled the Danes.

Tristan turned to Nuri. "We are from the Saint-Germain-en-Laye region, and on our way to Cluny now. My brother and I will be living there at the monastery."

At this, Nuri's daughter put her mouth to her mother's ear and whispered something. Nuri nodded and looked back at Tristan. "Ah yes, Cluny Monastery! Oh, all the world knows of Cluny. It's said to be the most magnificent place in all Christendom, outshining even the Vatican." Smiling, she pointed to her daughter. "It's one of Mala's dreams to one day visit Cluny. We discussed stopping there during our travel north, but it was out of our way."

"Perhaps one day you can come visit me then," said Tristan, failing to understand that he would likely never see these people again.

Though she said nothing, young Mala smiled at hearing this, nodding at Tristan with contentment.

"We have never seen people like you before," said Tristan, "nor even heard of the Romani. Are you the first of your people to enter France, then?"

"Si, I think so," Nuri replied, "but we won't be the last. The Muslims continue to advance and won't be content until they rule the world, so more Romani will follow. But these five brave warriors with you have saved our children and returned them to us. Tell them that my two sisters and I offer ourselves to them in gratitude."

Tristan shrugged, confused, then asked Nuri to repeat her last statement, which she did while pointing to her two sisters who were nodding in agreement. Still confused, he shook his head. "Matrimonio? But Senorita, you cannot offer such a thing, some are already married."

Nuri smiled. Due to the maturity Tristan had displayed since their brief acquaintance, she had forgotten he still possessed the innocence of childhood. Tousling his hair, she stood, giving Fairhair a nod, motioning for him to follow her to one of the wagons. Fairhair understood, and followed her path. Nuri's two sisters stood also, grabbing StraightLimbs and Guthroth the Quiet. StraightLimbs followed but Guthroth resisted, flushing red. Sitting back down by the fire, he stared into the embers, too timid even to look at Nuri's sister as she beckoned.

"Ja, don't worry then, Guthroth," said Crowbones, standing. "I'll take your place."

This seemed to embarrass Guthroth even more, causing him to walk away from the fire and disappear into the brush.

As transactions were occurring, the other Romani discreetly slipped from the fire and retired to their wagons. Still confused, Tristan looked at Orla. "Lord Ox, what is happening here? I think these women are asking to be married!"

"Oh no," said Orla, watching Crowbones as he followed StraightLimbs and Nuri's sisters into the dark, "I don't think so. It appears they're just telling us 'thank you', but wish to do so privately in the wagons there."

"Oh," replied Tristan, satisfied with Orla's response. But something had been worrying him since the previous night. "Lord Ox, that big examination you were telling me about…Guillaume never paid attention to the teacher nuns. I suppose you were right, he might not pass it."

Orla gazed into the fire, content that Tristan had so quickly changed the topic from the Romani women to Guillaume. He loved this boy as he would a son. Still, he took certain pleasure in keeping him at the edge of uncertainty. Nodding, he said, "Ja, Boy, too bad. And if he fails, they'll put him out. Poor lad!"

Tristan shuddered at this prospect. "Put him out?"

"Ja, instead of educating him, they'll stick him behind a mule in their fields to labor all his life."

Tristan shivered as the image of Guillaume slaving in the Burgundy sun swept to mind. "Oh," he said regretfully, "I wish we had brought one of the nuns with us to help him prepare for this examination as we travel."

"Me, too," said Orla poking at the fire. "Ja, that would have been a good idea, but too late for that now, huh?" As he said this, he happened to notice that Nuri's daughter, Mala, was still seated on the other side of the fire staring intently at Tristan, absorbing his every gesture, taking in his every word. Since Tristan had taken his place next to Nuri an hour earlier, the girl's attention had never once deviated from him. *Ah*, thought Orla, *Boy already begins to catch their eye.*

Minutes later Nuri appeared from the darkness and motioned to Orla, who stood and followed her back into the darkness, leaving Tristan alone with Mala at the fire. This made him feel immediately awkward. Though he had had no problem speaking to Nuri, the daughter, for some reason, was a different issue. This was the first time in his life he had ever been alone with a young girl. Accordingly, he refused to look at her.

Mala was not so timid. Standing, she circled the fire and took a seat beside him. "Thank you for saving us today," she said in Spanish.

Staring at the fire, Tristan replied, "Oh, but I did nothing. It was the Danes."

"Maybe you did, maybe you didn't," she said, moving yet closer. "I say you did." She studied him a moment then. "Are you rich? I've never seen such fancy clothes before except on the Spanish nobility."

"No," said Tristan, wishing the Danes would return to the fire. "Well, maybe I used to be, but there has been some trouble and—" Stopping, he said nothing more.

"Well then, how did you get so smart?" Mala asked. "I've been watching you. You speak French and Spanish, and I heard you talking some other language with these men in your company. You seem to know just what to do and say all the time. I think I'll start calling you 'Smart Boy'. I've never met anyone like you—that's so young, I mean."

This caused a flitter of pride in Tristan's chest, but embarrassed him also. Not knowing what to say, he said nothing.

She looked at him a long while as he sat there silently watching the fire, then said, "Here, I want you to have this." This forced him to look up, despite feeling weak in the stomach. She had taken something from her hand, apparently, and was offering it to him.

"What is it?" he said, his curiosity pricked.

"It's a ring of Moorish silver, see the little crescent moon carved there?" Mala said. "Other than my clothes, it's the only thing I own. It's yours now."

Tristan was touched. "B-but why would you give me the only thing you own?"

"Why do you think, Smart Boy?"

Tristan could not find his tongue.

"Because I like you," Mala said, "but we will never see each other again. Still, I don't want you to forget me.

Chapter Nine

Paris

As the Romani and Danes broke camp that next morning, Tristan was struck by a pang of unanticipated regret. He had enjoyed meeting the Romani, had been fascinated by their story, and had appreciated this opportunity to converse in Spanish with native speakers, but there was something else, something he failed to quite comprehend. As the Romani wagons pulled away, he stood there gazing at the last wagon, wishing it might stay just a while longer. On the back stoop of that wagon sat Mala, staring back at him.

They had ended by talking for hours the night before, long after the Danes and Romani women had returned from the dark and retired for the night. He could not even remember what they had talked about for so long—everything and nothing, he supposed. They had laughed a bit, too, which was something Tristan sorely needed in the wake of losing his mother.

Feeling vacant and disappointed, he waved at Mala as her wagon slowly began to gain distance, hoping she would wave back, but she did nothing. She merely sat there on the back stoop of the fading wagon, chin in palms, looking back at him with an expression of despondency.

***

A great portion of Tristan's education at the hands of Asta's nuns centered on the history of Christianity's development in France. As Orla led them into the great city of Paris and approached one of the bridges that led across the Seine onto the Île de la Cité, Tristan pointed excitedly to the island and said to the oxman, "The pagan Celts considered this island a sacred place, and held their ceremonies here amongst the oaks. They worshipped trees, you know. And it was the Romans who built the first two bridges onto the island, constructing a pagan temple to Jupiter on the very site of the cathedral we will be visiting."

Impressed that the young boy should know so much, the oxman listened with interest. "I've been to Paris before," he said, "but know little of its history. But I'll say this, I never could've imagined you were such a scholar, lad, speaking languages and knowing so much history."

"My mother says that learning is the foundation of light," Tristan replied.

As they crossed the river, the Romanesque cathedral of Saint Étienne rose above the tree-line, dominating the sky. "There it is," said the oxman, "the church your mother wanted you to see."

"Indeed," said Tristan, staring in wonder. He had never in his life seen such a huge and marvelous structure. "You know, sir, the nuns taught me that this cathedral was founded in the 4th Century, and has a front façade as long as ten ships."

As they drew nearer, the massive cathedral grew even more imposing. Orla and Crowbones halted their mounts, and craning their heads skyward, stared straight up at the peak of the building.

"These damned Christians," grunted Crowbones, "quite the temple builders, huh?"

Orla nodded. "Ja, I've never in my life seen stone piled so high."

StraightLimbs, Fairhair and Guthroth the Quiet reined their horses in next to the oxman and Tristan, also gazing at the cathedral with awe. "Who in the hell was this Saint Étienne, and what'd he do to be so honored by such a monument?" asked StraightLimbs.

"He was the first Christian martyr," said Tristan, "and was stoned to death for blaspheming against God and Moses."

"For blasphemy, the Christians stoned him and then honored him with this incredible building?" asked StraightLimbs, confused.

"No," said Tristan. "He was stoned by *Jews* for blasphemy, jealous synagogue elders. They were angry because they could not argue him into submission. During his trial he accused his accusers, telling them he saw Heaven open up with his Savior, Jesus Christ, ready to protect, receive and crown his servant. This angered the mob and they dragged him about the town and stoned him to death."

Fairhair shrugged. "Damned Christians, none of it makes sense."

"No," insisted Tristan, "it was the Jews, not the Christians, who killed him."

"But was not Jesus himself a Jew?" asked StraightLimbs. "And the apostles, and even Saint Étienne?"

"Yes, but they became Christians *later*, and were punished by the Jews and Romans alike."

"But were the Romans not Christians themselves?" asked Orla, also confused. "If not, why do you call yourself a Roman Catholic?"

"Yes, Romans were Catholics, but later. *After* they crucified Christ!" Tristan responded, frustration seeping into his voice.

"Jews, Romans, Christians, one and the same; all foolish and superstitious," snorted Crowbones.

"No, you don't understand," insisted Tristan.

"They're pagans, lad," whispered the oxman with a nudge. "You'll do no good trying to explain such things to heathens."

Tristan began to explain yet again to the Danes, but paused as the futility of discussing Christian doctrine to them dawned on him. "In any case," he sighed, "this is truly a grand cathedral, is it not?"

"Ja, certainly so," the Danes agreed.

The square was bustling with people and activity. It reminded Tristan of the local spring fair in Saint-Germain-en-Laye, except in scale Saint Étienne Square was thirtyfold more immense in peddlers, booths and visitors. Exuding a carnival atmosphere, sounds of haggling and friendly conversation filled the air while throngs of market-goers roved up and down infinite rows of food stalls and exhibits inspecting wares of unimaginable variety.

"Can we look?" asked Tristan.

"Aye, get down Boy and let's walk about," said Orla. "Then we'll go see the inside of your cathedral as your mother instructed."

Tristan jumped from the wagon and Orla followed, amused by the boy's enthusiasm. Coming to the first row of vendor displays, Tristan encountered leather pouches, pennants, carved wooden toys, whistles, linens and cook-ware. The vast array of offerings fascinated Tristan. Running from stall to stall, he wished to see them all.

The following series of rows was dedicated to food stalls where the smoky scent of roasting hog, mutton and goat wafted through the air, luring weary market-goers and travelers with food for the hungry and drink for the thirsty. Ducks, geese and herons hung flaccid and broken-necked from hooks, as did hares and weasels. And everywhere one looked, baskets and counters were spilling over with plump vegetables and colorful, fresh fruit smelling of recent harvesting.

It was the next row of displays that drew Tristan's eye the most, those reserved for the sale of religious mementos. As he meandered down the row, fascinated, unexpected objects for sale appeared. Due to their exorbitant prices, Tristan could not contain his curiosity. After wandering about a bit, he stopped at a booth where delicate swatches of fabric were lined across the table. Each appeared frayed and soiled, but was accompanied by an official looking parchment upon which calligraphic notations appeared in Latin.

"What are these, sir?" he asked the peddler.

"And why so damned costly?" added Orla, puzzled.

Leaning over, the peddler said, "Relics, of the most holy grade. Swatches from the tunic of Saint Étienne himself."

Tristan drew back, stunned. "From the good saint himself?"

"Aye, lad, very precious, and quite rare!"

Orla eyed the vendor with suspicion. "Ha! And how is it you came by such items, friend?"

"From the Vatican," the vendor replied. "I purchased them in Rome from certain cardinals of the Vatican." Then he pointed to the parchments. "Do you see these documents there? They're authentification certificates, each signed and verified by a cardinal of Rome."

"Indeed?" said Tristan, now even more mesmerized by the strips of fabric displayed on the table. His imagination began to drift as he thought back to his teacher-nuns' stories about Saint Étienne. "From the garment of the first Catholic martyr!" he whispered aloud, reaching to touch one of the swatches.

"Stop that!" shouted the vendor, pushing Tristan's hand aside. "You mustn't touch! These are extremely precious."

Embarrassed, Tristan retreated a step, issuing a meek apology.

"Precious, my ass!" snorted Orla, aggravated by the vendor's tone.

Continuing to examine the strips of filthy fabric, Tristan leaned closer and pointed to a faded blue swatch on the end. "Is that a blood stain there?" he said, his eyes flaring with wonder.

"Indeed, lad, the blood of Saint Étienne," nodded the vendor.

Tristan nearly swooned, determining that he must possess that holy swatch. "Lord Ox, could we buy it?" he pleaded. "I won't ask for anything else, I promise!"

The urgency of Tristan's voice was unmistakable, but Orla shook his head. "We'll not be taken in by tricksters, Boy."

The vendor shook his head, pointing again to the parchments. "Believe what you wish, sir, but the cardinals of Rome don't lie. These relics are authentic. And for each one sold, a portion goes to the rectory and the good arch-bishop of Saint Étienne himself. He, of all people on this earth, would not abide by trickery on the very grounds of his own cathedral!"

Tristan gazed up at Orla, bolstered by the vendor's argument. "Please, Lord Ox," he pleaded, pointing to the blue swatch.

But Orla's anger had been piqued. "You damned thief!" he exclaimed, pointing at the now startled vendor. "Thief!" he repeated, louder so others could hear.

Orla's commotion embarrassed Tristan. Looking with apology at the vendor, he began to walk away from the booth, signaling Orla to follow. Once at a safe distance, he stopped at another booth, surprised to find yet more swatches of cloth with similar accompanying parchments. Saying nothing, he examined the swatches and the parch-ments as before, but in closer detail. The calligraphic in-scriptions caught his attention first. They were in Latin just as at the previous booth, but the style was primitive, nearly childish. The signature at the bottom, which he assumed to be that of a holy cardinal of Rome, was utterly illegible. *Oh, but this looks like something little Guillaume might scribble.*

Looking at this new vendor, Tristan asked, "Sir, are these strips of fabric from the tunic of Saint Étienne?"

"Nay, nay," the vendor said, pointing in the direction from which Tristan had just arrived. "Saint Étienne's relics are over there, those ten booths down the aisle. No, these pieces are a bit more reasonable, and are from the tunic of Saint Jerome. You do know who he is, eh, lad?"

"Indeed," replied Tristan. "The healing saint, doctor of the Catholic Church. He pulled the thorn from the great lion's paw."

"Ha, the very same!" laughed the vendor. "Good lad!"

Orla glanced over Tristan's shoulders and spied the swatches of cloth, marveling at the foolishness of the throngs of Christians milling about, purchasing one worthless object after another.

Tristan next spied a series of ornately carved, inlayed wooden boxes that were wax-sealed and stamped with official insignia. There was no indication of price. "But what might these be, sir?" he asked.

"Reliquaries', my boy," said the vendor. "They contain extremely rare first-class relics. These two here each contain a tiny sliver of bone from the body of holy Saint Jerome. These slivers, as you can just imagine, possess untold healing powers. They're the finest relics you'll find within the entire square! And this reliquary here contains filings from the very chains that held Saint Peter captive before his crucifixion."

"Are they costly?" asked Tristan.

"Indeed!" sniffed the merchant. "So much so that only bishops, lords and other merchants can afford them."

"And," said Orla, who was listening, "I wager you purchased them from the cardinals of Rome, who've documented that these bone slivers and filings are real, eh?"

"Of course, sir," crowed the vendor. "Real bone of a real saint. Real filings from the real chain that bound the Rock of the Church."

"And," Orla continued, "I imagine that you hand over a portion of each sale to the good archbishop of Saint Étienne, huh?"

"Absolutely," said the vendor, sensing mockery.

Orla looked down at Tristan, smirking. "They're all in this together, Boy, don't you see? There's enough fabric of saints in this square to clothe all of Europe, and enough bone of Saint Jerome to reconstruct a herd of elephants!"

Tristan ignored Orla's comments, pointing to the far edge of the table. "Those clay pots there with the cheaper prices marked and no seal or documents, sir, what do they hold?"

"Dirt," said the merchant, "but very special dirt, extracted from the catacombs of Rome where the early Christians and many saints practiced the early faith and hid for safety."

"*Dirt?*" ridiculed Orla, shaking his head in disbelief. "And how do we know you didn't dig it up in the countryside?"

"Sir," said the merchant with indignation, "I'm offended. Surely you don't presume that I'd commit such a sin in the very shadow of Saint Étienne Cathedral, under the very gaze of our Lord and Savior! Come now, I'm a purveyor of relics, licensed and certified by the Church, not a common swindler!" Reaching into his blouse, he extracted a document. "Here are my papers and—"

"Bah!" groaned Orla, grabbing Tristan by the hand. "Let's go, Boy, I've seen enough. I won't have these crafty hooligans slipping their fingers into our purses!"

Tristan followed reluctantly, his heart still burning to purchase one of the many holy objects he had encountered. But Orla, wishing to get away from the relic sellers, dragged Tristan away.

Just as they were about to vacate the relic area, a stir arose as a strange looking monk atop a donkey came down one of the aisles. He was small in stature, possessing a rather feral look about his eyes, and his beard tumbled to his waist. He wore filthy, frayed trousers and hair shirt accompanied by a mantle that fell to his bare feet, which were black with filth. As he noisily advanced, he was shouting at the passing crowd, admonishing them.

"Sinners!" he cried. "Be gone from this false marketplace! The sale and purchase of holy relics is forbidden by the Theodosian Code and by God! This and simony are against God's Law! Half your bishops have purchased their miters and crosiers from the King! The Church is dissolving in a sea of sin!"

Onlookers were circling the donkey, and it appeared the gathering crowd was taking delight in heckling the man. "Kuku Peter! Kuku Peter!" howled someone in the crowd.

"Go back to Amiens, you dirty Gaul!" a woman cackled, laughing.

"Go back to your cave, you filthy hermit!" an old man brayed.

The monk remained undeterred. "Woe unto all in this marketplace following the practice of that evil sorcerer, Simon Magus, who offered payment to the disciples of Jesus to validate his magic! The sacraments aren't for sale! Relics aren't for sale! Holy office isn't for sale! And cursed be the clerics of the Catholic Church who condone and encourage your damnable behavior!"

"Now there's a man who makes sense," said Orla, taking in the unfolding drama with interest.

"No," objected Tristan, disturbed by the monk's rhetoric, "he's railing against priests and bishops. God will strike him down."

As the little monk became more animated, so did the crowd. Nonetheless, there seemed to be humor in their sniping, and it appeared everyone was rather enjoying the wild-eyed monk's presence. Reciprocally, despite the crowd's haranguing, the monk himself did not seem the least perturbed by the crowd's mockery, and was giving as good as he was getting.

But this entertaining exchange of mock-anger suddenly spiraled into a fracas as a priest and two soldiers broke through the mob, appearing from nowhere. "Get him out of here!" the priest shouted to the soldiers. Reaching out with a lunging fist, one of the soldiers punched the monk in the jaw, sending him flying off his donkey into the crowd. Before he could get up, the other soldier began kicking him. "Beat the hell out of him!" cried the priest.

Backing away, onlookers began to shout in defense of the accosted monk. "Leave him alone, it's just Kuku Peter!" a woman cried out.

"He's just a poor, crazy hermit! Have mercy!" someone pleaded.

"We're just having fun here, damn you!" cried another.

The beating continued. Orla watched briefly, but became disturbed as the pummeling of the little man increased despite his evident defenselessness. Shoving the priest aside and shaking one of the soldiers violently by the collar, Orla snarled, "Let this man be! He's done nothing but spout a few well-deserved insults!"

"He's blaspheming!" the soldier bristled, breaking from Orla's grip. "We were sent by the archbishop, damn you! He's ordered this lout imprisoned! He causes a public disturbance every time he shows up!"

Orla reached down to pick the monk from the ground. "Leave now! Your criticism of priests and monks is getting under some collars."

The monk, confusing Orla for one of the soldiers, went into a crouch, shifting left, then right, as though ready to strike out. Orla found this comical, and began to snicker, shrugging to those watching.

The monk found no humor in his own absurd defensive movements, and snorted, "Ho, you big piss-ant, move aside before I clobber you! You'll not quell the fire of God, for He Himself sent me here!" Balling his fists and waggling them about like fluttering birds, he let out a whoop and charged Orla, only to bounce off his massive chest as a pebble would ricochet off a fortress wall.

Orla grunted, dumbfounded at being thus assaulted by such a puny entity. "Don't be an imbecile, monk. I'm only trying to help you!"

Gathering himself from the ground, the monk waggled his fists again, but it was evident his balance was ajar. His attempt to bowl Orla over, along with his subsequent plummet onto the pavement, had rattled his senses. "God is my shield!" he shouted, teetering about as intoxicated, on the verge of collapse.

Seeing that the monk was not about to retreat despite his condition, Orla looked over at the two soldiers and said, "Touch him again and I'll wring your damned necks. And that goes for you, too, priest!" Taking Tristan's hand, he led him away from the mêlée, though the monk was still spouting garbled threats, wobbling about, threatening to knock Orla out.

Looking up, Tristan said, "You should not talk to a priest that way, Lord Ox. Still, thank you for helping that crazy monk, even though he was attacking the Church. I am pleased you refused to let the soldiers hurt him anymore."

"Very well then," said Orla. "It pleases me that you are pleased, Boy."

Tristan grabbed Orla's huge paw with his own small hand, content to be in Orla's mighty shadow. "Come then, Lord Ox. I wish to show you this wondrous cathedral. It might make you wish to be baptized!"

Chapter Ten

Cluny

After nearly a week of tedious progress on thirst-crusted roads leading south, Orla led his group east until finally entering the territory of Burgundy. Here the oxcart began to bounce and rattle violently, shuddering over the many rocks and stones strewn over the road ahead as it snaked its way through a series of valleys and low mountains. The wagon at times quaked with such violence that the oxman, Tristan and Guillaume were nearly thrown from their seats on several occasions.

Accustomed to such roads in his native Burgundy, the driver sat there glum and bored despite the incessant jostling brought on by the conspiracy of rocky terrain and rough-hewn wooden wheels of the cart. He was rather a dull man given to interminable bouts of silence, but on entering his home territory he came to life from time-to-time upon arriving at certain landmarks with which he was familiar. He then took sudden delight in delivering to his two young passengers a sporadic history of that church or this battle site.

These history recitals interested Tristan, who had been somewhat morose himself since departing Paris. He had been thinking of his mother, wondering how it was that she could have abandoned him and Guillaume. Then, too, oddly, he had been wondering about Mala, the Romani girl. He wished she was there to talk to, if for nothing else, to make time go by and make him laugh again. Indeed, though they had only been together once, he missed her for some reason.

Guillaume, upon reaching this rougher terrain, found the cart to be suddenly exhilarating. He laughed and shouted with each new bump, hoping the next would be even more raucous. "Tristan!" he would shout. "Hang on! This one's going to throw us over!" Then he would sink his little head down into his shoulders and glue himself onto his older brother's arm, his gray eyes shimmering with glee.

So it went until late one afternoon they entered an especially picturesque valley along the Grosne River where the fields, full of bustling peasants, began to look especially well-tilled and rich with spring growth. Well-groomed vineyards rolled endlessly along gentle slopes, and vast stretches of partitioned and cultivated farmland filled the entire valley. In the distance, on a large plateau halfway up a hillside, a great edifice rose to the sky, towering over all it shadowed. Its peach-cream colored stone formed the formidable appearance of a magnificent fortress, one many times greater in scale than anything Tristan had ever imagined.

He stared at the structure, awed. And as the cart drew nearer, the splendor of the structure seemed only to magnify. Pulling at the oxman's sleeve, he asked, "That palace, does it belong to the overlord of Burgundy, or perhaps even the King of France?"

The driver shook his head. "No, lad, that's the Monastery of Cluny, home of Benedictine prayer and center of God's light in France."

"A monastery?" Tristan questioned him, disbelief outlining his face. The monasteries of the Saint-Germain-en-Laye region were small and humble in nature. This majestic complex on the hillside was far more like a royal palace. "Is it here that you are taking us?" A flitter rose in his chest. "Guillaume, look! The Monastery of Cluny!"

Guillaume stared in wonder at the hill and pointed. "Cluny!" he shouted. "Cluny!"

Tristan gazed at the fields again, surveying the army of peasants working them. "These endless farmlands surrounding us," he said to the oxman, "who owns them?"

"The Benedictines," replied the oxman.

"But I see no monks working in the fields. In Saint-Germain-en-Laye the monks till the land."

"Oh, not here, lad. They touch neither tool nor earth."

"What is it they do, then?"

"Pray, my boy, day and night, for our souls and for the souls of the faithful departed. They also run the infirmary for the sick, feed the poor and offer hospitality to travelers and pilgrims. They've no time for farm labor or other such menial tasks."

Within the hour the road widened, taking an ambling turn up the hillside toward the monastery complex. The oxman turned his team up the slope, but as they neared the monastery gate they came upon a commotion. Two monks were struggling with a woman garbed in a long white robe, dragging her off. The woman had long black hair and possessed a demented look about her eyes. Fighting off the monks, she glared up at Tristan and Guillaume as the wagon passed, and hissed, "Allez-vous en, les enfants! Get away! Oh, don't enter that place, children! It's the blight of Europe!"

At the instant Tristan's eyes met hers, her anger seemed to dissipate momentarily. In its place arose a look of despair. He wanted to say something, but before he could open his mouth, one of the monks swung his fist, knocking her to the ground.

Pushing her face from the dust with both palms, gazing up with bloodied lip, she reached a hand toward the wagon. "Retournez chez vous!" she wailed. "Jump from the wagon, boys! Run!"

"Ignore her," said the oxman. "It's just the White Witch. She hates the Church. Some say the Devil's taken possession of her. She's from the village below and has been haranguing the Black Monks for years now, ever since losing her daughter."

"Her daughter?" asked Tristan. "What happened to her?"

"It's a sad story, lad, but never mind. It's not a story for children."

Flicking the reins, he drove his team through the gate, which was when Tristan and the Danes began to comprehend the actual immensity of Cluny Monastery.

"Damnation!" muttered Orla. "What a place this is!"

The oxman observed Orla's reaction, and a wave of Burgundy pride swept over him. "The scope and wealth of this place is unimaginable," he said, pointing to the abbey. "That cathedral has five altars, four major steeples and double aisles. It's the longest building in all Christendom, glorified with gold, silver and magnificent frescoes. And they say the great Abbot Hugh of Cluny is more powerful than any king in Europe, or even the Pope."

"Is it to the Abbot Hugh that we are to make our introductions?" asked Tristan, enthralled by the oxman's descriptions.

"Not likely," replied the oxman. "He's like an elusive phantom, slipping in and out of Cluny like a shadow in the night, performing secret embassies here and clandestine negotiations there. Though a monk, he's the leading power-broker of continental politics and carries unimaginable sway throughout the royal courts of Europe. No, you'll rarely see him, lad. He has no time for mere students here."

"Oh," said Tristan, disheartened. "I was hoping to meet him. My mother says he speaks to God through spiritual visions that he can conjure upon will."

Seeing Tristan's disappointment, the oxman said, "But, lad, you'll be introduced to a man nearly as celebrated as Abbot Hugh himself. Indeed, it's Prior Odo de Lagery who will interview you upon arrival."

Tristan shrugged. "Odo de *who*?"

"Odo de Lagery," the oxman said. "Next to Abbot Hugh, and then the Grand Prior who manages the wealth and treasure of this place, he is the master here. In fact, Odo de Lagery actually runs the day-to-day operations of this entire place. As much as you know about the Church, I'm surprised you've never heard of him. He's one of the most renowned clerics in all France."

"My mother has never spoken of him," said Tristan.

"Well, he's a good man, so you and your little brother are fortunate," asserted the oxman. "After all, lad, it'll be Odo de Lagery now who will be running your lives."

Chapter Eleven

Odo de Lagery

The oxman and Tristan dismounted from the driver's seat as Orla approached the rear of the wagon, reached beneath the bed, and pulled something loose from between the two rear wheels. It was an iron lever. Orla next crawled beneath the wagon, positioned his back to the ground, and began leveraging the iron bar against the bottom of the driver's seat. Tristan backed away as wood cracked and splinters began flying in all directions, exposing a secret compartment crafted beneath the driver's seat. Orla grunted as two planks broke loose and a heavy wooden trunk dropped down onto his chest. He then shimmied from beneath the wagon with the chest in tow.

As Orla stood to dust himself, a monk approached. "May I be of assistance?"

"We're here to see the monk known as Odo de Lagery," Orla replied. "We represent the Lady Asta de Saint-Germain and are delivering her sons here for schooling."

"Ah, the Claustral Prior," said the monk, motioning with a pass of his hand. "Come along, I'll take you to Main Parlour where new students are interviewed."

Interviewed, thought Tristan nervously, supposing that might be Cluny's 'code' for the big oral examination he and Guillaume would have to pass in order to be accepted by the Black Monks.

As Orla picked up the trunk to follow the monk, he said to the other Danes, "Asta told me before we left that I was to meet privately with the prior. As always, she offered no explanation. In any case, I'll get this business of turning the boys over as quickly as possible, bring them back to share farewells, and we'll be on our way to England."

As he said this, Tristan perceived a shift in Orla's mood. His voice grew gruff for some reason, and his face became somber, as heavy with worry. "Come along, boys," he groused, taking the monk's path.

The monk led them through a labyrinth of stables, guest halls and courtyards. With each passing step Orla and the boys began to further fathom the vast scope of the Cluny complex. Finally, they were ushered into the entry of the Main Parlour, which was located adjacent to the magnificent Chapter House.

"Wait here," the monk said, "Prior Odo will be along shortly."

Tristan gazed about the vast chamber, awe-struck by its richly decorated interior and ornate furnishings. Its walls were adorned with stunning mosaics, paintings and tapestries and huge candles taller than a man stood encased throughout the room in massive candelabra bases of pure silver, so brightly polished they perfectly reflected every aspect of every object throughout the Main Parlour. The walls extended high onto the ceiling, beautifully detailed every six feet by exquisite faux half-columns made of polished limestone extending to the ceiling where they terminated into masterfully carved capitals so delicate with detail that they could not help but draw the eye, making one marvel at the intricacy and finesse of the sculptor's chiselwork. The arched, vaulted ceiling was even more striking, bathed in stunning frescos of saints, holy scenes and interpretations of Heaven.

More than anything else, it was the books that overwhelmed Tristan. They filled the endless rows of wall shelving that stood between each wall column, lay in disheveled stacks upon the many tables within the room, and even littered the floor in waist-high stacks. He had only seen three books in his entire life, as they were so rare, so the sea of books now surrounding him seemed an impossibility. He had never even imagined that so many books existed in all France, let alone in a single room. Each was a masterful work of art, its cover crafted from finely polished hardwood or gold-embossed leather, many being trimmed with ornamental edgings of gold or silver leaf.

It was the collection of gold chalices arranged three deep and twenty across on the massive mantle that caught Orla's attention. Each was a masterpiece of craftsmanship, encrusted with a dazzling array of precious gems. Trying to calculate their total worth, he determined that he had never in his life seen so much bejeweled opulence in one space. Reaching up, he was about to examine one when a man entered from the opposite end of the chamber.

He was tall and wore the hooded black robe of the Benedictines. As he approached, it was evident to Orla that this man, in his early thirties, possessed that air of confidence characteristic of those who wielded authority and had lived a life of privilege.

Orla's mood had already turned foul upon leaving the wagon; the cold reality of leaving the boys behind had hit him. Scowling, he wanted to hate this handsome man, take his stunning height down a notch. "You are the Claustral Prior of Cluny?" he asked, showing little trace of cordiality. Setting the trunk onto the floor and opening it, he added, "The Lady Asta de Saint-Germain bids me to greet you with this gift. Beneath the gold and silver coins contained within, she has also included a private correspondence for your eyes only. On her behalf, I deliver to you her two sons, Tristan and Guillaume."

Orla was speaking in a tone and manner that Tristan found unfamiliar. It was cold and vacant, tinged with hostility. Anxiety-ridden as he already was, he began to fear that Orla's lack of deference might jeopardize his and Guillaume's introduction.

As Tristan fretted in silence, the prior looked down into the trunk, appearing unmoved, saying nothing. This baffled Orla, who expected that the monk would be immensely pleased with Asta's significant monetary offering, to the point of at least asking about the sum or taking a brief accounting of it. What Orla did not realize was that the sizeable wealth contained in the trunk was but a pittance to the monastery of Cluny, whose treasury, resources and holdings far exceeded that of most emperors of the continent.

Pointing to the trunk, Orla said, "You *have* received Lady Asta's previous correspondence on this transaction, have you not?"

Ignoring the trunk, Prior Odo stepped over to Tristan and rumpled his spill of fair hair, then did the same to Guillaume who stood in place uncharacteristically wide-eyed and shy, one foot atop the other. Watching, Orla thought he detected in the monk's expression a slight tug of affection, but it disappeared before he could be certain.

The prior continued to survey the two boys before him from head to toe. "Eh bien, quels beaux garçons, ces deux," he said. "So, the Lady Asta presents these two handsome lads, Tristan and Guillaume." Then he finally acknowledged the trunk. "Lady Asta *does* understand that this gift creates no favor, no expectations and no ties between herself and the Benedictines of Cluny, does she not? She does acknowledge that we accept this gift only as a free-will alm?"

Orla nodded begrudgingly. "Though I don't understand such a one-sided exchange," he replied, "yes, Lady Asta has acknowledged all you mention, and holds no expectation of return from the Black Monks. She does request, and I quote, 'that you educate her sons and use them to further the glory of her God and the Roman Church'."

The Prior listened to Orla's words with a placid, listening face. Tilting his head, he said, "Her God? Ah, I surmise you are not Christian nor do you hold our Church in high regard. This surprises me a bit, sir, because the Church counts the Normans as their greatest protectors. Are you not Norman?"

"No, I come from there but remain a Dane. I'm a free man and refute the yoke of the French, as well as of the Roman Church. I've seen what your holy men do. I therefore, am content to remain 'pagan' as you people so derisively call it."

This horrified Tristan, causing him to lift his eyes to Orla in sheer supplication. *Oh, please, Lord Ox,* his eyes implored, *stop being difficult.*

But Orla was not watching Tristan. His focus was on the prior, awaiting a rebuttal to which he was already prepared to counter. The truth was, he had since arriving at Cluny, become disconcerted beyond anticipation. He was filling with apprehension and pity for Tristan and Guillaume, two small boys who were suddenly lost to the wind, having lost their mother and their home, and would within the hour lose the protection of the Danes themselves. It had dawned on Orla all at once that Boy and Mite were about to be left in a stark world of regimen, indoctrination and probable abuse, yet the two young innocents suspected nothing. Orla felt stricken, suddenly, knowing there was nothing he could do. The political web that had given rise to all this was far beyond his control.

Gazing thoughtfully into Orla's eyes, Prior Odo said, "Well spoken sir. I, too, have seen what our holy men do, and the more I see, the more I am disgusted."

Of all responses Orla could have expected, this was not one of them. Thinking at first the prior was baiting him or engaging in mockery, he searched the cleric's mute expression, but detected neither deceit nor scorn,

"There are many amongst our religious who have lost their way," Prior Odo continued. "In fact, our Church is at a tipping point, spiraling into decay. Many of our clerics favor the secular over the spiritual, burying themselves in sin. But so you know, here at Cluny we make war against such spiritual decay each day of each week of each year."

These words came as yet another surprise to Orla, and his initial distrust began to melt away, by degrees. It then occurred to Orla that this monk standing before him lacked all pretension, as well as that condescending posture of those wielding authority or having the good fortune of inheriting wealth and power. Gesturing at the boys, Orla said, "My main concern here is how you shall accept these two boys."

Tristan, who had begun to drown in disquiet from the moment Orla had challenged the Church, misinterpreted Orla's statement, thinking Orla had said, 'My main concern here is *if you* shall accept these boys'. Swallowing hard, he glanced first over at Guillaume, then up at the prior, who had seemed to him since his arrival to be the tall, dark and omnipotent judge of doom. Then he grabbed Guillaume about the shoulders, as if to protect him. Unable to contain himself, words began to spill from his mouth. "Prior, I am ready for my oral examination! Ask me what you may! And I will speak for my brother also. I will answer his part!"

Hearing this pitiful plea, Prior Odo tilted his head. "Oral examination?" he asked.

"Indeed!" Tristan persisted. "Lord Ox warned me about it, and I am ready. But please, sir, let me answer for my brother lest he be forced to drive mules in the fields!"

"Mules in the field?" said Prior Odo, raising a brow in puzzlement.

Witnessing Tristan's frantic appeal, Orla reddened. But before he could clarify or intercede, Tristan continued to plead his case.

"Indeed, Prior Odo," said Tristan, "I am well prepared to answer about Church history, geography, Latin,

Spanish, or whatever else your examination entails! But my little brother is still young yet and—"

"Hold there," clucked Prior Odo, waving a hand to calm the boy. "Pray tell…what are you talking about?"

"The examination!" Tristan insisted. "You know, to see whether you will accept me and my little brother or not!"

"Examination?" echoed Prior Odo. "There is no examination. You are both here, and you shall both be educated."

"*No examination?*" said Tristan, shrugging with disbelief as color returned to his cheeks. Standing there dumbfounded, he fired a glance at Orla who was now as red-faced as himself. "Oh, Lord Ox!" he fussed, on the edge of tears. "I've been fretting for Guillaume since coming through the gates, and it was but a joke?"

"Not to worry," said Prior Odo, assuring the boy. "We accept you on the faith of your mother whom I met in the city of Rouen months ago. Her strong faith in God struck me during our first encounter. We had two days together there, and spent a good amount of time discussing her circumstances…and yours as well."

Tristan released Guillaume. "You know my mother?" he asked.

"Yes. It was in Rouen she approached me about the possibility of accepting you boys at Cluny."

Tristan dropped his eyes to the floor. "Then…you know my father was executed for treason, n'est-ce pas? My brother and I are no longer considered of noble blood because of what he—"

"Insperata accident magis saepe quam quae speres, Tristan," said Prior Odo. "Do you understand that Latin proverb?"

"Yes, Prior. What you did not hope for happens more often than what you hoped for."

Smiling, Prior Odo placed a hand on the boy's shoulder. "Très bien, Tristan, an excellent translation. The truth is, you are here despite your father. Such is God's path. Because of your mother's piety and obedience to God, you and your brother shall now begin your training here at Cluny with us, and perhaps one day join the order as I did."

"B-but, I do not wish to become..." Tristan stammered, then paused.

"Yes, yes, what is it you were about to say?" asked Prior Odo.

No reply.

"He doesn't wish to become a priest or a monk," said Orla. "He fears you will force him to become one."

Prior Odo looked at Tristan with empathy. "You are quite young and could not know yet what you wish to become, lad. Still, know that we teach other vocations here also." Then, turning to Orla, he said, "We accept this gift of coinage as a free-will alm from the Lady Asta. And I thank you, sir, for delivering these boys. I will take charge of them now, so assure Lady Asta upon your arrival in England that her sons shall be well educated."

Orla bowed, then waved his hand in a quick arc of farewell. "Boy, Mite, I hope to see you again at some point, but if I don't, remember me and the other Danes. Make us proud, lads." Turning, he quickly left the room. It was a poor farewell, Orla knew, but his heart had begun to swell as the prior said, 'I will take charge of them now'. The moment was so poignant for Orla that he could not bear to stay a moment longer, thus he simply fled, forgetting even that the other Danes had not yet said their own farewells to the boys.

Tristan, unprepared for Orla's hasty departure, dashed after him as a frustrated cry burst from his lips. But Orla was gone and had already closed the door. "L-Lord Ox!" Tristan bawled, tears swelling his eyes to bursting. "I wanted to bid you farewell and embrace you before leaving! Will you not even—" The words stuck in his throat, stinging like nettles, and he froze with every muscle locked, mouth ajar. Abandoned again, he shivered, dropping both arms limply to his side.

Standing mute and motionless, Guillaume watched. "Don't be sad, Tristan," the four-year-old said, feeling from within the stirrings of a deeply rooted sorrow for his brother. Even at his tender age, and despite the fact that Tristan was older, Guillaume already understood that Tristan was immensely more fragile than himself. "Don't be sad, Tristan," he repeated, holding both arms out to his brother.

"Indeed, Tristan, listen to your young brother," said the Prior. "Now come along, boys, your new life awaits."

Chapter Twelve

The Dorter

Prior Odo, his long legs moving forward at a quick pace, led Tristan and Guillaume out of the Main Parlour and took them south past the Ladies' Chapel and the Infirmary. "I am about to deliver you to Brother Placidus," he said, "who oversees the Dorter where our youngest students reside. He is old, but be not deceived. He is far more clever than you would imagine. Also, know that he has lived here at Cluny his entire life. He was abandoned here as an infant during the winter of the Great Freeze."

"Abandoned?"

"Yes," said Prior Odo. "He says little, but sees and hears all. The other boys make things difficult for him at times, but no need to join their mischief. Understood?"

"Yes, Prior," the boys replied.

As they entered the Dorter, which was tucked in the southeast corner of the monastery complex, Prior Odo led them to a small room where they encountered an elderly man sitting alone at a small workbench. The man shuffled about a moment as if to rise.

"No, Placidus, keep your seat," said Prior Odo, touching the man's elbow deferentially. "Here are the two new students we have been waiting on. This is Tristan, and this is his younger brother, Guillaume, from the Saint-Germain-en-Laye region in the north."

The old man started to speak, but the words caught in his throat, forcing him to issue that raspy cough of the infirm. "Saint-Germain-en-Laye?" he said hoarsely. "I heard there was some troubles up there a while ago. Executions by order of the Bastard…treason or some such affair. They say—"

"Never mind all that, Brother," Odo interrupted, positioning himself between the boys and the old monk to shield them from this talk. "Settle these two in and get them acquainted with the other boys. To earn their keep, I believe Tristan here might be good help in the scullery, and young Guillaume might be a suitable stable hand."

"Very well, Prior. Leave it to me. I'll take them to their quarters and show them about."

"Thank you, Placidus," said Prior Odo, bowing. Then he looked at the boys. "I will check on your progress next month. May God guide your way and be your light."

"Come with me, boys," said Placidus, slowly pushing himself up from the workbench with both palms. He led them down a narrow corridor into a large chamber filled with other boys engaged in lively play and a loud stream of chatter. "Boys! Boys! Quiet now!" Placidus cried out hoarsely.

"Boys! Boys! Quiet now!" a falsetto voice mimicked from within the group.

"Listen here," Placidus droned, ignoring the mockery, "these are the new boys Prior Odo told us about. They're from Saint-Germain-en-Laye, so make them welcome."

"Saint-Germain-en-Laye?" someone whispered. Then came a hushed exchange among the boys. Tristan thought he heard the word 'traitor' whispered.

"They'll take the end bunks," Placidus rattled on. "Respect their belongings, their bodies and their affairs, lads."

As Placidus limped out of the room, Tristan gazed about uncomfortably at the other boys who now stood in silence sizing up the new arrivals. There were about twenty of them, ranging in age from seven to eleven or twelve. This meant that he would be one of the younger boys, Tristan deduced, and Guillaume would be the youngest by far. *Not the best of circumstances in this strange new setting*, he thought.

Tristan offered up a meek smile to the group, but as he searched one face to the next, it seemed that each boy was scrutinizing him and Guillaume through narrow eyes. There was one older boy in particular, with reddish hair, whose eyes seemed swollen with resentment for some reason. This augmented Tristan's discomfort, and he shuffled about uneasily. Finally, he found the courage to speak. "I am Tristan de Saint-Germain, and this is my younger brother, Guillaume. He is about to turn five."

"I am Tristan de Saint-Germain, and this is my younger brother!" someone hidden within the crowd mimicked in a girlish voice. It was the same voice that had mocked Brother Placidus.

A burst of boyish laughter exploded. Then, oddly, all the boys seemed to lose interest in the newcomers and returned to their original state of chatter. The red-headed boy, however, continued to stare at Tristan with disdain.

Unnerved, Tristan took Guillaume by the hand and led him to the end bunks. But from the corner of his eye he could see that the older red-headed boy was following them. He hoped secretly that this was coincidental, but then he felt a violent push from behind that sent him reeling onto the floor, crashing into the wooden corner of his bunk.

Dazed, Tristan's eyelids fluttered limply as his vision became a constellation of spots. Gathering his senses, he tried to rise, but then came another push, more violent than the first. This sent his head crashing against the stone floor. All at once he felt the warmth of blood trickling through his hair and into his eyes. Despite this fog, he could still see the older boy standing over him, ready to pounce yet again.

At that moment, little Guillaume ran at the big boy and buried the bully's legs in a barrage of tiny fists and kicking feet. "Leave my brother alone!" Guillaume squealed, by now lost in his own blind fury.

Surprised at being attacked by one so small, the big
boy grabbed Guillaume by the scant meat of his neck and
shoved him down onto Tristan. Then he stood back, and
had just broken into derisive laughter when he felt a violent
blow to the back of his own head. Covering the back of his
crown with both hands for protection, he spun about to
strike back, but instead froze in place.

A larger boy stood there, his hands balled into fists.
"Hey, LeBrun! Let them be! They've not yet earned a beating from you or anyone else here!"

The red-headed LeBrun dropped one arm, and raised
the other to soothe the knot rising on the back of his skull.
"Damn you, that hurt, Letellier!" he hollered. "I didn't do
anything to you! Why'd you hit me, you big bastard?"

"Because you're a pig!" shouted a diminutive figure
standing next to the boy named Letellier. This second boy
was a dwarf, standing only three feet tall, yet seemed to
lack all fear of the red-head.

Letellier leaned down to gather Tristan and Guillaume from the floor. "We're getting sick of you, LeBrun,"
he said with heat. "If you want to fight, pick someone your
own size like me or Hébert!"

At the mention of his name, Hébert joined Letellier's
side. He also was larger than LeBrun, and a year older.
"Yeah, you lout!" he barked.

"Yeah," said the dwarf boy, "or try me you big ugly
shit!" Then he assisted Letellier in helping the new boys to
their feet.

Clearing his head, Tristan looked down on the small
figure of a boy who seemed full of bluster for one so small.
He had heard of dwarves before, but had never in his years
encountered one face-to-face. "Th-thank you," he mumbled.

"Why are you so short?" giggled Guillaume, fascinated by the boy.

"Hush!" said Tristan, mortified.

"Because I'm a dwarf," the boy replied to Guillaume. "They call me Scule. You know, short for 'miniscule'. My father was horrified upon seeing me at birth, but my mother loved me and said I was cute, so she dubbed me 'little Scule'. I'm the same age as Letellier and Hébert, just half their size." Turning toward LeBrun, he pointed. "But I can still beat his freckled ass!"

LeBrun, reddening, sized up the opposition. Fighting any one of the boys standing there before him would have been a challenge, even the dwarf who had already pummeled him a time or two. Consequently he retreated out of the sleeping quarters, muttering profanity beneath his breath.

"Sorry about that," Letellier said, patting Tristan's blood soaked locks. "I'm the Dorter Acolyte. Brother Placidus gave me that position because I'm the toughest one here. Say there, you're bleeding pretty bad."

"Yeah," agreed Scule. "I better go get Brother Placidus."

Tristan shoved Letellier's hand from his hair. "Thank you, but no," he said, shaking his head. "Best that no one knows about this. It would just cause more trouble." Then he dabbed at the fine stream of blood that was trickling down his forehead. "That boy, he called you Letellier. I know that name. Are you from the north?"

Letellier nodded. "Indeed, from just outside the Norman territories near Paris, like you." Letellier looked down at the floor then, his expression colored with abashment. "My father, Lord François Letellier," he said slowly, "was among those who turned your father in to the Bastard. He now possesses your family's former estate." Pausing, he placed his hand over his heart. "But don't entangle me in that mess, and never confuse me with my father. I barely know him."

"Nor did I know mine," said Tristan, stunned, thinking that only the most twisted of fates could create a circumstance as odd as being saved by the very offspring of the man who had caused his father's execution. "*Merci beaucoup*, Letellier, and you, too, Scule. Thank you for intervening." Giving a shrug, he said, "That boy LeBrun, he must be crazy or something."

Letellier nodded in agreement, content that there would be peace between himself and the newcomers. "Yeah, angry at the world, we've decided." Next he pointed at Guillaume and chuckled. "Your little brother, he's a feisty little badger!"

Tristan nodded. "He fears nothing."

"Huh, then," said the tiny Scule, "he must be like me, eh, Letellier?"

"Yeah, just like you," Letellier grinned. "And maybe since he's tough, he'll be lucky enough to join me and Hébert in the Stable Cohort."

"Stable cohort?" said Tristan.

"Yeah, each of us here has been assigned to a cohort according to what the Black Monks see as our future. The Stable Cohort trains to ride and care for all the mounts. We're also learning to clean and maintain armor and the four weapons: sword, ax, dagger and hammer."

At this, Guillaume stepped forward, ripe with anticipation. "Ax and hammer, like the Danes! I want to learn that! Can I be with you, Letellier?"

Letellier laughed. "Not my decision! The monks decide."

Tristan thought a moment. "Prior Odo said something to Brother Placidus as we entered about putting Guillaume to work in the stables. Do you suppose then that—"

"Ha!" exclaimed Letellier. "Then it's already been decided. Prior Odo's already assigned your brother with me and Hébert. It's a good group to be in except when we're not receiving our lessons." Pinching his nose, he added, "That's when we have to shovel mule and cow shit! But when we turn fourteen, we'll return to our families and our fathers will sponsor us as squires. Later, we'll become knights."

"Oh, I see," said Tristan, realizing that Guillaume did not and would not have an aristocratic father to sponsor him. He wanted to ask what would then happen to a boy in Guillaume's position, but felt it better to wait until Guillaume was not present.

"And what about you, Tristan?" asked Scule. "What did Prior Odo say?"

Tristan thought a moment. "Well, something about the...*scullet*? Or something like that, whatever that is."

Letellier and Hebert exchanged a glance, nodding. "You must mean the scullery," said Letellier. "That's where they store and wash cookware. You've been assigned to work with Brother Loiseaux and his boys in the Scullery Cohort to help the kitchen hands cook and clean for the entire monastery."

Tristan's face dropped. "Cooking and cleaning?" he shrugged, crestfallen. Unable to disguise his disappointment, he looked at Letellier and Hébert. "God gave me a fine start at birth, but life has taken a bad turn of late, and now this. I'm to be nothing but *kitchen* help."

Letellier shook his head. "Tristan, the Scullery Cohort is the finest assignment at Cluny."

"Don't play with me, Letellier," said Tristan, disheartened. "There is no humor in any of this. I'd rather work the stables than be a pot washer."

"I don't think you understand," said Hébert. "The Scullery Cohort is the most elevated of all cohorts here at Cluny. It's also known as the Academic Cohort. You'll receive the highest education possible in this entire life!"

"What?" asked Tristan.

"Yeah," said Scule. "You'll be with me! It's from the Scullery Cohort that Cluny develops its future Church leaders, diplomats and emissaries. They pick only the most intelligent lads for the Scullery Cohort. And you, it seems, have been chosen. Ay, it appears the Black Monks have decided that you are to be one of them!"

Chapter Thirteen

Life at the Abby, and LeBrun

The first night in the Dorter was difficult for Tristan. He lay there in a state of restless agitation, staring up at the night sky through the open window adjacent to his tiny bed. It seemed the moon was peering down at him with pity. Half hidden behind a darkening silver cloud, its ghostly pallor heralded specks of rain in the wind, leaving him feeling isolated and abandoned. In the bed next to him, he could hear his brother's soft breathing, rising and falling with the placid rhythm of a deep sleep. He envied Guillaume who did not dwell on things and was not as profoundly affected by events, or by others.

Wrestling against such unease late into the night, he finally began to feel the day slipping off him and descended into a half sleep. Part of him remained in the real world, but moment-by-moment reality began to fade as he slipped into the realm of the dream world. Edging his way there into half sleep, something weak and thready began to form. Then, coldly aware, he was back in that place, at the edge of the Seine River amidst the Danes and the Norse and their boisterous orgy of ale and drunken laughter. Knowing what was about to occur, Tristan stepped forward, shivering in desperation, wanting to warn the Norsemen to flee. But before he could utter a sound, mighty Orla burst forward from nowhere, his muscled neck-flesh thick and pulsating. His ax swung down in an arc of fury as the unsuspecting Norse captain, Frode, glanced up and smiled. Next his head was suddenly split in half and became a flushing, scarlet fountain of horror. The wind lifted then, carrying the screaming voices of other men being slaughtered by the Danes.

Startled, Tristan bolted in his sleep and started up on his elbows, moaning, only to find himself back in the Dorter. What he had thought was the screaming in his dream was actually a commotion that had broken out within the Dorter. Boys were scurrying about, shouting and lighting candles. Frightened, worried about his little brother, Tristan jumped over to Guillaume's bed. But Guillaume was fine, sitting erect in his bed, rubbing at his eyes. "What's going on?" he yawned.

Next came the ticking of wood against stone floor as Brother Placidus tottered into the candlelight of the sleeping quarters on his cane. "What the devil's going on in here, boys?!"

In the darkness, a falsetto voice broke out in mimicry. *"Wh-what the devil's going on in here, girls!"*

At this, laughter broke out. From a corner, several of the younger boys pointed toward a bunk just three spaces down from Tristan's. "Brother Placidus, it's LeBrun!" they shouted. "Look!"

Placidus moved toward LeBrun's bunk and poked his candle toward the red-head, who sat there dazed in the midst of clay shards and a foul mess of excrement and urine. He was intermittently crying, shouting and rubbing at his forehead. It appeared that one of the Dorter's many clay chamber-pots had been busted over his head as he was sleeping.

"Damn you, Hébert! Letellier!" LeBrun screamed, pointing at the two older boys.

Brother Placidus flung his eyes at them, but before he could utter a word Letellier retreated, raising his hands in innocence. "Oh, ho!" he protested. "Not *me!*"

"Oh, ho!" echoed Hébert, joining Letellier's side. "Nor me!"

Old Placidus glared about the room from boy-to-boy. "Aha," he muttered, "so all of you were sleeping, huh? Well, well, we'll just see about all this in the morning, then. Much as I hate to say it, this looks like a job for Brother Allaire...and there'll be a beating or two, I imagine."

At this the boys' eyes widened as they stepped back, hanging their heads. It was Brother Allaire who administered the monastery discipline, a merciless man who believed that severe punishment was God's answer to all things out of the ordinary. Sensing the boys' alarm, Placidus shook his head with irritation and turned, limping his way back out of the sleeping quarters. "Candles out," he barked.

***

Early that next morning, the boys found themselves standing in a row stripped to the waist within the Misericord, also known as the Penitent Chapel. It was a small edifice tucked in the back corner of Cluny where those who violated Cluny rules prayed for forgiveness and performed penance. Although it held the designation of 'chapel', and even had a small altar at the fore, the Misericord was more akin to a dungeon chamber. Five kneelers were planted directly in front of the austere altar, upon which stood a simple iron crucifix. The only other furnishing was a long table at the side of the altar upon which lay numerous instruments of punishment, to include paddles, rods and scourging whips.

As the boys stood trembling before the tight-lipped, dour monk known as Brother Allaire, it was the two paddles sitting atop the table that held their attention. Whereas the whips and rods were reserved for errant monks and laborers, the paddles were reserved for students—the boys knew this. They also knew Brother Allaire was an absolute master in the application of either paddle to the exposed flesh of a young sinner's backsides, whose hands were already trembling with anticipation as he began to speak.

And so, Letellier," he said, casting a sullen look, "LeBrun tells me you attacked him from behind yesterday. For no reason, he claims."

Letellier shook his head. "I had a reason, Brother Allaire," he offered meekly. "LeBrun attacked the new boy there over nothing, then attacked his little brother. I was just trying to keep him from hurting th—"

"*True*, LeBrun?" interrupted Allaire, his brows drawing down as he switched his focus onto LeBrun.

LeBrun appeared dumbfounded. "True," he muttered.

"Hmm!" Allaire snorted. "And why would you do such a thing, LeBrun?"

"Because I don't care for them," replied LeBrun, "especially the older one."

"Aha!" chirped Allaire, pointing to Brother Placidus. "So, Brother Placidus, surely God has given young LeBrun a reason for this distaste, eh?"

Placidus shifted on his cane. "If you say so," he rasped, showing little sign of conviction.

"His father's a traitor!" shouted LeBrun.

"Ah, I see," said Brother Allaire. "And we certainly don't like traitors, do we, Brother Placidus?"

Placidus shook his head no, then looked upon the forlorn troupe of boys trembling in terror. His old heart palpitated a beat as he began to regret having involved Brother Allaire.

Allaire returned to Letellier. "Was it *you* who broke the piss-pot on LeBrun's head last night?"

"No, Brother Allaire!" objected Letellier. "Upon my oath to God!"

"Then it must have been your friend, Hébert, eh?" smirked Allaire. "No one else but you two would dare do this to LeBrun…except our little friend, Scule, huh? Or maybe the three of you together?"

"No, Brother Allaire!" protested Hébert, wagging his head in the negative. "I w-was sleeping, and so was Letellier and Scule!"

"So then, if not you three, who else could have done such a thing?" asked Allaire, shifting his gaze to the other boys.

As his eyes roved from one face to the next, each boy began to shudder. Two of the younger ones standing next to Letellier began to sniffle as tears welled in their eyes and began a slow, streaming trek down their fat little cheeks. Though frightened, Tristan and Guillaume stood in silence, not moving a muscle.

"Very well then," sighed Allaire, "no one wishes to come forward, so I shall administer the justice of Cluny, which is to set an example by punishing the guilty as well as setting an example for the innocent." Moving to the table, he reached for the two long paddles that lay there. One was narrow in girth, and thin. The other was equally long, but thick. He held them up for the boys to see. "LeBrun, you should not have attacked the new boys. I therefore award you five kisses on the ass from Fat François here, or ten stings on the ass from Petit Paul. Which will it be?"

LeBrun sent Letellier a smoldering look, then eyed the two paddles. "Ten from Petit Paul," he sighed.

"And Letellier, you should not have broken the piss-pot on LeBrun in his sleep, so which paddle will it be for you?"

"But I did no such thing, Brother Allaire!" Letellier insisted. Then, dropping his hands in resignation, he said, "I choose five…from Fat François."

"And Hébert, you should not conspire with Letellier, so which one do you choose?"

"*Me*? But I'm innocent!" wailed Hébert.

Brother Allaire wagged his head sternly, a signal to Hébert that his pleas were futile.

"Ten stings from Petit Paul," Hébert muttered in surrender.

"And you, Scule?" asked Allaire.

The stubby Scule did not protest. "I'll take Petit Paul as well," he sighed.

Brother Placidus leaned on his cane, shifting his weight to the other leg. "Brother Allaire," he coughed, clearing gravel from his throat, "I believe you are about to punish the innocent along with the guilty here. LeBrun gets what he deserves, but I don't believe Letellier, Hébert and Scule are dumb enough to attack LeBrun in his sleep. Too obvious, don't you think?"

Allaire looked at Placidus with disdain, then gazed around the chapel at the other boys. "It is quite possible, of course, that I'm about to beat the innocent along with the guilty. But let us remember that Christ was the innocent of all innocents, and that it was He who set the greatest example of all by suffering for others. *Correct*, Brother Placidus?"

Placidus flapped his hand with disgust. Turning on his cane, he limped out of the Misericord, closing the door behind himself.

"Very well then, you four, let's begin," said Allaire. "LeBrun, step forward, drop your breeches and take the position."

Bending at the waist and exposing his rump, LeBrun complied, his face twisting like roots as he braced for the ten licks from Petit Paul. Then, with each following whoosh of the paddle as it split the air, he lurched forward, yelping as the paddle stung his bare flesh. He made a fierce attempt not to cry, but by the fourth lick he was bawling like a baby. When his thrashing was over, he returned to the line of other boys, unable to keep from snuffling and heaving.

"Very well, then, *your* turn Letellier," said Brother Allaire. "Step forward. You said five swats from Fat François, did you not?"

"Yes, Brother," Letellier replied, bending over and exposing himself as the monk switched to the fat paddle.

Brother Allaire reared back and was just about to deliver the first blow when a small voice rang out. "*Stop!* It wasn't him, Brother, or Hébert, or Scule! It was *me*. I broke the piss-pot over LeBrun's head!"

Surprised, Allaire turned and looked down at the confessor while the other boys backed away, distancing themselves from the culprit. They could have never suspected who it was, but the most shocked by this admission of guilt from the small boy was Tristan. "Guillaume!" he shouted, pulling his brother back in line. "*What are you doing?* Get back and hush!"

But Guillaume broke from his brother and stepped up to Brother Allaire. "It w-was me that broke the pot on LeBrun," he stammered, "because he hurt my brother yesterday! I waited until everyone was asleep last night, then snuck over to LeBrun's bed and hit him over the head with the pot. Then I ran back to my bed in the dark and pretended to be asleep."

Allaire stared at little Guillaume a moment, shaking his head. "Ah, a noble little squirt, but I don't believe you. I—"

"It's *true*," Guillaume insisted. "Don't beat Letellier! He didn't do it!"

Letellier, still bent over and exposed, turned and looked at Hébert and Scule. Shrugging, he next glanced at Guillaume, bewildered. "*I'll* take the licks Brother Allaire," he said. "I don't believe him either."

Rarely confused by anything, Allaire rubbed at his chin. Finally, he motioned to Letellier. "Pull up your breeches and cover that horrendous ass of yours. Hébert, Scule, you're off the hook, too." Then he motioned for Guillaume who stepped forward and bent over, nearly falling as he clumsily shoved his breeches down to his ankles.

"I'll take five from the big one, Fat François," Guillaume said, showing no emotion.

Allaire stared down at the boy's tiny bare rump. Though he was a stern and unforgiving disciplinarian void of empathy for rule-breakers, as he looked down at this little boy's bare butt, he grew reticent about beating this cherub who had so gallantly stepped forward to defend justice. Thus lost in thought, he gently slapped his own thigh several times with Fat François, weighing this predicament. With each of these meditative slaps of Fat Francois, the boys behind him winced, Tristan more so than the others.

After a full minute of rumination, Allaire stepped forward, having determined that cherub or not, noble or not, order must be maintained and examples must be set. Rearing back, he cocked Fat François behind his ear to deliver the five blows. As the thick paddle met Guillaume's tender flesh with the first blow, a dull thud split the air, sickening each boy in the room. Tristan winced upon hearing the thick wood of Fat François splat against Guillaume's flesh, then shivered as Guillaume gasped in agony. But Guillaume did not cry. Rather, it was Tristan's eyes that filled with tears as he stared in dismay at the thick, scarlet whelp rising on Guillaume's rump.

Allaire reared back again to deliver the second blow, but at that very instant the cathedral bells of Cluny Abbey rang out in a thunderous chorus of metered ringing. Allaire froze in place, as did the boys, cocking their ears toward the abbey steeple to count the spacing of the knells. One-two in quick succession, then repeated over and over...it was the 'assembly' signal being metered out by the bell tower, instructing all to gather within the walls of Cluny before the cathedral steps.

Along with Brother Allaire's lifelong zeal to maintain order, he was also extremely devout. Against his nature, he had been having second thoughts about paddling the little boy, and the bells had interrupted. He interpreted this as spiritual intervention. *Yes*, he reasoned, *a signal from above.*

"Quick, lads," he cried, dropping the paddle. "To the Square! Something's about!"

***

The square quickly filled as nearly two hundred monks, hordes of laborers and servants, and over a thousand visiting pilgrims assembled before Cluny Cathedral. For nearly half an hour the huge cathedral bells rang out their clamorous toll while field laborers and village dwellers continued to stream up the hill to enter the monastery. Finally, the bells fell silent, and the great Abbot Hugh of Semur, standing alone upon the steps of the grand church, addressed the crowd.

Having just returned from Italy, he was dressed in the fine fabrics and richly embroidered vestments befitting a high ambassadorial diplomat of the Holy Church. He stood there in regal grandeur, holding a large staff carved of burnished walnut and inlaid with intricate gold patterns and mother of pearl. Tristan watched, mesmerized by the cleric's very presence, as well as by the splendor of his dress.

Abbot Hugh struck his staff three times against the stone steps of the cathedral to command the crowd's attention. All fell silent. "It is with great sadness," he declared, "that I inform you of black news that I received while returning from Italy. I was notified by papal messenger that our Holy Father, Pope Alexander II, passed into Heaven several weeks ago—on the twenty-first of April in Rome!"

Cries of anguish and consternation arose from within the crowd. For these people, and others within Christendom, the Pope represented order and stability. The Holy Church was the bedrock of their civilization, and the Pope was its guardian against the horrific violence and treachery of warlords, nobles, and heathens.

"God save us!" someone wept aloud.

"Bless Pope Alexander!" shouted an old field hand, putting a palm to his forehead.

"Woe to Christendom!" wailed a woman from the edge of the throng, sobbing.

Abbot Hugh again tapped his staff three times. "Be it known also, faithful Christians, that as God has taken, he has given! On the very next day, April the twenty-second, as the obsequies were being performed in the Lateran Basilica, a great cry arose from all the people and the clergy assembled there. 'Let Hildebrand be Pope!' they hailed. 'Blessed Peter has chosen Hildebrand the Archdeacon!' they cried."

At this, a buzz swept through the crowd and the throng began exchanging questions and suppositions. "Hildebrand of Sovana?" someone shouted.

"Hildebrand who was here at Cluny many years ago?" inquired one of the older monks.

Abbot Hugh struck with his staff once more and continued. "And on the very next day, the College of the Cardinals selected him to be the Holy Father, Pope of all you faithful who love God. From now forward he shall no longer be referred to as Hildebrand, but henceforth shall be heralded by his new title, Pope Gregory VII!"

Cries arose as members of the crowd began to embrace each other, raise hands to the sky, or bend heads in prayer. Tristan watched in wonder. It was his first time seeing a large mob in action, and he was mentally dissecting each maneuver of Abbot Hugh. Here before him he was witnessing 'real' authority and power. The grand cleric was a virtual puppeteer, silencing the crowd, then exhorting the crowd, then filling them to bursting with emotion. It was as if the mob was childish in the thrall of the Abbot's manipulation of their fears and hopes.

In the midst of this noise, Abbot Hugh struck his staff once more against the steps, then raised it to the sky. "All hail the blessed Hildebrand!" he cried. "Hail to our Holy Father, Pope Gregory VII! I declare a holiday for all at Cluny! Start the fires! We shall roast hogs and calves! Bring forth the wine and the ale for all to share! Gather the musicians! Two days of celebration and feasting in honor of our blessed Pope Gregory!"

At this announcement the crowd burst into a wild chorus of shouting and dancing. For the peasants and village dwellers, the availability and consumption of meat was a rare occasion. "Bless you, Abbot Hugh!" the mob screamed, delirium spreading like wildfire. "Hail to the new pope!" they shouted in an orgy of jubilation. "Hail to the great Hugh of Cluny!!" cried others as they rushed forward to kneel before and embrace their beloved abbot.

This astounded Tristan even more than what he had witnessed before. He quickly felt himself being swept into the current's overwhelming pull as the boys around him began to jump up and down and slap each other on the back. It was a surge of rushing adrenalin he had never experienced before, which was making him dizzy with joy and anticipation.

Grabbing Guillaume by the waist and raising him in the air, Tristan swung his brother back and forth like a rag toy. "Hail the blessed Pope Gregory, Guillaume!" he cried. "Hail to the great Abbot Hugh of Semur!"

***

Over the next three weeks Tristan began to gain his feet in terms of the younger cohorts' routines at Cluny. He rose in the morning, worked the kitchen, attended class with Brother Loiseaux and an assortment of teacher-monks for most of the day, then returned to the kitchen for dinner.

Dinner was the big meal of the day, usually eaten at about eight o'clock in the evening, comprised of whatever was left over from the monk's evening meal. To Tristan's delight, he discovered that the Black Monks ate extremely well despite their vow of poverty and Spartan lifestyle. The bounty of their vineyards and farmlands produced an endless offering of meats, fowl, vegetables and fruit. Although he and Guillaume had eaten well in Saint-Germain due to their noble status, the infinite varieties of cheeses, sausages and breads produced by the monastery labor force made the end of the day meal a delight. Picking through the monks' bountiful leftovers each evening was nearly like a treasure hunt.

Guillaume's schedule as a member of the Stable Co-hort was far less rigorous in terms of academic structure, but not so in terms of actual labor. With the other boys of this cohort Guillaume cleaned and polished armor, filed tools and farming implements, and burnished saddles. Letellier and Hébert, adopted Guillaume as their pet 'little brother', and the three quickly became inseparable.

A good deal of Guillaume's day was spent with blacksmiths and leather crafters, so he became rather adept for one so young in the structure and mechanics of instruments with moving parts. Unlike the other boys who viewed their labor as a temporary exchange for earning their keep until they returned to their families at age fourteen, Guillaume eagerly anticipated learning these new skills. He listened carefully to the iron smiths and saddle makers, asking questions and picking up the finer points of their workmanship. He quickly became a favorite in the shops among the craftsmen.

Guillaume also spent time caring for the horses and donkeys of Cluny which were stabled separately from the field oxen and field mules. He found pleasure in feeding and currying these beasts, often carrying on entire conversations with them as they stood there staring back at him with dumb indifference. He named each beast under his care and learned their individual temperaments and foibles.

Tristan rarely saw Guillaume except late in the evenings back at the Dorter, and by then they were both exhausted. Nonetheless, they did manage to find time for limited fraternal banter. Yet there was something in all of this that disturbed Tristan. It seemed to him that Guillaume had plunged full bore into the Cluny life, had forgotten their previous existence. Although Tristan would bring up vignettes from their past in conversation, Guillaume himself seldom spoke of the manor or their mother. This troubled

Tristan who could not grasp that the simple difference of two and a half years in their respective young lives was like a great gulf. Whereas Tristan sorely missed Asta and thought of her often, such sentiments seldom seemed to enter his brother's mind. For him, she had already become little more than a distant memory.

Just as Guillaume had become a favorite in the workshops and stables, Tristan quickly endeared himself to Brother Loiseaux and the teacher-monks, regardless of their individual discipline of study. Tristan was attentive, engaged, asking questions, especially in terms of why things occurred and how people responded to these things. For one so young, it seemed to his teachers that he possessed an uncanny perception of how the human mind reacted to and interplayed with circumstance. Tristan's greatest strength was with languages, yet his teachers determined that history was his passion.

One puzzle remained unsolved for Tristan. Despite his own efforts to be cordial to the brutish LeBrun, it seemed the red-head's hostility toward him never waned the tiniest measure. This mystery did not consume Tristan by any means, but he pondered on the issue at times because it made little sense, and for Tristan, all things had to make sense. For every action, there was a stimulus, a trigger.

Accordingly, Tristan found it odd one morning in the kitchen when LeBrun came to him lacking his usual scowl. "They're rendering hog fat in the kitchen this morning," LeBrun said, pointing to the floor. "See there, it's slippery, so be careful. One of the cooks spilled a cauldron of oil on himself last month and got severely burned."

Brother Placidus happened to be foraging about in the kitchen and overheard this warning issued by LeBrun, thinking for a moment that LeBrun might have actually overcome his resentment of the new arrival. "Aye, Tristan," Placidus agreed, "LeBrun's right. Best be careful."

"So, listen," LeBrun continued, "we have to ladle the hot oil out of that big caldron and break it down into those clay pots on the table. Tonight when the grease has cooled, we'll be sealing them with wax for storage." Then LeBrun threw a length of cheesecloth over the slippery spot he had pointed out to Tristan. "Since we'll be tracking back and forth, this cheesecloth'll keep us from slipping and getting burned. But even with it covering the grease, move slow, it's still a bit slick."

Brother Placidus nodded. "Good idea, LeBrun. There may be hope for you yet." Then he turned and walked to one of the cupboards, burying his head in it to search for leftovers.

Struck by LeBrun's gesture, Tristan acknowledged this unexpected courtesy with a smile. "Thank you," he said, grabbing a ladle and a clay pot. Stepping gingerly across the cheesecloth, he moved toward the middle hearth where a large caldron hung simmering over red hot embers. The smell was thick and unpleasant, and the heat emanating from inside the caldron and radiating from the iron itself was unbearable. Leaning forward, he dipped the ladle into the bubbling fat, pushing aside thick curls of rendered pig hide. As he filled the clay pot, it warmed, then quickly turned hot. Despite LeBrun's counsel to move slowly, Tristan could see that he would only be able to hold the hot pot for only a few seconds. Throwing the ladle down, he turned and fairly danced across the cheesecloth to set the clay pot onto the table. Then, his palms taking on the appearance of flopping fishtails, he fanned his hands to relieve the burning.

LeBrun laughed at this, reached over, and threw a wool cloth at Tristan. "Here," he said, "wrap the pot in this next time. It won't be so hot in your hands." Then he picked up a ladle and cloth of his own and began working the oil. As Tristan watched, LeBrun did, indeed, take his time ladling the hog oil, and again took his time again traversing the cheesecloth. "See," LeBrun said, "nothing to it."

This was the first time LeBrun had addressed him in a civil manner. It so surprised Tristan that he strayed from his usual sense of wariness. Disposing of previous suspicion, he followed LeBrun's procedure and began working the boiling oil. If he had been watching LeBrun,   Tristan would have noticed that LeBrun was keeping a close eye on everyone else in the kitchen. So, at the moment he was satisfied that nobody else in the kitchen was taking notice, he made his move.

As Tristan finished loading yet another pot with the smoking oil, he slowly began to traverse the cheesecloth, treading gingerly so as not to slip just as he had done with his previous pot. LeBrun stepped up behind him, reached down quickly, and pulled at the end of the cheese cloth, jerking it out from under Tristan. Tristan teetered, then fell straight backward, his rear end crashing to the floor first, the back of his head following. The pot of seething oil wobbled wildly in his hands during this descent as Tristan frantically tried to control it from spilling on himself. But as he crashed to the floor, he lost all purchase on the bubbling pot, which swiveled backward, dumping its simmering contents toward Tristan's face and neck area. By good fortune alone, the padding cloth came between Tristan's face and the bulk of the burning oil. Throwing his arms up to cover his eyes, they absorbed the remainder of hot oil as it splattered about, severely burning and blistering his forearms, fingers and portions of his neck. Tristan screamed in pain and began flailing his limbs in a dance of agony on the floor.

All work in the kitchen came to a halt as several of the cooks rushed forward to assist him.

"He slipped!" cried LeBrun, pointing at the cheesecloth. "I warned him to be careful, but he never listens!"

"Quick, to the infirmary!" shouted one of the cooks. "Here, help me lift his legs, I have his head!"

Two men litter-carried him from the kitchen while others followed, rushing through courtyards and down walkways, urged on by Tristan's squirming pleas for relief. Finally, they burst into the infirmary. "Grease burns! It's bad!" shouted the cook holding Tristan's shoulders.

"Throw him on the table!" instructed an elderly monk while two others held Tristan to the table and began stripping his clothing. "Get the salve, Brother Luc, and bandages," the old monk commanded calmly. Examining Tristan's face and neck area, he said, "The blistering looks severe, but the boy is fortunate, his whole face could have been disfigured for life, and he could have been blinded." Turning, he asked, "How did this happen?"

The cooks began to speak at once, each over-talking the other. Failing to understand a word they were saying, the old monk waved them off, telling them to return to the kitchen. Resuming work on the patient, he gingerly lathered salve over the blisters, assuring the boy that he would survive; that he was extremely fortunate the hot oil had only sparingly caught spots on his face.

When the cooks returned to the kitchen, they found LeBrun diligently working the hog oil. "Be careful!" they told him. "We don't need any more accidents today."

LeBrun nodded. "I told him to watch out," he muttered, "but he seems to think he already knows everything. Maybe next time he'll listen, huh?"

Chapter Fourteen

The Infirmary

A rule of Saint Benedict mandated that the abbot of each monastery provide an infirmary for the ailing and organize care of the sick as a special Christian duty. Specifically, this rule stated that 'care of the sick is to be placed above and before every other duty, as if, indeed, Christ were being served in waiting on them'. Cluny, therefore, as the very heart of Benedictine monasticism, devoted inordinate time and resources to healing the sick. Its infirmary was one of the largest and best known in all of Europe.

It was to Tristan's good fortune, then, to receive medical attention at the hands of Cluny's infirmarians. As the old monk tending to him completed his treatment of the burn wounds, he said, "There, done for now. I'm Brother Damien, chief infirmarian here. It appears you'll live, at least for a few more days." At this the monk chuckled and shook his head. "That was a joke, lad. You're lucky, but you'll still be spending some time with us in the patients' chambers."

Tristan nodded feebly. The salve had relieved much of the initial pain, but he found it difficult to move his head and arms, and still felt a painful searing within all areas that had contacted the hog oil. Thus injured, he thought of his mother, wishing she was here in this moment of distress. In this helpless state, he felt consumed by her absence and ached for the previously simple existence at the manor that had been torn from him. He also missed Orla and the other Danes, and even felt his young brother, Guillaume, slipping between his fingers. *God has forsaken me,* he decided, woozy with pain. Then came a swell of resentment. *Mother has set me adrift in life. I will be forever alone.*

Shedding hot tears, he began to cry.

Watching, the old monk felt the pull of sympathy. "God has spared you for some reason," he said, feigning cheerfulness. "He must have bigger plans for you down the road, eh?"

Lost in his profound sense of abandonment, Tristan gave no answer.

"You'll recover from these wounds, but it'll take time," said Brother Damien, continuing to seek positive ground. "Your neck and arms will scar a bit, but these little blisters around your eyes and cheeks will heal and disappear. Some good news, then, the girls shall still flock to your handsome face one day!"

This encouraged Tristan a bit, as he wiped his eyes. He was little interested in his future with girls, but the tone of Brother Damien's voice soothed him. "Th-thank you for helping me," he said, gazing up at the monk. He had never encountered a healer before, nor even knew infirmaries existed. It had simply been the nuns back in Saint-Germain-en-Laye who tended to the injured. "How is it that one becomes a healer such as you, Brother?" he asked.

"Bad fortune, I suppose," clucked Brother Damien. "As a young man I followed the conversion wars against the Teutonics and the Nordic races. Though it was a bloody trail littered with the wounded and the slaughtered, I found myself thirsting for the fight. *Iucunda macula est ex inimici sanguine*…what a pleasant stain comes from an enemy's blood! But eventually the blood ran so deep, I rediscovered shame. That led me to healing, closing wounds instead of opening them. Recently I'd been doing the same in Spain, as our armies fight the Moors, but was sent here to Cluny a year ago." Stepping back, he took a closer look at his young patient. "You're not interested in becoming a healer, are you, lad?"

Tristan shook his head. "No, it's just that sometimes I wonder why people do what they do, how they become what they become."

"Deep thoughts for one so young. The wind plays a part, I'd say…and chance, but God directs much in life also. Maybe he'll direct you as he did me."

"Did he direct you into becoming a monk?"

"No, my parents left me and my two younger brothers in a monastery outside of Poitiers. We were all starving during the two-year famine, and I suppose they saw no future in keeping us. That monastery was Benedictine, so the monks cared for all three of us boys, along with many, many others. Educated us also. In the end, we all three joined the order."

Tristan thought a moment. "Prior Odo said Brother Placidus was abandoned also as a boy, right here at Cluny," he frowned. "It seems monasteries are a good place to dump children."

"You may be right. but the world's overrun with the hungry, the diseased, the war-torn, the lost. Monasteries provide food, shelter, healing and safety. They've always been a haven in difficult times, and still are."

"Did you ever see your parents again?" asked Tristan, thinking of his own separation from Asta. "And did you not hate them then for leaving you and your brothers?"

Brother Damien shook his head. "They did what they had to do. We three boys were starving just as they were. My brothers and I could well be moldering in a grave somewhere had they kept us. Our parents gave us a future, actually."

Tristan thought back on his last day in Saint-Germain-en-Laye. "My mother said something similar just before sending me and my little brother away. She said our future was here at Cluny. Then she left for England to marry my rich uncle, who refused us." He sucked in air then as another wave of pain overtook him.

"Ah-ha," sighed Brother Damien, "so you're feeling a wee bit left behind then, eh? My brothers and I did the same, for a while, anyway. But no fear, you'll be fine here. Cluny will prepare you for all that life throws your way, lad. You may even end by taking up the black robe yourself."

Tristan shook his head. "Of all things in life, I would not wish that."

"Very well, then," chuckled Brother Damien, "I can't fault you for that! Now try to stand up if you can, I'm taking you to the men's bay."

***

Brother Damien helped Tristan down a long hall that split into multiple wings. "These rooms on that end are the women's chambers," he pointed, "and that wing there is for the wounded coming up from fighting the Muslims in Spain. This other end is where you'll bunk until you heal."

Moving carefully so as not to aggravate his blisters, Tristan entered the chamber and was quickly overwhelmed with the odor of filth, vomit and urine. Muffling his nose, he found the room filled with ten rows of makeshift beds, all occupied with men in various stages of illness or injury. Many were moaning in pain while others begged for food, water or treatment. Still others were lost in sleep, snoring loudly, while those in better condition carried on conversations with each other or with attending monks.

As Tristan surveyed the scene before him, he swallowed hard. Most of the bed linens were drenched with blood; even the floorboards had been darkened by years of diseased body fluids and blood-stained misery. Everything before him was a ghastly image of human suffering and woe, reminding Tristan of a frightening painting he once saw of Hell in which the landscape was littered with tortured souls suffering the anguish of God's wrath. Lost to the horrors of that painting, envisioning himself as one of the suffering characters within it, he was jolted back to reality when a young monk jostled his shoulder. "There's your bed. Give them a minute or two and you'll be set."

Tristan watched as two other monks lifted a man from the bed. "Am I taking a bed from the sick, Brother?" he asked, concerned.

"No, that man's dead."

Tristan's heart contracted. "Am I to sleep in the d-dead man's bed, then?"

"Aye, unless you wish to lay on the floor or in bed with another. We pride ourselves on clean medical facilities, but we've been overwhelmed of late due to the Spanish wars, the spread of leprosy and an outbreak of pox."

Shivering, Tristan waited as the two monks lifted the corpse and hauled it away. When they were gone, Tristan approached the bed, sickened by the filthy linen sheet that lay rumpled on the bed, half covering the mattress. It was stained chocolate in spots, which Tristan imagined to be either blood or defecation. Worse yet, the sheet was heavily mottled in deep yellowish-green stains that appeared to be caused by puss, mucus, or urine, or a combination thereof. Running his hand over it, he could feel it was damp with sweat and body fluids. Staring at this mess, he trembled, reminded of the dead man who had just been hauled away.

"Here," said the young monk, "fresh linen for your bed." Pulling the filthy linen from the bed, he rolled it into a bundle. After helping the monk spread the clean linen over his mattress, Tristan slowly lowered his back onto the bed, only to smell hideous odors emanating from within the straw-mattress itself. Unable to endure the stench for even a second, he felt his throat filling with vomit. Gulping, he swallowed it, not wishing to make a scene. This only made him more nauseous, feeling more vomit on the rise. Blenching, he swallowed hard, gagging as only the remnants of a little vomit dribbled from the corner of his mouth.

That is when Tristan noticed the man in the bed next to his, lying there watching him. He was a grizzled, toothless looking fellow covered with sores and boils, possessed of a glazed look about the eyes. The man had been completely absorbed in every movement Tristan made. Tristan looked at him, then quickly diverted his eyes. *What kind of a place is this*, he thought, closing his eyes, wondering how he would ever find sleep in the midst of such wretchedness. Nonetheless, within half an hour the day's events overcame his disquiet and he fell into a deep sleep, finding himself happily running the hills outside Saint-Germain-en-Laye with Guillaume.

A deep sleep is a peaceful, affirming proposition, especially for the troubled. Therefore, as he was rudely jolted from this state of tranquility, Tristan struggled for several moments to linger there in his dream-world. But feeling pressure against his neck burns, he cried out and pushed at whatever it was that was pressing against his blisters. Blinking his eyes open, he discovered a man laying on top of him, naked, pressing his slathering lips against his own. It was the man he had seen staring at him earlier from the bed next to his. Tristan strained furiously to free himself, but the man's weight pinned him to the mattress.

"There, there, my little pretty," the man whispered, his gross breath forcing Tristan to gag. "Be still for me just a minute or so!" Then, reaching down, he forced his hand into Tristan's trousers and waggled his fingers, groping and fondling Tristan's genitals.

Aghast, Tristan cried out in terror, kicking upward with his legs and feet. This only caused the man to cackle and tighten his grip on Tristan's privates.

"Get away! Stop!" Tristan wailed.

"Now, now, be sweet to old Marceau," the man cooed, continuing to slather at Tristan's lips and mouth with his tongue while feverishly working his fingers beneath Tristan's trousers.

Tristan continued to struggle, but his assailant had now clamped his other hand over his mouth, suffocating him. Unable to believe that God would allow such a horrendous thing, Tristan was at the edge of blacking out when suddenly he heard the loud whack of a rod striking bare flesh. Tristan's attacker groaned, released his grip, and rolled over in agony.

"Get off him, you bastard!" someone cried.

Sitting up in the milky light of the patients' chamber, lit by only a single lantern, Tristan made out the silhouette of a black robe standing over his bed. It was Brother Damien. The monk swung down again with his rod, striking the man on the back of his bare buttocks, then across his back.

Cowering, the man scrambled from Tristan's bed in a flurry of limbs and jumped over to his own bed, curling as a fetus, covering himself with his linen sheet as if it might shield him from the rod. Staring up at Brother Damien, he then issued that mournful laugh of the deranged upon being disciplined.

"Stay there or we'll put you out for good!" Brother Damien barked, his eyes afire. Then, leaning over, he nudged Tristan on the shoulder. "Are you all right, lad?"

"Y-yes," Tristan shuddered, his body quaking. "That m-man, h-he tried to—"

"Yes, yes, I know," nodded Brother Damien, offering reassurance. "We've had problems with Marceau before. But he'll stay put now or get more of the rod, and he knows it. So go back to sleep, boy. I'll keep watch."

Chapter Fifteen

Monastery Management

Tristan's sojourn in the infirmary gave rise to multiple consequences. To begin, he established a firm relationship with Brother Damien. He also had the opportunity to converse with other healer monks, and could not help but admire their good work on behalf of the diseased and the injured. But the most significant impact of his confinement in the infirmary was shock of seeing so many of the helpless in life. The patients' chamber was filled with the aged, the infirm, the destitute and even the insane. They were ignorant, poor, covered with sores and disease, and smelled horrifically. The saddest aspect of their existence was that they lacked any hope of ever improving their station in life.

Tristan's convalescence in the infirmary also forced him, because of inactivity, to reminisce about Saint-Germain-en-Laye and miss his mother, as well as the Danes. This reminiscing inevitably culminated in reliving the journey to Cluny, which in turn led to Mala. This caused him, from time-to-time as he lay in the Patient's Chamber, to reach into his pocket to retrieve the tiny Moorish ring she had given him. Examining it fondly, he began to hope that he might encounter her again one day. She had said she had always wished to visit the famous monastery, so perhaps one day she would appear. *Strange thing*, he concluded, *this ring was the only thing she owned, and now it is the only thing I own.*

The experience in the infirmary did one other thing. Sharing time with victims of the world confirmed to him that education, or lack thereof, was what separated those who might control their own fate from those who were destined to be life's fodder. It was with complete contentment, then, that he was released from the Infirmary to resume his studies. As he returned to the Dorter, he found Guillaume with his gaggle of friends. Looking up, Guillaume ran over, eagerly wrapping his arms around his brother's waist. "Brother Placidus told us about the hog oil!" he exclaimed. "You're lucky to be alive, he said!" Next, he insisted on inspecting the bandages swaddling Tristan's neck and arms. "Does it still hurt, Tristan?"

"A bit," Tristan replied, "but I'll be fine."

"Good," said Letellier. "We've missed you in the Dorter."

"Yes, and in class also," said Scule, waddling up to Tristan with a smile. "Since your absence, LeBrun's been trying to act like the class genius. Shit, I'm tired of listening to him jabber on day after day!"

A short while later, Brother Placidus approached. "They're coming soon to gather the cohorts, boys. But Tristan, you've been taken off the Scullery Cohort. Follow me."

"But—" said Tristan, stunned.

"Orders from Prior Odo," Placidus grunted. "You can't move about or work properly in the kitchen with your sores, so he wants you to assist him in his office for a while with posting and filing."

"But what about my schooling?" Tristan objected.

"No worries," said Placidus, his voice full of gravel. "We shut down instruction in a few weeks so the boys can go home for their summer visit. You won't be missing much. And since you and Guillaume have nowhere to go, you'll be staying here with us over the summer. You just won't be serving as a scullion, that's all."

At this, Guillaume and the others cheered as LeBrun stood there in silence, dumfounded that Tristan would be working directly with Prior Odo. *How was it possible,* he seethed, *that my plan to eliminate this little bastard has reversed itself?* "Bah!" he muttered, storming out the door.

As the other boys left with their cohort monks, Tristan followed Placidus into the back entry of the Camera, which was the nerve center of the entire monastery as well as the office of records.

"Wait here, I'll just be a moment," Placidus said, entering Prior Odo's office, closing the door gently behind him.

Odo was seated at a large table surrounded by stacks of official papers, petitions and invoices. "Ah, Placidus," he smiled, "so how goes my faithful old teacher and mentor?"

"Quite well for an old man, Odo. I've brought the boy as you've requested. He's not happy about being shifted, though; worried his studies might suffer."

"Ha, good lad," said Odo admiringly. "No, his studies will not suffer. In fact, he may be about to learn far more than he ever imagined."

"So, you continue to incline toward the distressed," said Placidus, looking at Odo with curiosity. "You see something in the boy, huh, Odo? Yourself, perhaps?"

"No, something far superior than myself, Placidus. When I was a boy in my home village of Chatillon-sur-Marne in Champagne, my father insisted that I follow in his steps of knighthood and nobility, but I got injured one day in the stables. It was the village priest who cared for me within his parish rectory—good Father Dubois. He adopted me in a way; started having me assist him with some clerking. And quickly, to my father's fury, I lost interest in horses and weaponry and turned to books. It was Father Dubois, again, who referred me to study at Rheims where I first met you so many years ago."

Placidus pulled himself back in time, to his teaching years. "And you did well during my short time there, Odo. But even I never imagined that you'd so quickly become canon at Rheims, then archdeacon."

"If not for men like Father Dubois and yourself taking an interest, exposing me to greater things, I would have never risen from the darkness. I would still be somewhere in Champagne."

"Ha!" laughed Placidus. "Probably living the fine life of a seigneur on some magnificent estate!"

"The Church is my life. I would have it no other way."

"But this boy has no wish to join the clergy, Odo. Pitiful as it sounds, he hopes to one day return to Saint-Germain-en-Laye as a nobleman. Poor lad. It'll never happen after what his father's done."

"True, but God will direct the boy, Placidus. He has already given the lad unfathomable potential."

Placidus nodded, tilting his head. "Agreed," he said, rubbing at the stubble of his chin. "But while I'm here...something you should know, then, Odo. The burns the boy suffered—not an 'accident'."

"What?"

"LeBrun caused it all. There was a cheesecloth on the floor to keep the boy from slipping, and LeBrun pulled it out from under him, on purpose, as he was carrying hot oil. He deliberately tried to injure the boy. He—"

"Oh, impossible!" said Odo, shaking his head. "Cluny is a nursery of aspirations, and LeBrun hopes one day to become a Benedictine."

"So he claims, but only to curry favor while he's here. Odo, I was right there in the kitchen when the incident happened. LeBrun thought I was digging around in the cupboards, but I happened to turn at the very moment he stooped down and pulled the cloth out from under Tristan. Feigning innocence, LeBrun claimed Tristan 'slipped'."

"So disappointing," said Odo, passing his palm across his forehead as if to dispel a cloud. "How does one learn such corruption as this?"

"The malicious feed off of a dark happiness, Odo, which they find only in harming others. But you already know this."

"Yes, yes" scowled Odo, "but in my hope to find the best in others, I sometimes forget. Does young Tristan know about this?"

"No. Nor anyone else."

"Then we shall keep it between ourselves, Placidus. And keep an eye to LeBrun as well. But tell, what is the root of LeBrun's venom?"

"Simply put, LeBrun hates the lad. First there's the situation with Roger de Saint- Germain. The LeBrun clan is Norman, as you know, and has always been loyal to the Bastard. The LeBruns were among those crying for Roger de Saint-Germain's execution at the trial. And another thing, both Saint-Germain boys are handsome, strikingly, and LeBrun's as ugly as a mule's ass. Yet another source of antagonism. Then too, Tristan's far smarter than LeBrun."

"Ah, Placidus," said Odo, clasping the old monk about the shoulders, "ever vigilant in the shadows, watching and listening." Then he motioned to the door. "Bring him in, Placidus!"

***

Tristan's entry into the office of the Claustral Prior of Cluny that day was tantamount to rebirth. Just as the fetus has no way of knowing what exists outside the confines of the womb, Tristan possessed no concept of organizational structure or operational strategy required to run a monastery. Moreover, he had simply thought Prior Odo an authoritative presence at Cluny and a man of prayer. He had no idea that Odo was, in truth, a logistical genius, or that he himself was about to enter a new world.

"Good morning Prior Odo," he said, standing before the high monk, twining his fingers with discomfort.

"Good morning, Tristan. How are your burns?"

"Not so bad," said Tristan, feebly raising both arms a bit to show they were maneuverable.

"You are going to be helping me for while, with recording and inspections. But there is one trick you must adhere to: magna res est vocis et silentii temperamentum. Comprends?"

"Yes, Prior, the great thing is to know when to speak and when to keep quiet."

"Aha, excellent!"

"But I have no skills, and no idea even what a claustral prior does," said Tristan, shrugging his shoulders to his ears.

"The office of the Claustral Prior in any monastery," Odo began explaining, "is dedicated to the daily running of the entire organization. And since the Cluny Monastery of the Benedictine Order is the largest monastery in Christendom, the responsibilities and duties of this particular office are enormous, as you will learn. Serving God is in itself, of course, the foundation of all Benedictine life. But serving God includes tending to the poor and caring for the sick and injured, which you yourself witnessed in the infirmary as a result of your…accident." A slight, undetectible smirk crossed his visage at the last word.

Tristan nodded. "Yes, Prior."

"The healing monks perform their duties with devout fervor, which is why so many of the wretched come to us. Cluny has become a magnet for the destitute and the ailing. This, of course, creates an incessant need for increased crop production and the clearing of additional farmlands just to feed these flocks of helpless arrivals, as well as to feed our monks, our novices, students, the labor force and pilgrims. All of this is overseen by this office."

"But so many people! It must be difficult managing all that."

"Yes, so much so that I have circators who assist me. They are sub-priors, so to speak, who make rounds each day checking on various things and keeping me informed. Of course, I also make daily rounds myself, but there's much more. Due to its great spiritual significance and the magnificence of our abbey, we attract tens of thousands of visiting pilgrims each year, who also have to be provisioned and fed. Although many of these devout visitors find lodging in the village below, many prefer to stay in our Guest House along the northwest wall. It is divided into a gentleman's and a lady's wing, separated by a common dining hall."

"I didn't know there was a Guest House here," said Tristan.

"Yes, it is always filled to capacity. Unlike the destitute and the ailing, the pilgrims pay their own way, which generates a bristling flow of commerce that fills the Treasury Tower. Pilgrims also sustain us in the form of free-will alms, gifts and endowments. This office also manages the farmlands, which involves sheep, goats, cattle, fowl, rabbits and hogs. Too, there are teams of oxen and mules that work the fields, as well as scores of horses and donkeys for transport. This in turn necessitates the harvest of hay and other fodder crops as well the maintenance of a large granary. There is also the production of grain for cereals and breads, as well as for the distillation of drink to include spirits, ales and ciders. Furthermore there is the harvest of fruits, vegetables, berries, and the production of cheese and spirits."

Tristan's eyes widened. The vast scope of the monastery's operations had never occurred to him before, and as he listened, his awe grew.

"Another crucial role of the monastery is education," Odo continued, "which is reserved for novices and sons of the high aristocracy. Part and portion of this educational mission also includes the maintenance of records and the copying of manuscripts and books, which takes place in the

Scriptorium. Other than the cathedral itself, it is one of our most treasured and revered buildings. High education is an extremely costly enterprise that does not pay immediate dividends like the pilgrimage trade. It does fill the ranks of the Church and serve its purposes, thus ensuring that we maintain a strong force of capable and educated clergy. Then, of course, there is also our huge labor force: farmers, craftsmen, tailors, cobblers, cooks, gardeners and house-keepers."

"Am I to learn about all of these things?" Tristan asked, feeling inadequate.

"Indeed, and you start this morning. So follow me, there is much to see."

Chapter Sixteen

Brothers

Out at sea, a jagged finger of lightning burst through the dark belly of clouds ahead as the broad-beamed vessel heaved its way through the angry chop of the Channel, its prow slicing and groaning through ten foot swells.

"Rain's coming," said Orla to his brother as they both clung to the port side of the large Norman knorr commissioned to take them and their horses to England.

"Ja," agreed Crowbones, "but shore's not far off. We're nearly there, though I'm not looking forward to it."

"Nor am I," nodded Orla, shaking his head dismally. "Too bad about losing the Saint-Germain manor, eh, Ivar?"

"Aye, though I didn't give a shit for Roger de Saint-Germain, I enjoyed life with our families under Asta's wing. It's the most peace we've seen in years."

"It was a good time," said Orla, spitting into the wind. "And you know, I really miss Boy and Mite. I didn't much like leaving them there at that monastery. No telling what horseshit the Black Monks will drive into their skulls."

Crowbones nodded, then yelled aft. "Fairhair! StraightLimbs! You two still managing back there?"

"No problem!" Fairhair cried in reply, his long locks flung straight back by the pressing wind. "But Guthroth's still spilling his guts over the stern!"

Crowbones laughed. "What the shit kind of Viking is Guthroth?" he snorted. "Gets sick every time he sees water!" Then he looked back at Orla, seeing that he remained glum-faced. "Boy and Mite will be fine in Cluny, I suppose. Just be glad they're not headed where we go, for dark days lie ahead, I fear. Ever since we killed those Norsemen along the river outside Paris, I've had an ill feeling about England."

"The Norsemen? Damn, I'd forgotten all about them, Ivar. But look, we did what we had to do. They broke the Dane Code."

"I know," assented Crowbones, "but you remember the one that got away, fled into the woods? Frode's son?"

"Ja, he had a birthmark," said Orla. "They called him WolfPaw. What about him?"

"He's shown up in my dreams. Three times now since leaving the boys at Cluny." Crowbones patted the small leather pouch hanging from his neck before continuing. "And my bones, they reveal he's placed a curse on us."

"Ha, your guilt overcomes your brain, Ivar," Orla snarked. "No, we'll never see that frightened rabbit again! He'll never return to France after what happened to his friends. Besides, he—"

"But we're no longer *in* France," interrupted Crowbones. "We're bound for England, where roving Nordics still come and go there, raiding the northern coasts; now even making alliances with the Saxons against the Bastard."

"Ah, the Bastard," said Orla, changing subjects to distract his brother from the dark topic of the Norsemen. "He continues to drive our fortunes, eh? First we fight for him all over Normandy and France, but then he executes our lord, Guntar. Then we fight for him at Hastings with Roger de Saint-Germain, and he beheads Saint-Germain and expels us from the manor. And now we go to do Lord DuLac's bidding for the Bastard in the wilds of north England against ousted Saxons and invading Scotts and Vikings!"

"My very point; Norsemen still go to England"

"Dammit," chided Orla, "don't piss away time worrying about the escaped Norseman, Brother! I know you're blessed in omens and reading bones, but we've other problems to worry about ahead, such as how we'll manage with Asta's new husband."

"Bah! Desmond DuLac's an ass," said Crowbones disgustedly. "He was already in good stead in France, but gambled with shoring up the Bastard in England in the hopes of tripling his wealth. Then he had to spend years taming rebellious Saxons! Doesn't he see the Bastard's simply using him? Worse yet, this new system the Bastard's devised doesn't even give DuLac or the rest of the Bastard's lackeys full ownership of the land he rewarded them with for fighting at Hastings! They're not land owners, but tenants! Yet another scheme the Bastard's invented. Worse yet, the Bastard's given these same allies of his their estates piecemeal instead of as single large estates!"

"Aye," Orla replied, "so the Bastard's vassals can't easily defend their lands if they ever revolt against him. Clever man, the Bastard. And since Hastings, his vassals have been able to do little for the past seven years but defend their holdings and put down rebellions by the defeated Saxons and raiders from the north. And now, Ivar, we go to join in this madness.

"What does the Bastard care? He's back in France! Before conquering England he was vassal to the King of France. But now as King of England, the Bastard believes himself to be King Philippe's equal. More war to come, so maybe it's just as well we leave France."

Orla spat into the wind again. "You may be right. It may be a good thing Asta sent the boys to Cluny, no fighting there. Still, I feel bad for the boys, especially Tristan. Ivar, if you could have seen the look on his face back at the monastery as I turned to leave. I didn't dare look back. His heart was broken." At this Orla paused, staring into the oncoming storm. "I should've taken time to bid him a finer farewell."

"Ja, dammit," agreed Crowbones, growing miffed, "and you should have let us see him and the Mite, too, before we left Cluny. But shit, when you came back from meeting with the prior, you vaulted on your horse and shouted, 'Let's go! Now!' Then, when we objected, you turned into a raving ass! I've never seen you that way, Orla."

"It would've just made things worse for the boys, Ivar, prolonging their misery." He shook his head, then, giving Crowbones a hard look. "Odin's ass! And why couldn't Asta have explained things to the boys instead of just packing them up and sending them off as she did?"

"Because they're too damned young, Orla. She loves them more than life itself! But it wouldn't have done any good to explain, they still wouldn't have understood. So let it be."

"Look," retorted Orla, his jaw tightening. "It was a good thing she did. The boys should know about it! After Roger de Saint-Germain was beheaded, Asta lost name, title and possessions, as well as all hope for any kind of decent life. She married Desmond DuLac only to spare her sons' future, Crowbones, and ours, lest you forget! Between us of her Danish Guard and all of our wives and children, there's nearly ninety of us in all! We were blacklisted and put out right along with Asta. She married DuLac only to save everybody's ass. Her only other option was her and the boys scrabbling for crumbs, along with all of us!"

With each word, Orla's anger was rising. Nudging him with a foot, Crowbones said, "Ja, ja, everything you say is right. But DuLac refused her sons, so she laid down the conditions that he pay for their education at Cluny and that he employ and provision the Danish Guard and our families in England. It was a heavy toll she extracted from him. But then, she's the most beautiful creature in all

France, so he agreed to her stiff terms. Anyway, it's done, Orla. Let it be."

"Dammit," Orla insisted, "she still should've explained it to the boys before shipping them off so they'd not think she was just dumping them!"

Tucking his head down between his knees as the first drops of rain began to pelt the ship, Crowbones fell silent. Lifting his shield over his head for cover, he said, "All Hell's about to break loose overhead, Brother, cover yourself."

Orla complied sullenly, lifting his shield and tucking his ax beneath his knees.

Watching, Crowbones leaned over, placing a hand on his brother's shoulder. "They say the Saxons are good with the ax, Ivar. Is yours sharpened?"

Orla nodded, his eyes settling on the blackness now consuming the seas ahead. "We are good, too, Ivar," he said. "Ja, I've put my finest stone to the blade and now it's sharper than ever, just for the Saxons."

Chapter Seventeen

England

As it was late afternoon when their ship landed along the English coast, Orla determined it best to move inland a half league or so to find shelter from the east wind that was blowing a scything rain across the beaches.

To their good fortune, at the edge of the nearby forest, they came upon the stone ruins of a farmhouse that had been torched during the rebellions. Although its roof thatching had deteriorated, they managed to salvage a sufficient number of charred beams and rafters strewn about to create a makeshift shelter just large enough to protect the five of them from the rain.

While the others labored at this task, Fairhair gathered the horses, led them to the tree line which stood just thirty yards or so from the ruins, and tethered them to one of the smaller oaks. Minutes later, all five men were gathered in a tight huddle beneath their shelter staring into the rainfall until, shortly, night fell and blackness swallowed both countryside and sky. Within the half hour, all but Crowbones had fallen into a deep sleep, covered by their mantles, leaning into each other like a tight pod of fetuses.

Crowbones sat there awake like a stone statue staring out into the darkness, lost in mystical apprehensions of his own devise about the escaped Norseman, WolfPaw. This was unusual for Ivar Crowbones, as very few occurrences in life had ever frightened him. By age eleven, he had already been thrown into the role of warrior by circumstance; forced to fight to protect family and clan. From there, life evolved into a ceaseless struggle as battle followed battle, and war followed war, forcing him and his brother, Orla, to fight side-by-side over the ensuing three decades. Their massive height and formidable girth had made each of them fearsome enough, but together they were absolutely frightening, unstoppable. Still, despite braving this violent past, and relishing it, the slaughter of the Norsemen along the Seine three weeks earlier had for some reason begun unsettling him. Like those tiny unseen parasites that silently feed from within, this disquiet was slowly devouring him.

Lost in speculations about his bird bones and their foreshadowing of WolfPaw's curse, he was oblivious to the arrival of four shadows creeping along the edge of the rainy forest, moving silently forward on bent haunches, whispering in low murmurs and motioning with secret gestures. Nor did he see the huge Irish wolfhound quietly leading them.

The hound tracked forward one stealthy paw at a time, his back sloped lower than his shoulders, his nose keen about the nostrils. Irish wolfhounds, also known as wolf-dogs, were not actually related to wolves, but were used to hunt and kill wolves, along with boar and deer. Being the tallest of all dog breeds in Europe, also massive and muscular, they were highly prized as guard and war dogs at the time. Unlike the wolfhounds of later centuries that were bred to be more gentle and compliant, the Irish wolfhounds of the 10th and 11th Century were highly prized for ferocity and aggression.

Darkness concealed the approaching profiles, and the heavy sound of rainfall covered the movement of their feet as they padded along the heavily wooded tree line. But then one of the men stumbled, falling into the jagged stub of a downed tree limb. Grabbing at his pierced ribs, the man screamed, gasping to catch his breath.

This cry jolted Crowbones from his reverie. Thinking the sudden howl to be the cry of a wild beast going after the horses, he fumbled for his ax and sprang to his feet, taking a run toward the noise. "Hee-yaw!" he bellowed, thinking to scare the creature away.

This created panic amongst the interlopers, and three of them bolted despite their leader's command to gather the horses and stand firm to fight. Standing alone in the dark rain, he could make out the form of a man coming at him from the ruins, ax raised. Abandoned by all but his dog, the bandit leader uttered a guttural sound, signaling the wolfhound to sic through bared fangs.

Though Crowbones could hear the growling approach of an oncoming beast, he could not see it, but the wolfhound clearly saw him. Drawing near, the dog lunged forward and upward, heaving its massive weight against Crowbones' chest. Caught by surprise, the shock of the collision flung Crowbones backward onto the ground. Scrambling to gain his feet, he began to flail at the dark with his ax, having no idea what was attacking him. Then he felt the gnash of fangs ripping at his shoulder flesh, and realized the creature was going for his throat.

Groaning with desperation, Crowbones continued to flail about with his ax, but the beast was too close in for the ax to strike. Heaving himself into a body roll to escape the fangs now lunging for his jugular, Crowbones managed to arc his arm and bash the creature with a single blow. Although it was the side of the ax, not the blade that made impact, the wolfhound raised his snout, yelping in anguish. Bucking forward, Crowbones drove the beast from his chest and struggled to gain his feet.

By now Orla and the others had been raised from their sleep. Weapons in hand, they charged into the blackness toward the cries of Crowbones and the ruckus. Hearing their approach, the bandit leader issued another guttural sound, signaling his dog to retreat. Crowbones and the others did not hear this call over their own shouting, but the hound recognized his master's call. Its ears going erect, the monstrous hound turned and raced back into the trees. Once joined, dog and master fled.

"Ivar!" shouted Orla, charging to his brother's assistance. "What's going on here? Are you all right?"

Crowbones stood, blood running down both forearms in dissipating streams as it mixed with rainfall. "Something in the woods!" he stammered. "A w-wolf! I was attacked by a goddamned wolf!"

"No!?" said Orla.

"We heard snarling," said StraightLimbs, "and I saw something shoot off into the woods. Yeah, it could've been a wolf, but they travel in packs at night; seems we would've seen more of them, or at least heard some howling and baying from the pack if it was a wolf."

"Yeah," agreed Fairhair. "Could've been a wild dog, maybe."

"Ja," said StraightLimbs, "a wild dog."

"Damn you two, I'm the one bleeding here! I'm the one that got attacked!" snapped Crowbones. "I say it was a goddamn wolf!"

Orla nodded, trading looks with StraightLimbs and Fairhair, waving them off. "Aye, Ivar, a wolf it was. Aye, let's get back out of this damned rain." Pointing to Guthroth, he said, "Stand watch a while, then let Fairhair take over while you get some sleep."

***

By dawn, the rain had stopped and the others awoke to find Fairhair returning from the trees. "Found several sets of footprints in the mud by our horses, and paw tracks," he said, approaching the shelter. "Must've had visitors during the night. The bunch of them were probably after our horses until Crowbones awoke."

Crowbones shook his head. "Nobody was in the woods last night, except that damned wolf. If you saw footprints, they must've been there from earlier, before we arrived."

"Well then," Fairhair replied, "what was it that rousted you from your sleep if it wasn't thieves moving toward our horses?"

"I wasn't asleep like the rest of you. I was wide awake. Don't you think I'd have heard a whole group of goddamned thieves moving through the woods? Shit, I'm not deaf! I heard a beast, a wolf, the one that attacked me last night."

Not wishing to further fuel Crowbones' agitation, Fairhair kicked at the mud. "Ja, the tracks may have been made prior to our arrival."

Fairhair's remark assuaged Crowbones. "Ja," he nodded, "you simply missed them in the dark and the rain last night."

Thus the matter was settled, with four of them deciding that whatever had occurred was not worth bickering over. Gathering the horses, they took to the road.

As they rode toward DuLacshire, getting their first look at England since the Battle of Hastings, the Danes were taken aback by the Saxon landscape. The cottages and farms had regressed since Hastings. It became evident also that the native population, though already seven years into the Norman Conquest, remained bitterly hostile. Despite the Danes being dressed in neither Norman nor French garb, the Saxons seemed to somehow know the five were tied to the Norman Conquest. In each village the Danes encountered, the Saxon inhabitants would stop what they were doing and stare with resentment until the travelers were out of sight. Then the villagers would resume their activities while exchanging bitter declarations and curses about the unwelcome intruders.

"Do you feel the chill?" Fairhair asked Orla upon passing through their third village.

"Ja," nodded Orla. "And not even the first woman has smiled at you this morning! That tells us much, eh?"

"Yeah," agreed StraightLimbs. "It's been seven years and these people still have the look of hate on their brow."

"It's the Bastard," said Crowbones, still irritated over the others doubting his claim about the wolf. "Even though he himself returned to Normandy after the Battle of Hastings, he instructed his occupation force to be merciless on the Saxons, especially here in the north where the rebellions were the most heated. And these people know that any men riding about with weapons, like us, could only do so with the blessing of Normans, so they know we're hooked in with Normans. Shit, truth is, we *are* Normans in a way, I suppose."

"W-we are D-Danes!" stuttered Guthroth, who was listening.

"Well spoken!" said Orla. "You've found your tongue since leaving Saint-Germain-en-Laye, Guthroth. Ja, we'll always be Danes!"

Guthroth flushed at the collar, but Orla's remark made him smile a little, too.

"These people don't know that, or care," replied Crowbones. "As far as they're concerned, we're simply the hated Norman enemy."

"Perhaps it'll be different among the Saxons who live on DuLac's lands," interjected Fairhair. "In witnessing the kindness of Asta and the intentions of our families and the rest of her Danish Guard, they might appreciate that we're different from the French and Normans."

"Damnation, Fairhair!" Crowbones snorted. "Have you forgotten DuLac? *He's* the one who'll set the tone. Anything good that Asta does, he'll undo ten-fold!"

"Easy, Brother," Orla offered, shaking his head. "You've been in a foul way ever since leaving France."

Offering no reply, Crowbones kicked at his mount's ribs and cantered ahead of the others.

"Odin's ass," grumbled StraightLimbs, "what in shit's eating him?"

"Omens," said Orla. "His bird bones have put him off kilter. Remember the lone Norseman who got away from us that night along the river?"

"Ja," replied StraightLimbs. "Son of the Norse captain, eh?"

"His name was WolfPaw," said Orla, "and he's started showing up in Crowbones' dreams, and in his bones. Somehow he's gotten into Ivar's head, like a haunting, I suppose."

StraightLimbs nodded, thinking about Crowbones' adamant stand about what attacked him the previous night. "The beast that came after him, I'm certain it was a damn dog, tagging along with the men Fairhair thinks were after our horses. But Crowbones insists there were no men, that it was a lone wolf." StraightLimbs fell silent then, mulling over what Orla had said about the escaped Norseman, tying it to Crowbones' dark mood and the so-called wolf attack. A light breaking over his brow, he shrugged. "You don't suppose Crowbones thinks the beast that attacked him was WolfPaw, come back to life, huh?"

"J-ja, th-that's it," muttered Guthroth. He had actually made that same connection the night before while guarding the camp after the attack, but said nothing because it would require a lengthy explanation, which he had no wish to undertake. It would have required him to say more than five or six words in a sequence, which he found difficult.

"Ja, maybe," said Orla. "Anyway, Crowbones can't seem to let that damned Norseman's birthmark go. He believes WolfPaw has set a curse on us all for killing his father and clansmen. That damn curse now follows us to England."

"I went with Fairhair this morning before leaving the ruins to inspect the footprints," said StraightLimbs. "I also saw the paw prints, and in Crowbones' defense, those damned prints were huge, bigger than any dog I've ever encountered. Shit, who knows, maybe it *was* a goddamn wolf, eh?"

"Naw, not likely," replied Orla. "As Fairhair said, someone was after our horses and Ivar just happened to flush them. The paw prints were mingled with the boot prints, and wolves don't mix with people, you know that!"

At this, StraightLimbs began to chuckle, but then checked himself. "People have been known to breed dogs with wolves, especially here in England."

"Dammit, StraightLimbs," snorted Orla, "now you're making excuses for my brother."

"No, I'm just saying that anything's possible. Who knows, huh?"

Now it was Orla who guffawed, "Ha! Before it's all over, you'll be swallowing this WolfPaw horse-shit, yourself!"

"The fact is, Orla," said StraightLimbs, "your brother's bones have saved our asses more than once, so maybe I'll just keep a close eye to my back for WolfPaw's curse. Maybe you should do the same, eh?"

"Ha, not likely!" snorted Orla. Turning, he motioned to Guthroth. "So, Guthroth, what do you say about all this? That thing that attacked my brother last night, wolf or dog?"

Guthroth, who was rarely ever asked to settle an argument, was surprised by Orla's question. Stuttering in confusion at first, he collected his thoughts. "I th-think it was a h-hound," he stammered, "b-but a d-damn *wolf-hound!*"

"Dammit!" Orla snorted. "Well spoken again! Guthroth, you're becoming a regular goddamned orator!"

Orla and StraightLimbs brayed with laughter, then, as Guthroth shook his head, wishing he had kept his mouth shut.

***

By late afternoon, Orla and the Danes were halfway to DuLac's realm. "We'll set camp in another few hours,"

Orla told the others when they came to the edge of a small village.

As they nudged their horses past the first enclave of huts, from the opposite direction a contingent of French cavalry approached, moving at a brisk pace. In their path, an old woman was struggling with a large basket. Dragging it along with much effort, she was in a state of irritation and could be seen mumbling aloud, fussing at the basket. The French riders could clearly see her, yet they refused to slow down.

Seeing this, Crowbones flagged his hand at the riders and shouted, "Ho, there! Watch the woman!"

The French continued the pace of their advance. Fortunately, the old woman just managed to drag her basket across to the other side of the road. But in passing, one of the horsemen kicked at her, knocking her violently to the ground, causing the contents of her basket, wet laundry, to spill onto the muddy road.

This needless act of arrogance irked all of the Danes, but before the others could respond, Crowbones reacted. Still lost to his foul mood, he spurred his horse forward, charging into the midst of the French. Leaning forward, he slapped the offending horseman full across the face, sending him careening off his horse backward, straight into the mud. "Filthy bastard!" Crowbones bellowed, grabbing his ax. "Do you not have a mother?"

The other Frenchmen drew their swords, surrounding him, but Orla, StraightLimbs, Fairhair and Guthroth charged into their company with weapons also drawn. This outbreak upset the horses, and they began to bray and snort with fury, milling about wildly, rising on hind legs.

"Arrêtez!!" Orla cried in French. "Arrêtez tout ça! Put up the weapons! Ivar, damn it, stop!"

Hearing their own tongue spoken, the French settled, followed by the Danes. "You're Normans?" one of the cavalrymen shouted.

"We are, so to speak!" said Orla. "No need to fight here!"

The French cavalryman motioned to the others and they sheathed their swords. "I'm DuFresne, Captain of Lord DuLac's Guard. We're on the way to the coast to escort members of Lady Asta's Guard to DuLacshire. But I guess you're them, huh?"

"You're late," said StraightLimbs, ax in hand. "We thought to see you upon landing, but then struck out on our own. Yes, we belong to her Guard."

DuFresne nodded. "I can see by your dress. But still, you're Normans then." Next he glanced over at Crowbones. "Nonetheless, you there, best that you not assault any of my men again."

Crowbones pulled his horse next to DuFresne, nudging it into DuFresne's mount. "Best your men never kick old women then," he said, his eyes alight. Pointing to the offending horseman who was still picking mud from his trousers, he added, "If I catch that man doing such a thing again, I'll kill him! Comprenez-vous?"

Before Captain DuFresne could reply, Orla reined his mount in next to him. "This is my brother, Ivar CrowBones. And DuFresne, he never says anything he doesn't mean. Your man shouldn't have kicked the old woman. I hope you're not the sort of man who justifies such a thing."

DuFresne thought a moment, looking at the offending soldier. "Indeed, it was not at all necessary. But know this, these damned people hold a bitter hatred for France and Normandy alike, so you and I are equally despised here. You'll see. Come then, we'll take you to DuLacshire. Lady Asta awaits your arrival."

The old woman, along with others in the village, had stood there silently watching the exchange between the two parties of horsemen. Although the villagers did not speak French, they surmised that the two parties before them were somehow tied together despite the dispute that just taken place. Meanwhile, Crowbones glanced over at the old woman whose eyes had not left him since striking the French rider from his horse. She motioned for him.

Orla moved his mount toward her, and just as he reined the horse in by her side, she spat at him. "Dirty Norman bastard!" she cried in Saxon, her voice shrill with hatred.

Although Crowbones did not understand Saxon, he felt the reproach. Backing his horse several paces from the range of her spittle, he shook his head. "So," he muttered, "this is how it shall be in England?"

Leaving the village, the two groups of horsemen traveled another hour or so before setting camp. Orla and DuFresne rode together at the head of the column, which gave the French captain a chance to brief Orla on DuLac's activities in England since the victory at Hastings. "It appeared to be no victory at all those first four or five years," DuFresne said. "The Saxons refused to lay down, so there was one revolt after another. Finally, in the winter of 69-70, the Bastard ordered fire set to the entire north where the most vicious resistance continued."

"Ja, we heard about it," said Orla. "Was called the Harrying of the North, eh?"

"Yes, a bloodbath, and we were right in the thick of it. Razed the entire landscape to waste and massacred nearly everything that moved. Salted the earth, burned the crops, killed the livestock. Those Saxons we didn't murder were left to starve, to the point of cannibalism in some cases."

"No wonder the Saxons are bloated with hate," said Orla. "But DuFresne, you seem a level man, and don't strike me as one who tramples over the weak."

DuFresne shook his head. "I don't, generally. But it was a bad time back then, and the Bastard brooks no disobedience, nor does DuLac. Truth is, DuLac thrived on the misery, and was rewarded with an earldom. Me? I just did as told. Not proud of it. As a soldier yourself, I'd guess you've been in those same boots."

"Ja, certainly," nodded Orla.

Orla then gave DuFresne a brief history of Roger de Saint-Germain, Asta and the Danish Guard. As they shared thoughts, the initial discomfort incurred by the incident in the village dissipated. Soon each man determined the other to be both reasonable and engaging. The others did not share this sentiment. Therefore, when camp was pitched, the Danes claimed one side of the fire while the French staked the other. Fortunately, there were no further incidents.

That next day, they rode for another five hours before finally crossing the boundary into DuLacshire. Two hours later, Orla spotted an unusual stone structure seated on a rise in the distance. "DuFresne, what's that?" he asked.

"Home," said DuFresne. "Lord DuLac got unlucky. Whereas most of the Bastard's vassals had to build their own motte and bailey forts, DuLac received a Saxon castle."

"Unlucky?" said Orla, puzzled. "You have that backwards, don't you? Motte and baileys make for rugged living. Far better to have a castle already in place."

DuFresne shook his head. "Saxon castles aren't equivalent to Norman or French castles by any means. Especially this one. Haven't you been told about the history of this place?"

"We were only told in France that we'd be occupying a castle that previously belonged to a Saxon noble."

"After Hastings," said DuFresne, "the Bastard awarded this estate to Lord Bartholde, who immediately hung the Saxon owner from the south wall before moving his family and Norman troops in."

"*Bartholde?* I remember him...a tough bastard. But why doesn't he still own it? Did he relinquish it?"

"Indeed he did," said DuFresne. "By his own death."

"Bartholde's dead?"

"Five years ago," replied DuFresne. "A Saxon revolt. They got into the Keep at night, somehow, and murdered everyone inside. Some claim there's a secret tunnel somewhere leading into the castle from outside, but we've found no trace of such during our time here. Anyway, the rebels took Bartholde's corpse and hung it upside down from the south wall, the same spot where Bartholde hung the Saxon noble two years earlier."

"If that was five years ago, then the place has stood empty that long before being awarded to DuLac?"

"No," answered DuFresne. "After Bartholde's murder, the castle was recaptured and the Bastard then awarded the estate to Lord Charton."

"Charton? The Butcher of Hastings?"

"Indeed, the most violent Norman ever born."

"But if DuLac now possesses this estate, Charton must have fallen from the Bastard's good graces then, eh?"

"Ha! Yes, you might say so...by his own death. Scotch raiders from the north got into the castle at night somehow and murdered everyone inside. Then they took Charton's corpse and those of every member of his family and hung them upside down on that same damned south wall. Left them there for over two months for the crows. Norman troops finally reclaimed the castle, but by then there was nothing left of Charton and his brood but bones. In any case, because of its history, Lord DuLac's convinced there's a secret entrance into the castle, and is offering a handsome reward to anyone who discovers it. Me, I suspect both times it might have been Saxon servants opening the gates to the enemy from the inside."

"Odin's ass," said Orla, "I now understand why you say DuLac may be the unlucky one. This place appears to be a damned target."

"Not just this place, but the entire northern frontier. So you see, Orla, we're to be brothers-in-arms here at DuLacshire. Us against the Saxons, and the Scotts, and the

Irish, and the Nor—" Stopping himself, DuFresne shot Orla an awkward look.

"You were about to say the Norsemen," Orla chortled, "which includes raiders from Denmark, eh? DuFresne, we of Asta's Guard maintain our culture, but no longer have any ties to the Vikings from Denmark who still raid Scotland and England from time-to-time, so relax."

"Well, it's not so much me, it's my men. They don't trust Asta's Guard. Besides, resentment's already built up between the two groups to the point your Danes refuse to bunk with mine in the troop barrack. They've taken over the stable area instead."

"Of course they're not going to bunk in the troop barrack, DuFresne, we've got women and children in our mix."

"So do some of the French, Orla. I'm talking about the single troops who make up the majority on both sides. That friction aside, it seems Asta's Guard's despise Normans and French alike!"

"Well, hell yes! It was the Bastard and his goddamned Norman crew that executed our patriarch, Guntar the Mace, with the helping hand of the French. It was a filthy business, that betrayal, from both ends. Since it happened, we've trusted neither, and stuck to ourselves. What could you expect?"

"Look," shrugged DuFresne, "I can't help what happened in the past. But you Danes are stuck in the wilds now, along with us French. Our men are going to have to get along, Orla, or none of us will survive. We can't afford division in the midst of these pissed-off Saxons and raiders from every direction, or we'll end up hanging from that damned south wall just like our predecessors. The point is, I'm asking for your help here, with the men."

Assessing DuFresne's words, Orla nodded with assent. "You seem to be a steady man, DuFresne, and you're right about being stuck in the wild. So I've no problem with your proposition. I'll see what I can do to simmer down the

Danes, if you'll do the same on your side. But know this, I'll not make my single troops move into the troop barrack. We've always stayed to ourselves, and that's not going to change. Understand?"

"Fair enough," said DuFresne, satisfied that he and Orla could work together on the issue.

***

As they entered DuLacshire castle, Orla and Crowbones were greeted by their families. Fairhair, StaightLimbs and Guthroth, having neither wives nor children, stood by and watched as Orla and Crowbones were mobbed by fawning spouses and children ranging from near infancy to adolescence. Orla's wife, a large woman named Birgita, nearly swept him from his saddle, and when he dismounted, he was then accosted by his two sons. The first to grab him was six-year-old Hroc Five-Hands, so named because he had since birth begun to tightly grasp anything within reach. The second son, thirteen-year-old Knud, was exultant on seeing his father, but had been born with a streak of timidity and reserve.

Allowing time for this exchange of greeting, Dufresne and his men stabled the horses. Shortly, he reappeared and approached Orla. "Lord DuLac is absent," he said. "Apparently he and an armed accompaniment are scouring the surrounding forests for Saxon poachers who've been feasting on DuLac's game. But Lady Asta anxiously awaits."

As they walked, Orla surveyed the castle interior. The castle was larger than Orla had originally thought, but in a state of complete disrepair. Orla also found the structure to be rather odd opposed to what he had been accustomed to across the Channel. "What the shit kind of place is this?" he asked DuFresne.

"Started out as a hill-fort occupied by the early Celts. When the Romans came, they modified such forts into Roman style fortresses, but they never quite succeeded in taming the north, so they never completed this particular place. From there a succession of Celts and Scotts moved in and out, but none were castle builders so their dereliction left the place a pile of shit. Eventually the Saxons were recruited from Germany by the Celts as mercenaries during their tribal wars, and the damned Saxons ended up taking over England completely. Then around the late 800's, Alfred the Great came up with a national Saxon defense system he called the 'burh concept'. That's a lot of what you see now."

"Burh concept?"

DuFresne laughed. "Yes, to keep *your* ancestors out, the Vikings! Fortified burhs, or burgs, were built on high ground around a castle. They threw up walls around the towns and everyone was commanded to live within twenty miles or one day's travel from the burh. During raids the Saxons living beyond the burh all gathered within the burh with the villagers for protection."

"You seem to know a bit about castles, DuFresne."

DuFresne laughed again. "My grandfather and father were both stone cutters and worked the castles of France throughout their lives. I was raised on the history of fortress building throughout Europe from antiquity forward. It's all they ever talked about!"

"How did you not become a stone cutter, then?"

"Ha! Have you ever cut stone, Orla?"

"No."

"If you had, you too would quickly be looking for another way to earn your keep. Fighting made a hell of a lot more sense to me at a young age than whacking rock all day!"

"Ah, I understand. That shorter wall we passed coming through the outer gate, that was the old Saxon burh wall?"

"Yes."

Orla thought a moment. "But I saw no people or huts in the section between that wall and the gatehouse of the castle."

"DuLac ran all the Saxons out and leveled the huts because of what happened to Bartholde and Charton. He's obsessed with this thing about a hidden passage into the Keep; thinks if it exists, the entrance is probably concealed somewhere within the burh walls. Also, he makes the Saxon servants leave both the castle and the burh at night in case the passage doesn't exist; believes it was actually the servants who let the attackers in during the previous attacks. At dawn he lets them back in to work until nightfall again."

"Makes sense," nodded Orla.

"You noticed the makeshift huts outside the burh wall? Well, that's the village now. He has no wish to hang like Bartholde and Charton from the south wall. Nor do we, eh?"

Orla scanned the surroundings as they continued to walk, assessing the strange castle. "And what about all this other mess laying about?"

"Bartholde's and Charton's incomplete construction," replied Dufresne. Those are the stables over there. Those low structures standing next to them, that's living quarters for your families. And the single men of the Danish Guard have garrisoned behind that and the stables in some run-down shanties located there. Your single men prefer them to staying with the French. And that half structure you see poking up younger is the chapel, or what's left of it."

"Damn, what happened to it?"

"Destroyed during the Harrying of the North. Bartholde and Charton both began renovations of it and the rest of the original Saxon structure, but I've told you how they both ended. DuLac has re-begun the process and hopes to finish within a year or so, but these Saxon masons aren't worth a shit."

"And what's that next to the Keep?"

"The Saxons used it as an armory, but it's a garden house now. Lady Asta spends time there, helping some old Saxon woman from at times who's a healer. My men think the old hag's a sorceress."

Finally, DuFresne led Orla into the Keep, through the grand hall, then up to the second level where Asta was waiting. Upon seeing him arrive, she moved forward to greet him.

"Orla," she said, holding out her hands. Despite calling his name with beaming affection, she neither kissed nor embraced him.

Orla extended both hands and grasped hers, smothering them in his massive paws. "Asta," he said, also with great affection. "We're happy to finally be back at your side."

DuFresne was both puzzled and touched by the exchange occurring before him. It seemed profoundly heartfelt, yet strangely controlled. Also, seeing such a rugged bear of a man display such servility and reverence to such a strikingly beautiful woman of but twenty was not something he had witnessed before. He watched a moment longer, then excused himself.

"My boys," said Asta, her tiny hands still buried in those of Orla. "How are they?"

"Fine," replied Orla, shaking his head with affirmation. "And Cluny is impressive beyond belief. I never imagined such a place existed."

"And the Monk-Prior, you found him to be sincere?"

Detecting a trace of urgency in her tone, Orla nodded. "Yes, a reasonable sort, that one. I think you've left the boys with a good master, Asta. So, it's a good thing you've done for them."

Asta withdrew her hands from Orla's and turned away. "A good thing?" he heard her whisper.

Then he thought her shoulders heaved a bit, which left him feeling vacant, not unlike how he had felt just before leaving Tristan and Guillaume with the prior. Odd as it all was, this twenty-year-old girl standing there quietly dissolving at the loss of her sons had become an anchor for him in life, as she had for the other Danes and their families. But this brave and stout young soul before him had had her innocence and adolescence torn from her at the age of twelve, then was forced at that tender age to lead and care for others. For this reason, Orla, hulk of the man he was, now stood speechless and lost before her. He wished to console her with a fatherly embrace, but Asta shunned such displays. He wanted to say something comforting, but found his own throat filling with emotion. So they both stood there in silence, her staring at the floor thoughtfully, and he staring at the wall in discomfort.

Finally Asta spoke. "Did they ask for me during the trip south, Orla?"

"Oh yes!" Orla responded. "They both spoke and thought of you often."

Asta raised her eyes from the floor, leveling them at him. "*Orla*," she asserted frigidly.

Orla, whose eyes had met hers upon the question, looked away now to avoid her scolding gaze. "W-well," he muttered, knowing she had snared him, "other than mentioning a time or two what you had taught him, Tristan spoke of you...once. We were at the campfire and he didn't quite understand why you sent him and Guillaume away."

"Is that how he put it, Orla?" Asta probed.

Orla groaned a bit, exhaling heavily. "Damnation," he muttered. "Yes."

"Orla, you know I don't abide profanity of any sort. Now answer my question, with honesty this time."

"He said you sent them away because Lord DuLac denies them...and so you could...*marry* well."

Silence descended. The two stood there like stone sculptures for a long while, after which Asta spoke first. "None of what Tristan said was completely untrue, though you and I both know the real implications," she said, unable to disguise a trace of disappointment in her son's words.

"So good, I have taught him well, I suppose. He is not easily deceived and sees things set before him clearly, or at least as clearly as a seven-year-old could be expected to see. But a question, then. Did he cry during this discussion at the campfire?"

Orla looked at her, knowing it was useless to lie. "He was about to at one point, but he toughened up then."

"Good," Asta replied without conviction. "The fact that he spoke about me only once tells me he is not dwelling on that over which he has no control. It also shows he has no need to air his every private thought. I would not wish him to be weak. Would you, Orla?"

"No, certainly not."

"And Guillaume, did he speak of me during the journey?"

"No, Asta, not once."

This surprised Asta, but she passed it over as though such a thing was to be expected. "Then you agree the boys will weather this separation from me?"

"I hope so. But then, they are just children, Asta."

Asta watched him curiously as he gave this last response. "Orla, I see this discussion is making you uncomfortable."

"It was difficult leaving them." He shrugged. "I was fine until we got to Cluny, then...goddammit, I don't know."

He grumbled to himself as Asta's eyes raked over him for cursing again. Still, she said nothing about it. Instead, she said, "I would have accompanied you to Cluny with them, Orla, but determined my heart simply could not bear it."

"I understand," he said, though in truth, he did not. Since their birth, the two boys had been her entire life, yet rarely did she offer her touch, or demonstrate tenderness. It seemed her energy had been obsessively devoted to preparing them for something even she did not understand, something vaporous and intangible. *Perhaps she herself had simply been too hardened by the grist of life, refusing to allow them to be caught unawares as she had been. In any case, they're gone and on their own, thought Orla, so in the end, maybe Asta knew all along what she was doing.*

"So," Asta sighed, "all is well then, I suppose, now that they are in the hands of the Black Monks."

"Yes, probably so. But one other thing, Asta. On the first night we left Saint-Germain-en-Laye, your old nurse-maid and keeper appeared from out of the forest and walked right into our camp."

"Mielikki?"Asta questioned, stunned as if a thorn had caught on her breath.

"Yes, begging for food."

"Did she see Tristan?" asked Asta, growing uneasy.

"No, he was in the wagon, but he saw her. Of course, he had no idea who she was or what she had done long ago. And Crowbones and I said nothing to him about her."

"Good," said Asta, but the expression etching itself into her face since hearing Mielikki's name betrayed regret. "I loved her as my mother," she said, more to herself than to Orla. "It broke my heart to force her from the household. But the terrible thing she tried to do to Tristan…"

"Yes, good that Guthroth came upon her as she was bathing the boy. When he saw her trying to drown him, he'd have choked her to death on the spot had you not intervened."

Asta stared into space, lost in the memory of the day she had forced Mielikki from the clan. "Such a horrid day, Orla," she whispered. "I could scarcely believe any of it was true. But you know, since the day Tristan took his first breath, Mielikki became consumed with a strange dread, to the point of trying to murder him." She fell silent again. Then after a long pause, turned, saying, "Very well then, I thank you from the depths of my heart for taking the boys to Cluny, Orla. You may take your leave now." Pointing to a table, she added, "And take these gifts from me to your sons, Knud and Hroc. Such dear boys."

Orla collected the gifts, an ivory crucifix embedded in gold and a small bust of the suffering Christ, his temple crowned with thorns. "Yes, good boys," said Orla, "especially little Hroc." Bowing, he left.

Asta, now alone in the chamber, suddenly found that her lips had begun to tremor uncontrollably. Feeling faint, she flung herself onto a nearby chair. Throwing her arms and shoulders over its back, she dissolved into unrestrained weeping. "My Lord and Savior in Heaven," she cried, "you have taken from me all in this life that is dear to me! Whatever it is that I have done, forgive me my sins for I have only tried to follow your word!"

***

That next afternoon Lord Desmond DuLac and a party of horsemen returned to the castle with two ragged Saxons in shackles. The two were forest dwellers, a father and his son of about six or seven who had been scratching a living for the past several years in the wild.

DuLac made a great performance of dragging the two through the village as a gaggle of old men, women and children watched. The villagers knew the pair, but stood in silence not wishing to reveal their acquaintance, except for one old woman leaning over her cane, her back so horribly bent that it appeared she was staring straight down at her toes even as she craned her neck to look up at the prisoners. Her name was Heidi the Elder, the village healer. Signaling to them, she held her hands over her breast in desperation.

Around the father's neck hung a dead hare, and around the son's a snared bird. "Caught them with the blood of my animals on their very hands!" DuLac crowed for all to hear. "I'll deliver justice within the half hour. This forest belongs to me alone, Earl Desmond DuLac. Hunting by others is forbidden by Norman law!"

The villagers listened, but beneath their breath each was cursing this vermin of a man who had taken over the territory. They loathed his name, his authority and even his appearance. He possessed short arms, a long nose, squinty eyes, and a pointy face. Mocking these features, the Saxons had contemptuously dubbed him the 'Mole'.

The Norman procession slowly worked its way up the hill, entered the burh gate, then the gatehouse of the castle. DuLac dismounted and shouted for his men to drag the prisoners to the butcher's stump where a broadax stood embedded in the top, its blade stained with blood now caked black. Prying it loose and pointing it at the father, DuLac cried, "Gather me the bucket of pitch! Lay his arms over the block and extend them!"

The soldiers grabbed the man's arms and pulled them over the stump while the Saxon struggled in futility to free himself. The son, wide-eyed, burst into tears as all activity within the castle walls came to a halt. Masons, laborers and passing servants stood motionless, knowing what was about to come. The Norman troops appeared amused.

Orla and Crowbones, who were currying their horses outside the stable, stopped what they were doing also. "A pity," Orla said without emotion. "The boy, I mean."

Crowbones shook his head, but resumed with his horse, disinterested.

"You choose not to watch, Ivar?" asked Orla.

"No. I'm tired of bloodletting. Even if the Saxon was hunting on DuLac's land, has he earned such a severe penalty? A man must eat to live. Odin's ass, flog him, but don't take his arms!"

"Ja, maybe the boy deserves mercy, but the man, he knew better," Orla insisted. "He broke the law and gets what he deserves."

Crowbones stopped brushing and turned to his brother. "Ah, just like the Norsemen on the Seine River?" he said, his posture beginning to bristle. "Orla, have you never just once thought that perhaps it is the laws that are corrupt, or the *men* who make the laws?"

"Ivar, we live by the law. *Man* lives by the law."

"Really, Orla? It seems to me more and more that man *dies* by the law!"

Orla did not respond. He had been noticing a strange softening occurring within his brother since leaving France. Failing to understand it, he thought, *It must be the bird bones. Still, where had the hard-shelled Crowbones crept off to? And when would he return?*

The struggle at the stump continued. "Goddammit, secure the prisoner's feet, you imbeciles!" shouted DuLac with increasing impatience. When his soldiers finally secured all four of the poacher's limbs, DuLac raised the ax over his shoulder, preparing to strike.

Seeing this, the man's son went berserk, kicking at the soldiers and cursing them. Not comprehending a word of Saxon, they collared him, laughing. As they got the boy under control, additional soldiers grasped the father's limbs as he also began to struggle more furiously, knowing that within seconds he would be rendered helpless by the severing of both arms. Then, in a moment of surrender, seeing there was no hope, he screamed, "Kill me you bastards, but have mercy on my son!" Raising his eyes to the sky, he cried, "God in Heaven, help my boy! Oh Lord Jesus, have mercy on him!"

Asta, who happened to be near the south window of the Keep, heard this pitiful plea for holy intervention and peered down into the courtyard, quickly surmising what was about to occur. "No, Desmond!" she shrieked. "No! Stop this madness!"

DuLac was just at the point of beginning his downward thrust with the ax. But hearing Asta's cry, he stiffened, and froze. He had never once, since first encountering Asta, witnessed such emotion coming from her.

Seeing him pause, Asta cried out again. "In the name of God, *mercy,* Desmond! I beg you!"

All in the courtyard stared up to the window, then down to DuLac. Whispers ensued. "Oh, what will DuLac do?" breathed a female servant. "Will he listen to her?"

Hearing this, DuLac dropped the ax to his side and stood erect, staring up at Asta. "Come down!" he bellowed. "If you wish to spare these outlaws, then have the decency to speak to me directly rather than screaming at me from the Keep like a common wench!"

Asta disappeared from the window and soon appeared in the yard. Kneeling, she grasped the outstretched woodsman about the neck and looked deploringly at DuLac. "I beg you for this man's arms, Desmond," she said with a sudden calm. "And the boy's as well."

"To what purpose, Asta?" sniffed DuLac. "If I spare their arms, they'll only poach my game again."

"Then *feed* them, Desmond," snapped Asta, "and give them work so they may survive. This man cried out to God for salvation, so be God's instrument, Desmond. You sent my sons away, and I agreed! You dragged me to England, and I agreed! As I've surrendered so much to you, could you not give me this token, at least, in exchange?"

There is no predicting, at times, the effect of a woman's words on a man. And even less so the words of an extremely beautiful woman upon a man smitten. As he watched Asta pleading there on her knees, mesmerized by the gaze of her stunning grey eyes, and taken by the very movement of her luffing silver hair in the breeze, DuLac faltered. She was the most alluring creature he had ever encountered, and he knew that he would never cross her likes again if he were ever to lose her. He had coveted her upon first sight, which was her betrothal to his own brother eight years earlier as a twelve-year-old bride. There was something so remarkable about her that she had never left his consciousness from that moment forward. For these reasons, even in the company of his men-at-arms, he dropped the ax.

"Very well," he grumbled, "for you alone, Asta, I give these poachers mercy." Signaling to the soldiers, he said, "Release them both, and feed them, *dammit*." Next, gazing about the yard with irritation, he shouted, "And the rest of you gawking asses there, get back to your god-damned affairs!"

Asta released her hold on the poacher's neck and stood, then embraced the man's tearful son. The boy threw his arms tightly about her waist and began to sob. "Oh, thank you, my Lady!" he snuffled. "Thank you!"

Asta held the boy a moment and caressed his spill of thick, blondish hair that so reminded her of Tristan and Guillaume. Perplexed, DuLac watched. He had never seen her embrace or caress even her own two sons, and this sudden comforting of an unknown child seemed a lapse of her glacial character. But Desmond DuLac had never suffered loss during his greed-driven existence, and failed to understand that the sheer grief of losing what one loves can change a person's world, as well as their heart.

Releasing the boy to his father, Asta approached DuLac, not to embrace him, but to reach out and lightly place one hand on his. "God will remember this day, Desmond," she said.

DuLac shook his head, wishing she could be more demonstrative, knowing that she wouldn't. After a moment he finally muttered, "To hell with God, Asta! It's *you* I hope remembers this day."

Chapter Eighteen

The Black Monks

In working as Prior Odo's intern, Tristan became engrossed in the intricacy and complexity of monastic operations. He also learned that Prior Odo was a skilled logistician, masterful in dealing with people. Each day after the early morning walk-about with Prior Odo, Tristan would report to the teacher-monks where he continued his studies with the Scullery Cohort until dinner and his nightly report to Prior Odo. In going about this regimen, Tristan soon discovered he had become the root of division amongst his classmates. There were those within the Scullery Cohort who much admired his new appointment, and those who resented it. It was LeBrun who stoked fires against him; undoing Tristan had now become an obsession for the envious red-head. Initially, LeBrun attempted to outshine his young nemesis intellectually, but this proved disastrous because LeBrun invariably ended up looking the fool. In the end, LeBrun abandoned this intellectual challenge and settled for undermining Tristan through rumor and ill report.

When the other boys of the Dorter left Cluny for six weeks of summer break, Guillaume contentedly continued to work the stables while Tristan was afforded the opportunity to focus entirely on developing a more detailed knowledge of monastery operations. A quick learner, it took him little time to identify and compartmentalize each individual phase of operations, the resources required, and the personnel involved. "Everything is interdependent," Prior Odo lectured daily as they moved from one area to another. "No one thing stands alone."

As summer ended and the other boys of the cohorts returned to Cluny, there was still one aspect of the Cluny operation that remained somewhat of an enigma to Tristan: prayer. More specifically, the amount of prayer that took place within the monastery walls. Each day at Cluny was divided into the eight sacred offices, which meant the monks met in the cathedral and began prayer each day with three o'clock-in-the-morning Lauds. This was followed by Prime, or early morning prayer, at six o'clock. They then reconvened at nine o'clock for Terce, or mid-morning prayer. Sext occurred at noon, the sixth hour after dawn. This was in turn followed by prayer at the ninth hour after dawn, or None, at three o'clock in the afternoon. Vespers was the evening prayer service, which took place at six o'clock when candles were lit. Compline, coming from the Latin completorium, was the prayer service at the end of the day, which was considered to be nine o'clock. Finally, the night prayers, or Matins, were recited at midnight.

Although Tristan, for his age, was already a devout Catholic due to the early efforts of his mother and teacher-nuns, he was astounded that men would actually agree to spend so much time on their knees. Yet more questionable, he learned the monks were not allowed to receive correspondence from their families or to receive visitors. Furthermore, they were not allowed to leave the monastery or travel without specific written permission from either the abbot or one of the priors. Although the Benedictines did not adhere to as austere a vow of silence as certain other monastic orders, hours of strict silence were set, and silence was maintained as much as practically possible except by teacher-monks and other designees. Though he dared not question such piety, he secretly wondered what it was that drove the Black Monks forward with such fervent devotion.

***

When the instruction cycle started again, Tristan immersed himself back into his academic regimen while continuing his internship with Prior Odo when not in class. By September, he had become completely buried in his new existence at Cluny, and though images of his mother continued to arise periodically, thoughts of her began to wane. His burns had completely healed also by September. Although some scarring had developed below his neck and over one shoulder, these markings were not visible beneath his shirt.

Prior Odo, increasingly struck by the unusual talents and focus of this mere boy, determined that Tristan would continue in his office throughout the fall and winter. That next spring, Abbot Hugh removed Odo from Claustral Prior duties and appointed him to Grand Prior, which meant Odo's role moved from monastery logistician to monastery treasurer. This appointment as the overseer and manager of Cluny's financial affairs meant that Odo de Lagery now directed one of the greatest amounts of accumulated wealth in all Christendom. Whereas Abbot Hugh of Semur was the political and spiritual figurehead of Cluny's power, the power brokers of Europe clearly understood that it was Odo de Lagery who collected and distributed Cluny's vast wealth and accounted for its immense property holdings throughout Europe. Thus Odo de Lagery now found himself thrust onto the grand stage of international affairs, his name quickly developing continental significance.

Odo's first official act as Grand Prior was to remove Tristan from his duties as intern to the Claustral Prior and appoint him as intern to the Treasury. In other words, Tristan would continue to be his personal assistant. "As I rise," Odo told the boy, "so shall you rise, as long as you remain faithful to God."

So it was in March of 1074 that young Tristan de Saint-Germain, now inextricably hinged to Odo de Lagery, would unwittingly and by chance happen into a great chain of events that would ultimately transform the political maps of Europe and affect the future direction of continental history. There was no way on earth that young Tristan could have foreseen such a path, but Odo de Lagery might have already suspected such a possibility.

Even the most catastrophic of earthquakes signals its arrival with but a tiny tremor so slight that only the insects notice. This initial tiny tremor is then followed by another, only a microscopic measure more intense, perhaps. Upon this second tremor, there may only be a rare individual or two who recognizes that something extraordinary is about to develop. In the case of Tristan de Saint-Germain, it was Odo de Lagery who felt this tremor, in the form of a lost but extremely gifted child. Odo felt these things for reasons that even he himself did not comprehend. Perhaps it was his own innate and highly cultivated sense of perception and expectancy. *But perhaps it was also the will of God*, he thought, *silently loosening the decay and silt of Europe in the year 1074.*

Chapter Nineteen

Visitors

Odo and Tristan were sitting at a table lost in paper-work when a structured burst of coded knocks rapped at the door of the Treasury Tower.

"Tristan," said Odo, "see who it is."

Tristan stood and moved toward the door, pulling a large key from his pocket. "Who's there?" he called.

"Percunia non satiat avaritiam, sed inritat!" came the answer.

"Very well. And what message does that convey?"

"Money does not satisfy greed, it stimulates it!"

Hearing this secret response, Tristan opened the lock and struggled to pull open the heavily reinforced door. A young monk stepped inside, addressing Odo. "Grand Prior, there are visitors in the refectory of the Guest Hall, led by a woman who seeks audience."

"A woman?" asked Odo.

"The most beautiful woman who has ever entered our gates."

"Here to see *me*?" asked Odo, puzzled.

"No, Prior," the monk said. "She asks for young Tristan."

Tristan shoved his work aside. He, too, seemed sur-prised, but seconds later the clouds parted and he broke into a burst of motion. "It's my mother!" he shouted, afire.

"She's come to get me and Guillaume! Perhaps my uncle has relented and will allow us to go to England!"

This naked and uncharacteristic burst of emotion from Tristan caused Odo to laugh with contentment. "Ah, come then, Tristan, let's greet her!"

Tristan became a blur of motion. As they exited the Treasury Tower, he ran ahead, his heart thumping like a rousted rabbit. Minutes later, he burst through the doors of the Guest Hall dining area. "Mother!" he cried, glancing about with unbridled anticipation. "Where are you?"

There was no reply, which caused immediate anxiety. Then he spotted the figure of a woman sitting in the midst of others rising from the back of the refectory. He ran to her with outstretched arms, tears beginning to stream down his face. But then he froze, nearly stumbling.

"Tr-Tristan? Is that *you*?" the woman said...in Spanish.

When Prior Odo entered the guest-hall refectory, the look of sheer woe flooding Tristan's face told him immediately that Tristan's mother had not come to Cluny. Seeing Prior Odo watching him, Tristan gathered himself and wiped at his eyes. Then, stepping forward, he greeted the woman. It was Nuri, the Romani woman he and the Danes had encountered along the Seine River.

"Oh, good to see you," she said in broken French, bending slightly to embrace him. Smiling sheepishly, she said, "I speak French now, but not so good as my daughter, Mala."

"B-but what are you doing here?" Tristan asked, too surprised to even issue a greeting.

"We go back to Spain, to gather the others of our family."

Remembering her stories of the Muslim troubles in Spain, Tristan said, "You were seeking a place to live, to the north. Did you find a home?"

"Si!" Nuri smiled, reverting to Spanish. "A beautiful place just a half day's walk from where we met you along the river—near Saint-Germain-en-Laye."

"What?" Tristan stammered, stunned.

"Yes, we met a lord there, Lord Letellier. He lets us stay on a corner of his land. Our men work his fields, and my sister and I, we cook and work in the castle for him. Did you not yourself come from somewhere in that area?"

"Si, my brother and I were born in that…general territory," said Tristan, not wishing to mention being removed from the very estate where Nuri and her people had now settled.

Nor did Nuri wish to explain that the lecherous Lord Letellier was, in truth, actually bedding her and her sister to satisfy his pursuit of stray female flesh.

As Prior Odo approached, he heard Tristan and the woman speaking Spanish, introduced himself and welcomed her in that language fluently. She reciprocated with a mixture of Spanish and French.

When this exchange was completed, Tristan spoke up again. "Your daughter, did she come with you?"

"Si!" Turning, she called to the back of refectory where a young girl stood smiling, and was already approaching.

This caused Tristan to flush a bit as a strange pang loosened something in his belly. Embarrassed, he deflected his eyes from her. "Senorita Nuri and her people are Romani," he blurted, turning to Odo.

"I have heard of the Romani," said Odo, "but had no idea any had come north into France."

Tristan was not listening, but slipping a look toward Mala as she came toward him. Pleased, yet nervous, his eyes centered back at Prior Odo, pretending not to notice Mala's approach.

But Mala saw through the ploy. Refusing to be ignored, she stepped within inches of his face. "Hello, Smart

Boy!" She beamed. "I *told* you I'd come to Cluny one day!"

Forced to look at her directly, Tristan felt tiny palpitations beating at his chest. He remembered that she had been as beautiful as her mother, but now as she stood there, her dark, almond eyes penetrating his charade, it seemed she had since their first encounter eclipsed even the stunning Nuri. He stared, paralyzed.

"Well then," she smirked, feigning a scolding tone, "have you nothing to say?"

Whereas it is true that in the very young there is no comprehension of sexuality or love, it is also true that even in pre-pubescence one can feel attraction, or at the least a strong and immediate connection. This brief reunion and exchange of eye contact between the eight-year-old boy and the eleven-year-old girl was precisely such an occurrence. Their mutually handsome appearance aside, both of these children carried within their heart a sense of dispossession, she on the constant move and in a foreign land, and he separated from his mother and sent to a distant place not of his choosing. Each felt unrooted, as tossed to the wind. The human heart can perceive a similar loneliness in others, somehow, and this silent, shared desperation can give rise to an irrational bond. As the two youngsters stared at each other, they could detect that their lives, though very different, had converged onto common and unstable ground.

"H-hello, Mala," mumbled Tristan, nodding awkwardly with a mix of sheepishness tinged with elation.

The two stood there quietly then, looking dumbly at each other, as people do when surprised to the point of quiescence.

"Tristan, why don't you take the young lady into the courtyard," suggested Odo, "and show her about while I meet the rest of Nuri's people?"

Tristan's heart soared despite suppressing his reaction to a polite nod. "Certainly, Prior Odo," he said, quietly motioning her to follow.

Mala, too, demonstrated reserve upon following Tristan out of the refectory door, but once outside, her face blossomed into a wide smile. Playfully taking his hand into her own in that natural fashion not uncommon of a girl stuck between childhood and adolescence, she twittered, "Indeed, Smart Boy, show me this monastery! But I must tell you right off, I've thought about you a thousand times since that night at the campfire. Yet, I still I can't believe you're to be a monk!"

"No," Tristan objected, very conscious of Mala's grip on his hand, "I am just here to learn from the monks, not to become one!"

Mala laughed, taking full delight in Tristan's concerned expression as he said this. There were no boys her age within her clan, and despite being three years older than him, she found his manner and intelligence to be arresting.

"So what are you learning here then, Smart Boy?" she chided with an elbow to his ribs.

Mala's close proximity was creating a small degree of discomfort for Tristan, but only due to his fear that others might see them holding hands. In particular, he did not want any of his classmates or Dorter mates spotting them, especially LeBrun. Accordingly, he avoided the open courtyard and stuck to the covered cloister walkways where visibility was obstructed by dense shrubbery. "I am the Treasury Apprentice to the Office of the Grand Prior," he declared, boasting for the first time ever about his status at Cluny.

"Really?" Mala replied. "I thought you were just a student here."

"Well, I am," said Tristan, falling humble, "but I have been lucky enough to help Prior Odo since my accident."

"Accident?" asked Mala.

"Yes, I was burned badly in the scullery while draining hog fat."

"But you don't *look* burned."

"You can't see scars because they are under my shirt." At this, he pulled the bottom of his shirt up to his throat, and pointed to his chest and shoulder. "See there, not a pretty sight, huh?"

Mala looked, running a finger over the barely visible scar tissue. "Poor, poor Tristan," she sniffed.

Tristan dropped his shirt back and responded stoically, as though explaining a grievous battle wound. "It was a horrid ordeal, and the pain was terrible, but I never cried a single tear." But this lie did not set well with himself, so he retracted it. "Well, Mala, actually, I *did* cry. But just a little."

Mala admired him even more for this admission, hugging his neck, which made Tristan flush pink, then purple. Pushing her away gently, he glanced about to see whether anyone was watching.

Mala feigned a pout. "I was just letting you know how brave and honest you are, and you push me away? Well then, maybe you're not as smart as I thought. Now take me back to the guest-hall before my mother calls. We'll be staying in the woods just outside the village. We haven't set camp yet."

"Camp?" said Tristan. "But we have a guest house here. Why don't you stay there?"

Mala rolled her eyes. "Foolish boy," she shrugged, "that takes money, and we've barely enough to make it to Spain and back."

Tristan thought a moment. "Maybe I can talk to Prior Odo. He could make an exception if he wished."

This delighted Mala to the point of issuing a tiny squeal. She had never experienced the luxury of an inn; had rarely ever had a roof over her head other than that of her mother's wagon. "You could manage that?" she said, her eyes turning to saucers.

Seeing her excitement, Tristan suddenly regretted pushing her away. "Certainly," he said, though in his heart he suspected he might well have overstepped his bounds. Nonetheless, he grasped her hand and, leading her back to the refectory, said, "Mala, be sure to thank Nuri for me because no one has ever come to visit me here. I am glad she thought of coming by the monastery."

"Silly boy!" Mala sniggled, delivering another elbow to his ribs. "It wasn't her that decided, it was *me*. Cluny was out of our way, but I insisted over and over that I wanted to stop by to see you. I've wondered about you a lot, you know, since the river."

When they joined Mala's clan within the refectory, Tristan called Prior Odo aside and whispered something in his ear. As he did this, Mala, in turn, whispered into her mother's ear to explain what Tristan was doing. Nuri's brow creased as she listened, then flared with jubilance. Within seconds she was passing word along to the other Romani, whose reaction was identical.

Noting this as Tristan pleaded his case, Prior Odo smiled. It would be a small concession on his behalf to grant this favor, yet to the Romani, it would be monumental. Besides, for all his good labor, Tristan had never once requested a favor. "Yes, yes, most certainly!" nodded Odo, patting Tristan on the shoulder.

That evening Prior Odo invited the Romani to dine in his private chambers, and asked Tristan to join them. Nuri and Prior Odo did most of the talking during the meal while Tristan and Mala, seated beside each other, listened, only occasionally adding a comment or two. When dinner was over, Tristan and Mala walked out to the Square and sat alone together on the steps of the Abbey, sharing stories and laughter until nearly midnight. This was a breach of practice for boys of the Dorter, but Prior Odo had made the exception on Nuri's request.

"Please, Prior," she had pleaded, "I haven't heard my dear Mala laugh in such a long time, and this beautiful boy is so entertaining to her. She's talked my ears off about him since last year when they first met. Give her a little time with him. What could it harm?"

That next day as Tristan carried out his morning walk with Prior Odo, he caught sight of Mala as the Romani were about to tour Cluny Abbey. Raising his voice so as to be heard, he took on an officious air while scribbling notes on his tablet, pointing here and there. Stealing a glance in Mala's direction, he was pleased to see she was watching. Nonetheless, he did not see her the rest of the day as he had class until his evening walk-about with Prior Odo.

Noticing the boy was antsy, Odo said, "Had you rather spend some time with your visitors, lad, than finish our circuit?"

"Oh, no, certainly not," Tristan lied.

Shaking his head, Odo grinned a bit, then gave Tristan a slight shove toward the Guest House. "Go on, our business can wait. They will only be here another two days, so take some time, maybe even miss class until they leave for Spain, eh?"

Too stunned to reply, Tristan took off at a run toward the refectory. Halfway there, without stopping, he turned and shouted, "Thank you, Prior Odo!"

***

The two youngsters spent every moment of the next two days together as Tristan helped her explore the monastery grounds, explaining the many different buildings, the operations of Prior Odo, and the stiff regimen of the Black Monks. As they moved from one place to another, words fairly tumbled from them both in a communion of comfort and contentment. Despite the many differences dividing their respective worlds, each somehow recognized that the other possessed a similar heart. This sparked in them both a wave of exuberance that was as foreign as it was compelling.

On her last night there, Mala took on a look of concern as they sat together on the Cluny Abbey steps. Reaching over, she took Tristan's hands in hers. "Oh! But I almost forgot. Tristan, do you still have my ring?"

"Yes, of course," Tristan replied, fishing into his trouser pocket. A moment later he held it in his hand, showing it to her. "I keep it with me everywhere I go," he said, beaming a little.

This pleased Mala to no end, and she leaned over, kissing him on the cheek.

Mortified, Tristan froze.

Tittering, Mala kissed his cheek again, closing his fingers about the ring he was holding. "Do you remember why I gave you my ring, Smart Boy?"

"Y-yes," Tristan stammered, taken aback by her two pecks on his cheek. "So I would not forget you."

"Well then, since you still have it, I guess it was a good idea giving it to you! Next time I see you, I'll be asking about it again, so you better have it, eh? And here's what else I'm going to do, when my mother finishes this business in Spain, I'm going to talk to her about moving to this part of France, maybe even here in Cluny village. Then we could see each other all the time!" At this, she kissed him yet a third time on the cheek, her eyes alight with happiness. Turning, she then ran toward the Women's Guest Hall, laughing as she went.

That next morning, as the Romani wagons departed and began winding their way down the hill, Mala was sitting on the rear stoop of the last wagon, just like the year before when she left Tristan. Standing at the gate watching her, Tristan waved. But as before, Mala did not wave back. This distressed Tristan, although he did see her suddenly wiping something from her eye…a tear, perhaps.

The two youngsters stared longingly at each other until the distance became too great. When Tristan could no longer make out her figure at the back of the wagon, he was overcome with a devastating vacancy in the pit of his stomach. That first separation along the Seine had been difficult enough, but this one was far more so, for some reason. *Oh, it would be comforting to have Mala and Nuri living nearby.*

This brief sojourn together made a powerful impact on them both, each feeling a hurtful loneliness that morning after Mala's departure. For Tristan and Mala, this time spent together had been a rare relapse into childhood, a time that had been snatched from them both through different circumstances. In each other's company they had at least, if only for a moment, retrieved a fraction of their respective loss of innocence. But now, in bidding farewell, they both grieved a bit.

***

Over the next month Tristan had difficulty focusing on his studies as well as on his accounting in the Treasury Tower. He was consumed with a vaporous emptiness. It made little sense, he knew, as the root of it was a girl he barely knew. Still, he found himself thinking of her at all hours of the day.

But time quietly erodes hurt. After several weeks passed, Tristan found it more and more difficult to remember the precise features of Mala's face, or the lilt of her voice. Finally, it was only the idea of Mala that haunted him at times. Still, he missed her terribly.

Chapter Twenty

Kuku Peter

As summer approached, Guillaume turned six. Even though the two brothers had spent less and less time together, for Guillaume, Tristan was a shining beacon to be revered. Tristan's accomplishments at Cluny were a tremendous source of pride for Guillaume, so much so that he never allowed a cross word to be spoken of Tristan, not even from the older boys. This resulted in the fearless Guillaume receiving a cuffing or two from the bigger boys outside the Stable Cohort, but his fervor for defending his brother never waned.

Oddly, Tristan had it in his mind that Guillaume had abandoned him in favor of Letellier and Hébert. In truth, it was Tristan who had become overly occupied, buried in studies and duties in the Treasury Tower. It was Tristan who was too tired by day's end to share fraternal play, and it was Tristan who at times seemed to forget he had a brother.

Nonetheless, Guillaume doggedly forgave his brother this blind spot because, having never known his father and by now having forgotten his mother, Tristan was his only family. Tristan, on the other hand, had not forgotten his mother. Even though he was but two-and-a-half years older than Guillaume at the time they left her, those extra years had made a world of difference in impact.

There was another difference. Unlike Guillaume, Tristan had found surrogate family in the form of monks. In Prior Odo he had cultivated a father figure. In the teacher-monks he found not only academic mentors, but uncle figures. And in Brother Damien, Chief Infirmarian, he acquired a wise and seasoned war veteran who was grandfatherly.

Unconsciously, with lack of ill intention, these men levered Tristan from the freewheeling days of boyhood into the weighty world of adults, further prying the two brothers apart. Tristan, having spent so much time in the company of responsibility-laden elders, was no longer entertained by boyish romp or foolishness. He was more interested in how human systems operated, how efficiently they worked, and who ran them.

Yet another adult was about to enter Tristan's existence. This man was to further fuel Tristan's interest in the human condition, not through intellect or reflection, but through bedlam and confusion.

***

One hot September afternoon, a small bedraggled individual rode up the hill to Cluny on a donkey, wearing a ragged hair-shirt, wool breeches, and no shoes. His filthy long hair was disheveled, he possessed a barbarous beard falling to his waist, and there was something feral in his eyes. On entering the monastery gate, this peculiar looking man halted his donkey and began shouting with the abandon of a banshee. "It's Peter of Amiens, arrived at last! Fetch me Odo de Lagery immediately! I wish to speak to the Grand Prior!"

Unaccustomed to such racket within the placid confines of their walls, several monks quickly approached him. Due to his unkempt appearance, which indicated he was not an individual of substance, they roughly pulled him from his donkey and took him to the ground. "Quiet down, you little lout!" one of them commanded. "This is a place of worship!"

This only served to infuriate the man who grew even more boisterous. "Unhand me, you piss-ants disguised in monk's garb!" he cried, flailing about. "I've come to see Odo de Lagery!"

"He hasn't time for beggars and vagabonds!" one of the monks shouted. "Now settle down or we'll have you placed in chains!"

"Chains don't quell the fervor of God!" the man shouted, struggling back to his feet, rabid with fury. "I'm Peter of Amiens. God has directed me to give counsel to Odo de Lagery! Unhand me!"

Despite the man's small frame, and seeing that their efforts to collar the man were making little impact, the monks cried out for reinforcements. Several more monks appeared and joined the effort to subdue the rambunctious little man.

Just as the violence reached a peak, and the wild visitor had managed to break free after knocking two monks to the ground, a stern voice rang out. "Peter! Cease this nonsense immediately!"

Hearing this command, the combatants stopped their jostling and looked up. It was the Grand Prior.

"Aha! Odo!" the ragged visitor said, suddenly turning civil. Dusting his chest and shoulders, he turned to the other monks. "Be off, you robed jackasses!"

They did not move.

"Be patient, Brothers," Odo said to them. "This man is Peter the Hermit. He is a monk."

"A monk?" said one of the monks who had been sent careening to the ground, lifting his face from the dust.

The other monks were equally surprised, but then began to snicker amongst themselves.

"Well, Peter, don't just stand there, come along to my office," said Odo. "I suppose you have come a long way and are either hungry or thirsty."

"Both!" the Hermit replied. Stuffing the reins of his donkey into the hands of one of the other monks, he barked, "Here, take my steed to the stable. He's my faithful companion, so don't cast a spell upon him in my absence!"

This infuriated the monk, but Odo intervened. He then asked one of the other monks to bring bread and wine to the Treasury Tower, then led the Hermit to his office where Tristan sat, stooped over a ledger.

"Tristan," said Odo, "this is Peter of Amiens, also known as Peter the Hermit. He is a monk and has come to…well, I'm not exactly sure. Peter?"

"Yes, I've come to counsel Odo!" the man said loudly, extending a dirty hand to greet the boy.

Tristan stood and extended his hand in return, but then withdrew it, surprised. "You!" he said.

Peter looked at the boy, raising his shoulders in puzzlement. "And so, what is it, boy?" he sniffed. "Satan got your tongue?"

"What's wrong, Tristan?" asked Odo.

"I *know* this man," said Tristan.

Peter shook his head. "Eh? Impossible!" he said loudly, which was for him a normal tone. Forming his fingers into a claw and combing them down his beard three strokes, he snorted, "Never seen you in my life, boy."

"Were you not in Paris at the Saint Étienne Cathedral about a year and a half ago?" Tristan asked, now sure that this was the monk he had seen haranguing vendors in the market square. "Did they not beat you there, for interfering with commerce?"

The Hermit thought a moment, then a light broke upon his face. "Aha! Yes, I *was* there!" he exclaimed. Next his eyes began that circuitous side to side shifting that was an incontrollable characteristic of his speech. "Aye, found myself surrounded there by Beelzebub's fold itself! They were going to *hang* me!"

"Hang you?" said Tristan. "Oh, I don't recall that, sir. I—"

"Aha, yes, *now* I recall," he interrupted, his eyes shifting in their sockets again. "The hanging attempt was in Dijon. Saint Étienne is in Paris. Yes, yes, it was the selling of relics! Correct?"

"Yes, sir," replied Tristan, "and they were beating you."

"Aha!" A tiny light glinted in the Hermit's eye then. "Yes, and a blessed troop of God's angels saved me that day! Do you remember, boy?"

"Angels?" shrugged Tristan. "Uh, no, sir. It was Lord Ox that saved you. A big Dane from my mother's Guard."

"A Dane, *you* say. But *I* say a troop of angels, *disguised by God*, as a big Dane. You see, God allows me to see *into* things more deeply than others. *You* saw a big Dane, but *I* saw the truth, a band of angels!"

"No, sir. Lord Ox is no angel. He is pagan."

"Oh," replied the Hermit with certainty, "but do you now see how clever God is? He deftly concealed his entire angel troop as one big Dane, who *appeared* to be pagan!"

"No, sir. The man's name was Orla. He—"

"Never mind," sighed Odo, gesturing for Tristan to be seated. "Peter sees things differently than the rest of us, I fear. It seems God saw fit to give him unusual eyes and ears."

Tristan thought for an instant he spotted a glimmer of fun in Odo's voice as he said this, but when he looked more closely, there was no humor in his face. "Should I leave while you visit, Prior Odo?" Tristan asked, realizing that the Grand Prior had taken on an expression that Tristan had never seen. There was no trace of patience.

"No, continue your work there," replied Odo. "Anything Peter might wish to relate to me does not merit confidentiality."

This comment surprised Tristan. It sounded harsh coming from the tongue of the Prior Odo.

"Confidentiality?" echoed the Hermit. "Indeed not! In fact, what I have to say, I want to shout aloud because the entire world should know! Just as the so-called White Witch in the village below refuses to keep the Church's foul secret to herself, nor will I keep *my* secret to myself. Fact is, I've already begun to spread the word in the north, and have come south to do the same!"

The Hermit's mention of the White Witch snared Tristan's curiosity, making him want very much to ask about her, but the increasing gravity of Prior Odo's expression made Tristan uncomfortable to the point of leaving. Nonetheless, he followed instructions and sat down, attempting to count figures again. Unfortunately, the Hermit's loud speech accompanied by wild gyrations and hand movements made this impossible.

Odo set his hands on the table, and without awareness, his finger tips began to drum the tabletop with impatience. "So, Peter," he sighed, "what is this grand news you must share?"

"What's it about?!" the Hermit shouted, gazing toward the ceiling. Turning his palms upward as though finally feeling those first precious drops of rain at the end of an interminable drought, he cried, "It's about *you*, Odo de Lagery!

"What?"

"Yes. It's about you becoming the pope!" the Hermit shouted.

"Outrageous!"

"Indeed, God came to me in a sacred vision two months ago," the Hermit said. "He spoke to me, Odo, in his own Holy Voice. He said that blessed Pope Gregory is getting old, and will within a matter of years pass on. Then, God told me He would place the papal tiara onto *your* head. Ah, it was like the sweet music of the angels' harps! He next declared that you'd lead the entire Western and Christian world against those locusts of Satan's fiery Hell who have infested this world!"

"Who?" asked Odo.

"That vile horde of vipers bred by Beelzebub himself, the Muslims!"

Tristan, pretending to concentrate on his ledger, could not help but fall into the Hermit's rant. The wild monk was comical, yet there was something compelling about his personal fire. Every word he uttered was spoken with drama, and no matter how clownish the delivery, one could not help being taken in by the blazing conviction burning in his eyes. And the effect this man was having on Odo was evident testimony that through words alone, the Hermit could boil the blood of even the most even-tempered of men.

Odo shook his head and fired a finger at the Hermit. "Peter, you actually mean to tell me that you have been preaching that I will be pope?"

"Indeed. And you shall!"

"Peter!" Odo huffed, raising his brow to his hair-line. "You once told a farmer outside Poitiers he would be king of France, remember? The poor fool believed you and in-stigated an uprising in his village against the real king, then was beheaded in the town square two days later!"

The Hermit fell silent, but a light soon broke in his eyes. "Ah, yes, but that fellow *is* a king now. Not in France, but in Heaven!"

At this, Odo broke into a fit of derisive laughter. "You are *impossible!*" he cried, flagging his hand back and forth. "No matter how asinine your predictions, you find some way to twist them into being true. I *demand* that you stop telling others that I will be pope! Others will only as-sume that it is *me* putting you up to this nonsense, and quite honestly, I have neither design nor desire to leave my post here at Cluny. To even think that I would be pope would be both pompous and preposterous!"

Odo's words did nothing to deflate the Hermit. "Tis the word of God that directs me!" he insisted. "Plead as you wish, Odo, but God listens to no man. He—"

"No, Peter!" Odo interrupted angrily. "It is *you* who listens to no man! God has nothing to do with this!"

There was so much blood in his expression and furor in his voice upon saying this that Tristan sat erect, startled. He had never seen or heard Odo lose his composure, but the Hermit had now driven him to that point.

"Tristan," Odo snapped, "I have heard enough! Accompany Peter to the stables where he can stay the night."

At that moment a monk appeared at the door with bread and wine. Within moments he could detect that tension filled the room. More importantly, he could also tell that Grand Prior Odo was angry, which was a rarity. "Uh, I brought this as you instructed for the...guest," the monk said, feeling ill at ease.

"Thank you, my good Brother," said Odo. "Give it to Tristan for he is about to accompany the Hermit to the stables."

Tristan accepted the basket from the monk, motioning to the Hermit. Knowing the Hermit had flustered the Grand Prior immensely, Tristan thought for a moment that perhaps Odo had misspoken. "Prior," he said timidly, "I heard you say to direct the Hermit to the stable, but did you not mean to say the Guest Hall?"

"No, I meant exactly what I said," said Odo, looking directly at the Hermit. "Tristan, if I give Peter the luxury of the Guest Hall, he will within the course of the evening anger every pilgrim within, which will result in bedlam or rioting. And this claim I do not exaggerate because the Hermit is not content unless he is either leading the masses toward self-destruction, or infuriating them. This has cost him banishments, beatings and even attempted assassinations, yet he still persists. It appears he simply cannot help himself. Even by allowing him the stables tonight, he will undoubtedly have the horses revolting by dawn!"

Hearing this, the monk delivering the basket snickered. Detecting that Prior Odo found no humor in his own words, the monk stifled himself and retreated from the room, anxious to share with others the exchange he had just witnessed in the Treasury Tower.

The Hermit looked at Odo. "Ah, but the horses' ears are more open than your own, Odo! We'll speak again in the morning, not of you being pope, but of all the things that are beginning to stir across the continent. A great wind is gathering! The world is either on the edge of collapse or the threshold of rebirth, depending on which way we spit, you and I!" Then he turned to Tristan, laughing, and in his ever boisterous, gesture-filled style, he said, "Come, lad, the stable will be just fine! Wouldn't want my donkey to get lonesome!"

Tristan accompanied the Hermit to his stable lodgings and helped him fashion a palette of straw in an open corner of the stable. During this time, as the Hermit prattled on, Tristan found himself drawn in even more deeply by the Hermit's words and mannerisms. The man was entertaining, but also deceptively magnetic. Tristan found himself wanting to believe his wandering flow of discontent. Though unconventional, there was just enough truth in each of the Hermit's diatribes that Tristan began to feel the bedrock of his own confidence in the Church cracking a bit.

Returning to the Treasury Tower, he found Odo sitting by the window, red-faced, chin cupped in hands. "Are you feeling ill, Prior?" asked Tristan.

Odo stood, and shedding his frustration upon seeing the boy, said, "No, not ill-*sick*, but ill-*tempered.* Things have been sliding along so nicely this past year, but now the Hermit shows up. He's a locust arrived in the garden!"

"You don't especially care for the Hermit, do you, Prior Odo?" Tristan asked.

Odo did not reply immediately, but after some thought said, "It is not so much that I don't care for Peter, it is just that he is so—*exasperating.* He is the ultimate example of the man who always talks and never listens. On the other hand, I have never met a man who possesses more passion or love of the Lord. But he is so overzealous and uncompromising that many believe him to be mad."

"Do *you*, think that, Prior Odo?"

"I sometimes believe he is a bit touched, perhaps. Yet, there are things about him that defy explanation."

"Oh?"

"Yes," nodded Odo. "Just as he makes ridiculous predictions that turn to smoke, he has also made ridiculous predictions that have actually come to fruition. And this has happened with *just* enough frequency to keep others off balance. Even me."

"He told me that God speaks to him, Prior Odo. Is that true?"

"Anything is possible, of course," replied Odo, "but even if God does speak to him, it could not possibly be to the extent Peter claims. Church history documents that God has appeared to certain blessed individuals over the ages, but the Hermit makes it sound as though he maintains a running dialogue with the Almighty on a daily basis! And that, lad, is preposterous."

***

That next morning, Tristan went to the stables to check on the Hermit, and found him grooming his donkey.

"Ah, the donkey!" the Hermit said on spotting the boy. His eyes flared wide and he made a grand gesture of smoothing the brush over the animal's hide. "One of God's finest gifts to man!" he exclaimed.

The Hermit's facial expressions and gestures as he said this amused Tristan, making him marvel at how this man could turn the most mundane of statements into theatre. "I just came by to see how you were doing," Tristan said.

"Now don't hurry off, boy, take a seat on the bench there and keep me company awhile. But tell, did Master Odo send you to spy on me?"

"No, sir. I came on my own."

"Really? Hmm…" The Hermit craned his neck forward, taking a closer look at his guest. "You have an *aura*, boy," he said crouching next to him, as inspecting a goat. "It circulates all about you. Felt it yesterday, but said nothing because I was too busy trying to pry Odo from the darkness!"

"An aura?" asked Tristan.

"Yes, yes. And it *draws* people in, like the fisherman who foregoes the net to slip fish into the palm of his hand with slow, gentle movements of his fingers. You appear to be such an innocent lad, but there's a danger about you."

"What?" asked Tristan, mortified by the accusation.

The Hermit stooped lower, forcing himself to now look up into the boy's eyes. Extending a hand, he ran his fingers through Tristan's golden locks. "Oh, yes, it's *there*, hidden in that little head of yours, concealing itself from world. But it'll soon leap free, breaking its way out like some starving carnivore that will one day devour the world!"

The Hermit's facial contortions both frightened and tickled Tristan so much he could not help but burst into a nervous spat of boyish laughter. "But I am just a boy!"

"Aha!" replied the Hermit. "When Ramses began, he was but a boy! And Alexander the Great, as well as Emperor Caesar. Yay, yay, they all started as boys. But oh, who can count so high as to number the dead they left in their wake, huh?"

Tristan found this disturbing. "I would not want to cause anyone to die."

"Ah, but great men can't perform great deeds without inflicting great suffering!" insisted the Hermit. "Perhaps the outcome of your actions will, in the end, lead to a better world." Closing his eyes as though cast into a trance, he began waving his hands about at the level of the boy's shoulders. "Yes," he whispered, "I see you there, sowing the seeds of *war*!" This last word he said so sharply that it caused Tristan to jump. Reopening his eyes, the Hermit stared at him, his head cocked to the side, his eyes dilated beyond reason. "So, is there a black robe in your future, lad? Is that what my sacred vision exposes this morning?"

"No, sir, certainly not," Tristan replied. "A nobleman, perhaps, or an agent of some king, for I am greatly interested in the affairs of men and government."

"Aha! Do you see now?" declared the Hermit triumphantly. "I was right! It is especially men such as *that* who bring war upon others. So come hither, let me give you a special blessing in the hopes that your future actions will be for the good of the Church, and not for its downfall!"

Tristan stood silent, trembling, as the Hermit approached him, placed his left hand over Tristan's heart, and made a sign of the cross with his right. "Late ignis lucere, ut nihil urat, non potest," the Hermit muttered, "a fire cannot throw a great light without burning something, so may God make this boy's flame burn brightly, but with mercy upon the innocent." Then the Hermit withdrew his hands and threw himself down onto the straw, exhausted, as though the blessing had depleted him of his final drop of blood. "Sit, boy," he wheezed, pointing to the straw. "If this, then, is the future, I must give you counsel."

Tristan began to think it wise to flee the confines of the stable, but the Hermit's insistence held him in place. "Yes, sir," he said.

"So, boy, you know the great Church is divided now, huh?"

Tristan shook his head no.

"What? You don't know about the Cluniac reform revolution that's raging even as we speak? Or that Pope Gregory has joined in this blessed crusade against priests and monks who've been turning the Church into a corrupt market-place of whores?"

"Whores?" asked Tristan, raising his shoulders to his ears. "What does that word mean, sir?"

His steam diminished by Tristan's naiveté, the Hermit went blank. "Uh, very well then, a corrupt market-place of *merchants*. Understand *that* image, boy?"

"Yes, but I lived in the church parish of Saint-Germain-en-Laye before coming here, I recall no corruption there."

"Saint-Germain-en-Laye, you say?" cried the Hermit. "Ha, a den of iniquity led by a certain Bishop Villier. Ever heard of him?"

"Yes" replied Tristan, "a good and holy cleric loved by all in Saint-Germain-en-Laye."

"Ha!" sneered the Hermit. "I spit on him! He has a house full of sluts and sells their services on the side to boost his income! A whore-monger he is, and needs to be excommunicated! Been filing complaints about him to Rome for two years now! Yes, our greatest enemies are men just like Bishop Villier."

This was news to Tristan. "But how is that possible?" he asked.

"Ah, the boy asks *how*!" the Hermit cried, his eyes widening again as he slapped his thigh. "*Sin*, that's how! The sinning cardinals and bishops who, like painted whores, endorse the selling of relics, most of them fake! The whoring high clerics who support the selling of religious offices. I've met bishops just a couple years older than yourself whose parents purchased the position from crooked high Church officials, or the King. God in Heaven, bishoprics and miters sold to the highest bidder like whores in the night! And then there's the marrying of priests, and the whoring of the flesh by both monks and priests rutting about!"

Whatever this word 'whore' stood for, it was evident to Tristan that the Hermit believed it to be a great problem. But the Hermit's escalating rant about the Church reminded Tristan of the woman in the white robe ranting at the gates of the monastery when he first arrived. "Sir," he said, "when you were talking to Prior Odo yesterday you mentioned the White Witch, that she would not keep silent her secret about the Church. I have seen her on several occasions now. She sounds a bit like you, angry at the Church, I mean."

The Hermit grew still a while, but shortly burst into motion again. "Aha, the White Witch! No, no, she's *not* a witch! I said the 'so-called' White Witch. So-called because of the ignorance of men and the deceit of certain Church officials. No, she's simply yet another poor woman victimized by Church corruption! Do you not know her tale, boy?"

Tristan shook his head.

"Aha, let me enlighten you then. She had a beautiful daughter, Gisele, who had the misfortune of catching a certain young Lord Matisse's eye. Have you heard of him?"

Tristan shook his head again.

"That makes sense, boy, because people don't like to mention his former name! Indeed, he's now known as the Bishop of Montrey, a small diocese near the Pyrenees. Any way, Lord Matisse was the favorite nephew of the Duke of Burgundy himself, who rules all those lands outside the Benedictines' vast Cluny territory. This lusty young rooster and his friends came upon the lovely Gisele one morning in the forest while hunting. She and her mother were gathering herbs. He threw himself upon Gisele and raped her while his men raped the mother.

"Raped?" shrugged Tristan. "I am not familiar with that word, either, sir."

This quelled the Hermit's fire, but only for a moment. "Never mind such details, boy. What you need to know is that while that young bastard Matisse was doing his filthy deed, the girl slapped him. He pulled his dagger and stabbed her in the heart before the eyes of her mother, shouting that no peasant had the right to strike a nobleman!"

This appalled Tristan. "But, surely, he was punished wasn't he?"

"Punished? *Him*, the favored nephew of the Duke of Burgundy? Ha! You truly are a little boob, aren't you! No, lad. One year later his uncle purchased for him the office of bishop, yet the young Matisse did not even know his prayers, nor could he even speak Latin!"

Tristan sat back, stunned. "Surely not," he whispered, shaking his head. "No, the Church would never allow such a—"

The Hermit slapped Tristan across the arm, as though to raise him from some distant reverie. "Wake up, boy! This is why we need reform! Oh, how twisted we've become! And now, since ascending to the papacy just a year and a half past, Pope Gregory is under constant siege from that foul German, King Heinrich IV, and his ungodly hooligans! We don't need a cleansing of all these sinners, we need a *gutting*! Excommunicate them all, I say. Let them run their wicked, ungodly marketplace amongst the flames of Hell. Damnation to King Heinrich and the Church whores! We should blast the bugle and press forward like a wrathful and righteous army!" Then, from his seated position on the straw, the Hermit threw himself straight backward, flattening the heap of straw behind him. He lay there silent and motionless, eyes closed.

Tristan stared at the Hermit, certain he would soon rise and resume his evangelical tirade. But the Hermit did not move. Tristan waited a few moments longer, but still the Hermit did not move, nor did he even sound as though he was breathing. Alarmed, Tristan leaned over and shook the Hermit's shoulders. The Hermit remained motionless.

My God, Tristan thought, his heart flooding with panic, *he's dead*! Rising, he stumbled through the straw and raced out of the stables, crying out with desperation. "Help! Help! It's the Hermit! He's dead!"

Two monks appeared from behind the stable and ran to Tristan, but they could barely make out his words. Then Odo appeared from the cloister walkway. "What is it, Tristan?"

"The Hermit!" Tristan wailed. "He's dead in the stable!"

Odo grabbed him. "Quickly, take me there! Oh, Saints of God! What happened?"

"He was just talking, shouting, about whoo-ing or whorr-ing or some such thing, then he just collapsed and died!"

Upon reaching the stable, Odo held Tristan back. "Wait here, I'll go see!" he said. He ran into the livery area, looking about for the Hermit, and found him…standing next to his donkey with a brush in hand.

"Good morning, Odo!" the Hermit cried out in that boisterous tone that so irritated Odo. "A lovely morning for grooming asses, huh?"

Chapter Twenty-One

The Western Meadows

Since arriving in England, Asta's fluency in Saxon became a valuable asset to Desmond DuLac and his troops who frequently came to depend on her for translations. She was also depended upon by the Saxon labor force, very few of whom understood French, which helped her garner a degree of favor from the villagers.

On the first day of September, in her second year at DuLacshire, Asta was tying the ends of harvested yarrow cuttings together for drying. "Willy, take these out and help Elder Heidi hang them on the south side of the Keep," she said, motioning to the boy who had been assisting her. "We'll be needing them to treat illness over the winter."

"Yes, Mum."

As Willy left, Asta watched his movements with careful consideration. She couldn't help but think that, from a distance, he could pass for Tristan, or even an older version of Guillaume, which is why she found solace in having him around. Since saving the boy and his father that day her husband had dragged them in for poaching, she had made Willy a house servant, a role the boy relished. He looked upon her adoringly as the only soft presence in his own rough-hewn existence, and considered her a guardian angel

Asta had also seen to it that the boy's father, Jack Forest, was employed. As he was a skilled woodsman and poacher, she suggested to her husband that he could serve as a gamekeeper. DuLac had balked at the suggestion, but after reflecting upon her line of reasoning, thought it a clever idea and commissioned Jack to oversee the forests and wildlife of DuLacshire. Jack quickly agreed to DuLac's terms, but any allegiance he felt was reserved entirely for Lady Asta alone because the woodsman harbored a profound hatred for the haughty DuLac.

Asta had over the past year developed a relationship with the Saxon healer from the village called Elder Heidi. The old squatty nurse had for generations tended to the ailing of the village, and was strongly versed in the mixing of herbal medicines that addressed illness, pain, fever, wounds and melancholia. Although wrinkled, arthritic and severely stoop-shouldered, the old woman was still active and lucid of mind. She had a habit, nonetheless, of mumbling to herself in a tongue that others did not understand, which tended to frighten the children of the village.

Asta became fascinated by Elder Heidi's knowledge of treating illness as well as by her understanding of the medicinal capabilities of all things that grew directly from the earth: plants, foliage, roots, seeds and soils. Despite the old woman's absolute loathing of Lord Desmond DuLac, she seemed quite content to mentor his wife in the art of healing. Elder Heidi was aware of Asta's intervention at the butcher's block on behalf of the woodsman and his son, so the old hag consequently developed a special affection for the new lady of the Keep.

As Asta began to stow away Elder Heidi's assortment of mortar and pestle instruments, she heard Elder Heidi shuffling toward the garden shed. But the dragging of her old feet against the cobbles suddenly stopped and Asta heard her speaking in a hushed voice. This struck Asta as odd because the old woman tended to bark whenever she spoke. Her curiosity aroused, Asta peeked out the garden shed window and spotted Elder Heidi engaged in what appeared to be a whispering match with young Willy. Though their words were unintelligible, Asta could tell that the top-ic of discussion between the two was creating an exchange of emotion. Stooped nearly in half and leaning forward on her willow cane with one hand, Elder Heidi shook her other hand with vigor and appeared almost to be scolding the boy, though Willy did not appear to be taking offense. On the contrary, it appeared as though he was agreeing with the old woman despite the fact his face had turned crimson and he had become anxious about something.

"What's going on out there, Willy?" Asta shouted.

This caused Willy and Elder Heidi to move closer to-gether, as if to conceal their discussion.

"Did you hear me, Willy?" Asta shouted with more assertion.

"It's nothing," Willy replied. "We're just talking about…the herbs."

Asta did not believe for one second that herbs could generate such an exchange between the boy and the old woman. Still, she suspected she would not be receiving the truth at that particular moment. "All right then," Asta re-plied, "come help me clean up this mess and pack Elder Heidi's tools."

***

After finishing the cleaning chores, Willy said, "I'm done, Mum, so I'll help Elder Heidi make her way back down to the village."

"Willy, you know well that Elder Heidi takes offense at people treating her as though she cannot manage on her own. So why would you—"

"She asked me to, Mum," Willy interrupted with hes-itancy.

"I see," said Asta, detecting deceit. "That's fine, Wil-ly, but when you return I'll want to talk to you a bit."

"Yes, Mum," Willy replied, suspecting that he had best invent a suitable explanation upon his return.

Hearing this exchange, Heidi stepped toward the shed door. "Asta!" she barked. "We were talking about the Western Meadows near the coast, Dearie, where the most potent wild herbs in all England grow. Winter's approaching and it'll soon be too late to harvest that area. It's only a day's ride from here by wagon, and I want Willy to accompany me there!"

"Oh?" said Asta.

"Yes, and I'd like you to come with us with some of your personal Guard for protection. Women and children don't dare travel alone in those parts."

"The Western Meadows?" asked Asta, curious. "I've never heard you speak of them before, Elder Heidi."

"My own grandmother and mother harvested herbs there years ago because of the rich mineral soil. But the previous Norman lords who owned this land before your husband forbade travel since taking over this land, just as your husband has. As I said, it's only a day's travel from here, but it may as well be a world way because we Saxons aren't allowed to come and go from DuLacshire. But I believe you can change that, or at least get me access to the Western Meadows for a few days. If you accompany me, perhaps I'll be allowed to go there. I see how your husband bends to your will. Winter's coming and there'll be much sickness this season. We'll be needing those herbs."

"Much sickness this season?" said Asta.

"Yes, as forecast in the fall clouds. This winter's going to be especially harsh and the village will need strong medicine, as will your husband and all his French louts."

Having no reason to doubt the validity of Elder Heidi's claims, Asta nodded. In fact, the story rather intrigued Asta, and she quickly forgot the previous dubious exchange between the old woman and Willy.

"I will consider your request, Elder Heidi," said Asta. "But know this, my husband does not always do as I wish."

The old woman leaned into her cane and shuffled in place with duck feet, her head nearly on her chest. "Oh, I know about your sons. We *all* know about your sons. I watch you quietly endure this loss day after day. Every time you look at that husband of yours, I see the bile brewing in your blood. You're helpless about it. Still, you exact a toll from him one drop at a time for your surrender of your sons. Yes, if you request it, he'll agree to it because it'll cost him nothing."

Asta did not reply. The blunt force of Elder Heidi's statements had taken her breath away, and the naked honesty of the old woman's words had pierced any veil of discretion that Asta could have hoped to devise.

"It's all right, Dearie," the old woman rasped, her tone softening. "It's men that force us into such predicaments, but God knows the truth. You're a good woman and God hasn't forsaken you completely. Shed your guilt and move forward. Your sons are lost. DuLac will never change his stand on your boys because they'd simply remind him that another man once possessed you, and he couldn't bear such a daily reminder. One day, perhaps, God will restore your boys. If not on earth, then in Heaven. And there is a Heaven. But until then, Dearie, we need medicine for the village."

***

Although Desmond DuLac depended on Elder Heidi to tend to his soldiers from time-to-time, and begrudgingly acknowledged her ability to heal, he could scarcely tolerate the old Saxon nurse. Moreover, he resented Asta spending so much time with her. "Her head's stuffed with superstition, brimming with old pagan ideas though she purports to be Christian," he complained. "And I don't like the way she looks at me; there's neither respect nor deference in her eye."

"But Desmond, she knows the seasons and she knows sickness," countered Asta, dismissing such concerns as she pressed for the trip to the Western Meadows. "These herbs will be critical come winter, she claims."

"Dammit, the outlands are still full of outlaws and vengeful Saxons," he said.

"Orla and part of my Danish Guard could accompany me and Elder Heidi."

"Hell, Orla's seen less of the outlands than he has the hole of his own ass, Asta!" DuLac huffed. "How in Hell's *he* going to lead this expedition?"

"No, he and the Guard would be for protection, Desmond. Jack Forest, your gamekeeper, would lead the caravan. He knows the countryside like the palm of his hand."

"The gamekeeper?" blenched DuLac.

"Yes, Elder Heidi suggested it, and it makes perfect sense."

As Elder Heidi had predicted, Asta was able to convince DuLac that the trip might be a worthwhile endeavor. Delighted by the thought of traveling beyond the Keep, something she hadn't done since arriving there, Asta began organizing and provisioning a caravan of three wagons for the trip. Elder Heidi assisted in these preparations, barking specific instructions on what to take along and how to pack it.

Asta, as a woman of noble birth, had never before been on the gathering end of a camping expedition, but took to the task with enthusiasm. Orla and Crowbones were unaccustomed to seeing Asta hauling and loading boxes and crates, but whenever they tried to help, she shooed them away. "Leave this to me," she insisted. "Besides, I find that I rather enjoy it."

Scratching his head after several such rebuffs, Orla stood watching her from the stable. "Ivar," he said, "I haven't seen Asta this happy since she was a young girl."

"Ja, I remember those good days when she was small and Guntar was still alive," nodded Crowbones. "Wasn't that long back, but it seems a life time ago, eh?"

"Aye, just like Tristan and Guillaume," Orla said. "They've been gone two years already, and now it seems we barely knew them. Dammit, I wonder how they're faring."

"Stop worrying, Orla. To their good fortune, they have their mother's heart. They'll be fine."

***

Two days after Elder Heidi's initial mention of the Western Meadows, the wagons were loaded and Asta was prepared to leave as planned. Strangely, Elder Heidi came to her and said, "Oh, but we must wait five days yet before leaving."

"What?" said Asta, dumbfounded. "But you said time was critical, because the herbs had to be harvested immediately lest it be too late."

"I did, Dearie," replied Elder Heidi, staring down at her feet, "but we must pull them from the earth at *just* the right time." Pointing skyward, she said, "I've been watching the moon these last two nights. It tells me to depart in five days."

"But—"

"No, Dearie, we leave when the moon dictates."

Asta knew it would do little good to argue. The old woman gauged her decisions on the moon, stars or clouds, and nothing could shake her faith in the mysterious code she seemed to interpret from them.

Later that morning, Asta shared her disappointment with Willy. "I just do not understand," she said to him. "I thought she was in a hurry to go."

"Elder Heidi knows about things that no one else understands," offered Willy. "If she says we wait five days, there's a good reason."

"You like her a lot, don't you, Willy?" said Asta, having noticed how quickly the boy always jumped to the old woman's defense.

"Yes, Mum, of course. She's my—" Halting mid-sentence, he said nothing more.

"She's your what?" asked Asta, seeing that Willy's cheeks had colored.

"Oh, nothing," he replied, looking away. "I was just going to say that everyone in the village likes her a lot, except the little children." Wrinkling his nose, he added, "*You know*, when she jabbers to herself in that strange tongue and scares them!"

When the morning of departure finally arrived, Asta was giddy with anticipation. As they departed, Orla and Crowbones rode at the head of the column with Jack Forest, the gamekeeper, and ten other members of Asta's Guard; Fairhair and StraightLimbs took up the rear with eight other Danes. Orla instructed Guthroth the Quiet to remain at the castle, which disappointed Guthroth. Disappointment faded, though, when Orla asked him to 'take charge' of the Danes remaining at the castle. It was the first Guthroth had ever been left in command.

Like Asta, Orla and Crowbones were more than content to break from the confines of the castle. Nonetheless, the two brothers also shared certain concern about being led to the so-called Western Meadows by Jack Forest. Though neither of them had seen much of the gamekeeper since the day DuLac nearly lopped his arms, both harbored suspicions about the man. There was nothing they could actually put their finger on, yet there seemed to be something furtive about Jack—his manner, perhaps, or his gaze during those occasions he appeared at the castle. Moreover, though he played the part of poverty-stricken poacher and bumpkin, there seemed to be more substance to him than he wished to expose.

As Asta's caravan left the castle, Orla and Crowbones agreed it would be wise to keep a close eye to him. "Let's be sure he doesn't happen to wander off," said

Orla, "just in case he has friends hiding out there in the thickets."

Since becoming gamekeeper, Jack had continued his existence in the woods, without his son, returning to the castle only once a fortnight to report to DuLac on poaching, trap locations, predators and baiting stations for hunts. Other than missing Willy, who now remained under Asta's wing at the castle, this suited Jack fine. As a conquered Saxon, he had no wish to be in the company of those who were militarily occupying his country. Moreover, he held a special hatred for Desmond DuLac, one that extended back well before the poaching incident.

Regardless, Jack honored the terms of employment that had spared him and his son—because of Lady Asta. Accordingly, he determined that he would remain civil to the Danes accompanying her on this outing, even though he knew they had fought beneath the Bastard's banner at the Battle of Hastings. Of course, there were other things about the Danes that Jack questioned. For one, their status and stance at DuLacshire seemed oddly ambiguous. Jack knew that all Normans were originally Danes who had acculturated decades earlier into Frenchmen, adopting Gallic customs and language. Yet, Asta's Guard seemed to refute the French ways, which were now actually also the Norman ways. More dubious yet, though the Danes had joined DuLac's French forces in England, the two camps appeared divided. As with other Saxons of the village, it was evident to Jack that there were two distinct cultures co-existing within DuLac's castle, which seemed to be struggling somewhat to hold together a workable truce. Complexities aside, Jack still could not help but see the Danes as Normans, even if they themselves refused to see it that way. Oddly, he held no such sentiments about Lady Asta, even though she was the leader of their clan.

As a matter of logistics, despite their ambivalent feelings toward each other, Orla and Jack rode side-by-side all the way to the Western Meadows. Jack, being familiar with the terrain, was leading the caravan; Orla, as leader of the security contingent, was riding advance-guard.

The two men had ridden in near silence throughout the course of the day, exchanging only perfunctory comments about directions. Unbeknownst to Orla, as he and Jack rode along ignoring each other, Jack had been spending much of his time pondering the conundrum of the Danes, wondering exactly where they stood within the scheme of things at DuLacshire. Finally, unable to resist temptation, Jack turned to Orla and ventured a question. "Say there, Dane, does it ever occur to you and the others of Lady Asta's Guard to *leave* this place? It doesn't appear you particularly enjoy working for DuLac."

Orla shot him a pointed look, feeling the question was a poke. "That's a queer question, Saxon," he grumbled, his expression souring. "I might ask you the same thing, because it doesn't appear *you* enjoy working for him either. I see the itch on your brow every time you look at the man."

Feeling poked himself, Jack retorted, "Not just him, Dane, *all* invaders from across the Channel. Since the Harrying of the North, I'll *never* forgive. Nor would you, if you're any kind of a man, or if it was your own dead piled up like cord-wood—women raped, babes skewered like rabbits on a spit, men blinded and castrated. Our lands north of the Humber were turned into a barren desert, our Saxon clergy was removed and replaced with foreigners, our churches were sacked, our nobility slaughtered or exiled."

"Such is the price of rebellion, gamekeeper," said Orla. "Had you lain down, the north would have been treated less violently, as happened in the south."

"Lain down?" said Jack, his voice rising. "Ha! But then, what could I possibly expect from someone like you? Sure, it would have been easier on you invaders had we lain down after Hastings."

"Watch your mouth, gamekeeper," Orla snorted, feeling the seeds of irritation rising. "Ja, we Danes were at the Battle of Hastings, carrying Roger de Saint-Germain's banner. But then we returned to France and played no part in the Harrying of the North."

"The hell you say. Maybe not directly, but it was the Danes that sold us out!"

"Eh? How do you make such a claim?"

"During the rebellion we enlisted Denmark to come south to our aid. Cnut, son of Danish King Swein, brought a fleet down to block the coastlines and assist against the Normans and French. But then Cnut took bribes from the Bastard and sailed off north again, leaving us to *rot*. He sold us out for gold. But that's a time honored profession amongst you Danes, eh?"

"So, you hate Danes also then, eh, Jack?" said Orla with a controlled grunt.

Jack shook his head. "No. Mistrust them perhaps, but there's no hate." Taking a breath, he sat back in his saddle. "Disappointment, I suppose, for what could have been. King Malcom of Scotland was also with us, and had Cnut's Danes followed through with their part, we'd have driven the Normans out!"

"Best to put your damn simmering on a leash, Jack," Orla replied. "The Normans and French are entrenched now. There's little good in dreaming of a dead Saxon past. Anyway, it's agreed, neither of us are especially pleased to be working for DuLac, but you wouldn't want to leave your son behind, huh? Well, nor would we leave Asta and our families behind. Truth is, there are few options out there for us other than becoming raiders or mercenaries."

"And what's wrong with that?" asked Jack. "After all, isn't that how the Danes originally came to both England and France?"

"Aye, but your goddamned people are no different, gamekeeper," said Orla, feeling heat again. "You stinking Saxons came over from Germany as mercenaries hired by the Celts during their tribal wars, but then you grabbed England for yourselves, driving the Celts straight into the ground! Everybody came from somewhere else, dammit, moved someone out, took over. So don't throw your sanctimonious Saxon shit at me, gamekeeper!"

Blunt response, thought Jack, *but truthful, and the Dane had a point.* "We Saxons notice there's a bit of a rift between your bunch and the French," Jack continued. "We're wondering just how long before the fighting breaks out."

"Don't you worry yourself about that, Saxon. Captain DuFresne and I keep the peace. And Asta keeps the peace." Then Orla grinned a bit. "Besides, it's to our mutual benefit to stick together in the midst of you goddamned Saxons. Know what I mean?"

Orla's eyebrows had lifted to the top of his head as he said this last bit, and that seemed to amuse Jack somewhat. "Ah, shit then," Jack muttered, breaking into a tiny smile, "yeah, I know what you mean. Still, you can't fault us for hoping, huh? In any case, my people are fortunate to have the Lady Asta in our midst even if she *has* turned French. She's generous and kind."

This remark softened Orla, turning him a little. "Ja, a good woman. But know this, in her heart she remains a Dane. And me, too, until the day I die."

"Well then, let's hope that's not any time soon," said Jack. "We've actually gotten used to having you and the others of Asta's Guard around. If something were to happen to the French here, we'd wish no harm upon you, I suppose." Reaching across his saddle, he extended his hand to Orla. "No need to call me '*Saxon*', my name's Jack. Jack Forest."

Orla returned the gesture. "Ja, and I'm Orla Bloodaxe."

"Very well then," said Jack, satisfied the two would now at least be on speaking terms, "and if you don't object, I'll ride back and speak to Lady Asta about the Western

Meadows since we're nearly there." Jack turned his horse then, not waiting for Orla's reply, and spurred him back to the lead wagon.

Although Asta was heavily engaged in conversation with Elder Heidi as Jack came alongside the wagon, she couldn't help but notice an odd glance passing between the gamekeeper and Elder Heidi. She dismissed it, though, nodding politely. "Good morning, sir," she said.

"Good morning, Mum," Jack replied. "Jack Forest, here. I'm your husband's gamekeeper."

"Oh, I know who you are," said Asta.

"And indeed you should," smiled Jack. "You saved my livelihood, dear Lady." He extended both arms into the air, waggled them, and laughed. "Life would be difficult without these. But I beg your forgiveness, my Lady, I've never even taken the occasion to personally thank you!"

Since that day at the butcher block, Asta had rarely set eyes on the gamekeeper. "No need," she said, "your son, Willy, has thanked me a thousand times." Looking at the gamekeeper more closely as she said this, she realized he was much younger than she had thought, early thirties perhaps. Perhaps that was because on the day he had been captured, he looked bedraggled and forlorn. But now his eyes were bright and he seemed handsome in a rugged manner of speaking. Moreover, he carried confidence despite his low status in life.

Then the unexpected occurred. Her heart flittered a moment in her chest, and she dropped her eyes, as though embarrassed by his appreciative smile. She had grown accustomed to men staring at her since childhood, and it had never bothered her, but this look from Jack, for some reason, was different…and somehow touched her.

Interpreting her sudden look of discomfort and silence as a signal to leave, Jack turned his horse back toward Orla. "Good to make your acquaintance, Mum," he cried, "and thank you for taking in my son!"

Jack led the caravan into a scenic, rolling series of hills covered in wild flowers and herbs. "Behold the western meadows!" he proclaimed.

Gazing across the lush fields, Elder Heidi could barely contain her excitement, and nearly fell from the wagon as she hurriedly attempted to dismount from her seat.

"Careful!" cried Asta, reaching over to steady the old woman. "We have plenty of time, Elder Heidi. My husband has allowed us several days time to work the fields and is not expecting us back until the end of the week."

Pointing here and there, Jack gave instructions on setting up camp while Orla and Crowbones scouted the surroundings to determine how best to establish a defensive perimeter in case of bandits. Meanwhile, the two Saxon cooks prepared a fire and began pulling out meat, bread and smoked fish, creating great anticipation amongst the other Saxon laborers; most had not tasted meat since the Harrying.

"Damn," one of them whistled, "perhaps Jack'll even scare us up some fresh hares to add to tonight's feast!"

"Aye, if we're lucky," replied another. "Haven't tasted game in seven years because of the goddamn Normans!"

After dinner, the laborers and Danes settled in for the night. Asta prepared a palette in her wagon next to Elder Heidi, but the old fossil's heavy gasping and the bray of her snoring would not allow Asta to sleep. Outside the wagon, she could still hear Orla and Crowbones seated by the fire deep in discussion, which also kept her awake.

"Good to be away from the Keep, eh, Ivar?" she heard Orla say.

"Ja, I was beginning to feel like a prisoner," said Crowbones. "Being out like this reminds me of our days at Saint-Germain-en-Laye." He kicked at the fire then, looking about. "Where's the gamekeeper? We said we'd keep an eye to him. And you know, I still find it odd he speaks French so well. Saxon peasants don't speak French. And did you see him looking through the thickets all the way here, as though expecting company?"

"Aw, relax. He's a poacher and a woodsman," said Orla, "and those types always keep a keen eye and ear to the wind, especially when they've been reduced to scratching a meager living from the forest like he was for years."

"Huh?" said Crowbones, surprised. "You're making excuses for him now?"

"No, but I talked with him a bit just before getting here and…Hell, he's not all that bad."

"Yeah? Well, I didn't like the idea of camping in the open like this, and when I disagreed with him on it, he claimed a stealthy opponent would have easier access to us camped in the tree-line, that the cover provided by the trees would cripple our defensive capabilities and help the enemy."

Orla laughed. "He's right, Ivar!"

"Maybe so, but does that sound like the talk of a peasant woodsman? Dammit, sounds like the talk of a man-of-arms to me!"

"Aye, it does sound like he's familiar with close quarter fighting. But still, many of these Saxons fought against the Normans and French, or against other invaders at one time or another, and even amongst themselves. Maybe he *was* a soldier, but those days are long past. But if you're concerned, give your bones a roll, eh?"

"Ja, I will."

Orla looked at his brother and started to speak again, but hesitated.

"Well, what is it, Orla?" said Crowbones. "I've known that look my whole life!"

"I was just thinking about your bones. Haven't heard you speak about wolves, or that Norseman, WolfPaw, lately. Seems he was on your mind quite a bit after we killed his clan on the way to Cluny, but you haven't spoken of him in over a year now, nor have you rolled your bones."

"Ja, he was on my mind then, and in the bones, day and night, but then the bones fell silent. Maybe the blood of the Norsemen was still too fresh in my mind back then, playing with my brain. But I'm no longer worried about it."

Since she couldn't sleep, Asta had been listening to Orla and Crowbones as they chatted by the fire. She followed their exchange until mention of the Norseman named WolfPaw and the killing of his clan. This vein of the conversation suddenly disturbed her, and she wondered why Orla or the others had made no mention of it upon their arrival from France, especially since her sons had been with them. *Surely my boys were not entangled in any of that, or witnessed it.* She sat up in the wagon, determined to question Orla and Crowbones about it, but then heard another man approach the fire. It was Jack.

"Well, gamekeeper," said Crowbones sourly, "I give you credit for guiding us here, but where've you been?"

"Not out organizing an ambush if that's what you're leading to," Jack laughed. Then he looked at Orla and shrugged. "Your brother there seems to have his doubts about me."

"Not doubts, just concerns," said Crowbones. "Haven't met the Saxon yet that doesn't concern me."

"Ha, I feel the same about your kind," Jack replied. "Yet, man-to-man, I suppose I'd be willing to give you the benefit of the doubt now that I've gotten to know your brother a bit. Maybe you could extend me the same courtesy, eh?" Jack spoke these words with conviction, and despite the size difference between him and Crowbones, he spoke without trepidation. "And if for no other reason," he continued, "then perhaps you should trust me because of Lady Asta. She saved me and my son. Do you suppose a Saxon forgets such a thing? No! So rest assured, I'd never allow harm to come to Lady Asta."

Crowbones looked at Orla, then nodded back at Jack, snorting, "Dammit, well spoken, Saxon. I'd not considered that."

"Ja, me neither," added Orla.

"Good," said Jack. "Now that we have that out of the way, how about I sit and share the fire, eh?"

Fascinated, Asta listened as Jack opened up, sharing the history of his upbringing and background, describing his recent years of living off the land, setting snares and squeezing a living out of the forest. "It was once called 'hunting' until the Normans came," he said ruefully. "Now it's called 'poaching'."

Orla and Crowbones had been raised on hunting as youths and still enjoyed chasing game through the wilds when given the opportunity, but such occasions had become rare of late. Nonetheless, as they shared tales with Jack of memorable past hunts, the three men seemed to develop that kindred appreciation that arises from discussing a common passion. Asta listened as the three exchanged stories, boasted and laughed, and began to enjoy the upbeat lilt of Jack's voice. Having never in her life been privy to the private conversations of men, she found spying on their conversation amusing.

The more Jack talked, the more Asta became curious about the gamekeeper. Taking care not to awake Elder Heidi, Asta slid out from under the blanket and peeked out of the wagon to take a closer look at him. Watching him sitting there spinning stories by the fire, she thought for a moment to exit the wagon and join the conversation. The idea melted away as the image of DuLac came to mind. He would feel such a thing improper, and would become furious at learning his wife had spent time by a campfire in the middle of the night with three men, even if two of them were like uncles. *Besides, I know nothing of the forest or hunting and could contribute little to the conversation.* Finally, yawning, she retired to her palette and fell asleep, feeling comfort for some reason in knowing that she would see more of Jack in the morning.

***

Each person on this earth wakes up at least once in life without any expectations, falling upon a day that is nearly perfect. Such was that next day for Asta as she arose and went to the campfire where Orla and Crowbones were seated. She looked at these two hulking pillars of her life, and in a moment of uncharacteristic affection, reached down and hugged each of their heads. Speechless, they exchanged a look of surprise.

"Great stars of the gods," Orla said, "what have we done to deserve such a greeting this morning, Asta?"

Asta clasped her hands, gazing about the meadows flowing from verdant hill to hill. "Is this not absolutely beautiful?" she said, ignoring the question.

She knew her gesture had surprised Orla and Crowbones because it had surprised herself. Perhaps it was being away from the castle and DuLac. Perhaps it was merely the donning of casual clothing, or engaging in something as mundane as harvesting herbs. Or perhaps, even, it was just the simple fact that for once in her life she was able to arise in the morning and put aside that devastating yoke of responsibility that had been crushing her since the age of twelve. Life had gotten away from her: the loss of her father, the marriage to Roger de Saint-Germain, the caretaking of the Danish Guard and their families, the marriage to DuLac, the loss of her sons. But on this sunlit morning in the Western Meadows, those shackles seemed distant, for the moment at least. Feeling liberation, she determined that she would rejoice in it because she also knew that every moment in life meets its end. Once they returned to the castle, the yoke would once again be braced onto her shoulders.

Then Jack appeared, lightening Asta's spirits even more. "Good morning, Sir Forest!" she proclaimed, bowing slightly.

Jack looked at her, recognizing that Lady Asta seemed not to be herself. "Good morning," he replied clumsily. "You look especially—brilliant this morning."

The moment he said this, he chided himself for sounding foolish. *Brilliant? Could I not have found a better word?*

But the comment, rather the awkward manner in which it was made, tickled Asta, making her laugh. "Brilliant? I have been called many things, but never that!"

Orla, too, laughed, as did Crowbones. They were not laughing at Jack, but at Asta, ever pleased to see her brimming with frivolity, a sight they had not witnessed since her childhood. Soon Elder Heidi shuffled up to the fire along with Willy in tow. They, too, saw that the Lady Asta was in high spirits, though they could not imagine why.

Thus that special morning began, with all being thrown into good humor by Asta's joy. Elder Heidi led the group into the fields to harvest herbs, giving effort to show Orla and Crowbones how to differentiate one herb from the other. She didn't speak French, so the two brothers had no idea what she was babbling on about. "What's she saying?" Crowbones asked Jack.

"She's trying to show you which herbs to pick."

"Surely the old hag doesn't suppose Orla and I will be picking herbs with the women, does she?" snorted Crowbones.

Jack translated this to Elder Heidi, and she erupted into an animated reply, pointing her cane angrily at the two brothers.

"Now what the shit's she saying?" grumbled Crowbones.

Jack gave no reply, but Asta, who heard the exchange, said, "Elder Heidi just said to tell you two hairy bear-brothers to kiss her Saxon ass!" Bursting into laughter, Asta covered her mouth to excuse herself for repeating Heidi's profanity. "The two hairy bear-brothers!" she repeated again, nearly drawn to tears. "Never in my life have I heard such an accurate description of you and Crowbones, Orla!"

Jack began to laugh also, settling his eyes on Asta as she pointed to the two Danes. But as her own eyes swept from Orla over to Jack, something occurred. In that instant their eyes connected, Asta thought she detected a moment of lingering in the gamekeeper's glance, which caused her own eyes to rest there a moment longer also.

This made Jack conscious of his action, causing him to quickly avert his gaze. Looking toward the ground, he pretended he had not noticed the silent exchange that had just occurred. He knew his place, and well realized that his worthless station in life did not allow him to look upon a 'lady' with anything but humility and servitude. Yet he also felt his own heart bolt nearly from his chest, thinking he had spotted something in Asta's glance. Thinking again, he dropped to reality, chasing that impossible supposition from his thoughts, thinking himself a fool.

In truth, Asta had felt her own blood stir during that moment; had been struck with a mercurial wave of confusion that was entirely foreign to her. Having been married off at the age of twelve to an older man, then having married another older man for the sake of others, she had never once had time or occasion to experience actual attraction to any man. This sudden, unexpected lifting now heaving in her breast, therefore, took her by surprise. But then, just as quickly, reality doused this fire and she flushed pink with shame.

All of this occurred between Jack and Asta in the frame of only an instant, going unnoticed by all except Elder Heidi. Even she was not completely convinced of what she had just witnessed, but she suspected that whatever had just transpired could lead to no good, which gave rise to a pang of disquiet as she continued to pull herbs from the earth in silence.

God help us all, if there's a trace of substance to what I think passed between the two, it would be the ruin of Lady Asta and the Danes, it would be condemnation for the village, and the death of Jack Forest, my last remaining son.

Chapter Twenty-Two

The Attack

As midnight fell over the Western Meadows, the last of those sitting about the fire retired for the night and fell into a deep, comforting sleep. Posted in hidden positions along the perimeter of the camp, watchful members of the Danish Guard kept guard.

Twenty miles to the east, atop the ramparts of Desmond DuLac's castle, the guards were less vigilant. As they conversed, rolled dice, and intermittently dozed off, they took no notice at one hour past midnight that a small army of heavily armed men was edging silently toward the castle. The leader of this clandestine band was an outlaw Scotchman named Aengus MacLeod.

As his band reached the outer burh wall, a Saxon was guiding them. Dropping to his knees, the Saxon pointed to a small tree about seven feet in height and whispered, "Here's the spot. We transplanted it after the last attack to re-conceal the passage opening."

"I see nothing here, Harold," hissed Aengus. "And I'll have your ass on a pole if you've led us here for nothing."

"Dammit, Aengus," the Saxon rasped with irritation, "I grew up in this goddamn village and lived here until joining your bunch three years ago! The tunnel's beneath the tree, I say! We'll uproot it and dig down four feet. There's an iron plate there. Lift it and we'll drop down into a tunnel. It'll be tight, but once we're in, we'll light the horn-lanterns and follow it another hundred feet or so until we come to the end where, straight up, there's another plate. It's heavy and covered with several feet of earth, so it'll take five or six of us to pry it loose…but once we hoist it free, it opens inside the castle wall next to the Keep. We'll be able to take the garrison by surprise and loot to your heart's content, just as has been done twice before."

Straining his eyes, Aengus grimaced, trying to read the Saxon's face in the sparse moonlight. "Very well, then," he grunted, "let's get started. But Harold, if you've led us into a trap—"

"No trap!" snapped Harold. "I hate the goddamn Normans and French like the plague. And this bastard, DuLac, he's the worst. He and his French bastards did more than their share of dirty work during the Harrying. I'd love to slice his balls off and shove'em down his gullet!"

"And you're sure no one from the village has ratted us out, huh?" asked Aengus.

"Dead sure. Rest assured, these people hold a special hatred for the Mole."

Aengus gestured for several of his men to begin excavating around the tree. As Harold had indicated, after pulling the tree loose, they encountered an iron plate. This they lifted, and one by one, they followed Aengus and Harold into a narrow hole opening to a tight passage leading beneath the burh wall. There were about ninety men in all, primarily Scotts, but also a mix of Saxon rebels, outlaw Irish and stray Scandinavians. Representing no cause or nation, it was a bastard army of opportunity interested only in looting the riches of the Normans and French. This they did under the banner of Aengus MacLeod, an angry, dispossessed second born son of a Scotch nobleman of the highlands bent on making his mark through piracy and plunder.

As they approached the end of the tunnel, Aengus called to his second in charge. "Alf! Move up, we're nearly there!"

"Ay! I'm coming," the man replied. Throwing his head over his shoulder, he said, "You men there, have sword and ax at the ready! We're outnumbered, so when we clear the hole it'll be kill fast or die."

The tunnel widened at the end, and above, a framework of latticed timbers formed a supporting roof. "There's the plate," whispered Harold. "Gather round and we'll hoist it up, but keep it slow and quiet so's not to raise the alarm. And put out your lanterns!"

Loosening the plate took much effort, but once pried loose and lifted, Aengus, Alf and Harold quickly squirmed out of their rabbit hole, followed by others. Through the sparse moonlight, they detected three guards atop the castle parapet. Though the guards were supposed to be strung along the ramparts in separate positions keeping watch, they had assembled and were lost in animated conversation, completely unaware of the infiltration occurring below them.

"The garrison quarters are just over there," Harold said, pointing to the west corner of the yard.

Aengus nodded to his second. "We've caught them sound asleep in the barrack, Alf," he whispered. "When the rest of the men clear the tunnel, we'll attack at once together. It'll be like butchering lambs."

At that very moment, across from the French barracks outside the stable, Guthroth the Quiet spotted shadows crawling from what he thought was a hole in the earth. He had awakened from an uneasy sleep just minutes earlier and stepped outside to the stable to urinate. Confused at first by what he saw, he soon realized the castle was under attack. Looking about in the filmy light, he slipped over to the blacksmith's anvil and, picking up a hammer, furiously beat down on the anvil three times, and cried out. This sudden clanging of hammer against anvil surprised the French guards posted on the parapets, as well as the raiding party itself.

"Goddammit! No time to wait for the others!" Aengus swore to those behind him. "Attack the barracks straight away!"

As the barracks door was breached, the French soldiers located near the entrance were caught in their sleep, and quickly slaughtered. This precipitated a chorus of yelling, shouting and wailing that awoke the French troops in the middle and rear of the barrack. Streaming out of their beds while hollering, lighting lanterns and seizing weapons, these French troops charged blindly into the mayhem that had broken out near the entrance.

Meanwhile, because of Guthroth's actions at the anvil, panic broke out within the tunnel itself amongst the raiding party. Men near the opening broke into a mad scramble to exit the hole, while those immediately behind them began to push and shove their way forward, forcing a stampede. As this chaos erupted beyond control, those toward the rear of the line, realizing that surprise had been lost, began to fear being trapped in the tunnel. The howl of survival raised its head, quickly overcoming the hunger for plunder, and these men began to flee. Shimmying their way backward through the tight space in pandemonium, they were soon trampling over others in the ensuing stampede of constricted retreat.

Across from the besieged French garrison, behind the stables, the Danes had been awakened by the combination of Guthroth's hammer and the savage ruckus occurring in the barrack. Soon they came storming out into the yard, weapons in hand. Bursting into battle, half rushed into the French sleeping quarters, catching the raiders by surprise from behind, while the other half attacked intruders still crawling out of the tunnel. Harold, the former Saxon villager guiding the raiding party, was unaware the castle had two different troop contingents quartering in separate areas due to tensions between French and Danes, and had not warned Aengus of any such possibility. During previous attacks on the castle, all castle troops were sleeping in one location, the barrack, which is exactly what Harold had told Aengus while planning the attack.

The French barrack quickly became a bloodbath as men blindly slashed and hacked at each other in an orgy of confusion and fury, guessing foe from friend only through the language being shouted by the man standing before them. The Danes and DuLac's men cried out in French, while the raiders cried out in Saxon or Norse. From within the Keep itself, the guards alerted DuLac from his sleep, expecting him to lead them in a charge to defend the castle. Instead, he instructed them to lock the Keep door and prepare for an interior defense should the attackers breach the Keep entry. "Goddammit," he shrieked, "bar and reinforce that entrance lest they break through!"

The bloody battle within the barrack and by the tunnel mouth raged for another half hour. Aengus, sensing his cause was losing momentum, cried out to his second, Alf, and the two fled from the barrack, somehow managing to slip into the hole and flee down the passage with a handful of other men, including Harold, the Saxon. Scrambling out of the tunnel on the other side of the burh wall, they made for the forest where they met up with other stragglers of their party.

"Goddammit, Alf!" Aengus bellowed, glaring at Harold, not grasping yet exactly how things had gone afoul. "It's all fallen to shit somehow! Let's get the Hell away from here!"

***

Nor did Desmond DuLac, that next morning, grasp what had actually occurred during the surprise attack of previous night. Yet, as often happens among men of weak character in the wake of debacle, rather than seek answers, he began to cast blame. At dawn he placed his entire garrison in formation, placing the smaller Danish contingent to his left, and his French contingent on his right. "I am absolutely *disgusted* with each and every one of you," he began, his tone rife with contempt. "So to begin, Captain DuFresne, I order that each man posted on the parapets keeping guard last night be flogged. They should have been more alert, by damn! Twenty lashes apiece should get their attention, I believe."

DuFresne looked at DuLac, dismayed. "But, Lord DuLac, the attack came from underground," he objected. "The guards couldn't possibly have suspected that any—"

"Captain," fumed DuLac, "if you choose to question my commands, then I'll have you join these incompetent guards at the flogging post."

All guards assigned the previous night happened to be French, and as the remainder of the French contingent listened to DuLac, watching him strut back and forth before them like some belligerent peacock, they thought him a fool. Furthermore, they had learned by now that instead of coming to their aid, DuLac had locked himself within the safety of the Keep, so they also now thought him a coward.

"And," DuLac continued, "the fact that we nearly lost the castle last night tells me that French and Dane alike were unprepared! So, Captain Du-Fresne, you shall begin a series of night drills with *all* the men that will continue until I'm satisfied that we within the castle can more effectively repel a surprise attack. Understood?"

"Yes, my Lord," replied DuFresne dutifully, though inside he was seething. "But, my Lord," DuFresne continued, "just one word for your consideration, if I may?"

"Goddammit! What is it now DuFresne?" DuLac scowled.

"Actually, drills would not have helped us last night. The attack came from a tunnel in the ground, not from a direct assault. Even at that, we made an extremely good account of ourselves and repelled the enemy. Perhaps you might…reconsider the night drills?"

"Dammit, DuFresne, my order stands!" DuLac shouted, wagging his head in anger, throwing his stubby arms to his hips.

This action, and the resultant picture DuLac struck, tickled Guthroth who was standing at the head of the Danes. Trying to stifle the chuckle arising in his throat, he ended by making a snarking noise, then nearly choked as he tried to subdue it. This infuriated DuLac who stamped over to Guthroth and stuck his face nose-to-nose to the hapless Dane.

"What's *your* goddamn name, soldier?" DuLac shouted.

Guthroth, finding himself the focus of attention of the entire garrison, flushed red as mortification filled his face. "G-Gu-Goot... " he stammered, unable to even utter his own name.

"Speak, imbecile!' DuLac cried. "What are you, a goddamn idiot?"

Standing at attention, daring not to look DuLac in the eye, Guthroth continued to stutter until, mercifully, DuFresne spoke up. "My Lordship, this soldier is called Guthroth the Quiet. He has since birth had a hard time expressing himself. Orla the Dane has informed me that he suffers from a speech impediment."

DuLac glared another moment at Guthroth, then said, "I don't give a shit what kind of impediment he's got! Have him flogged along with the guards, for disrespect!"

"But Lord DuLac," DuFresne insisted, "it was Guthroth who sounded the alarm last night. He saved us all."

"That has no bearing on the disrespect he has just demonstrated toward *me*, DuFresne!" countered DuLac. "Give him the same flogging as the others." This caused a ripple of grumbling among the other Danes, but DuLac continued. "And there's one other matter, Captain DuFresne. The villagers."

"Yes, my Lord?"

"I suspect complicity between the village and those who attacked us last night, so we need to establish an example for future purposes."

"But amongst the bodies of the slain enemy, Lord DuLac, we found no men from the village. If indeed the village—"

"We need to establish an example," fired DuLac. "Whether you found any among the slain enemy or not, I'm certain they assisted in this assault one way or another. And I'm also now convinced that they've all been aware of this goddamned tunnel for years, thus they've also contributed to the murder of the Norman lords, Batholde and Charton. Therefore I want you to select ten men at random from the village, ten women, and ten children for punishment."

"Flogging, my Lord?" asked DuFresne.

"No," said DuLac. "Execution by rope…to be strung from the parapet walls and left there for the other villagers to witness day after day, as a reminder that treason of any form will be punished by death."

"Women and children, my Lord?" asked DuFresne. "Would it not be better to take thirty men instead?"

"No, fall harvest approaches, and I'm also in need of stonecutters and masons as I rebuild this shambles of castle. I wouldn't wish to deplete the labor force. Besides, the execution of women and children sends a more chilling message. It worked well during the Harrying when the Saxon uprisings were at their worst, so we'll revive the tactic!"

This order did not set well with DuFresne. Asta's Danish Guard was even more revolted. They had not been in England during the Harrying, nor had they participated in the Bastard's merciless policy of Saxon genocide throughout Northumbria and the St. Cuthbert lands. As DuFresne reluctantly began selecting men to take down to the village to gather victims for execution, every Dane silently simmered, cursing DuLac's ruthlessness.

As for DuLac, his anger sated, there remained but one question in his mind—the coincidental absence of

Asta. Although DuLac gave voice to this concern to no one, he could not help but wonder how it was that there had not been a single assault against his castle until Asta's first absence from the castle. Every time this unwelcome suspicion crept upon him, he chased it away. Still, he was unable to make it dissipate completely.

This created much angst for DuLac because, worm that he was, he truly loved Lady Asta and still hoped that one day her frigid heart might soften, that she might yet actually return his affections. This love for her had actually by now become a searing obsession, rooting itself in the deepest crags of his soul, becoming stronger even than his unbridled pride and unquenchable greed. Even he didn't understand this thing with Asta, but she had now become the one thing in life that he treasured above all else. To know that she felt little affection for him was difficult enough, but to suspect that she might be entangled in betrayal was unbearable.

***

Asta was not entangled in betrayal. Her trip to the Western Meadows was purely in response to Elder Heidi's plea for winter medicine. Subsequently, it was with great surprise that, upon her return from the trip, Asta discovered a crowd of Saxon villagers stirring with agitation beneath the castle wall. Upon further inspection, she and members of the returning caravan saw that some of these people were on their knees, wailing, while others pointed to the parapets above them where a long line of corpses hung.

Gasping at what she saw, Asta also pointed to the castle parapets. "My God in Heaven!" she cried. "What is this horror?"

Elder Heidi looked up at the bodies strewn along the wall, squinting, then spat. "Your husband's work, no doubt," she snorted.

Orla and Crowbones noticed the corpses at the same time as Asta. "What in Hell?" cried Orla.

"Something happened during our absence," offered Crowbones. Turning, he shouted back to Jack who was riding just behind Asta's wagon. "Dead hanging from the parapets," Crowbones cried, pointing to the wall.

Jack was further back in the caravan, thus unable to clearly identify who was hanging from the walls. Peering toward the castle, he gave little evidence of reaction. After stopping his horse and leaning forward in his saddle to get a better look, only then did he discern that the victims were villagers. "Saxons!" he bellowed.

Crowbones watched this reaction, then glanced at Orla. "Who the Hell did he expect to see hanging from the walls? Frenchmen? Danes?"

Orla failed to hear his brother because he was watching a figure riding toward them from the burh gate. "It's DuFresne," he said.

Shortly, DuFresne reined his horse in next to Orla. "We were attacked three nights ago," he said, "and damn lucky to live through it. Guthroth and the Danish Guard saved our asses."

"Attacked?" asked Orla. "By the villagers?"

"No, by outsiders. Not sure who they were or where they came from."

"Outsiders?" Crowbones said. "Then why in Hell are village women and children hanging from the wall?"

DuFresne shook his head with disgust. "Because DuLac's convinced they knew the attack was coming, maybe even helped set it up. Remember that secret passageway into the castle we kept hearing about? It was real, a damn tunnel. DuLac, in retribution, ordered the hanging of thirty villagers, including women and children."

"Huh," muttered Orla.

"Glad you left Guthroth behind," said DuFresne. "He sounded the alarm in the middle of the goddamn night. We'd be dead if not for him."

"My good lad, Guthroth, eh?"

"Yeah. But in the end, DuLac had him flogged anyway," frowned DuFresne.

"Flogged for saving the garrison?" Orla asked, dumbfounded.

"No," said DuFresne, "for laughing."

***

As Orla and DuFresne conversed, Asta left the wagon, her eyes never leaving the figures hanging from the castle wall. Moving toward the wall in silence, she made her way into the midst of the grieving Saxons. As she did this, she happened across a stone mason she recognized from the castle repair crew. She was about to inquire about the corpses hanging from the wall, but the man was so distraught, she said nothing.

"M-my son, my d-daughter," the man muttered over and over, tears streaming down his face in rivulets, gathering in the rough-shaven furrows of his cheeks. "M-my s-son...my d-daughter!"

Asta, stung by this scene and by the weeping of others, became overwhelmed by the sight of the victims hanging from the wall. Dropping to her knees, she stared dumbly up at the parapets and clasped her palms in prayer. Hanging there just twenty feet above, she saw a little girl, broken-necked, staring into open space with dead eyes, her arms hanging limp. This, Asta simply could not bear, and tears began to fill her eyes. The little girl appeared to be about five-years-of-age, and next to her hung a young boy several years older with similar facial features and hair color, undoubtedly her brother. Her eyes hopelessly glued to the two young victims, she could not help but think of Tristan and Guillaume. Bowing her head, Asta made the sign of the cross and whispered a prayer as her shoulders began to heave. Soon she was sobbing heavily.

Orla watched, disturbed. He had never seen Asta dissolve like this and was unprepared to see her openly weeping, especially for people she didn't even know and in plain sight of others. "Asta!" he said, moving toward her. "Come away from the wall. Such a sight is not for your eyes!"

"Orla!" she hissed, turning. "Do not interfere with my prayers! Step away!"

This stunned Orla, who had never experienced such severity directed at himself from Asta.

Crowbones watched this exchange, then turned to Jack. "I don't know what's come over her. It's not like Asta to be so emotional. She's an iron-willed woman."

Jack shook his head. "Maybe not so iron-willed as you suppose. For my part, it's understandable that she would weep upon seeing the butchery of children. But then, we Saxons have suffered such slaughter before at the hands of the Normans and the French."

"Ja, a terrible sight, I agree," assented Crowbones. "But Asta watched her own father's head severed by the executioner when she was but twelve, and stood there like a stone statue refusing to let others enjoy her agony. And when it was done, she stared coldly ahead without showing a single tear to either the executioner or William the Bastard who had ordered it done. Yet now she weeps like a child for people who mean nothing in her life."

Jack shook his head again, his face turning dark. "Perhaps those people hanging there mean more to her than you suppose. It's begun to occur to me that you may not know the Lady Asta as well as you imagine."

Crowbones bristled at this and was about to fire a reply, but at that same moment Desmond DuLac and a contingent of French riders galloped from the castle gate, making their way toward the caravan. Glancing about, DuLac smiled as he cantered his horse toward the wagons, eager to see Asta. Then he spotted her kneeling at the foot of the castle wall beneath the executed Saxons, and his smile faded on seeing that she was weeping. Spurring his horse her direction, he shouted, "Come away from there, Asta! Those Saxons hanging there are traitors!"

Refusing to move, Asta continued to pray.

This angered DuLac, especially with so many people watching. Bounding from his saddle, he grabbed Asta by the arm and pulled her from the ground. "Did you not hear me, dammit? Come away from the wall! These savages tried to murder us in our sleep!"

Asta pulled herself free, her eyes aflame, shooting DuLac a withering look. "Did you order this, husband?" she hissed, flinging a finger to the parapets.

DuLac grabbed her again and pulled her toward him. "Yes I did!" he shouted. "And you'll not question it. I'm the lord of this manor, and you're but a goddamned woman!"

Asta broke free a second time. When DuLac fumbled to seize her arm yet again, she furiously swung her free hand around, slapping him full across the jaw. Stunned, DuLac stood motionless, as around him all motion came to a halt as those within the burh froze in place. Not a breath stirred for several long moments as DuLac and Asta stood staring blankly at each other while others, in turn, stared at them. Then, in a blur of motion, DuLac came to life, swinging his balled fist into Asta's face, crushing her cheekbone. This sent a shiver of fury through everyone watching as a gasp arose from the crowd. Before anyone could absorb what had just happened, Orla and Crowbones charged forward, hurling themselves onto DuLac. An instant later they were pummeling him in a blind fit of rage.

As DuLac collapsed to the ground covering his bloody face, he cried out for assistance. This quickly prompted the French to dismount and charge into the melée. Cursing, kicking and grappling, they struggled to free DuLac from the two huge Danes who continued their vicious battering of him.

"I'll kill you, DuLac!" Orla bellowed.

"You'll never touch her again, you filthy bastard!" screamed Crowbones.

Seconds later Fairhair, StraightLimbs and Guthroth were in the fray, slinging Frenchmen here and there.

This forced DuFresne's hand, so he charged into the fracas. "Arretez! Stop this madness!" he shouted hoarsely, only to be kicked in the stomach and thrown to the ground. "Goddammit!" he swore. "Stop this! Have you lost your minds?!"

The Saxons had backed away from the brawl at the onset of fighting—all except the stone mason next to Asta who had been grieving for his dead children. Standing in place, he stared ahead dumbly, eyes glazed, as the fracas erupted. Then, as if lit afire by seeing DuLac laying broken nosed and bleeding on the ground, the stone cutter reached into his blouse, withdrew a dagger and threw himself onto DuLac, stabbing at him while screaming a stream of Saxon profanity.

That such a violent fight between the ferocious Danes and the war-seasoned French had progressed thus far without the first weapon being drawn was a miracle in itself. Upon now seeing the stone mason's knife plunging in and out of Lord DuLac's shoulder and chest, Danes and French alike paused in disbelief, then together joined in separating the stone mason from his victim. Orla grabbed him first, by the hair, and pulled him backward off DuLac. Despite his fury at DuLac, Orla had never intended to kill him. Soon Crowbones, DuFresne and others grabbed the Saxon and dragged him to the side, beating and kicking him from all sides. Seeing that the Saxon gone berserk still had possession of the dagger and was swinging it savagely back and forth, Crowbones pried it loose, sweeping it into a downward arc. This motion inadvertently pierced the Saxon's heart, erupting a fountain of blood, spraying Crowbones' face and beard in a gory wash.

At the same moment, Asta's voice rang out. "Stop it!" she wailed. "All of you, stop it now!"

Pulling the dagger from the Saxon's chest, Crowbones paused, his hands scarlet with blood. Orla, DuFresne and the others also stopped, stood erect, as though ordered to attention. DuLac, still writhing about on the ground, tried to groan a command but halted mid-word, slumping forward while grabbing at the back of his shoulder where blood spurted from a patchwork of deep punctures.

"Are all of you satisfied now!" Asta yelled hoarsely. "Husband, you have killed the innocent! Orla, you and Crowbones have attacked your master, such as he is! And now that Saxon father of two slain children lies dead! I am repulsed by all of you! Your shameful, maddening manliness is not a virtue as you all seem to suppose! You have made life on this earth a living inferno for women and children alike, so may you all one day burn and suffer in the fires of Hell!"

She turned then, holding her face in her hand, then stormed from the burh into the castle gate, never once looking back.

The wild melée at the castle wall had suddenly thrown the entire future of DuLacshire into flux. The French, seeing DuLac hemorrhaging on the ground, gathered him up and threw him into the nearest wagon, whisking him through the castle gate and into the Keep. Orla and Crowbones stood in place staring at each other with that confounded look of two prisoners awaiting their turn on the gallows, while the other Danes, equally dumbfounded, shook their heads while exchanging concerns about what had just occurred.

The villagers set aside their grieving and summoned enough sense to retrieve the body of the stone mason for burial before DuLac could order mutilation of the corpse. But with each step down the hill they grew more fearful, knowing that should DuLac survive, he would now exact an even more terrible retribution on the village than after the surprise attack. Indeed, they supposed the stone mason's assault may have well spelled the village's imminent doom.

After entering the Keep, the French flopped the writhing DuLac belly-down onto the table and began tearing his blood-soaked blouse from his back.

Then Asta entered the room. "Get away from him!" she shouted, angrily striding through the knot of attending soldiers. "And *you*, husband, stop yelping like a whiny pup! You'll live, thanks to this Saxon woman." She motioned to Heidi the Elder who was standing by the doorway. "Come save this wretch," Asta said, though pain washed through every syllable, her eyes turned to embers. "And you Frenchmen there, go cut those dead Saxons down from the castle wall immediately! And may God forgive you for hanging helpless women and children!"

Hearing this, DuLac feebly attempted to raise up to countermand her order, but the pain rifling through his upper back and shoulder nearly made him faint, so he was able to only gasp in agony.

"Did you men not hear me?" Asta shouted. "Heidi the Elder will tend to my husband! *You* go tend to the wall!"

The soldiers looked at each other with uncertainty, then filed out of the room. This infuriated DuLac, but his pain was so severe he was barely able to communicate. "D-d-amn you!" he moaned. "G-get back here, you men!"

Heidi the Elder moved to his side and began cleaning the wound with rough, rapid motions, impervious to DuLac's pleas for gentleness. "Silence, DuLac," she grunted, "tis not becoming for all in the castle and down in the village to hear you whining like a blubbering child!"

"Indeed," echoed Asta, who stood with crossed arms behind the old nurse, blinking back tears of pain from her swollen face. "You who hung the helpless so mercilessly, try to act like a man!"

Heidi the Elder worked for another half hour on DuLac's wounds. As she progressed, DuLac, by degrees, began to feel some of the pain subside. But the loss of blood weakened him, so that he finally gave an exhausted heave and lost consciousness. Hours later he awoke in a fog, but sensed someone seated next to his position on the table. "A-As-ta, is that you?" he muttered, unable to make out the figure beside him.

"No, Sire, it's me. DuFresne."

DuLac raised his head and eased himself over onto his side. Grimacing, he blinked several times. "G-good," he said finally. "Just who I need to see. I have s-some orders to be c-carried out."

"Orders, Sire?"

"Y-yes…the man that stabbed me. I w-want him executed immediately."

"He's dead already, my Lord."

"Dead?"

"Indeed, and already in the ground. Killed by Orla and Crowbones. They saved your life."

At the mention of the Danish brothers, DuLac's eyes flared and he started up on the table, but his wounds quelled his motion. "Th-those bastards! By God, they *attacked* me! Oh, but they'll have to pay, DuLac. Round them up! I want their heads on the stump at dawn. Commoners are forbidden from raising a hand to a lord!"

DuFresne listened patiently, then shook his head with equal patience. "Sire, it's not my place to interfere with your commands. I've always done your bidding and always been your loyal soldier. But I implore you, think about what you're saying."

This so immensely displeased DuLac that he was able to do little more than sputter despite feeling a fire building. "Merde, alors, DuFresne! Qu'est-ce que vous dites!"

Again, DuFresne listened patiently. When DuLac was done, DuFresne replied with cautious deference. "Orla and Crowbones, despite their attack on you, saved your life. If not for them, you'd now be a cold corpse. They were only protecting the Lady Asta after you struck her. If you execute them, there'll be an uprising of the entire Danish Guard and—"

"G-goddammit! They *h-have* to be punished! Now! They—"

"And without the fearsome Danes," DuFresne continued, "we could well be in dire straights. Indeed, Guthroth and the Danes saved us from annihilation just the other night. We lost a good number of our own men in the night attack. If word gets out that the Danes are no longer here and that we are only half strength, that will invite new attacks."

"Damn you, DuFresne! Are you suggesting that I let this go? Non, c'est impossible, ça!" He trailed off then. "I can't just—"

DuFresne continued, his voice softening. "If you execute Orla and Crowbones, I promise you, Lady Asta will gather the remaining Danes and abandon DuLacshire."

This gave DuLac pause, but only for an instant. "She wouldn't! She can't! She has no means, nowhere to go!"

"Can't?" echoed DuFresne, his voice gaining certainty. "Then perhaps you should know, she's already instructed the entire Danish contingent to begin gathering their belongings."

"What!"

"Yes, she's ordered them to be prepared to leave with her at dawn. I spoke with her at length about all this while you were sleeping. She knows you intend to punish Orla and Crowbones, and she simply won't abide by it. Also, she heard you had Guthroth flogged during her absence and she..." Here DuFresne paused and looked away, muttering to himself.

Looking at DuFresne, DuLac growled, "Well, dammit, DuFresne! She *what?*"

DuFresne weighed the wisdom of continuing, but decided that in this instance truth might trump deceit. "She brought up her two sons; that you forced them away from her. Each day without them is a bitter and unbearable solitude for her, she said. Still, she accepted the separation only in the hopes that her boys might find a better life…away from you, Sire."

At the mention of Asta's sons, DuLac reddened at the throat, which crept up his entire face. "Those little bastards! Shall they blacken my marriage for the remainder of my existence? Goddammit, even the wolf doesn't accept the cubs of another, nor the bear! There's no future in raising the offspring of another. Does she not understand that?"

DuFresne shook his head. "There's a great difference between a man and a woman as pertains to family, Sire. As I said, she accepted you refusing her sons, but she told me she'd never endure another such loss at your hands, under any circumstances. She'll not lose Orla and Crowbones to you, Lord DuLac now that she's lost her sons."

"She's bluffing! She has nothing out there without my shelter! I saved her from a life of filth and poverty. She was about to lose everything!" He closed his eyes then, thinking, but in his heart he knew there was no bluff in Asta; she was a woman of profound resolve.

"Sire," said DuFresne with a shake of his head. "As beautiful as Lady Asta is, should she leave you, how long do you think before other men came to her assistance? Quickly, I'd guess, and in droves."

DuLac sighed, pausing to reflect. Wilting, he gazed at DuFresne, one of the few men on this earth whose opinion he valued. DuFresne had been his battle counselor and captain for over a decade now, proving himself to be both judicious and practical. "So you suppose, DuFresne, that she'd actually leave?"

Without hesitation, DuFresne nodded. "I'd bet my life, and yours. She has lost much already. After a point, one no longer gives a damn about anything. She's nearing that bridge in life."

"Goddammit, DuFresne," DuLac muttered. "Where do I go from here, then? Orla and Crowbones have to pay for what they did! And dearly so."

DuFresne pulled his stool closer, scraping it across the stone floor. "I have a plan," he said, "but you'd have to stretch a bit, Sire."

"Stretch?"

"Aye. When you recover, I think you should hold a ceremony, perhaps." Here DuFresne paused, measuring DuLac's expression.

"Ceremony?"

"Yes, in honor of Crowbones and Orla."

Stunned, DuLac's face fell blank. "Bon Dieu! Have you lost your goddamned mind? What the shit are you thinking?!"

DuFresne pressed forward. "It's quite simple, Sire. Orla and Crowbones saved your life, so *honor* them."

DuLac shook his head, so offended that when he began to speak, he choked. Then he threw DuFresne a stern glare. "They assaulted me, dammit!" he snapped. "They've violated the law! My God, what would people think if I don't execute them?"

"Just pretend that Orla and Crowbones didn't do anything," shrugged Dufresne.

"That's *preposterous*, DuFresne!"

"Pretend that they did nothing...but save your life," said DuFresne. "Then decorate them for bravery and swift action. Everyone would be satisfied—Asta, the Danes, even your own soldiers. After all, even though your men don't hold the Danes dear, they owe a debt to them for the night we were attacked. You'll be seen as magnanimous, Sire. Aye, you might then even wish to hold a feast in honor of you surviving the stone mason's attack."

DuLac, red-faced, was bewildered by the suggestion. Still, DuFresne's logic did, in some respects, crack the door in terms of resolving a hopeless predicament. Weighing DuFresne's words carefully, he nodded with reservation, his pride remaining the only barrier to DuFresne's unusual ploy.

DuFresne sat back and folded his arms. "The Lady Asta," he said with calculation, "would be very pleased, Sire."

DuLac exhaled deeply and his face dropped onto the table, his blood-caked cheek flattening on its surface. "Ah, you're a sly son-of-a-bitch, DuFresne," he sighed in surrender. "So be it then. Go fetch Lady Asta; tell her I wish to talk."

"Certainly, Sire," said DuFresne, nodding. "But such as her temperament is at the moment, I don't know whether she'll heed your request."

"P-perhaps not, but tell her this, that I *implore* her to come, that we will talk of forgiveness."

"Forgiveness, Sire?"

"Yes, dammit! Forgiveness."

***

Begrudgingly setting aside his fury at Orla and Crowbones for attacking him, Desmond DuLac heeded DuFresne's counsel. A fake ceremony was thrown together in which DuLac honored the two Danes for killing the Saxon laborer who had attempted to kill him. It was an odd affair in that neither French nor Danish troops could forget that Orla and Crowbones had lain hands on the Lord DuLac, an act so taboo that immediate execution was the accepted standard. Yet, DuLac now acted as though the assault by the two Danes had never occurred…and treated them as heroes.

For their part, Orla and Crowbones awkwardly submitted to the ceremony, though they could not help but flush red with embarrassment throughout its staging. DuLac delivered a lengthy, flowery speech in which he lauded their courage and quick thinking in dispatching the stone mason, while never once referring to their attack on his own body. As DuLac then pinned medals across their chests, Orla and Crowbones could virtually feel the seething heat of DuLac's eyes. Nonetheless, copying DuLac, they feigned silken smiles.

DuLac's French troops and the Danes were lost to consternation throughout the ceremony ordeal. Regardless, they stood stone-faced and at full attention throughout the proceedings, acting as though DuLac's generous actions constituted the most natural thing that could be expected after an attack on himself by common soldiers. In the end, no one dared question either DuLac's actions, or his motives.

Asta clearly understood that DuLac had ceded ground by sparing Orla and Crowbones, a gesture for which she was grateful. That aside, he had still struck her in the face, an act that was unpardonable. It also made him more repugnant than ever in her eyes.

Orla and Crowbones came to learn that it was DuFresne who had framed their salvation, so their admiration for him elevated. Nonetheless, in private the two brothers agreed that should anything like this ever occur again, it would be best to actually kill DuLac and flee rather than to again gamble with fate.

Jack Forest had been certain that DuLac would wreak vengeance upon Orla and Crowbones, and was rendered so mystified by this ceremony that, instead, honored them as saviors. In the back of his mind he had envisioned DuLac ordering an execution which would in turn create a violent schism between the Danes and the French—a bloodbath, in other words. When the tables turned, he pretended to approve of DuLac's resolution to the issue. Privately, though, he cursed the fact that DuLac had not set his own house afire.

Chapter Twenty-Three

The Chasm Opens

The Dark Ages of Europe were characterized by ceaseless migrations, invasions of barbarian hordes, bloodletting and violence. Through this blackness, it was the Catholic Church alone that offered hope and stability to the common folk, thus positioning itself as the social and political anchor of Western Europe. By the year 1066 and the Battle of Hastings, most of the barbarian invasions had run their course and the landscape of Europe had changed considerably.

A good number of major nobles and kings had managed to carve out considerable territories and establish widespread power bases, which gave rise to the birth of the feudal system. Yet, the flow of blood abated very little as these nobles and kings continued to plot against and attack each other. Many of these power-driven royals had also taken possession of many aspects of long-established Church authority and independence, thereby giving rise to a growing struggle between emperors and the Church.

For the common man, life was still an extremely dangerous and tenuous proposition. Peasants and village dwellers found themselves living at the mercy of ruthless or bickering nobility, and continued to look to the Church for stability. The position of the nobility concerning the Church tended to be more divided, however. Whereas the nobility was often at odds with the power of the Church, many of their number also feared the fires of Hell. Consequently, members of Europe's nobility often found themselves torn between either defending the Church or siding with emperors whose tactic was to split the power of the Church. The most effective tactic for accomplishing this was for emperors and kings to appoint their own bishops, archbishops and anti-popes.

Pope Gregory VII had ascended to the Papacy in April of 1073, the same month Tristan and Guillaume arrived at Cluny. By 1074, when the Hermit arrived there to visit Prior Odo, Gregory had been in office for just over a year and had already begun his bold campaign of establishing complete Church independence from kings and emperors. As a result of this strong and controversial stance, Pope Gregory made a bitter opponent of Heinrich IV, ruler of most of Germany and northern Italy. Despite being the most powerful royal in Europe in 1073, Heinrich was but twenty-four-years-of-age and hobbled by impetuous character and inexperience. Also, many of his energies and resources were being seriously sapped by rebellions within Bavaria and Thuringia.

Sensing an opening, Pope Gregory quickly secured alliances with Heinrich's enemies, then demanded that King Heinrich appear in Nuremburg in May of 1074 to humbly perform penance in the presence of papal legates to atone for supporting Gregory's enemies in the past. This severely embittered the young king. Nonetheless, he complied with Gregory's demand and feigned amicable relations with the new pope because the German rebellions in Saxony were gaining momentum against him at the time; Heinrich could ill afford to simultaneously quell rebellions while also taking on the Vatican.

That same year Pope Gregory condemned simony, confirmed clerical chastity and opposed marriage for the clergy. These reforms outraged many clerics throughout Europe and led them to support Heinrich against the Vatican. Pope Gregory's most loyal allies were other reform-minded high clerics like Abbot Hugh and Prior Odo de

Lagery of Cluny Monastery. Accordingly, Gregory developed an open line of communication with Cluny and called on Abbott Hugh to spread the reform doctrine, recruit military and political allies and provide financial support.

This political upheaval, then, became the wellspring from which young Tristan de Saint-Germain's future would flow. From a noble birth, to loss and dispossession, to striking an unusual mark in an academic and reform-centered monastery, he would unsuspectingly slip into the raging currents of political discord arising from the seeds of a personal dispute between Pope Gregory and King Heinrich IV.

***

By October of 1074, Tristan and Guillaume had been at Cluny for a year and a half. On the first Tuesday of that same month, Abbot Hugh received an urgent message delivered by one of Pope Gregory's underground couriers. After reading the correspondence, Hugh sighed, then summoned Odo de Lagery.

When Odo arrived, Hugh held up the recent communication and said, "The Holy Father's agents have discovered there is to be a secret conclave of nobles and clergymen held at the foot of the Italian Alps a month from now. It smells of conspiracy, so Pope Gregory and I would like for you to attend, maybe smell the wind."

Odo nodded, detecting concern in his superior's tone.

"The meeting will take place at the castle of Lord Franzio. You know the place."

"Will you not be attending then?" asked Odo.

"No, because I was not invited and neither was the Countess Mathilda of Tuscany who stands firmly with the papacy."

"I see," frowned Odo. "Then who *will* be in attendance?"

"Nobles who remain undeclared in this growing schism between Pope Gregory and King Heinrich, and some high clergymen also. The invitees apparently include certain Romans, some Spaniards, Germans and Italian-Normans like Duke Robert Guiscard the Wily."

"Robert Guiscard?" said Odo. "That doesn't bode well for Pope Gregory. Did he not just this year excommunicate Guiscard?"

"Yes, for attacking Vatican holdings in southern Italy. But if Duke Guiscard makes proper restitution, Gregory has indicated he might lift Guiscard's excommunication. Yet, we continue to receive word that Guiscard is still furious at the Holy Father, which explains why Heinrich has invited him to the conclave."

"Heinrich? So, this conclave was called by the German king?"

"Not directly, but through envoys."

Odo shook his head with disappointment. "But Heinrich just performed penance in June at Nuremburg and swore allegiance forever to the Pope, did he not?"

"True, but our agents have learned that all is not as it appears. Heinrich's penance was a public humiliation, and to Heinrich's temperament, that is unforgivable. We fear he is now conspiring against Gregory."

"But King Heinrich is your godson, and has always demonstrated affection for you."

Abbot Hugh shook his head ruefully. "Yes, and I for him."

"Strange then you were not invited, considering your good relationship with Heinrich."

"Heinrich already knows well where I stand on independence of Church and pope. And on the issue of investiture, I don't like kings picking our bishops and filling our high offices. The Saxony rebellions were going badly for Heinrich, but recent reports indicate Heinrich has regained the momentum and is about to rout the Saxon princes. If true, Heinrich will cast aside his Nuremburg vows completely. He is not attending the conclave himself, but is sending his envoys to test the wind and seek allies for a possible future attack on the Pope, which would mean war across the continent."

Odo made the sign of the cross. "Let us pray this does not occur, Abbot, but this stewing pot over investiture has been boiling for over a century now." Then he rubbed thoughtfully at his forehead. "But, Abbot, won't my appearance at this conclave create a stir? Everyone knows that I, too, stand firmly with the Holy Father."

"Yes, true, but Lord Franzio is a friend and frequently does business with us. He is expecting a shipment of three wagon loads of our monastery's wine and spirits to arrive later this month in preparation for Christmas season celebrations. You will simply show up at his estate with the wine convoy during the conclave, claiming that we bestow upon him the three wagons of wine at no cost this year because we wish to thank him for his past generosity to Cluny."

"But I will do little good simply dropping in and leaving," said Odo.

"Oh, but Franzio will then most certainly invite you to remain and rest for several days as he always does whenever I arrive there with a wine shipment. You have been far less vocal than I have on the matter of politics, so he will think none the worse of your presence. While there, simply listen because it is only information we seek—who thinks what, who stands where. Take Brother Bernard, our linguist, since there will be Italians, Germans and Normans at the conclave. Have him mill about inconspicuously serving as another pair of ears."

"I understand," said Odo, staring thoughtfully at the floor for a good while, suddenly lost in reflection.

"Something on your mind?" asked Hugh.

"A thought has just occurred to me, Hugh. This is a sensitive mission. The arrival of two Black Monks of Cluny may well put others on their guard. Rather than take Brother Bernard, what if I were to take as an extra pair of ears...a boy?"

"A boy?" said Hugh, amused. "But to what earthly purpose, Odo?"

"A boy dressed as my personal attendant could circulate with greater ease than Brother Bernard, and would raise no suspicion. The nobles and clergymen will all have personal attendants there; many of them boys."

"Yes, but what could a boy possibly know of political intrigue and the rising poison spilling across the continent?"

Odo nodded agreeably, but raised a finger to the air. "But what if this boy was extremely clever? What if this boy, unknown to others, spoke all the continental tongues required for such a mission? What if this boy was so innocent appearing and pleasant to look at that he immediately disarmed those around him? And what if this boy was so unusually adept that he even often exceeds what we here at Cluny believe to be his limitations?"

"Ah!" cried Hugh. "You speak of that little wonder from Saint-Germain-en-Laye!"

"Indeed, Abbot."

"Brilliant, Odo," clucked Abbot Hugh. "Yes, clever maneuver. By all means, move forward. And be prepared to leave by week's end."

"Thank you, Abbot," said Odo, bowing and excusing himself.

As he closed the door, though, he was struck with a twinge of concern and began to question the wisdom of the proposal he had just offered to Hugh. By the time he had crossed over to the covered walkway of the cloister that concern had already been replaced with assurance. *Yes,* thought Odo, *Tristan is capable of successfully disarming and deceiving some of the most powerful men in Europe, and this he would do without a single misstep.*

Tristan was sitting in Brother Bernard's German class with the Scullery Cohort when Odo appeared at the door. Surprised to be pulled from instruction, Tristan looked up at Odo and asked,

"But where are we going? You just pulled me from German class."

Odo laughed. "Actually, we are going to *go speak German*, and speak Italian, and speak Spanish!"

"What?"

"Yes, I am taking you on a little trip where you can put all your hard work with languages into practice. And while we're there, we're going to see just how clever you actually are!"

The venture to Lord Franzio's estate began at the monastery tailor shop where Tristan was measured and fitted by a team of fussy clothiers who created four new wardrobes made of elegant, decorative fabric. Since arriving at Cluny, he had worn nothing but the drab wool trousers and shirts designated for students. Prior Odo was also being fitted. Tristan had grown accustomed to seeing him only in the simple black robes of the Benedictines, but as the Grand Prior slipped in and out of fanciful layman's garb, Tristan realized for the first time that Prior Odo easily and naturally struck that classic stance of an imposing high lord.

This trip was Tristan's first opportunity to break from the walls of the monastery and he found great delight in wearing something other than his student garb, being freed from the confines of the monastery, and seeing the Alps for the first time. Also, he found the wagon teamsters to be lively and full of spit, laughing at how they ribbed and poked at each other without mercy. They reminded him of the Danes. And Odo, upon departing Cluny, began to speak and laugh more freely, even taking occasion to joke and tease with the crusty teamsters. It was as if he had shed the grave responsibilities of serving as Grand Prior and slipped into the role of a common man.

Along the way, Odo would step back into his persona as Tristan's mentor, reminding him of the purpose of the trip to Lord Franzio's. "You are not serving Abbot Hugh," he said, "but the Pope. The Vatican is headed into a dark time, I fear, and you may well help establish which direction is taken."

This was impossible for Tristan to fathom, as he had no understanding of the great forces that were already aligning themselves, one against the other. Nevertheless, it pleased him to know that Odo was counting on him for assistance, so he listened intently as the wagons hobbled their way day after day into the mountains and through the valleys.

Asta and the teacher-nuns had drilled into Tristan a keen awareness of courtesy and decorum. Odo's lessons were different. "The ear cannot listen if the tongue is wagging," he said. "If you are the one speaking, then the one standing before you cannot freely empty what is in his head. Silence, is a mighty weapon." Odo also taught him tricks to more easily recall names and titles by making little mental connections through rhyme, physical features and gestures. He emphasized the importance of listening for background information. "If you wish to understand what a man wants, then you must learn what it is that he does, because this tells you where he is headed."

Arriving at the gates of a beautiful castle constructed in the Italian style, they were met by Lord Franzio, a hefty, jovial soul who welcomed them with open arms. As Abbot Hugh had predicted, the Italian lord was delighted to learn of the arrival of his Cluny wine, even more so that Abbot Hugh had bestowed the barrels as a gift.

"Oh, Prior, mille grazie!" Franzio cried, smothering Odo in hugs and kisses. "You and Abbot Hugh are so thoughtful about old Franzio!"

"No," replied Odo, embracing him in return, "it is *you* who is so thoughtful, Lord Franzio. We bring this as a humble gesture for your great generosity and gifts to Cluny." Indeed, Lord Franzio was a most generous benefactor of the Black Monks. Feeling sure that the more gifts he heaped upon the Church, the less time he would spend in Purgatory, he poured endowment after endowment into

Cluny. Having inherited all his wealth, having never been to war; having always caved to temptations of both flesh and drink, his life had always been one of utter debauchery. Still, he held in great esteem the austere lifestyle of the Black Monks, and remained ever thankful that he would never share in it.

Lord Franzio, interestingly, had no interest whatsoever in politics even though he agreed to host the conclave. His motivation had simply been to entertain, which other than bedding women of all ages, shapes and sizes, was his greatest passion in life. Therefore, as Abbot Hugh had predicted, Lord Franzio quickly insisted that Odo and his party spend the week at his palace with his other guests.

"Thank you, Lord Franzio!" said Odo. "We are weary from our trip and would take great pleasure in resting here a while."

"Perfetto!" Franzio said, nearly shaking Odo's hands from his arms. Tristan, who had been watching the affective movements of Franzio since arriving, found his mannerisms infectious, and could not help but utter a boyish giggle. Franzio heard this. Looking up, he was taken by the boy's striking appearance. "Ah, Prior, who is this little cherub?" he cooed, clasping his hands.

"This is young Tristan, a student at Cluny, Lord Franzio," replied Odo. "He is my attendant."

"Excellente!" exclaimed Franzio, looking at Tristan, his eyes growing wide. "Mi scusi, parlo Italiano?" he asked.

Tristan glanced at Prior Odo, then looked back at Franzio and shrugged as though he did not understand.

"E' un peccato! The poor lad doesn't understand Italian," Franzio said, disappointed. He then motioned for a servant. "Take Prior Odo and his guest to the east wing next to the great hall and make them comfortable," he said.

That evening Lord Franzio's fabulously adorned Grand Hall was filled to brimming with lords and bishops from Central and Southern Europe. As these dignitaries moved about in fluctuating groups, heads drawn together in lively conference, an army of servants flittered about serving wine, fruit and delicate meats piled high on silver platters. Other servants carried platters of gold upon which were arranged roasted pheasant, heron, crane and goose; each fowl sitting atop a decorative mound of rose petals surrounded by a ring of freshly cut lily blossoms. As a flourish of trumpets sounded, four separate teams of exquisitely dressed valets carried forth from the kitchen four roasted pigs, each splayed belly-down on a slab of finely polished granite.

Franzio, his cheeks flushed with wine and his voice nearly hoarse from talk and laughter, moved about the hall with the joy of a man relishing the finest moment of his lifetime. Although Franzio was lost to entertaining others and could have cared less about the political division rising its ugly head in Europe, others in attendance knew exactly why they had gathered in the Italian Alps. Many had already clearly chosen their stand while others were as of yet uncommitted, eager to learn more details about developing circumstances and who would be pitted against whom. Consequently, conversation flowed freely as men of different countries and different stations in life questioned or lectured each other on the approaching battle of Church versus Crown.

As instructed, Tristan expressed an interest in assisting Lord Franzio's servants as they served the guests, a ploy to enable Tristan to circulate amongt the many guests without raising suspicion. "Si, certo! Of course!" Franzio replied with delight. "Besides, this way you won't have to listen to boring adults talk your ears off!"

Listening to adults is exactly what Tristan did—and with great attention. Moving freely about the grand hall that first evening, he matched names and titles with faces and kept note of who spoke to whom. He especially enjoyed hearing the different languages being spoken, and experienced no problem understanding what was being said as conversation slipped from one language to another.

That next morning, Odo sent Tristan out into the courtyard and garden areas to slip about small groups of two or three envoys who might be engaged in conversation that appeared more private than the previous night. In doing so, Tristan discovered that what one said the night before did not necessarily hold water the day after; that many of these men tailored their comments to the company at hand. He found it astounding to see men of such vaunted stature dance about so dishonestly, especially the high clerics. Being so young, though, he failed to understand that in the world of these men, a word misspoken could lead to disgrace and ruin, or even death.

By the fourth day, three individuals in particular had drawn Tristan's attention. The first of these men was Duke Robert Guiscard, a Norman lord of great military significance controlling southern Italy and Sicily. Dubbed Guiscard the Wily, this man was exceptionally tall and broad-shouldered; carried about himself an air of tyranny and fierceness. On one occasion Tristan happened to be listening to Guiscard when suddenly the Norman reached over and throttled him by the collar. "Hey, boy!" he snarled, "What are you doing there!"

"S-sir?" Tristan stammered, caught off guard.

"Are you *spying* on me?" Guiscard barked, his dark eyes flashing about the room as if rooting out possible accomplices. "It appears you're listening a bit too closely to my conversation!"

This so stunned Tristan, he was unable to respond. "I, uh—" Finally, gathering his wits, he said, "Sir, I am a student from Cluny and today offered to help serve the guests. And yes, I was listening, sir. Your tale of war against the Saracens in Sicily fascinated me. I apologize, and will be on my way."

"Indeed," scowled Guiscard, "away with you!"

This encounter frightened Tristan, although he had thought himself unnoticed by all, this fearsome Norman war lord, of all people, had come close to rooting him out. From that moment on, any time Guiscard was in his vicinity, Tristan steered clear because it seemed the Norman war lord always glared at him or followed him with his eyes. This unnerved Tristan, but Guiscard also intrigued him. Guiscard made no attempt to be pleasant or political, yet he seemed to inspire fear whenever he walked onto the scene.

Tristan learned that Guiscard had originally come to Italy as a mercenary when the Lombards were battling the Byzantines for control of Southern Italy. He left Normandy with only five riders and thirty footmen. Arriving in Langobardia in 1047, he became the chief of a roving robber-band. Later he conquered Apulia and Calabria while also rousting the Muslims from Sicily. When Pope Gregory VII ascended to the papacy, he accused Guiscard of military incursions on papal provinces and excommunicated him. Guiscard, therefore, did not hold Pope Gregory in high esteem and at times during the conclave launched into tirades against Gregory. At the same time, it appeared to Tristan that Guiscard regretted his excommunication. "God knows," he said one day, "if there's really a Hell, I don't wish to dwell there! I wish the Pope would consider reconciliation."

The second of the three men who had caught Tristan's attention was Guibert, Archbishop of Ravenna. In earlier days he had shared ties with Cardinal Hildebrand, who was now Pope Gregory. It was Hildebrand who had saved Guibert's career during Pope Alexander II's papacy. Since those days Archbishop Guibert had developed a strong relationship with King Heinrich and had become the religious figurehead of Germany and northern Italy. It appeared to Tristan that Archbishop Guibert of Ravenna was now abandoning his old friend, Pope Gregory, in favor of the German king.

The third man was Cardinal Candidus of Rome. He also had shared earlier ties with Pope Gregory as they both, in younger years, navigated their way up the treacherous currents of the Church hierarchy. But Gregory was a reformist and Candidus, like Guibert of Ravenna, was not. Furthermore, Cardinal Candidus was heavily allied to the nobles of Rome, many of whom opposed the reform movement of Pope Gregory and the Benedictines.

Politics aside, the sheer, naked opulence of Lord Franzio's castle was a new experience for Tristan; just the thought that this magnificent estate belonged to one man was staggering. This new awareness of raw personal wealth was further compounded by the power of the men upon whom he was spying. They did not speak of controlling mere estates or cities, but of entire regions and countries. The stark contrast of these men compared against the helpless men he had encountered in the infirmary after the hog oil incident was mind boggling, if not offensive. This forced Tristan to wonder why God could allow the existence of such blatant inequity, yet Tristan also determined he preferred to be among the blessed than among the abandoned.

At conclave's end, as the Cluny caravan returned to France, Tristan shared in depth with Prior Odo all he had heard, citing names, titles and accompanying comments. Most significantly, he emphasized what he had heard about Duke Robert Guiscard, Archbishop Guibert of Ravenna and Cardinal Candidus of Rome.

Prior Odo smiled, patting Tristan on the head. "Ah, a fine job, son. What you have told me lights the corridor. Yes, as the fox approaches, the quail seek cover and huddle together. It appears that for Pope Gregory, his two friends, Cardinal Candidus and Archbishop Guibert, will become enemies, and his enemy, Duke Robert Guiscard, may yet become a friend. I have suspected the possibility of war, but after this trip tied to what you have shared, I now see it is inevitable!"

"War?" said Tristan, looking up at Odo as the wagon jostled and jumped down the alpine road. Looking away then, his face turned to paste. At Franzio's castle, he thought to be simply eavesdropping a bit for the Black Monks. He had no idea that war and violence were in the mix.

"What is it, Tristan?" asked Odo.

"The...Hermit," Tristan mumbled.

"Kuku Peter?"

"Y-es, Prior," Tristan stammered. "In the stable one day he said I had a 'look' about me; that I was dangerous and would cause destruction and war. And now because of what I said I overheard at Lord Franzio's, you say that war is coming." Tristan shivered a bit then as a chill skittered up his spine. "I don't feel so good," he said, closing his eyes.

"Oh, but set him aside, Tristan," clucked Odo with a shake of his head, smiling. "He is *touched*, you know that."

Tristan nodded weakly with agreement, but within the screen of his closed lids, the Hermit was crouching there, waving his hands, shouting in that raucous tone of his. "You will sow the seeds of war!" the Hermit cried, pointing at Tristan with an accusatory finger. "I see it in your future!"

* * *

After returning from the opulence of Lord Franzio's castle, the closed confines of the monastery began to seem a bit suffocating, which became disconcerting to Tristan. In some respects, he actually began to feel somewhat imprisoned, and this sent him spiraling into an unwelcome trough of melancholy and introspection. The experience in Italy amongst great lords, high clerics and enormous power had lit a fire of sorts within his soul. *I have lost my birthright because of my father's disgrace,* he realized coldly, *therefore I shall never wield power and authority, or even be the master of my own fate. Though I love God, I do not wish to wear a robe or a collar, yet that appears to be the only door left to me. Otherwise, I will end like those pitiful men in Brother Damien's infirmary.*

Thus drawn toward self pity by his foray into the Italian Alps, he was sitting on his bunk one night lost to woe when Guillaume slid over from his own bunk and quietly took a seat beside him. "You've hardly spoken to me since your return," he said, unable to mask disappointment. "I guess with all the important things you do around here with the Grand Prior nowadays, you don't have time to think about me or the rest of the Dorter anymore, huh?"

Tristan felt the reproach, but denied it. "Me, forget about you?" he objected. "Guillaume, it is you who are always busy, running about with your friends Letellier, Hébert and Scule."

"They're my friends, but you're my brother, and you spend all your time with the monks, so what else am I to do? In a few years they will be leaving to become squires, sponsored by their wealthy families, but I'll be left here to tend mules and donkeys. And you, with your high education, you'll be leaving me, too." Turning, Guillaume crawled into bed, his back toward Tristan.

This struck Tristan with a pang of shame; the realization that his younger brother was on the mark. Sitting there in reflection, he stared at Guillaume's back as a flood of forgotten emotions washed through him. The image of his mother arose first, resurrected from the shallow grave of a previous life. He had scarcely thought of her during the past year because of his pursuit of academics and tasks on behalf of monks. Now, as he struggled to remember the details of her face, it occurred to him that those shadowy details of her face he was trying to recreate had stood before him just moments before, in the face of Guillaume. Whereas Tristan's hair was blond, Guillaume possessed that same thick, silver hair of their mother, as well as her perfect facial features. This stunning combination of hers was now duplicating in Guillaume. This gave Tristan a measure of comfort because, though Guillaume was not as blessed in the intellectual arena, his fearlessness and striking appearance would provide him other advantages in the future.

Then Orla and Crowbones came to Tristan's mind, along with Fairhair, Guthroth and StraightLimbs, but the memory of the river massacre arose and he became disturbed. Nonetheless, he missed these men who had served as uncles since his birth; hoped that they had not forgotten him. *Indeed, when I grow up, I shall hunt the ends of the earth for my mother and the Danes, so we can be a family once more like back in Saint-Germain-en-Laye.*

As he began to lay down, it was the thought of the beautiful gypsy girl, Mala, that struck him. Digging in his pocket, he felt Mala's ring and pulled it out, examining it. As he turned it one way, then the next, he wished that she, more than anyone else, could be there with him that very moment. He missed her dark, mischievous eyes and luminous smile, as well as the lilt of her playful voice. They had only been together twice, yet he felt profoundly connected to her for reasons he could not grasp. Still, as he now thought of her, he hoped that she felt the same. *Yes*, he decided, putting the ring back into his pocket and closing his eyes, *when I grow up I shall also hunt the ends of the earth for Mala, because whenever she is with me, I forget my loneliness.*

That night he forgot about the Italian Alps, even the monastery and Peter the Hermit, for it was Mala's face that sent him into a deep and restful sleep.

Chapter Twenty-Four

The Investiture War

One year after contritely performing the penance demanded by Pope Gregory VII in Nuremburg, King Heinrich defeated the rebellious German-Saxon princes at the Battle of Homburg on June 9th of 1075. As suspected, he then abandoned all intent of cooperating with Pope Gregory or following his decrees. This infuriated Gregory and caused him to respond with a volley that thundered across the entire European continent. He excommunicated certain members of Heinrich's Imperial Court, and on December 8th sent a harsh and threatening letter to Heinrich in which he accused the young king of 'enormous crimes' that would make him liable not only to the ban of the Church, but to deprivation of his crown.

Gregory sent this correspondence at a time when he himself was in a tenuous political situation and under fire from many enemies in Italy who had sided with Heinrich. Gregory found himself carried off several weeks later on Christmas night as a prisoner of Cencio I Frangipane, a hostile Roman nobleman. Gregory was shortly freed by a mob of Roman citizens, but he angrily accused King Heinrich of instigating Frangipane's actions. Although this initial series of push-pull events between King Heinrich and Pope Gregory was nearly comical in nature, it was but a foretaste of the vicious ebb and flow that was about to unfold.

That next year at the Lentan Synod of 1075 in Rome, Pope Gregory decreed excommunication for violating his 1074 condemnation of simony, his confirmation of clerical chastity and the banning of marriage for clerics. These edicts were controversial, but it was Pope Gregory's next announced reform that absolutely enraged King Heinrich. Gregory decreed that only the Pope could appoint and depose bishops, thus giving official birth to the Investiture Controversy.

This bold political move by Gregory, in essence, meant the loss of nearly half of the imperial crown's territories as well as the loss of the crown's traditional appointment power to Church positions, which were among the most powerful positions in Europe. Furthermore, Heinrich saw this maneuver as a death knell for German constitutionality. Gregory's decree also infuriated many powerful elements within the German clergy, especially those who had received their appointments from King Heinrich.

Heinrich enlisted the support of these German clergymen, consolidated his military capabilities and confirmed treaties with other nobles disgruntled at the Pope. He even managed to forge alliances with non-German bishops and cardinals such as Cardinal Hugo Candidus of Rome who had at one time been on intimate terms with Pope Gregory. Heinrich then called these parties together and hastily convened a national council in Worms, Germany on January 24th of 1076. Accusations by this group were written, the attending bishops renounced their allegiance to Pope Gregory, and the assembly announced that Gregory had forfeited the papacy. King Heinrich boldly pronounced that Pope Gregory VII was deposed and that the Romans were required to select a new pope.

This German council then sent two bishops to Italy and procured a similar decree from the bishops of Lombardy in the synod of Piacenza. On February 21st, priest Roland of Parma boldly appeared at a synod that Pope Gregory himself was holding with a hundred and ten bishops. In a speech there within the Lateran Basilica to the Pope and others, Roland of Parma audaciously declared that Pope Gregory was dethroned and that those in the assembly must select a new pope. "This man before you," he said pointing to Pope Gregory, "is not a pope, but a ravening wolf!"

This announcement at first frightened those in attendance, but then such a storm of fury and indignation broke forth that only Pope Gregory himself was able to keep the mob of prelates from murdering Roland of Parma with their swords. That very next day, Pope Gregory pronounced a sentence of excommunication against King Heinrich IV, divested him of imperial dignity and absolved all of his subjects from all oaths they had sworn to him.

These respective actions by King Heinrich and Pope Gregory threw the continent into flux. Even Heinrich and Gregory themselves discovered that the earth beneath their own feet had begun to crumble and give way to chaos and violence. In Germany, Heinrich soon found he lacked the support of the common people; that a rapid and general feeling arose favoring the Pope. Moreover, the German Saxons viewed Pope Gregory's decree as a golden opportunity to renew their uprisings against Heinrich, so their numbers began to swell again. Nonetheless, military might remained Heinrich's primary strength against the Pope.

Pope Gregory also suffered from the destructive effects of this chaos incurred by his own machinations, losing the support of many clergymen. Yet, despite Pope Gregory's military inferiority, he equalized this disadvantage by rattling at his opposition the stark terrors of heavenly damnation and an eternity spent burning in the fires of Hell.

In other words, it was an evenly matched fight.

Chapter Twenty-Five

The Gamekeeper

History is littered with vanquished nations and races living beneath the boot of invading hordes whose occupation forces wreak brutality, humiliation and dispossession. In the wake of such defeat, conquered populations simmer with dreams of retribution and liberation...until, usually, time erodes hope. By the year 1077, eleven years after the Norman conquest of England, most Saxons had attained this ugly realization. But in Jack Forest, the fire of liberation had not diminished a single degree over time. In truth, that fire now burned more brightly than ever, fueled by Norman tyranny and the hopelessness they had thrust upon England's native population.

As with all Saxons, Jack was forced to bury such feelings, voicing them only to those he dearly trusted, such as his mother, Elder Heidi. "Be careful, Jack," she would scold at such times. Time has a way of dulling the clarity of dreams in people as they age. This very erosion had worn Elder Heidi into surrendering the dead past of a Saxon England. "Let it go, Jack!" she counseled. "That bastard, the Mole, is here to stay. There's nothing to be done about it anymore."

But Jack, like his father before him, was a dreamer, and dreamers refuse to abandon hope because they steer themselves into vaporous, imaginary places where dreams actualize. So it was that after Dulac's farce of a ceremony,

Jack went to DuLac requesting permission to cross north into nearby Scotland.

"But that's hostile territory," said DuLac.

"Not for Saxons, Sire," replied Jack. "Truth is, I've elderly relatives who fled there after Hastings. I'd like to see them before they pass."

DuLac cared little for the gamekeeper, but decided not to begrudge him a small reward because of his faithful services as gamekeeper. "Permission granted," he assented, "but be back within a week."

Jack decided to leave that very next day, but for some reason felt compelled to make Lady Asta aware of his pending absence by sending word through Willy. Hours later, he was surprised when Willy returned with a message from Asta. The note indicated that she wished to see him in the garden shed that next morning prior to his departure.

Entering the shed at dawn that next day, Jack rather expected that Lady Asta would be in the company of servants. Instead, he found her standing alone next to the cutting table. In that moment, he grew uneasy and glanced about, as expecting someone to catch him alone in the presence of the Lady Asta

"Will you not at least say good morning, Jack?" asked Asta, seeing that he seemed distracted.

"G-good morning, my Lady," Jack replied, his nerves jangling in his chest.

"I am curious about this trip of yours," said Asta. "Or more exactly, why you felt it necessary to let me know you were leaving."

Jack shrugged, his face falling blank. "I d-don't really know, my Lady. My absence means nothing to you, but for some nonsensical reason, at the final moment, I just wanted you to know, at least, that I was gone. A fool's thought, I now realize, so I beg your pardon."

Asta smiled, but it was a weak and tenuous one filled with unspoken expression. "I believe, perhaps, I understand, Jack," she said, lowering her eyes. "Thank you for thinking of me. And just so you know, I would have noticed on my own that you were gone, even had you not sent word."

Jack's eyes narrowed as he looked away to absorb these words. After a long moment, he offered a weak smile, pleased by the implication. His eyes returned then, and were met by the direct gaze of Asta's piercing grey eyes boring through him, which sent a flitter through his chest. His cheeks colored.

This reaction caused a similar stir in Asta, and she also flushed, which made both of them realize, simultaneously, that something silent had indeed arisen between the two of them during the Western Meadows. This realization frightened them both; each wishing to be away from it. Nonetheless, like the moth to the candle's deadly flame, each was also drawn to it. Thus, as Jack raised his hand in farewell, perceiving an undeniable look of regret in Asta's eyes, he moved around the table and took the back of her hand, kissing it.

"I adore you, my Lady," he said, his voice low and trembling.

Surprised, Asta began to withdraw her hand from his, looking to the door. Seeing no one, the tautness of her fingers slackened and she left her hand in place. "I adore you also, Jack Forest," she said beneath her breath.

This exchange, though swift and chaste, was more than either could bear. Jack retrieved his hand and turned to the door. He started to say something, but the words stuck in his throat so he said nothing and left, his face red, his heart pounding out of control.

"Until your return," whispered Asta, watching him vault onto his horse and spur it for the gate.

***

Scotland was known at this time as the Kingdom of Alba, and since 1058 had been ruled by King Malcolm III, later nicknamed Canmore, meaning 'long neck' or 'big head', depending on the source. Historically, the Romans referred to the wild tribes of this northern region as 'Picti', translated as 'Painted Ones' in Latin. These tribes managed to repel both the conquests of Rome and swarming Angles and Saxons, thus creating a true north-south divide on the English isle. These tribes later disappeared, their culture being swallowed by the Gaels.

King Malcom was disturbed by the Norman invasion of England and granted asylum to many English exiles. Nonetheless, in 1072, he delivered his own son to the Bastard to guarantee peace while recognizing Norman authority south of Scotland. Still, many Scottish clans refused to respect this agreement, especially the southern clans sharing the border with the Normans.

After crossing out of DuLac's territory into Scotland, Jack Forest cut due west, urging his mount toward the town of Dumfries near the mouth of the River Nith. Once arrived, he located his cousin, Harold Forest, who had fled England during the Harrying. Harold was two years younger than Jack and had been raised by Elder Heidi, thus he was more Jack's brother than cousin. After a brief exchange of jovial greetings, Harold then led Jack to a large farm just beyond Dumfries where they met Aengus Mac-Leod, chieftain of the outlaw branch of the MacLeod clan. This farm was also a military camp of sorts, frequented by raiding parties that were the scourge of the Galloway territory and north England.

Aengus MacLeod was a burly man, sporting a thick red beard and a bushy mane of fiery hair. Rough-mannered and violent, his entire existence had been one long fight against anyone and everyone from whom he stood to gain. Nor did he even respect his own ancestral highland clans of the north-country, or even King Malcolm himself. "Aha, Jack-boy!" he bellowed, as he and another man took seats about the table with Jack and Harold to share ale. "Good to see you again, Captain!"

Jack took a deep drink, then locked his fingers together and placed his elbows on the table. "You made a miserable effort on your raid in DuLacshire, Aengus," he said. "I expected a finer outcome."

This angered the man sitting next to Aengus. "No help from you, Saxon, if you be Jack Forest, the gamekeeper!" the man said in a Norse accent.

This man was stoutly built, possessing that imposing stature of Scandinavians. Jack had never seen him before. "I did *my* part," he fired back to the stranger. "I set the timing and saw to it that a portion of the garrison was away from the castle. The rest was up to you two!"

"Easy now, both of you," grunted Aengus, tipping his drinking horn to his snout. "No point in kicking old shit. It's simple, we thought to catch them asleep, but someone raised the goddamned alarm. Misfortune, that's all."

"Ja, one that nearly cost us our goddamned lives!" huffed the Norseman. Looking Jack square in the eyes, he said, "I was told you guaranteed that this raid was foolproof, Saxon!"

This angered Jack and he unlocked his fingers, turning them to fists. "God's spine!" he shouted, leaping up. "Just who the Hell are you?" Firing a hand to his hip, he pulled his dagger and drove its point into the table-top. "I'll gut you like a spring hog, you bastard, and carve that goddamn mark off your filthy face!"

"Hey now, Jack!" said Harold, throwing his hands to the air.

Continuing to flag his hands, Aengus leaned forward. "Stop it, both of you," he snorted. "No point in casting blame. Aye, it was a good plan, but it didn't play. Jack, put the knife away, my friend. And Alf, back off!"

The Norseman cast a sullen look across the table at Jack and Harold, then backed his stool from the table, crossing his arms with resentment.

"Jack," Aengus continued, "this lad beside me is Alf. He's only been with me a short while, but I've put him second in charge since Macklin got speared down in York. Alf's mean as a rousted badger and a good man to have in a fight." Turning, he looked at his second. "And Alf, I'll say the same damn thing about Jack, so no more about the raid, huh?"

Alf nodded, but the purple roots rising along his neck could not disguise his fury.

"Alf's an interesting case, Jack," said Aengus. "And you two have a bit in common, I'd say. He's full of poison, too, for the Normans."

This statement seemed to placate Alf somewhat, and normal color returned to his neck. "Ja," he said, "I hate the Normans! Danish bastards who forgot their past and now think they're French!"

Aengus continued. "Alf's father, two uncles and other kinsmen were killed by Normans a few years back."

"Not killed," retorted Alf, "but slaughtered!"

"Aye, Jack," Aengus said, "just as you lost your father, uncles and kinsmen at Hastings and the Harrying to the Normans, Alf lost his to them, too. So his hatred of them runs as deep as your own."

"How's that?" asked Jack. "The Normans aren't battling the Norse, nor have they ever invaded Norway." Turning, he looked at Alf. "Aye, so explain it."

"It didn't happen in Norway, but in France," said Alf, closing his eyes, retrieving the memory of that night. "We'd slipped down the Seine through Norman lands and just into French territory. We came across a party of Normans, an odd band of throwbacks, actually, who had kept the Danish ways. We took them in as kinsmen that night, but the filthy bastards turned on us just as my father raised his horn to toast them." At this Alf's lips drew back and his eyes turned to slits. "I was the only one to escape. For weeks I hid in the forests and along the river, working my way back to the coast. I boarded a vessel leaving for Norway, but we caught a gale halfway there, and again, I was the only one spared. The Gods, therefore, have twice spared me. I'm sure so's to avenge my father and kinsmen. I floated about on a spar for days until fortune landed me on Scotland's shore. Some days later, by chance, I encountered another Norseman. He was a member of Aengus' band and brought me here. My name is Alf," then he pointed to his cheek, "but my father dubbed me WolfPaw at birth because of this mark."

Jack looked at the birthmark and nodded. "Aye, I see his logic," he replied, scratching his temple with sudden curiosity. "These men that killed your father and kinsmen, you claim they were Norman, but maintained the Danish traditions?"

"Ja, they spoke Danish amongst themselves, not French. And their garb was more Viking than French or Norman. They were traveling south with two young boys, taking them to a monastery."

At this, Jack squinted and shook his head, bewildered. "I'll be damned to all Hell," he muttered. "Do you remember whether one of them was called Orla or Crowbones, perhaps?"

Alf sat erect, looking as though he had been struck across the forehead by a hammer. "What!" he screamed, thunderstruck. "Orla? How the Hell! Yes, their leader was called Orla! Orla Bloodaxe!" Springing from his seat, he pointed with fury at Jack. "But how could you possibly know this!"

"Sit down, Alf!" Aengus commanded, sensing things were about to turn ugly.

Jack, still in a fog, tilted his head, assessing Alf's connection to the Danes. "I know these men. They're at DuLacshire; members of Lady Asta's Personal Guard, now answering to Desmond DuLac."

"They're at DuLacshire?" cried Alf, stunned.

"On the night you attacked the Keep, half of them were among the troops I drew off to the Western Meadows. I'd planned to lead them off five days earlier, but receiving word that Aengus' men had not yet arrived from the Shetlands, I had to put them off for a few days. In the end, it was my mother that arranged the delay."

"Oh, but the gods are kind!" shouted Alf. "He's put those killing bastards right here in my palm! Aengus, a call to arms! We'll attack right off again!"

Aengus shook his head. "Hold there, Alf. We barely escaped with our asses on that last raid, even with Jack luring some of them away. I'll not have dirt tossed over my corpse for purposes of your personal vengeance."

But Alf was on fire and reason had fled. "Oh, I'll have each of those bastards' heads on a pole!" he seethed. "I can see their faces now! Orla the big one, and his brother, nearly a twin. And the fair one with long hair to his waist, and a strange-looking son-of-a-bitch with long arms and legs that looked misshapen! There was one other that never spoke and always stayed back. Damn you, Aengus, a call to arms I say! And if you're too much of a woman for it, I'll lead the charge myself!"

"Sit down and shut up!" said Aengus, stung by this insult. "Best you not forget who's in charge here! You might get your revenge at some point, perhaps even with my help, but dammit, for now you'd best settle back or I'll boot your dead ass from Dumfries and ship it back to Norway!"

"Aengus is right," said Jack, looking over at Alf. "Another attack right now would be madness, especially with the tunnel discovered. I want DuLac dead more than anything in my life, but now's not—"

"I don't give a shit about DuLac, it's the goddamned Danes I want!" cried Alf, tears of rage welling in his eyes. "Oh, father! Frode Longsword! Do you hear me! I—"

"Sit down, Alf!" shouted Aengus. "Grab a hold of yourself, man!" Looking at Jack, he stuck a finger across the table. "And let me remind you both that I hold nothing against DuLac *or* the Danes! My only interest here was and still is the loot in DuLac's castle. But I don't care to pay for it with my ass. Is that clear?"

Alf gave no response, but Jack said, "Agreed, Aengus. But if things come right and we take on DuLac again, I also want to make one thing clear. His wife, the Lady Asta, is *not* to be touched."

"Huh?" grunted Aengus.

"Eh?" said Harold, looking at his cousin. "But she's as much the enemy as DuLac himself. What interest do you have in sparing DuLac's bride, of all damned people, Jack?"

"Very simple," Jack replied, trying to appear detached. "She saved me and my son from DuLac's ax. Is there a man at this table who can't understand that? Is there not enough decency left in each of you to extend this same loyalty for such a selfless act?"

Aengus sat back a moment. "Eh, yeah, a good thing, that," he mumbled. "But old Aengus here makes no promises."

"Nor do I," spat Alf. "It was members of her own Guard that killed my people, so I owe her nothing!"

Jack's knife was still stuck in the table top. He extracted it with a swift pull and pointed it at Aengus' throat. "Oh, my fine red-headed friend, I've known you for years and fought at your hip at Hastings and in a score of other points. I've twice saved your life and put you onto God-only-knows how many raids against the Normans and the French, but if you refuse this one request I now make, I'll gut you where you squat!"

"Whoa, whoa!" said Aengus, raising both palms in the air. "Easy there, Jackie-boy! I didn't realize this woman carried such weight with you. Sit, sit! Yes, you and I are friends in this life, and years ago vowed allegiance to each other. She saved you and she saved your son, so good enough for me, then. It's a square deal. Aye, I honor your request."

Jack then looked at Alf who had slipped a hand to his sword. Removing that hand, he shrugged. "She means nothing to me either way," he replied, shaking his head.

"It's only the five men who murdered my kinsmen that I want. Agreed then, I'll not touch her."

"And you, Harold," said Jack.

"Of course, Jack," nodded Harold. "It's a reasonable request."

"Very well then," said Jack, sheathing his dagger. "I've several people I wish to see before heading back south. Aengus, I'll send word when I see how things shake out, agreed?"

Aengus raised his goblet. "Agreed." Smiling, he added, "Ah, but those were good days back then, eh, Jackie-boy? You, Captain of the Shire Fyrdd, and me at your side, both of us slicing Normans to bits up and down England. We almost had them a time or two, didn't we, lad?"

Jack looked at Aengus and reached down to his goblet, raising it to meet Aengus'. "Yeah, Aengus, we almost had them a time or two; maybe we'll have them yet."

Chapter Twenty-Six

The Walk to Canossa

A strange pall settled over the European continent in the immediate wake of the power schism created by King Heinrich of Germany and Pope Gregory. Like two angry scorpions suddenly ensconced in a dance of elimination, the two greatest figures of Europe raised their stingers in a deadly standoff while the remainder of Europe collectively held its breath.

The anti-royalist Saxon princes of Germany quickly sided with Pope Gregory under the guise of respect for the papacy and God's law. Regathering momentum, they moved against Heinrich as soon as he was excommunicated by Gregory. By early fall, the rebel princes had forced Heinrich's forces into retreat. Next, they convened in October at Trebur with the intention of electing a new German ruler.

King Heinrich, licking his wounds in Oppenheim, began to figure his days as King of Germany were numbered. Then fate intervened. The Saxon princes began squabbling and failed to agree on the new ruler. Frustrated, they postponed any decision, fully expecting Heinrich's excommunication to be permanent. They also decided to invite Pope Gregory to Augsburg to help them select the new German ruler. The proposed date for this meeting was established to be the anniversary of Heinrich's excommunication.

These were dark days for Heinrich since dethroning Pope Gregory. He sought to make amends with the Saxon princes in hopes of ending civil war. The princes rebuffed all diplomatic solutions, which left Heinrich with but one recourse—reconciliation with Pope Gregory. As humiliating as this might be, Heinrich knew that only the Pope could extract him from this morass of their own mutual devise.

It was at this point, also, that Gregory began to weigh his excommunication and dethronement of Heinrich. This feud had by now cost him both credibility and validity, and had also much emboldened his opponents within the Church itself, especially the powerful German Bishop, Guibert of Ravenna.

Nonetheless, with Heinrich cornered by the Saxon anti-royalists and on the verge of defeat, it appeared that Pope Gregory could have check-mated Heinrich while he sat languishing on the banks of the Rhine. Unbelievably, despite the Saxon princes' overtures to him for mediation and guidance in selecting a new ruler, Pope Gregory failed to take timely or decisive action.

The Benedictines, including the Black Monks of Cluny, were staunchly allied with Pope Gregory's reformist philosophy. This aside, Abbot Hugh found himself in a personal quandary. Though sharing intimate political ties with Pope Gregory, he also happened to be King Heinrich's godfather. Subsequently, despite Abbot Hugh's support of the Pope, many suspected that Hugh secretly hoped for a peaceful resolution between Heinrich and Gregory.

In November of 1076, Abbot Hugh summoned Odo de Lagery to his chambers. "Ah, Odo, did you bring the boy?"

"Yes, he is waiting outside."

"Good, good," Hugh responded, smiling. "As you know, I will be leaving for Augsburg in several days to meet the Holy Father in Germany."

"Ah, the long awaited Diet at Augsburg," nodded Odo. "I suppose the rebel German princes will be there also?"

"Most assuredly," said Hugh. "And since Pope Gregory has not lifted his ban of excommunication nor his dethronement of Heinrich, they are impatient to select a new German ruler. The Holy Father has been asked to officiate, then anoint and bless the new king."

"Do we know who it will be?"

"Duke Rudolph of Swabia, most likely," said Hugh. Then, dropping his gaze, he sighed. "This horrid civil war in Germany has been such a bloody affair, and now threatens to spill into Italy. Lord against lord, cleric against cleric, the damage is irreparable, I fear."

Looking at his superior, Odo noticed the fatigue-laden furrows outlining his eyes. "Heinrich's cause is lost, it appears," he said.

Hugh shook his head. "My godson is not to be underestimated. His greatest weakness is pride, so he will lead his troops to slaughter before actually abdicating."

"Let us hope not," said Odo, "but I believe the compass is set. It is God's will that the Church wins this struggle over the crown!"

"Agreed," sighed Hugh, "but I am now caught in a tricky situation of sorts. Heinrich has been sending letters pleading that I help him with the Pope. He begs absolution."

"Certainly he does!" said Odo with disgust. "*Paratae lacrimae insidias, non fletum, indicant*—easy tears show treachery, not grief. He is adrift and has no options left but to now seek forgiveness from the Holy Father. Lest we forget, he has played that hand before. Surely you know that yourself."

"A possibility," nodded Hugh. "Yet, I like to believe that he has seen the error of his misjudgment. That aside, I have a favor to ask. I have been keeping an eye to your lad, Tristan, of late, and am impressed beyond belief. In fact, I am interested in taking him with me to Augsburg, to serve as my page. Did you not tell me you hoped to see him don a black robe one day?"

"Yes, I pray each night that the Almighty might guide him into our service."

"Indeed," nodded Hugh, "the lad has frightening intelligence for one so young. He will achieve unimaginable things in his lifetime, if given the chance. We need to keep him in our fold. A trip like this to Augsburg will move things along. So bring him in then, Odo. I shall tell him he is about to meet the Pope."

Tristan was waiting in the corridor, nervously guessing his purpose for being brought to the great Abbot Hugh. Moments later, he was standing before the high cleric, keeping a brave face.

"Ah, but come forward, come forward, son," gestured Abbot Hugh with a broad sweep of his palm. "So now, you are indeed Tristan de Saint-Germain, the Wonder of Cluny, are you not?"

Tristan clumsily offered his hand. He had never heard himself referred to as the Wonder of Cluny. "I, well, yes, my name *is* Tristan de Saint-Germain, Holiness."

Abbot Hugh laughed. "Not Holiness, my boy! After all, I am not the pope. Simply call me Abbot."

"Yes, sir."

"Abbot Hugh has called you here to request a service," said Odo. "He wants you to accompany him to Germany as his assistant, just as you did for me in Italy."

Tristan thought a moment. "Am I to spy on others?" he asked, frowning.

"Ha! Spy?" said Hugh, amused at both the boy's tone and his posture. "Spy is such a strong word, boy, and uncomely for anyone from Cluny. But no, you will simply come along to assist with dressing, serving food, errands and such."

At this, the knot in Tristan's stomach loosened as his discomfort faded. "Most certainly, it would be my honor and privilege to serve you in such a manner, Abbot Hugh," he said reverently.

This response impressed Hugh. "Aha, Odo," he clucked, "a polite, clever boy, this one. And so well spoken! Very well then, we leave in a week."

Tristan started to speak, but the words caught and he stopped.

"Well now," said Hugh, "you must have something on your mind, boy. What is it?"

"May I be so bold," Tristan said, "as to ask what our mission is in Germany?"

Hugh's brows collected, creating a deep crease just between them and his lower forehead. "Mission?" he asked, leaning forward in his chair. "But what makes you think we are on a mission and not simply on a visit, my boy?"

"Because," said Tristan, pointing at Odo, "the Grand Prior has taught me that every action has a purpose, no matter how insignificant. And a trip of such great distance must, therefore, have great significance, or so I would suppose."

"My, my," said Hugh, glancing at Odo, "it appears the lad has soaked up all you have thrown in his direction."

"A stellar student," said Odo with a swell of pride. "Tristan listens, but he also thinks. He is quite analytical."

Hugh smiled. "Perfect," he said. "Once in Augsburg, I must introduce him to the Pope."

"The Pope?" said Tristan, feeling his stomach knotting again.

"You asked what our mission is in Germany," said Hugh. "We are to meet the Pope, and elect a new German king!"

"A new king? With the Pope?" Tristan stammered, feeling faint.

"Yes," said Hugh. "And just as you surmised, this is a mission of great importance. You will see much, take in much, and also walk away with much."

"But this will not lead to war, will it?" asked Tristan.

"Ah, but the war has already begun," replied Hugh. "Germans slaughtering Germans, Italians slaughtering Italians. Maybe even others joining in very soon. Clergy making charges against fellow clergy. But with God's help, this mission could well *end* the war and return peace and order to Christendom."

"Yes, Tristan," said Odo, reassuring the boy. "You will be on a mission of peace. The Holy Father, Pope Gregory, will lead the way. No need to worry."

This soothed Tristan. But as they left Abbot Hugh's company, he whispered, "Is it really true that I will not have to spy on anyone in Augsburg?"

"Heaven forbid!" said Odo. "Tristan, do you not trust the words of Abbot Hugh?"

"Yes, or at least I want to," said Tristan. "But is it not you who always tells me to trust no man, no matter how exalted, until I know the full lay of the landscape?"

Odo slowed his gait, thinking perhaps to chastise his young liege for doubting Hugh's word. After a moment's thought, he resumed his pace. "Exactement, mon fils," he said, looking straight ahead, "that is exactly what I have told you time and time again."

Then he smiled to himself.

***

Nature unleashed its fury on Europe during the winter of 1076-1077, freezing the Rhine River into a solid mass from November to April, creating one of the longest and most severe winters in the memory of men. Upon departing Cluny for Augsburg, Abbot Hugh's wagon train began an interminable battle against brutal winds, frozen roads and slashing snow storms. For the teamsters, each day was an arduous struggle against freezing temperatures, mountainous snow drifts and ice. Nonetheless, they tenaciously wormed the wagons toward Augsburg.

Simultaneously, Pope Gregory's entourage began its trek north from Rome toward Augsburg, encountering similar conditions as they moved toward the mountains. Suspecting that King Heinrich might still possess the capacity to launch a surprise attack from his position on the Rhine, the Pope had urged the Saxon princes to provide a military escort to meet him on January 8th in Mantua, the capital of Lombardy in northern Italy. Benedictine agents had reported that King Heinrich enjoyed enthusiastic support in Lombardy, thus added security would be required traversing this hostile region and the rest of the way to Augsburg.

Tristan was given the privilege of riding within Abbot Hugh's customized wagon; quickly discovering that Abbot Hugh was a fascinating conversationalist who was highly intellectual and well-traveled. Tristan's apprehensions about riding with this man of such vaunted repute soon vanished as he also learned that Abbot Hugh possessed extraordinary wit, loved to play devil's advocate, and was even capable at times of displaying unbridled bursts of joviality.

Abbot Hugh found Tristan equally engaging. The boy possessed frightening intelligence, was highly versed in Church and European history and demonstrated a freakish sense of perception. Alone in the comfortable confines of the wagon day after day, they struck up a grand friendship while the teamsters fought their way forward through blizzards and ice.

On the eighth day of travel the caravan stopped to rest upon the crest of a treacherous mountain pass. Abbot Hugh was steeped in conversation with the head teamster when he heard Tristan's voice ring from atop the wagon where he had temporarily perched himself. "Riders coming!" the boy shouted.

This created a stir, so the head teamster himself quickly climbed atop the wagon. Shielding his eyes from the blinding glare of noon sun against snow, he stared down the mountain. Soon he spotted riders coming up the heavily drifted pass, their horses slowly plodding ahead one struggling hoof at a time through snow that came to the stirrups. "Only two of 'em! No soldiers following!" he shouted to the others.

This calmed the other teamsters who were keenly aware that the road to Augsburg was filled with danger due to the political and military circumstances surrounding their trip. Nonetheless, the platoon of Burgundian guards accompanying the Abbot's caravan kept their swords at the ready. "Possibly just travelers," warned the captain, "but keep your guard up, weapons at the ready!"

After nearly an hour, the two riders made the crest. "We seek Abbot Hugh," the lead rider said, dismounting in utter exhaustion.

As he said this, he shoved his hand into his coat. Thinking the man was reaching for a dagger, the Burgundian captain sprang forward and drove the man down into the snow, placing the tip of his sword against the man's throat. "Ho, there!" the captain cried. "Hold still and open your coat or I'll stick you like a pig!"

"No! Wait!" the man shouted as the other rider raised both hands in surrender. "My papers! My name is Dieter Muehler! I'm just reaching for my papers!"

"We're agents of the Pope! Benedictine Underground!" said the second man, flagging both hands while backing away. "His Holiness has sent us to alert Abbot Hugh!"

The captain backed away, allowing the first rider to stand. Gaining his feet, the man reached back into his coat and retrieved two documents. "Our papers," he said, shoving the documents toward the captain.

The captain carried them to Abbot Hugh, who was by now seated on the wagon stoop. Hugh examined the documents, checked the seal and looked for Pope Gregory's secret verification, two nondescript ink marks placed discreetly on the document, one in the center of the page and one near the bottom left corner, then he began reading.

"They're clear," Hugh said to the captain. Motioning for the first man to come forward, he said, "Your name again, sir?"

"Dieter Muehler of Bavaria," the man said, "agent of the Benedictine Underground these past two decades. My partner here is Jurgen Handel, also an agent of the Vatican."

"So, Muehler, do you know the contents of this message from the Holy Father?" asked Hugh.

"Yes, Abbot. I'm the one that acquired this particular information from our agents along the Rhine. And I've sent two of them to intercept Pope Gregory's caravan, while Handel and I came to warn you."

Hugh nodded. "Bless you for doing the Lord's work in such weather." Turning to the captain and the lead teamster, he said, "We'll be changing course."

"Changing course?" asked the teamster.

"But what about Augsburg?" asked the captain. "I thought—"

"King Heinrich is suddenly moving south with his forces," interrupted Muehler. "He's already crossed Mont Cenis and we suspect he's trying to capture Pope Gregory's caravan before he gets to Augsburg to help elect the new king."

Hugh said, his eyes widening, "Hold on there. What about the reports that Heinrich may simply be seeking an audience with Pope Gregory prior to the Augsburg Diet? And what about the Saxon princes who were instructed to send forces south to meet and escort the Pope through Lombardy? Surely Heinrich would not dare engage them in battle at this point to attack the Pope's party."

The agent shook his head. "The Saxon princes never showed up! Could've been the weather since many of the mountain passes are blocked. But then, it could also be because of Heinrich, too. Anyway, to be safe, the Holy Father has been instructed to take flight."

"Back to Rome?" asked the captain.

Muehler shook his head. "No, due west a short distance to Canossa in the Apennine foothills. Countess Matilda of Tuscany has offered him refuge in her castle at Canossa. They've shut themselves within with her troops."

"If you are correct about Heinrich's motives," nodded Henry, "then God bless the ever faithful Countess Matilda for providing the Pope safe haven. Her fortress is impregnable, not to mention that it is also protected by the Qattro Castelli: Montezane, Montelucio, Montvetro and Bianell. Getting by those four castles is nearly impossible in itself, let alone getting up the mountain to Canossa."

Still atop the wagon, Tristan was listening to every detail being exchanged below. The thought of the Pope being captured or possibly even executed by a king was horrifying to him. At that moment, he was seized with concern for the Holy Father as well as for the future of Christendom.

"Indeed," continued Muehler. "Thank God the Countess remains so faithful to the Pope despite being surrounded by traitorous Lombards. But to answer your question, yes, we're aware of claims Heinrich wishes to seek forgiveness from the Pope. But we've also just received reports that the Lombards are welcoming King Heinrich as a hero and arming themselves. Worse yet, they're urging him to take the Pope prisoner, volunteering in droves to join his ranks. It's also reported that Heinrich's lackey, Bishop Guibert of Ravenna, is moving south with a separate army, possibly to make a drive on the Pope in a pincer movement. Heinrich could very well be presenting all this forgiveness drama purely as a ploy to get in close, then snatch Pope Gregory. I take it then that you were not aware of all the movement going on by Heinrich and Guibert of Ravenna's troops?"

Hugh shook his head. "No, not at all. I have taken Heinrich purely on his word that he seeks forgiveness from Gregory. But Bishop Guibert is dangerous. I don't understand why German troop movements are going on all over northern Italy at the moment." He sighed then and clasped his hands. "Heavens, I could have never anticipated such confusion and division. Germans turning on a German King, Italians turning on the Pope!"

Muehler agreed, saying, "We were hoping to bring this to an end in Augsburg, make a fresh start with a new king. But this latest twist changes everything." Tightening the wrapping around his neck and pulling his mantle tighter, he signaled to his partner, Handel. Mounting, he said, "Abbot Hugh, we must be on our way. What do I tell the Holy Father?"

"Tell him we will meet him at Canossa as soon as we can. And if Heinrich arrives and attempts to storm the castle, I shall try to reason with him. Heinrich is my godson, and we are close."

"Good luck, then, Abbot," said Muehler as he and Handel turned their horses and began their long trek back down the pass.

Abbot Hugh gathered the teamsters. "We leave immediately. When we clear the pass, we change course for Canossa!" he said. Looking atop his wagon, he beckoned to Tristan. "Jump down, lad, it seems you will be meeting the Pope sooner than expected!"

***

Over the next several days Hugh's caravan struggled over frozen roadways and through heavy snowfalls and howling winds. Several pack animals were lost to the slopes, but the wagons and teamsters miraculously remained intact through this ordeal. On the afternoon of the fourth day, after encountering the Vatican agents at the pass, the caravan began snaking its way up the twisted approach to Countess Matilda's fortress in Canossa.

It was at this point that Abbot Hugh gave Tristan the history of the Countess. "She is the Grande Dame of all Europe at only thirty-years-of-age," he told the boy. "They call her la Gran Contessa here in Italy. Men bow to her and even fear her, though she is a Godly and pious woman. She maintains a strong army, and is well versed in military matters and other manly arts, such as hunting, riding and the arms. She was taught these skills under the tutelage of the notorious Arduino della Padule, and possesses two personal suits of armor, which she dons when war calls."

"She is a woman and she fights?" asked Tristan. "I did not think such was allowed."

"Ha! She does as she pleases. No man dares tell her otherwise. Her upbringing was hard, which is why she is so willful. Her father was murdered in 1052 when she was six, and a year later her older sister died. In order to protect Matilda's and her brother's inheritance, Matilda's mother quickly married Godfrey the Bearded of Upper Lorraine. At the same time, they betrothed Matilda, as a child, to one of Godfrey's sons, Godfrey the Hunchback, who was actually also her stepbrother due to her mother's marriage."

Tristan nodded, reminded of his own mother's betrothal while but twelve, and also her sudden marriage to Lord DuLac upon the execution of her husband. Hearing Matilda's tale shed a glimmer of light on what life had forced upon his mother. "It must be difficult to be a woman, I suppose," he said. "But, was Matilda's husband-to-be really a hunchback?"

"Aye! But even with her mother's marriage to Godfrey the Bearded and young Matilda's betrothal to Godfrey the Hunchback, the mother, brother and Matilda were captured and dragged off to Germany by King Heinrich III where they lived as prisoners for a time."

"Was King Heinrich III not the father of King Heinrich IV who now threatens the Holy Father?" asked Tristan.

"Yes, lad, the same. And as the nephew of Matilda's mother, Heinrich IV is Matilda's first cousin. *His* father, Heinrich III, was infuriated that Matilda's mother married his enemy, Godfrey the Bearded, so he imprisoned her and the children. Matilda's brother died during this imprisonment, though it was said that Heinrich III treated him much better than the mother and Mathilda. Eventually Matilda and her mother were returned to Tuscany; that is when she, as the sole legitimate heir of her father's lands, inherited one of the largest tracts of territory in all Europe."

This story fascinated Tristan, making him think back to what Brother Damien had once said about men taking what was not theirs, and other men reclaiming what they had lost. In this case it was a woman who had reclaimed her rightful place, which suddenly made the possibility of him one day reclaiming his former noble status seem within reach.

"She also eventually *married* the hunchback," Hugh continued, "for political reasons only, of course. But they shortly separated because God willed it. He was killed just this past year. So you see, the Countess Matilda has lived a very different sort of existence. And you should know that she is highly educated and prides herself as a linguist, speaking German, Italian, French and Latin. Then, thankfully, she is now and always has been a fervent champion of the Church."

"She sounds a bit like my mother," said Tristan.

***

After making the rise to Canossa, Abbot Hugh ushered Tristan through the courtyard, which was seething with armed men. Then they entered Huntsmen's Hall where the Countess welcomed her guests in winter. It was a massive structure featuring two monstrous fireplaces, both ablaze with logs and stumps. The walls of the Hall towered over thirty-five feet high, and were adorned with countless stag-horn displays, deer and boar heads, bear skins and an assortment of impressive tapestries and paintings featuring hunting, wildlife and war.

Twisting through the mob of soldiers and guests, Tristan soon spotted the Countess, the only woman in the entire Hall. She stood by one of the fireplaces surrounded by dignitaries steeped in animated discussion and laughter. She was a large woman, draped in a thick, deep-violet gown. Her head was crowned with a cone-shaped head-piece trimmed at the base with trailing pieces of fine fabric adorned with glimmering gold thread. Her hair, also adorned in gold thread, hung in two long braids that fell to her waist. Despite her elegant wardrobe, the Countess herself was somewhat coarse-looking, and also appeared bored and disengaged. But spotting Abbot Hugh, she sprang into motion and cut a path out of her circle toward him. "Ah, my dear Hugh!" she exclaimed, throwing her arms around the Abbot's neck with the abandon of a ruffian.

"Contessa!" reciprocated Hugh. "May God bestow blessings upon you for providing shelter for the Holy Father in this time of confusion and dread!"

Tristan stood watching the exchange, absorbing the profound affection that obviously existed between the two.

Still holding the Abbot in her embrace, Mathilda noticed the beautiful young boy in Hugh's company. "Ah, Hugh, who have we here?"

Pushing Tristan forward, Hugh said, "Go on, lad, introduce yourself."

Stepping forward, rigid and formal, Tristan bowed with the grace of a practiced diplomat. "Tristan de Saint-Germain," he announced, "a student of languages at the Benedictine Monastery of Cluny."

Student of languages? thought Abbot Hugh to himself. *Aha, the boy was listening closely in the wagon, and has now used that information to aim straight for Matilda's heart!*

"And what do you speak, my sweet boy?" said Mathilda, clasping her hands.

"Danish, French, Spanish and Latin quite well; Italian and German less well."

"Perfetto!" Matilda exclaimed, throwing her arms in the air, overcome with a tug of affection for the young image of perfection standing before her. In her world of greed-driven men and political snakes, he appeared an oasis of innocence and purity.

"But I don't see the Holy Father," said Hugh, looking about the chamber.

"He's in his quarters, overcome with melancholy," said Mathilda. "He's completely distraught about Heinrich's advance southward and feels the King is plotting to imprison him or worse."

"But this looks like a merry time tonight with all these guests," remarked Hugh. "Won't he at least come down for a cup of wine?"

"No, not him," chuckled Mathilda. "As you know, Hugh, he is not one for festivity! Indeed, he has never understood gaiety, far preferring the dark clouds of doom!"

At this, they both laughed. "But tell, have you received communication from Heinrich these past months?"

"Yes, of course. My cousin begs me to plead his case before Pope Gregory. He professes to deeply regret the error of his ways and hopes Gregory can find it in his heart to forgive him." Then she smiled a little. "But then, Heinrich also knows that only Gregory can redeem him now, under the circumstances."

"Ah, he pleads that I do the same," said Hugh. "But what of this flight into your fortress here at Canossa? Do you not trust Heinrich's intentions?"

Mathilda gave the question consideration. "You know, Hugh, you can never tell for sure what Heinrich will say or do. Besides, he's as unhappy with me as he is with the Pope at the moment, as I've fully taken the Vatican's position in this feud and provided money, munitions and troops. I thought it wise that Hildebrand and I seek immediate sanctuary, especially after learning that Bishop Guibert of Ravenna is himself lurking about in the mountains with his private army. Such a foul man, that one! And he's stated publicly that *he* should be the new pope now that Heinrich has deposed Gregory. Horrible!"

"Bishop Guibert and Gregory were once friends," nodded Hugh. "Sad how the struggle for power cuts even the tightest bonds of friendship."

This statement struck Tristan, making him think of the deteriorated relationship that had existed between his father and Desmond DuLac. Though brothers, they had been driven apart by jealousy and competition. Silently, Tristan vowed that such a wedge would never split him and his own brother, Guillaume.

"Well then," said Matilda, taking Hugh by the elbow, "let me introduce you to my generals and guests who have come to reinforce the castle. We'll have an audience with Gregory in the morning and devise strategy since Heinrich's army is apparently now only a day's march away or so." Then she signaled to Tristan. "Come, sweet angel, I wish to introduce you to some of my men," she said, smiling, "to remind them what they once were, and how beastly they've now become!"

***

Hildebrand of Sovana was born the son of an Italian blacksmith in 1015 in Tuscany, which contributed to his lifelong description by opponents as 'a rough and violent peasant'. In adolescence he was sent to his uncle in Rome, abbot of a monastery on Aventine Hill, where Hildebrand developed into a highly educated, sober-minded and pious clergyman. Quickly adopting the philosophy of radical Church reform, he aggressively pushed agendas for Church independence from emperors while also espousing sexual morality, celibacy within the clergy and the banning of simony and investiture.

Reforms such as these threatened to weaken the privilege and power of many Catholic clergymen. As much of this power was owed to political, moral and spiritual abuse, many clergymen vehemently opposed Church reform under any format. Simultaneously, this reform movement also threatened the power of emperors by threatening kings' rights to appoint bishops and other high clerics.

Hildebrand of Sovana had already been engaged in this bitter struggle for reform for decades prior to his appointment as pope at age sixty when most busy men begin to long for rest. It was inevitable, then, that Hildebrand would become a formidable opponent to both a corrupt Church and to emperors who interfered with Church autonomy.

Despite Tristan's age and limited information, he was by now becoming more aware of the political backdrop surrounding the schism between Church and State which had pitted Pope Gregory and King Heinrich against each other as mortal enemies. Tristan's personal allegiance, due to his mother's upbringing and his education at Cluny, was unquestionably entrenched in the camp of Pope Gregory.

As Tristan retired that first night at Canossa on January 20th of 1077, his anticipation of meeting Pope Gregory was already running amok. Thinking that he was about to be in the same room as the Father of the Holy Church consumed all thought, so much so he could barely sleep. At dawn he awoke like an expectant child on Christmas morning, anticipating great things. Taking special care in grooming himself, he selected his finest wardrobe and hurried to Abbot Hugh's chamber, but Hugh was still asleep. Disappointed, Tristan descended to the dining hall where the servants were bustling about preparing the morning meal for over a hundred guests.

They paid him no mind, but then a voice addressed him from behind. "Aha!" the brusque voice said. "Why awake so early?"

Turning, Tristan discovered Countess Matilda. "I am waiting to see the Holy Father," he said, "because you said last night that we would have audience with him this morning. So I am ready!"

The Countess issued a deep, rich laugh, sounding nearly like a man. "Ha, Gregory will not rise for hours yet!

He's not a youngster, you know." Then, motioning him to approach, she continued. "Come here, my boy, and give the Countess a big hug. You are such a beautiful boy! I hardly ever see children! My existence is a world of ruffians, soldiers and politicians. Just looking at you gives me respite from such vipers!"

Tristan moved toward her awkwardly; he was unaccustomed to demonstrating affection, as taught by his mother. Nonetheless, he issued a tepid embrace about the shoulders.

Mathilda pulled him in closer, nearly smothering him in her ample bosom. "There now," she clucked, "that's much better! Don't be afraid of your Auntie Matilda."

"Auntie Mathilda?" asked Tristan, confused.

"Indeed, from this moment on I declare myself your adopted auntie, and shall remain so throughout your life. I've no children of my own, you know; a personal sacrifice in the name of service to my people and the Church."

Unsure how to interpret this, Tristan tightened his embrace, clumsily patting the Countess about the back of shoulders. "Thank you, my Lady," he muttered. "I am most fortunate to have an aunt so greatly respected and adored as yourself! God has blessed me!"

Delighted, she squeezed him once more, then held him away at arm's length. Staring into his face, she was mesmerized by the purity of his clear grey eyes. "Indeed, God has blessed you," she said, "but he has also tested you, according to what I learned last night."

"You know me, Contessa?" he asked, surprised.

"Yes. Last night Abbot Hugh told me about your father's execution, your family's humiliation and loss of property, your mother's marriage to your uncle, and your separation from her. I became weepy listening to it all. It reminded me of my own upbringing; things gave me thick circumstances beyond my control, people leading me hither and yon. But such are walls, Tristan. These trials God has set in your path will strengthen you, as well. So, I decided after listening to Hugh last night that I must be your ally for life, because with your gifts, you will most surely be one who advances our Church in the future, and you will need life-lines. Do you understand?"

Tristan nodded politely, comprehending only a portion of what she was suggesting. "You know, Countess," he said, his face growing grim, "I have a younger brother named Guillaume. He has been tested, too, and certainly needs a life-line such as yourself also."

"Ah yes, Hugh mentioned your brother," said Matilda. "Hmm, but I wonder, is he as beautiful as you?"

This embarrassed Tristan. "They say he is far more handsome than me," he answered.

"More handsome than you? Impossible! But if so, surely he's not as *clever* as you, huh?"

"He is not so interested in academics," said Tristan, "yet clever."

"Very well, then, I must meet him. I will expect you to bring him to Canossa when you come to visit me next summer. Perhaps he shall be my nephew also."

"Visit next summer?" asked Tristan.

"Of course! All aunts expect visits from their nephews. I'll instruct Abbot Hugh to send both of you to Italy after the weather warms and your lessons break for the summer."

Pleased, Tristan rewarded Matilda with a beaming smile that nearly dissolved her heart. "Do you suppose I could inspect your suits of armor?" he asked. "Abbot Hugh told me all about you, too."

This delighted Countess Matilda so it led her to spend the next hour discussing her military abilities and interests with Tristan. As they talked, it would have been impossible to detect which of the two enjoyed this conversation more.

When Abbot Hugh finally appeared in the dining hall, a bell was rung and everyone gathered for a formal breakfast. Mathilda insisted that Tristan sit next to her. Although the other guests had no idea who he was, they supposed from her display of familiarity with him that he was somehow related to her. Upon hearing la Gran Contessa address him as 'nephew' that morning, all who associated with Matilda from that moment on believed Tristan to be exactly that, never questioning the actual origin of this bond.

After the meal, Matilda gathered Hugh and Tristan for audience with Pope Gregory. Excited beyond words, Tristan could feel his heart palpitating beyond control as they mounted the steps to the Pope's quarters.

"I'm nervous," he whispered to Abbot Hugh.

"Be calm," said the Abbot.

Matilda overheard this exchange. "Yes," she chortled, "although he represents God on this earth, he is *just* a man, Tristan."

There are times in life when humans develop such great anticipation for an event that reality cannot possibly match expectations. This is precisely what occurred as Tristan walked into the Pope's chambers. There, seated on the bed with his back against the headboard, his head covered with a wool nightcap, sat an old man who appeared nestled in his death bed. He looked tired and extremely ordinary. Unprepared for such a sight, Tristan at first thought perhaps they had entered an antechamber and the man in the bed was a valet who was late in rising.

But then the Countess bowed and said, "Good morning, Holiness!"

Abbot Hugh followed with, "Ah, my dear Gregory, it warms me to see you again!"

Tristan had been expecting an imposing figure garbed in luxurious robes topped with the three-tiered, bejeweled papal tiara. He had anticipated an authoritative voice issuing profound words of wisdom. But as the old man, small in stature, greeted them, his voice hacked and sounded raspy, like Brother Placidus back at the Dorter. "O-oh, good morning," he groaned. "Moving a bit slow I'm afraid." Struggling to straighten his gown, he spotted Tristan. "And just who are you, lad?"

Tristan's mouth fell ajar and he could find no words. Though disappointing in stature, this was still the Father of Christendom, and he was directly addressing Tristan.

"This is Tristan de Saint-Germain," interjected Hugh. "We call him the Wonder of Cluny."

"And a wonder he is, Your Grace!" smiled the Countess.

"Humph," grunted the Pope, offering no trace of a smile. "And why is it, son, they call you the Wonder of Cluny?"

Tristan, standing in ashen silence, was unable to answer.

"Don't be shy," urged Matilda.

"I-I do well with my studies," Tristan stammered, "and I speak many languages and know the history of Europe and the Church. I—"

Hugh laughed. "He is rarely this reserved, Hildebrand. But then, he has been very excited meeting you."

"Exceedingly excited," echoed Matilda.

"I see," said Pope Gregory, making the sign of the cross in the air. "I bless you, my boy," he said. Motioning to the chairs arranged about the opposite side of his bed, he said, "Be seated, please. You, too, lad."

"Such difficult times for you, Hildebrand," said Hugh, shaking his head.

"My entire life has been little else but difficulty," replied Gregory, his tone glum. "Born into a world lying in wickedness; where princes prefer their own honor over God's honor; where hardly a bishop south or north has obtained their office through regular means or whose conduct corresponds to their vocation; a world where the high clergy, in their thirst for gain and glory, are the enemies, not the friends of religion and justice."

"But you are making your mark, changing such things," said Hugh.

Ignoring the remark, Gregory continued his lament. "The Eastern Byzantine Church has fallen from the Catholic rite, calling itself the Greek Orthodox Church, and is now being attacked by heathen Muslims. And these foul Lombards, Romans and Normans among whom I live are worse even than the Jews and heathens. I live as a dying man suspended between sorrow and hope like a sailor on the high seas surrounded by darkness. I often pray to God to release me from this present life."

Tristan was struck by the Pope's plaintive tone. He had thought to be meeting a robust, vibrant leader of men, not listening to tales of woe.

"And now Heinrich seeks to take me prisoner!" Gregory moaned. "May God have him burn in Hell for eternity for taking such liberties."

"Now, Hildebrand," said Hugh, "are you so certain that is his intention? It makes little sense that he would be so bold as to take you prisoner under his present conditions. France and Spain would both rise up against him and join the rebelling Saxon princes if he did such! Besides, I've been told he seeks absolution and forgiveness from you."

"Lies!" Gregory retorted, suddenly on fire. "He is a scheming worm of a man whose word holds no weight!"

"But I have heard the same as Hugh," countered Matilda.

"Was it not you, Matilda, who said I should hasten to your fortress upon hearing of his approach!" said Gregory, his face reddening.

"It was, but only as a precaution, Your Grace."

"And now that we are behind your walls," Gregory continued with sourness, "do you *now* side with your German cousin?"

"Certainly not," said Matilda, "but I do agree with Hugh that to attack you makes little sense—impetuous, in fact."

"But he's been impetuous since birth!" insisted Gregory. "No, he is not to be trusted!"

As he said this, a knock came on the door and a guard entered. "Your Holiness," the guard said, "a messenger has arrived. He said his name is Muehler."

"Muehler?" said Gregory, his focus shifting. "Yes, yes, send him in!"

Muehler entered the room, brushing snow and moisture from his cloak. He bowed upon seeing Abbot Hugh, saying, "Happy to see that you made it here safely, Abbot." Looking at Matilda, he bowed again. "Countess, you look lovely this morning."

"Enough of that, Muehler!" barked Gregory, now sitting erect in his bed, waving his hand with impatience. "Where is Heinrich now?"

Muehler approached the bed. "Actually, Your Grace, he arrived with his entourage and troops at the foot of the mountain three hours ago, and now stands just outside the gates of Canossa."

"What!" exclaimed Gregory with alarm. "He has marched his army up the mount? My Lord, Matilda," he shuddered, "we are under attack! Gather your forces!"

"Holiness," said Muehler, "he came up the approach with only a handful of diplomats. His troops remain at the foot of the mountain."

"Eh?"

"Yes, Your Grace," said Muehler. "He claims to come with only humble intentions, but requests to first meet with Abbot Hugh and the Countess."

"Deny him entry into the gate," Gregory exclaimed. "He is an excommunicate! I refuse to give him an audience now, or in the future."

"Yes, certainly, Your Eminence," replied Muehler. "But something unexpected, the Benedictine Underground reports that Heinrich has taken on the behavior of a penitent. He wears the woolen garb of a monk and allegedly walks with bare feet through the snow as a sign of humility. They say many in his entourage have also removed their shoes."

"That's preposterous," grunted Gregory. Looking at Muehler with curiosity, he said, "And your thoughts on that, Muehler?"

Muehler scratched his chin. "Our agents, on the other hand, also report that upon leaving each town, Heinrich and company get back in their coaches until the next town, then remove their shoes again and walk."

"S-o, it's all for show, huh?" snorted Gregory. "Just another reason to keep him outside the gate!"

Matilda and Hugh exchanged looks. Then Matilda said, "Muehler, please tell Heinrich that Hugh and I shall see him shortly. Alone, no diplomats."

"Yes, Countess," replied Muehler, turning to leave the room.

"No, Mathilda!" complained Gregory, showing displeasure. "You are ill advised to meet with a serpent!"

"We must at least hear him out," replied Matilda with certainty.

"I agree," added Hugh.

Gregory uttered a sigh of frustration and shrugged. "Then beware his trickery. I tell you now, he and Archbishop Guibert have troops hidden everywhere, for they play at deception!"

"We'll take care," said Matilda. Signaling to Tristan, she said, "Dearest, could you keep the Holy Father company while we speak to the King?"

Finding himself alone in the presence of the Pope, Tristan attempted to say something, but his words tumbled out in an incomprehensible jumble.

This seemed to amuse Gregory a tad, because he nearly smiled. "Well then, lad" he said, "tell me a bit about yourself and why you wish to become a monk."

***

Matilda and Hugh greeted Heinrich just outside the gates of the fortress. Seeing them, Heinrich rushed forward and embraced both. He was a handsome man, young and of good stature. "My sweet cousin Matilda!" he cried. "And Godfather Hugh! What fortune to see you here. God's generosity alone has brought you both here to assist my pleas for forgiveness from the Holy Father!"

Regardless of one's station in life, being snared in the midst of a blood-feud between friends or family creates confusion and discomfort. Accordingly, Matilda and Hugh had both struggled in navigating their way through the hopeless rift between King Heinrich and Pope Gregory. Matilda, despite all the philosophical, military and financial support she had thrown toward the Pope, was still related through blood to Heinrich. She also, as a royal, understood his responsibilities and obligations to subjects and country. This aside, she had since childhood felt an odd affection toward Heinrich despite his impossible pride and shortfalls.

For Abbot Hugh, this schism had already cost him the allegiance of German archbishops and cardinals, many of whom he had known for decades. Hugh's political hemorrhage also included losing the German nobility of Heinrich's camp as well as many in Rome and northern Italy. Nonetheless, Hugh also held affection for Heinrich. "Ah, my poor godson!" he said. "Bless you in these troubled times!"

Heinrich dropped his arms to his side, gazing at his feet. "I come with a heavy heart," he lamented. "I have committed a serious grievance against the Holy Father and the Holy Church. The fact that both of you have taken his part hurts also. Yet, it has shed light on my own misjudgment." Raising his eyes, he began to weep. "I pray now that you will speak on my behalf to Pope Gregory. Oh, this dreadful excommunication! I am lost with the doors of God's Church closed to me."

Listening, Mathilda's heart began to swell, having never imagined the fierce Heinrich in such a piteous state. "I want to believe you, Cousin," she said, "but Gregory has reason to doubt you after Nuremburg. Still, I will speak on your behalf." Looking over at Hugh, she added, "And I believe the good Abbot will also. But you have created a great disturbance, Heinrich, and dragged half the continent into this fire with you."

"I know, I know!" Heinrich snapped. "I should be flogged, dragged about the streets of Rome itself. And I would have it done, if I thought it would help. But only you and Abbot Hugh can reverse the wheel now, restore peace to the land. You are the only voices on this earth that can sway the stone-willed Gregory. He despises me, you know, and always has!" Falling to his knees, he began to sob again while kissing and tugging at the hem of Matilda's garment.

This act, so unexpected and contrite, brought Matilda to tears. She understood the extreme depth of Heinrich's predicament. He was not weeping just for himself or his loss of power and entitlement, he was weeping for his country, the German clerics, and tens of thousands of others who now suddenly stood to lose everything to the Saxon princes and Pope Gregory.

As Matilda's tears streamed, Hugh's eyes also began to dampen because he loved la Gran Contessa as he would a daughter. "For the sake of peace" he said, "and because it is God's will, we will try to help, Heinrich."

Heinrich stood, still bawling like a lost child. "Heaven be praised that God has provided us two saints as pure as the two of you in this life!" Dabbing his eyes, he held his forehead in his palm. "I will, in prayer, await your word on the Holy Father's judgment."

***

Over the next two days Matilda and Hugh sought to sway Gregory toward absolution for Heinrich, but Gregory responded with bitterness and acrimony, even flying into a rage. "Would you thus betray me in favor of your foul cousin!" he cried furiously at one point to Matilda. And to Hugh he exclaimed, "Would you throw me to this wolf and allow the Holy Church to crumble beneath Heinrich's boot?"

By the third day of Heinrich's arrival, Gregory was exhausted by continuous supplication from Matilda and Hugh, as well as by opposing supplication from others insisting he continue to shun the King. In a fit of frustration, Gregory threw his hands above his head and shouted, "I will consider absolving Heinrich only on the condition that he surrender his crown forever and resign the royal dignity!!"

This proclamation brought cheers from Heinrich's opponents within the fortress who thought this edict spelled the end for King Heinrich. But the ever hopeful Abbot Hugh heard something in this proclamation that others did not. Ignoring the first part of Gregory's demand involving Heinrich 'surrendering his crown forever', Hugh focused only on the second part, which involved 'resigning the royal dignity'. He knew Heinrich would rather fight and be slain than surrender his crown. Yet, Hugh reasoned, this dance of death between King and Pope, despite the grandiosity of its scope, was in fact simply a dispute between two men. And men, concluded Hugh, did not actually wish to hasten their own end, which was now exactly the point to which Heinrich and Gregory had arrived.

Thus convinced, Hugh went down to the village at the foot of the mountain and translated Pope Gregory's angry public proclamation to Heinrich, who responded by becoming infuriated. But Hugh delved into semantics, emphasizing the human capacity to work through even the most complex of circumstances through the power of 'gestures'.

When Hugh had concluded this lengthy lecture, Heinrich nodded. Though this nod was laden with skepticism, it also signified a degree of resignation. "Well then," Heinrich sighed, looking at Abbot Hugh with a glimmer of hope, "I shall, as always, follow your wise counsel."

***

As darkness and the faint glimmer of dawn stars began to fade on the morning of January 25th, Tristan was aroused from his sleep by what he thought was the voice of his mother calling him from another room. Coming fully awake and crawling from the bed, he realized he was but dreaming. Disappointed, he dressed and ventured out to the fortress ramparts where he was met with a light snowfall. Thinking to hear a faint voice directly below the rampart, he leaned over the wall to peer down into the inner court standing between the main outer gate and a secondary inner gate. Standing there was a lone man, bearded, mumbling to himself.

Despite the freezing temperature and the snow, the man was clothed only in a common hair-shirt and wool trousers. To Tristan's greater surprise, the man was bareheaded and wore no shoes. Tristan thought it to be Peter the Hermit, but on closer examination concluded that this man was more clean-shaven with neatly cropped hair. Whomever this poor soul was, it was evident that winter was taking its toll; the man's face was whitish-blue from the freezing wind, and his lips had turned a ghostly purple color. Tristan also saw the man's shoulders shaking as in the thrall of seizures. What pained Tristan the most was the sight of the man's bare feet standing atop the ice that had glazed over the cobblestones of the small court.

Tristan stared on, entranced. He wished to call out and offer a blanket or some other cover, but remained silent on realizing the man was praying. Shortly more guards appeared along the rampart, along with a few dignitaries who had received word about someone standing bareheaded and barefoot in the snow. As they gawked at the sight below, some pointed while others exchanged whispers and comments. All appeared appalled.

Tristan wedged his way through the knot of onlookers, nudging back to the edge of the rampart. Suddenly, the woman standing beside him began to sob. "Oh, but I can't bear to watch this horror! No king should endure such suffering, not even Heinrich!"

"Ha!" snapped a priest standing nearby. "He reaps his own harvest. No king is above God. I pray Heinrich freezes to death where he stands!"

King? thought Tristan, thunderstruck. *Was this pitiful figure below really the fearsome King Heinrich who had raised his hand against the Pope and Christendom? Was this the man Pope Gregory suspected of coming to take him prisoner?*

Soon Abbot Hugh, Countess Matilda and Muehler arrived with a small entourage led by Pope Gregory, who was now clothed in full papal regalia. *Gregory now cuts an extremely regal figure,* thought Tristan. Indeed, Gregory now reflected every part of his high office. As he worked his way through the crowd, onlookers opened a swath before him, bowing and crossing themselves. When he reached the wall, Gregory leaned forward and glowered. "Oh, Heinrich, I see you there!" he shouted. "But what mischief are you about now?"

Heinrich gazed upward and fell to his knees with outstretched palms. "Oh, Holy Father," he implored in a tremulous voice, "I beseech you, mercy on this poor sinner! I beg your forgiveness for my trespasses!"

Countess Matilda took Gregory by the arm, huddling against his shoulder. "Such a pitiful sight," she sighed, shaking her head. "It hurts to see my cousin in such a state of suffering. Can you not see that he's in earnest in his quest for absolution?"

But it was Muehler who responded. "Don't be deceived, Your Grace. If I were about to lose everything in this world, I too would stand barefoot in the snow for a few minutes to improve my position! This is but theater to save his crown!"

"Humph!" grunted Gregory. "You are correct. He fooled me at Nuremburg, but never again."

"This is different from Nuremburg," pressed Matilda. "No man would endure such humiliation and agony were his actions not straight from the heart. End this now, Holiness, and welcome him back!"

"Humph!" Gregory snorted again, turning to leave the wall. "Muehler, keep an eye to Heinrich and his troops below the mount. Sound the alarm should they advance."

"Holy Father, My Pope!" cried Heinrich on seeing Gregory taking his leave. "Don't thus forsake your lamb! I will wait here and fast until either forgiven, or the arrival of my own death!"

This plea fell on deaf ears as Gregory left the rampart and instructed his entourage to follow. "Enough of this horrid spectacle," he muttered.

Matilda remained at the wall, and just as Tristan was about to follow the others, she caught him by his coat sleeve. "Stay here with me," she said, taking his hand, "and pray that God might yet soften Gregory's heart."

Pope Gregory, now in a foul mood after seeing Heinrich, decided to separate from his entourage for the solitude of his private chambers. He had no wish to be hounded by the inevitable chatter of a dining hall aroused by the drama of Heinrich in the snow. Hugh tried to accompany him, but Gregory brushed him aside. "Hugh, you will only continue pleading for Heinrich," he sniffed, "so leave me in peace."

Heinrich's appearance in the court quickly created upheaval within the fortress, becoming the sole source of conversation. Although those within Matilda's castle supported papacy over crown, these conversations often grew heated; some believed Heinrich's actions indicated sincere submission to the Pope while others smelled a ploy. Yet others were confused and floundered from one side to the other, then back again.

Tristan and Matilda remained at the rampart all morning on their knees in prayer while Muehler and two soldiers stood nearby, watching the castle approach. "Suppose his troops'll come up?" one of the guards asked.

"No, that'd be folly," replied Muehler, "especially with Heinrich trapped in the court between the two gates."

The guard laughed. "Yeah, hell of a bad position! But you know, I can't believe he's still standing there. Thought he'd give it up after an hour or so. Didn't you?"

Muehler nodded. "Yeah, I was sure of it. Just look at his damn feet! But he'll pass out soon and his bunch'll drag him off and it'll all be done."

But Heinrich did not pass out. To all's bewilderment, as the sun settled and darkness approached, Heinrich was still standing in the court. Finally, attendants covered him with blankets and pried his feet lose from the ice. Lifting him to their cradled arms, they carried him to a wagon awaiting outside the main gate and moved him down to the village.

This caused many in the evening dining hall to crow. "Aha, it's over!" they exclaimed. "Heinrich's gone now and the Holy Father prevails!" Such talk aroused anger from certain quarters; Heinrich's perseverance was admired by some. Listening to the ongoing debate, Abbot Hugh remained silent. Conversely, Countess Matilda made it clear that she believed Heinrich's high degree of suffering that day was an unquestionable act of contrition.

"Perhaps so," replied a dour cardinal, "but the sinner has now returned down the mount, seeing that he's been defeated by the will of our Holy Pope. Heinrich will return to Germany in the morning to await his fate amongst the Saxon princes. God be praised!"

But Heinrich did not return to Germany that next morning. To the astonishment of all, as dawn's winter sun cracked the horizon, Heinrich was standing again within the two gates in hair-shirt and wool trousers, bare-headed and bare-footed. And as the cruel mountain wind cleared the ramparts, blustering down into the court, it ruffled Heinrich's sparse garments and lifted his hair in tufts, causing Countess Matilda to break down. "Oh, not another day of such suffering!" she sobbed. "Men have frozen to death in lesser conditions!"

"He said that he would seek forgiveness or his own death," said a guard standing nearby. "I didn't believe him yesterday, but today I—"

"He cannot possibly survive another day!" interrupted Matilda. "Quick, someone go gather the Pope to end this!"

As she said this, Gregory happened to arrived, having heard that Heinrich was back in the court. Going to the wall, he glowered down at Heinrich. "It is not God's will that you die!" he shouted. "End your foolishness and return to Germany!"

"Forgive me, Holy Father, I beseech you," moaned Heinrich, raising his eyes to the ramparts, "or my death is by your own hands! And perhaps you should know, Your Grace, I feel its icy fingers approaching. But I would rather come to my own death than offend you any further in this life!"

"Humph!" Gregory snorted. Turning, he left the wall, which caused Heinrich's head to drop to his chest in defeat. But as Gregory left, his own immovable conviction of the day before was rattled. "That fool intends to martyr himself," he hissed, confounded by Heinrich's persistence. "They will point to me after his death and accuse me of lacking all humanity!"

This was precisely the direction taken by certain elements within the fortress. "The Pope is murdering the King," some grumbled. "Heinrich's blood will be on the Pope's hands," others claimed. Still, most continued to support Gregory's firm stance.

As the day dragged on and onlookers shuttled back and forth, it became more and more evident that Heinrich had no intention of surrendering his painful vigil in the cold. It also became evident that the weather was worsening, endangering Heinrich even more. Still, he stood there like some ghostly apparition, his eyes and face appearing already dead. At several points during the late afternoon, some actually pronounced Heinrich deceased. "Look," they clamored, "no breath coming from his mouth. He's frozen to death where he stands!"

Yet somehow Heinrich survived that second day in the court. Near nightfall, his attendants appeared again, covered him and took him to the village.

Most within the fortress were relieved that Heinrich had not perished that day, including even some of the King's bitter enemies. These enemies, like Gregory, did not wish to see Heinrich become memorialized as a martyr.

Matilda and Hugh celebrated Heinrich's survival by attending mass in the Cathedral of Saint Nicholas within the fortress. As Tristan sat next to them, he tried to balance how this duel of wills might end. He wanted the Pope to prevail in this war against the crown, but he also had no wish to see harm come to Heinrich.

So it was that night that everyone within the fortress was content for one reason or another that Heinrich had survived. More than ever, they were now also convinced that, in the morning, Heinrich would appear at the gate to inform all that he was withdrawing to Germany. Yes, he would appear in royal regalia making some haughty announcement either blaspheming or threatening the Pope.

But when the fortress awoke, they discovered Heinrich yet again standing in the court at prayer; hair-shirt, wool trousers, bare head and bare feet. And as word quickly circulated, nearly all who heard found it beyond belief. No one was more bewildered than Pope Gregory.

The climactic moment of all great, historical events has always been well documented and noted, but it is often forgotten that the actual wellspring of that climactic moment is usually little more than a series of ill defined minor occurrences that build, one upon the other, until circumstances eventually become untenable or intolerable for all involved. At that point, due to some irreversible catalyst, the avalanche suddenly begins to career down the mountain. Such was the case on that third day of Heinrich's appearance in the court.

The roots of his self-inflicted penance in the snow had actually sprouted years before on Hildebrand's ascendency to the Vatican as Pope Gregory. These fledgling roots were then nurtured by a series of philosophical disputes which augmented into verbal and political posturing that, ultimately, escalated into a war that placed King Heinrich on the defensive against the Pope and the Saxon princes.

History has not recorded what it was precisely that altered Pope Gregory's compass on January 28th of 1077, the day after Heinrich's third day of penance in the court. It may have been the entreaties of Countess Matilda and Abbot Hugh, or fear of contributing to Heinrich's death, or political expediency, or even an unexpected attack of altruism leading Gregory to an act of personal charity. Regardless, Gregory's original position of 'no compromise' collapsed, and the stern, old Pope suddenly offered ground. Upon the condition that Heinrich promised to abide by the Pope's decision as arbiter with the Saxon princes, and with Heinrich's agreement to grant the Pope and his deputies protection on their continued journey north to Augsburg, and Heinrich's promise to abstain from exercising the functions of royalty, Gregory offered to lift the ban of excommunication and promote Heinrich's reconciliation with the Saxon nobility.

Heinrich joyfully promised to meet these conditions as two bishops and several noblemen, on his behalf, swore on sacred relics that he would keep the agreement. Abbot Hugh, who as a monk could not swear, also pledged his word before the all-seeing God that Heinrich would abide by his word. Then he, the bishops, the nobles, the Countesses Matilda and Adelheid signed the written agreement.

After completion of these preliminaries, the inner gate was flung open and Heinrich advanced, throwing himself at the feet of the gray-haired pope. Bursting into tears, he sobbed, "Spare me, Holy Father, spare me!" This moved the entire company to tears; even the iron-willed Gregory began to show signs of tenderness.

Tristan, perched high along a rampart, watched this entire series of events in wonderment. It was a scene that he would replay in his mind a thousand times over years to come because it's implications defied reality, proving that what one believes to be unthinkable is indeed, thinkable. There, before his very eyes, the powerful and proud King Heinrich, in the prime of his life, as the most powerful emperor in all of Europe, had been reduced to weeping at the foot of the Pope, who was himself but a man of small stature and low origin—yet had managed through his will alone to humble an entire empire.

Gregory, with Heinrich still on his knees, next heard Heinrich's confession, after which he raised him up from the ground, embraced him and bestowed both absolution and his apostolic blessing. The entire party then moved to the Chapel of Saint Nicholas where Gregory sealed this reconciliation through the celebration of the sacrifice of the mass. Mass completed, Pope Gregory entertained Heinrich and his legates at a formal dinner. Upon evening's end, he dismissed Heinrich with several fatherly counsels and a final apostolic blessing.

***

After the reconciliation with Pope Gregory, Heinrich withdrew from Canossa for other parts of northern Italy. Meanwhile, the Saxon princes had been gathering in Augsburg, anxious for the Pope to arbiter the selection of a new German king on February 2nd. When word reached them that Gregory had holed up at Canossa, then, of all things, forgiven Heinrich and retracted the excommunication, they fell into stunned chaos. Nonetheless, recovering from their shock and overcoming bitter dispute, most still felt it paramount that Pope Gregory help them select a new German king. But to their added dismay, Pope Gregory cancelled his trip to Augsburg and remained in Tuscany with Countess Matilda. Worse yet, he fell completely silent on the topic of selecting a new king.

Abbot Hugh, now having no purpose in continuing to his original destination of Augsburg, directed his teamsters to pack and made back for France.

***

During their return, Tristan had many questions, the primary of which was why Pope Gregory had seen fit to reconcile with Heinrich, his most bitter enemy and the greatest threat in all Europe to Church autonomy. Tristan also wanted to know how this unexpected reconciliation would play out since a state of war still existed between Heinrich and the Saxon nobles.

Abbot Hugh was impressed with the depth of Tristan's curiosity, and was more than pleased to address the boy's questions, most probably because it gave the high monk an opportunity to himself consider the mystery. "In the end," Hugh sighed, "it is my hope that peace will prevail and that order will be restored throughout Germany and northern Italy."

"But what about the Saxon princes?" Tristan insisted. "Will they now simply lay down their arms?"

"They might if the Holy Father commands it."

"And what about King Heinrich?" Tristan pressed. "Will he keep the pledges he so humbly made in the court of Canossa?"

Hugh stared out thoughtfully at the passing drifts of snow, launching into reflection. Finally he said, "My signature on the document he signed says he will comply, as does that of Countess Matilda and the others. The Holy Father has, despite his deepest fears, welcomed Heinrich back into the Church and allowed him to partake in the sacraments again. This was a bargain struck in God's name. So yes, I expect Heinrich to keep his bond."

***

Several weeks later, many of the Saxon princes who had been awaiting Pope Gregory at Augsburg grew impatient and assembled with other opponents of Heinrich at Forcheim on March 13th. Without Gregory's authority or permission, they offered the German crown to Rudolph, Duke of Swabia, Heinrich's brother-in-law. Rudolph accepted the crown on March 26th at Mainz from Archbishop Siegfried, but the omens turned bad immediately. During the coronation mass, the consecrated oil ran short and the Gospel was read by a deacon who practiced simony. Then the citizenry began to form mobs, raising such violence that Rudolph and Archbishop Siegfried had to flee by night.

Still in Italy, Heinrich became infuriated by this action of his Saxon enemies, immediately demanding that Pope Gregory excommunicate Rudolph, the robber of his crown. Gregory refused. Heinrich retaliated by beginning to act as king again, which directly violated the pledge he had made on his knees at Canossa. Next, Heinrich crossed the Alps with his troops into Germany and renewed his war against the Saxon princes.

Pope Gregory, meanwhile, refused to become embroiled in this new outbreak of war and insisted on maintaining papal neutrality. This further alienated Heinrich who had been counting on the Pope to sway the Saxons into accepting him as king. Worse yet, Gregory's neutral stance also now infuriated the very Saxon princes who had previously comprised his base of support.

Hearing of these developments, Abbot Hugh collapsed, utterly devastated by Heinrich's breach of promise, especially since he himself had vouched for Heinrich's word to the Holy Father, both verbally and in writing. He was also severely wounded by Gregory's indecision and failure to act. "Oh, how is it possible that Gregory could allow such deterioration to occur!" he lamented to Odo behind closed doors. "Gregory had everything he has so earnestly sought all these years at the very tip of his fingers right there in the court of Canossa! How could he let it slip away so quickly?"

Odo, who held neither respect nor affection for Heinrich, placed all blame on the German king. "Heinrich was not to be trusted from the very beginning," he replied dryly, shaking his head. "Gregory should have never lifted Heinrich's excommunication. His mistake was trusting a serpent!"

"But Gregory pledged to work on Heinrich's behalf in reconciling with the Saxon princes!" insisted Hugh. "Instead, Gregory remained in Tuscany, and after returning to Rome, continues to remain silent on the issue!"

Odo looked at Hugh with raised brow. "Surely you do not question the Holy Father, Hugh. Gregory has dedicated his life to freeing the Church from the boots of kings. God must always come before a king. No, only Heinrich is to blame here! He is like a wild boar loosened upon the village."

Hugh dropped his head in discouragement. "I thought things were settled at Canossa, but now the blood flows again and things are worse than before. I—"

"Divest yourself of your godson, Hugh," said Odo, "he refutes God's will. If the Church is to prevail, then you must shed your affection for him and stand squarely with Gregory."

Hugh placed his palm to his forehead and shrugged. "Indeed," he lamented, "all middle ground has vanished. Oh, but hope is such a fleeting thing!"

This deterioration of political events hounded Hugh through the remainder of winter and well into the spring. His urgings on behalf of Heinrich at Canossa had turned out to be a huge personal miscalculation. Although Heinrich, now chasing the Saxon lords about Germany, was thankful that Abbot Hugh had taken his part at the fortress, many of Hugh's supporters and friends began to doubt him.

In the end, the entire Canossa affair had become a costly hemorrhage to the revered high monk, and raised questions among many about his motives.

For Tristan, Canossa also became a seminal moment. Aside from being exposed to many of the main characters of the European stage, he learned first-hand how drama can force a sudden shift of the pendulum. As news filtered into Cluny about King Heinrich's newly successful war against the Saxon princes and about Pope Gregory's lack of action, Tristan began to see that Pope Gregory's forgiveness at Canossa was a huge mistake. He also understood Abbot Hugh's role in opening this Pandora's Box, which taught Tristan that even the most brilliant of political or spiritual leaders could be deceived through 'emotion'.

Chapter Twenty-Seven

Mathilda

Amongst other things, Canossa opened a new door to Tristan: the entry into the world of la Gran Contessa Matilda. As promised, that spring Matilda sent word to Cluny that she expected to have the Wonder of Cluny and his younger brother spend a month of summer with her in Tuscany. Thus, as the other boys of the Dorter departed for their homes that summer, Tristan and Guillaume boarded a coach for Tuscany.

Upon their arrival at Canossa, Matilda and her entourage met them with great fanfare. As Tristan stepped from the coach, Matilda ran to him, burying him with affection. "Ah, my handsome nephew!" she cooed. "And *this* must be your beautiful young brother!" She then grabbed Guillaume and pulled him to her breast, rocking him back and forth with the strength of a hardened field hand.

Guillaume, struck dumb, tried to return the hug but found that she had so completely wrapped him in this bearhug that he was unable to move. He next attempted to issue a greeting, but was so completely engulfed in Matilda's bosom that he could scarcely manage a sound. His helplessness did not go unnoticed by Matilda's servants and friends, and forced a round of laughter from the crowd. Matilda then led the boys into the dining hall where a sumptuous feast of mutton, pheasant, quail and freshly caught trout awaited.

It quickly became apparent to Mathida's court that the arrival of the two young Saint-Germains was a moment of delight for the Countess, as testified to by the animation and happiness the boys brought out in her persona. When certain women take it upon themselves to throw their wing over children they perceive to be unfortunate, these women become clucking hens of protection and pride. Such became the case for la Gran Contessa as she showered the boys with gifts and attention such as her acquaintances and servants had never seen.

The summer of 1077, then, was memorable for both Tristan and Guillaume. It also did much to re-cement their fraternal relationship, which had been flagging in Cluny. As the Countess was extremely pious, the brothers began each morning attending mass with Mathilda in the Cathedral of Saint Nicholas. From there, Tristan and Guillaume kept themselves occupied within the fortress while the Countess tended to business and politics. Nonetheless, she reserved most afternoons for the boys, periodically packing wagons to take them on excursions to her other estates scattered throughout Tuscany.

Guillaume, had not ventured beyond the walls of Cluny since his arrival there. Now nine, he was awestruck by the wealth that suddenly lay open to his eyes. He would frequently nudge Tristan to point out certain furnishings and decorative features within the manors they frequented. Tristan, more accustomed to such environments, pretended for his brother's sake to be impressed.

Mathilda was surprised to learn that Guillaume possessed a good knowledge of horses and all things relating to them, including a background he had picked up in Cluny about the manufacture, repair and maintenance of riding equipment. As an avid rider, huntress and militarist, Matilda held horses in high esteem, and marveled at how one so young could have already absorbed so much knowledge about horsemanship. Impressed, she granted him open access to her stables, allowing him to ride her horses, which constituted the most exceptional horseflesh in all of Italy. She also took him on her many hunts and taught him the finer points of hawking, tracking stag and rousting wild boar. As he displayed unexpected acumen with both bow and spear, she then introduced him to Vincente Morelli, her private weapons trainer. "Teach him the sword," she instructed. "He's a natural!"

Among the most gifted men-at-arms in all Europe, Morelli tutored only high nobles. Nevertheless, he agreed to work with Guillaume and found the boy to be unusually coordinated and athletic for a nine-year-old. "Quick and agile," Morelli reported to Countes Mathilda, "and showing unbelievable promise. He will be deadly one day."

Pleased by this report, she pulled Guillaume aside one day to inquire how he liked working with Morelli.

"Oh, he is the greatest swordsman in all the world," responded Guillaume, beaming. "I wish I could grow to be as skillful as him in all arms." But then his smile vanished, replaced by a wistful frown. "But I'm afraid I will be stuck tending to farm animals instead of fighting beside knights."

"Oh? And why is that, Guillaume?" asked Matilda.

"Well, Auntie, you know Tristan and I have no home except Cluny and have been denied by our mother's new husband, Lord Desmond DuLac. Unlike the other boys of the Stable Cohort at Cluny, I don't have a noble father to sponsor me."

Matilda felt the boy's regret beating at her heart. Grasping his hand, she shook it a little. "*I* shall be your sponsor then!" she said. "You shall return here to Canossa each summer to ride, hunt and learn about all forms of arms and weaponry. And when you turn fourteen, I shall put you forward as a squire. When of age, into knighthood you'll go. I'll dub you…well let's think a moment." Pausing, she put her fingers to her lips, closing her eyes, while Guillaume stared at her with anticipation. "Ah, yes," she continued, "I shall dub you the Dangerous Sir Guy, short for

Guillaume. You'll become one of my fierce Golden Knights of Tuscany!"

This sent Guillaume's heart soaring and he grabbed Matilda about the waist, entering into a wild dance encircling her torso. "Sir Guy the Dangerous!" he cried. "Oh, beware you troublesome outlaws!"

Guillaume's dance nearly knocked Matilda over, which she found to be amusing. *Ah,* she thought, laughing, *such a different creature than my lad, Tristan, this one!*

Tristan had little interest in horses, hunting or weaponry, and was content to remain at Canossa digging through its massive library, which rivaled even that of Cluny. He also enjoyed discussing religion and politics with the many noble guests streaming through Matilda's various Tuscany palaces. These guests were invariably taken aback by the boy's knowledge of affairs, both temporal and spiritual. Before long, they found themselves engrossed in profound exchanges with the eleven-year-old prodigy.

It was with sadness in mid-August that Guillaume and Tristan loaded into their coach to return to France. The Countess, herself, appeared rather distraught as she closed the coach door, so when tears began to stream down Guillaume's face, she, too, became weepy. "Oh, boys, no tears, please! I'll see you again soon!"

As the coach jostled and bounced its way out of sight, Guillaume was inconsolable, snuffling and pouting for the better part of that entire day as the coach moved west. Though Tristan had thoroughly enjoyed this pleasant sojourn in Tuscany, he was ready to resume his studies. He dearly missed Grand Prior Odo, and longed to be in his shadow once more.

Chapter Twenty-Eight

The Unraveling

The brutal winter of 1076-77 sweeping over the continent during King Heinrich's penance at Canossa also created severe hardship in England. As Heidi the Elder had predicted, much sickness struck the villagers of DuLacshire. With the assistance of Lady Asta, the old woman spent a good deal of time tending to the women and children, the masons, the field hands and DuLac's troops. Asta became indispensable in these efforts, and by doing so, continued to gain favor among the Saxons.

Yet, there seemed to be a sadness about Asta that winter, as detected by both Orla and Heidi the Elder. Asta had never been demonstrative, but she now became even more remote as winter continued. Orla at first attributed this to fatigue incurred by her tireless devotion to nursing duties alongside the old Saxon woman. But as the weather hardened and the season extended, he decided the real root of this remoteness was the continued absence of her two sons. The boys had now been gone four years, and even though Asta seldom mentioned them, Orla often caught her sitting alone, gazing into space, her eyes carrying that desolate grief of those in mourning.

Elder Heidi also suspected the loss of Asta's sons was responsible for Asta's descent, but only partially. The old healer recognized that Asta's demise was more complex. Elder Heidi had endured much over time and had a keen eye for bitterness. She recognized in Asta that numb, womanly stare incurred by the ceaseless infliction of one defeat after another in life. Asta's real demise, in Elder Heidi's estimation, centered around the fact that outside circumstances had year upon year forced and shaped every turn of her existence. The effects of this slow suffocation were now finally conspiring to erode her personal resolve.

It had been a slow process, supposed the old woman, *that probably began with the execution of the girl's beloved father, then deepened after being forced into a loveless marriage devised to meet the Bastard's political ends. From there her husband's treachery had forced disgrace and denouncement, which in turn precipitated a second loveless marriage devised of necessity. In Desmond DuLac, Asta had purchased a future for her boys through the Black Monks of Cluny, but also now endured the denunciation of her sons by her new husband and was suffering from a crushing guilt. Indeed,* concluded Elder Heidi, *Asta was grappling with many, many personal demons.*

Elder Heidi was on the mark. Time and the futility of Asta's past were conspiring to sap the very strength that had carried her through previous difficulties. In past years, she had pushed herself beyond life's snares through prayer. But now, added to these interminable trials by fire that God had thrust upon her, there arose yet one more impossible assault on her heart, the gamekeeper, Jack Forest.

After his return from Scotland and throughout that entire winter, he frequently consumed her thoughts. And she, his. Knowing that such an impossible relationship could only foster disaster, she fought to refute these emotions. Jack was in the same predicament and deliberately steered clear of the castle whenever possible, choosing instead to spend the cold months alone working DuLac's woodlands in order to stave off temptation. But starvation only exacerbates hunger, so he found himself thinking of her every moment of every day. Sensing her deep isolation and sadness, he felt even closer to her because he also very much suffered from a profound loneliness brought on by personal loss and inability to drive his own future.

That two people of such utterly different thread as Lady Asta and Jack the gamekeeper could fall in love is one of those impenetrable enigmas of the human soul. Such couplings defy all reason, as well as the established order of things. Moreover, the continued pursuit of such relationships breeds chaos and even, in many cases, threatens self-preservation. Still, the nascence and pursuit of impossible love has occurred throughout history because, in every man and woman born onto this earth, regardless of stature or station, there exists in the heart a secret backwater of hope.

Jack and Asta were both drifting into these backwaters, each realizing that imminent peril awaited just beneath the surface. Both also knew that backwaters die from lack of oxygen, invariably stagnating because still waters choke off life with a black, covering of scum. Thus they both saw, with bitterness, that to come together would cause an unraveling of their very existence as well as of everyone and everything around them. They determined, then, that it would be better to suffer in isolation through this cruel winter than to risk having the earth collapse beneath their feet.

***

Desmond DuLac knew well that all men could not help but fall under the spell of the beautiful Asta, and desire her. This was actually a source of pride for him because he knew he possessed the most beautiful woman in all of Europe. Yet, he could have never in his wildest ravings imagined that Lady Asta now dreamed of the lowly gamekeeper. Thus lost in his own fog, DuLac's attention was entirely focused on maintaining his high position and going about the duties befitting a prosperous earl of the English countryside.

His top priority now was to finally complete the stonework of the castle, so upon the onset of the spring thaw he sent word to surrounding burghs that he was enlisting additional stone masons and laborers. Within weeks so many men seeking work appeared from all over the countryside that he had to turn many away. Even housing the ones he kept became an issue, forcing him to construct new huts and shanties. During this process, he decided to rename the village in his honor with a formal ceremony. With much fuss and festivity, he carried out this self-serving effort. What he and the French had referred to for years as simply 'the village' was now renamed 'DuLacville', in his honor.

DuLac's other major project as spring arrived was the state of his woodlands, which involved Jack Forest. The harsh winter had decimated many of the large hardwood thickets where he enjoyed his best hunting; much fallen timber now lay strewn about the forest floor creating hazards to both men and horses engaged in the fleet pursuit of game. Moreover, during recent forays through his woodlands, DuLac noticed a dearth of stag, boar, fox and pheasant.

"What the hell's happened to my wildlife out here, Jack?" he asked, storming up to the gamekeeper's shanty with an armed escort one morning. Sitting pompously astride his horse with both fists on his hip as posing for a portrait, he cried, "Holy Christ, man, it must be that you've been lax on the goddamned poachers this winter!"

Jack, who was shaving his ax-head against a millstone, looked up, much wishing to lodge the implement he was sheering straight into the Frenchman's skull. "No, sire," he said, "I've held them at bay even though they starve. It's winter that's taken a toll on your game. I've lived here my entire life and never recall such severe conditions as we just came through. The bigger issue, though, is predators. Three large wolf-packs have moved into your territory over the winter and they're devouring everything they cross."

DuLac scowled. "Well, *you're* the goddamn game-keeper, so tell me what's to be done. Shit, this summer I'll be hosting a good number of Norman dignitaries and churchmen. I've been touting my woodlands as a prime hunting zone. So, Christ, it won't do to be scant in game!"

"We'll need to clear out the wolves then or they'll cut into your spring breeding stock," replied Jack. "When I was younger, we once had an unusually destructive infestation of wolves here, even to the point of attacking the farmers. My father organized the village and conducted a drive against them. I remember how he did it, but I'll need help and it'll take time. Wolves are wily. They avoid snares and can run all day long. We'll set up a chase-trap, camping men in groups throughout your woodlands at interception points. And then I'll lead a roving party and drive the wolves—"

"Holy Christ, I don't need the goddamned details!" interrupted DuLac, his voice dripping with condescension. Looking toward his escort to ensure they were watching, he said, "I don't really give a shit *how* you do it, Keeper, just get it done! I've been turning men away looking for stone-work at the castle by the flock, and still they come. So, go gather some up and get to it!" Then, for no apparent reason other than to make a show, he spurred his horse violently, trampling over Jack, and rode off as though charging into battle. Surprised, the men of his escort looked at each, shrugged, then set their horses at a gallop in chase.

Picking himself from the ground, Jack dusted his trousers. "Bastard!" he seethed. Returning to sharpening his ax, he began, begrudgingly, piecing together the details of how his father had rid the shire of wolves. As the memory collected itself, Jack's throat was still red with resentment at DuLac's treatment, which gnawed at Jack's effort to re-construct that wolf hunt of olden days. Thus entangled be-tween wolf strategy and resentment, he was suddenly stricken by a thought. Focusing on that thought, it began to occur to him that, if managed correctly, a trap to eliminate the wolves might also ensnare the French. The idea was thready and disconnected at first, but the more he thought, the faster his hands honed the ax blade. By the time the ax edge was razor thin, the concept had crystallized.

Setting the ax aside, he put a hand to the stubble of his chin and nodded to himself. *Aye, the end of my misery, and that of Lady Asta. And in the end, perhaps, she would flee to Scotland with me where we could both begin a new existence.*

***

Initially, on realizing the possibility of luring DuLac's occupation force into a trap under the guise of killing wolves, Jack was afire with anticipation. But as he began to engineer the details of the strategy, he began to identify barriers to the plan. First there was his son, Willy, and his mother, Elder Heidi. Even if Jack devised a means of overcoming the castle, the Normans would send an even larger force to retake it. Then there would come a bloody retribution.

There was also the issue of the Danes. Jack's hatred burned hotly for the French and the Normans whom he saw as the scourge of England. This hatred burned so violently that killing DuLac and his French troops was more important than keeping long-term possession of the castle itself. His mother was probably correct, conceded Jack. The conquest itself had rooted for keeps and was not going to be overturned. But if he could kill DuLac and wipe out his French troops, at least a portion of his raging personal fire would be assuaged and he could then flee north to Scotland, or even west to Ireland, taking his son and mother with him. Living as an exile could be no worse than ending his years as DuLac's lowly gamekeeper.

But how would the Danes come into play upon setting this gambit into motion?

Jack had by now come to accept them, in particular, Orla and Crowbones. Jack knew they held no loyalty to DuLac, so there existed the remote possibility they might even become complicit with Jack's plot. Yet the more Jack explored this idea, the more he thought of DuFresne, whom Orla and Crowbones had befriended, and to whom they both owed a huge debt. In the end, Jack could not see the two Danes turning on DuFresne even if they did despise DuLac.

These complexities aside, the greatest barrier to Jack's plan was Asta. He knew he was drawn to her more deeply than anything he had felt in years, and hoped she might feel the same, even though they had never spoken it—nor had they shared intimacy or carnal knowledge. But she was a married, and a devout woman of the Church, possessing a goodness and a purity that might be offended by Jack's conspiracy against her husband, DuLac. So, how *would* Asta react? Would she even consider a life of flight as a fugitive, or was she too accustomed to the fat life of French nobility? On the other hand, she might also see life without DuLac as a means of recovering her sons.

Thus Jack wrestled with himself day after day, trying to determine how others would be affected and how they would react upon the crossing of swords. He even imagined himself being killed during an assault on the castle, thinking this in itself would be a simple and acceptable outcome. But the more he thought of Asta, the more he wished to live.

After a week of driving himself in circles, he went to Elder Heidi and laid bare his thoughts. The old woman listened patiently without uttering a word. When he finished and gazed up at her for a response, she spoke. "Jack, it's a brilliant plan you have there to take the hill and end DuLac's reign of misery. And killing him and a few Frenchmen might well serve as a salve on your blistered soul, but *think*, your entire existence would be thrown to the wind. When the Normans show back up seeking blood, there'll be Hell to pay. Have you forgotten the Harrying?"

"No, mother, how could I?" he replied, his tired eyes turning ablaze at the mention of that hated word. "The rape, the burning, heads tumbling like apples from a storm-tossed tree. You weren't there to see, Mum, but I watched father get castrated, then gutted, set afire, then his charred corpse urinated upon!"

"I know. I heard of it from others. The horror has never left you, nor the hate."

"It was DuLac that held the knife, you know, and set the torch." At this, Jack's eyes watered and his shoulders shook. "Oh, but I *hate* that vermin."

"I know, Son. It's a black, boiling bile that's eaten at you a while now, Jack."

He looked at her, placing his hand over hers. "Do you not hate the Mole as much as I, Mother?"

"Aye, more even," she said. "I dream of a slow, hurtful death for that bastard, but not at the cost of you and Willy, or the village. God will see him punished one day, Jack."

"God?" asked Jack. "Ha! And where has He been these last ten years? I wonder, does God even exist? How could He allow such horrors?"

"Jack! Don't blaspheme!"

Jack settled back on his stool, shaking his head. "Will you follow me and Willy once it's done? I won't leave you here, you know."

"Go? But to what purpose? I don't have much longer in this world, Jack, and won't be dragged hither and yon in my final time. No, I'll not go."

At this Jack clenched his fists. "Dammit, Mum, please!"

She withdrew her hand from Jack's shoulder. "The one you'd best ask to go is up on the hill, Jack," she said.

"Huh?"

"Don't play stupid, Jack-boy," she said, a glint appearing in the corner of her eye. "I'm talking about Asta. If you could talk her into leaving with you, I'd say yes, put your plan into action, kill the Mole, and release the poison that's owned you all these years, then off to start a new life together. You, Willy and her."

"Oh, were it only that simple!" sighed Jack, his discouragement rising.

"Ha! It's more simple than you think, and more simple than *she* thinks. It's so simple I can't believe either of you have wasted a second thought on it! Aye, I've seen how you look at each other. Yes, it's simple—*you're* miserable, *she's* miserable. *You* despise the Mole, *she* despises the Mole. *You've* no future, *she's* no future. And you both hold the same dream. Ha! Where's the complexity in that, Jack? And so you know, I don't oppose your plan. I just don't want it to bury you. I helped you last time, didn't I? As long as I knew you and Willy would be away from the castle when Aengus attacked, I was for it. And the Lady Asta, I wanted her to be away also. She's a good soul, Jack, but a tormented one."

"But I don't dare tell her about any of this because I'm not sure what she'd do! If she informed—"

"Of course you can't tell her! If you did, even if she agreed, then she'd be part of the crime. No, Jack, at the final moment you just *take* her."

"Take her?"

"Yes, just throw her on a horse and off you go. You can sort things out later in Scotland. Jack, your plan to take the castle is brilliant, and it'll work. I've always been proud of your soldiering, as was your father and our good King Harold that was slain by that accursed arrow in the eye at Hastings, God rest his soul. And it'd be good for people in these parts to see dead Franks hanging off the wall again. Now go set your wheels in motion, boy, and may God be merciful."

***

Jacks's plot to overtake the castle was ingenious. He sent word across the border to Dumfries and managed to have his cousin, Harold, and Aengus slip south into the forests of DuLacshire to meet him at his shanty.

After hearing the plan, Aengus shook his head with approval. "Ah, a clever devil you are, Captain!" he exclaimed, winking at Harold.

"Your second, the Norseman, Alf," said Jack. "Might be best if you left him north for this one, Aengus."

"Eh?" Aengus replied. "Ha! All he's talked about since you left Dumfries is gutting those goddamned Danes. If I told him he couldn't come, I'd have to kill him or else he'd surely murder me first! No, he's coming, Jack. And like I told you, he's a damn good man to have when the blades come out."

Jack's plan required cool, calculating action, and he feared that Alf's temperament could create problems. Also, in the depths of his heart, Jack really didn't want Orla or Crowbones to end on the point of a sword even though they might well take to DuLac's banner in the end. Yet, Jack also understood Alf's thirst for revenge, and concluded that only fate could determine the outcome of the Norseman's score with the Danes, so he didn't argue with Aengus. "Very well," he said. "Now look, I need your army to start filtering into the forest four days from now, Aengus. I'll meet them at DuLac's boundary and show them where to camp. DuLac's brought a bunch of new men in to finish the castle, so seeing new faces about has become a frequent thing and won't raise any alarm."

Aengus nodded. "Be looking at the border then, Jack-boy. I'll have them pouring across in droves."

***

One week later, having already reviewed his strategy to DuLac once for eliminating the wolves, Jack met with DuLac again to report his progress. "I've hired men as instructed, Sire, and stationed them in the woods at a dozen locations, nine and ten to a camp."

"Holy Christ!" DuLac complained. "Why so many? Didn't you say three or four to a camp when you first talked to me about this?"

"I did, Sire, but the more men, the quicker we're done. I'll have them out within the week if things go right."

"Very well," snorted DuLac, "I suppose you know what the Hell you're doing, eh?"

"Indeed," Jack smiled, "I *do* know how to rid DuLacshire of wolves. But let me remind you, Lord DuLac, I'll also need the assistance of your horsemen on the day of the drive."

"Christ, you already have half the countryside enlisted to help with this thing! More yet you need?"

"I do. And one other thing I should tell you. These fellows I've hired are lowly and unkempt. I believe some of them have even been poaching while waiting for the drive to begin in two days even though we've provisioned them with grain and bread. That's why I wish to hurry this thing along and be done."

"Goddammit, Jack, they're supposed to be *saving* my game, not devouring it!"

"I know, Sire. But if you could spare about six or seven riders per camp to serve on the roving team, we'll be done in a day or so instead of a week."

"Six or seven riders per camp?" said DuLac. "Christ man, that's..." Performing quick calculation in his head, he looked at Jack and frowned, "That's more than seventy horse count!"

"Yes, Sire, but only for one day."

"I'll give you fifty horsemen, and I'm not happy about that," scowled DuLac. "Now tell me again about these roving teams again, Jack. How's it going to work?"

"The men I've hired are set in the woods at interception points. I've located the wolf dens, so the roving teams will drive the wolves from the dens. As the wolves split and run, the teams will drive the wolves into interception points, which is why I need your horsemen. Once the wolves are driven into the interception points, the help I've hired will be waiting with bow and lance to kill them."

"I see," nodded DuLac. "Sounds workable. But if you need so many roving teams, who'll be leading them? You're the only one familiar enough with the landscape."

"Of the rabble I've hired, I've picked a handful of the most reliable and shown them the routes we'll take."

"Are they horsemen?"

"Yes, Sire, but most have no means, therefore no horses. These men will double up with your own horsemen and direct the chase from behind the saddle."

"Well," clucked DuLac, "it seems you've thought of everything. It's a good strategy though I've never heard of wolf hunting being done in such a manner."

"Will you be accompanying us on the hunt, Sire?"

DuLac shook his head. "No. I'm having problems with my stone masons, so I'll remain on their backs here at the castle and leave the wolves to you." Jack bowed, then took what DuLac considered too long of a look back at him. "

Well," DuLac grunted, puzzled by Jack's lingering stare, "get about your business, Keeper, and be on your way!"

Chapter Twenty-Nine

The Reckoning

At dawn on the day of the wolf hunt, Jack led fifty horsemen out of the castle. Of these riders, there were only five Danes, including Fairhair and StraightLimbs. After reaching the bottom of the hill, Jack split them up into twelve roving teams of four or five riders each, turned them over to the men he had enlisted, and directed them into the forest.

Crowbones was standing atop the ramparts of the castle watching as the groups separated and disappeared into the thickets. "Orla" he said, "look to the west there just below the hill. See that flock of crows quarreling in the trees?"

"Ja."

"A troublesome omen for this hunt, don't you think?"

"Just birds fighting over perches," said Orla, disinterested.

Crowbones shook his head. "Do you not remember watching an entire flock of pitch-black ravens fighting and bickering atop a huge oak just before our charge at the Battle of Hastings? Minutes later blood flowed in rivers."

"Aye, I'd nearly forgotten that, Ivar. Ja, you said it was a bad omen at the time, but we *won* that day. So much for the ravens then, eh?"

"Ja, we won that day, but at such a cost. We lost half our Guard to the Saxon ax. And another thing, did you see the gamekeeper dispatching all those hunters below? It appears he leads easily and knows how to maneuver men, don't you think?"

"Aye, you've always thought he's more than just a woodsman."

Crowbones cupped his chin with a palm. "And when's the last time DuLac released over fifty cavalry through the gatehouse?"

"Not often that I can recall since we've been here. Why?"

"That's half of DuLac's cavalry," muttered Crowbones. "And though they're armed with sword and lance, they're bare of helmet and shield. Only leather tunics, hose, and caps."

"It's a damned hunt! It'd be ridiculous to wear battle gear in a chase."

"Ja," agreed Crowbones with reluctance, "but I feel strange about so much cavalry out and about, bare as babes."

"No worries. DuLac's still left with the other half of his cavalry, plus well over a hundred footmen within the walls, not to mention us of the Danish Guard." Then Orla chuckled. "And each of us is worth ten Frenchmen!"

"Ja, I suppose," Crowbones replied, his voice devoid of humor.

This caused Orla to survey his brother a moment. "Something nagging at you?" he asked.

"Just wondering about a few things. Have you ever heard of hunting wolves in such a fashion as Jack has set out, Orla?"

"No, but the Saxons have funny ways of doing things I've noticed."

"Ja, maybe so," said Crowbones, scratching at his beard, then pulling at it. "Perhaps I'll go roll my bones," he said, grasping the leather pouch about his neck. "I've let them languish lately." But he continued to stand in place, tugging at his beard. "Remember that wolf that attacked me the night we arrived in England?" he asked. "I was already in an agitated state back then about the Norseman's son who escaped. WolfPaw he was called."

"And so? What makes you think of that?" asked Orla. "That was nearly four years ago."

"Dammit, Orla, I don't know!" Crowbones snapped. "I just remember that damned wolf mark on his face. Then later, I was attacked by a wolf the night we landed in England, and now there's a goddamn wolf-hunt going on and I—"

"You what?"

"Odin's ass!" Crowbones growled with heat. "Never mind, Orla!" Turning with agitation in his step, he abandoned the rampart.

***

DuFresne was on the other side of the gatehouse rampart and had just ordered the castle gate to be closed and locked. Standing alone, he had also been watching the hunting sortie from the castle with interest. He felt no concern, yet just as the last riders vanished into the trees, he looked across the gatehouse, spotting Crowbones storming down the ramp and disappearing into the stables. When he reappeared, he was carrying broad-ax and shield, and took a seat at the butcher-stump. DuFresne became curious. "Clipping rooster heads?" he cried down to Crowbones.

Crowbones looked up. "Make sure the day guard stays alert today, DuFresne," he said curtly. "Some of your fellows have been getting sloppy lately!" Setting his ax and shield aside, Crowbones then opened the pouch about his neck and got down on one knee. Soon he was rolling his bones across the flat of the stump.

DuFresne was unaccustomed to hearing such a short tone coming from the usually jovial Crowbones. "Expecting something?" he asked.

Continuing to roll the tiny bones, Crowbones muttered, "Ja, something's in the air...coming our way."

DuFresne liked Crowbones, but the French captain was a practical soul and had concluded that Asta's Danes were at times overly superstitious, still holding too much faith in the occult by giving credence to omens, sorcery and such. Perhaps it was because they had never been baptized. Regardless, DuFresne dismissed Crowbones' comment and found amusement at the sight of the huge Dane playing at reading destiny with bird bones at the butcher stump, worrying about nothing.

***

Jack led the first roving band of mounted hunters, which was composed of five Frenchmen. Casually cantering his mount toward the nearest wolf lair, he bantered and joked with the riders, setting them at ease. Coming to a small stream, he suddenly cupped his ear to the woods ahead and pointed down the trail. "The wolves! Quick lest they escape!" he shouted, kicking his horse in the flanks.

Riding aside and behind Jack, they saw nothing. Nonetheless, they trusted the woodsman's instincts and spurred their horses to a gallop as Jack flew down the trail ahead, waving and shouting. Members of DuLac's cavalry had seldom been given the opportunity to hunt as it was a nobleman's sport, so their enthusiasm soared as they drove their horses through the forest chasing what they assumed were wolves. As they were about to catch Jack, there came a bend covered with long arching branches forming a canopy lush with new budding growth over the entire road. They saw Jack disappear around this bend, trailing somewhat off the path, and followed in full pursuit, shouting and laughing with the abandon of boys on a rabbit chase. Just as they made the corner, the earth disappeared beneath their feet. Horses dropped into the ground braying with fright, and riders went asprawl in shock and confusion. Seconds later a swarm of armed men dropped from the trees above, falling upon them with clubs and swords. More appeared from the brush.

"Use the flat of your blades and axes!" Jack yelled from his horse, watching the ambush. "I don't want blood on their tunics!

Within minutes all five Frenchmen were slain, their heads bashed to a bloody pulp. "Strip 'em down, get into their clothes!" cried Aengus, kicking one of the corpses aside. He strode up to Jack's mount and slapped him across the ribs. "Easy as twisting the necks off baby chicks, this was!" he laughed. "What's next, Jack-boy?"

"The other nine roving groups have further to ride, so we'll wait them out at my shanty. If they do as told, they'll have an easy time of it." Extending his hand and shaking Aengus about the shoulder, he smiled. "Good to snare the French again after all this time, eh!"

"Aye, Captain, nothing like a good goddamned slaughter to repay old debts!"

One mile to the west a second roving team galloped into a similar trap, as did a third and a fourth. Thus the morning went, DuLac's unsuspecting horsemen lured into ambush after ambush, only to be bludgeoned to death by Aengus' outlaws.

To the east, with one roving team, things differed. Fairhair and StraightLimbs were in this group. Within an hour of entering the deep woods, they sensed something afoul. Their first suspicion was aroused by the man Jack had appointed to lead them. "This fellow's Irish," whispered StraightLimbs as they rode toward their appointed wolf lair, "and I noticed several Gaels in the group that met us this morning. Those seeking work in DuLacshire as masons were all Saxons."

"Ja," responded Fairhair, "and this Irishman, have you noticed that shifty gaze about his eyes, like a cat slipping upon rats in a grainery, eh? Wonder how DuLac came by such an assortment of ruffians as this?"

StraightLimbs shook his head. "It wasn't DuLac that came up with them. Captain DuFresne told me they were hired by the gamekeeper."

"Jack?"

"Ja," nodded StraightLimbs.

"Shit. DuLac would've done better to lop the damned gamekeeper's arms off that day," said Fairhair. "I've never liked the way he looks at Lady Asta."

"Lady Asta?" asked StraightLimbs. "What're you talking about? I've never seen him give her even a glance."

"Well, that's because you don't know shit about women, or men who hunt them."

"Shit on you, Fairhair!" objected StraightLimbs. "I'm not a goddamn virgin, you know!"

"Aye, and far from it. But you lay with whores and wenches and know nothing of seducing *good* women. And I'm telling you, there's something going on in the game-keeper's head about Asta."

This conversation progressed several moments longer until the Irishman seated in the saddle behind the lead French horseman cried out, "There, the wolves! They scatter! Give chase!" Grabbing onto the waist of the French chevalier seated before him, he shouted, "Quickly, damn you! Run'em to the interception point before they get away!"

Spurring his horse with a swift kick, the Frenchman drove his mount into a full gallop while the two other Frenchmen in the group followed suit. StraightLimbs and Fairhair exchanged puzzled glances and held their place. "I saw nothing," said Fairhair. "Did you?"

"No," StraightLimbs replied. "Nor did I hear anything."

"Well, Seas of Fire, then, I'm not going to run about chasing shadows like a damn ground-squirrel, are you?"

"No, let's just keep our pace," said StraightLimbs. "We'll catch them down the road. Then we'll see if it was wolves or what."

As the lead Frenchman charged around a turn in the road, neither he nor the Irishman seated behind him noticed that the two Danes had lagged behind. Just as the horse made a turn in the road, the Frenchman felt his rider leave the horse. Not knowing that the man had deliberately leaped from the horse, and thinking that he had simply slipped, the Frenchman turned to look. At the same moment his horse gave way beneath him, stumbling into the meter deep depression that had been dug into the road and covered with branches and leaves. From behind him, the two French riders who were following collapsed into the same pit and their horses came careening into him, killing him instantly. The other two riders, having crashed into a tangle of branches, lances and panic-stricken horses, somehow pulled themselves from the heap and regained their feet, dazed. As the first was regaining his senses, he spotted men approaching him. Thinking they were coming to his assistance, he offered a weak smile and attempted to raise his broken arm in greeting. Then he noticed the look on their faces and saw their weapons. He knew in that instant that he had fallen into an ambush. The second Frenchman, standing now beside the first, never had time to clear his head, therefore had no idea what was occurring. Both met death within seconds.

The outlaws began stripping the corpses of their victims' tunics and caps when the Irishman looked about, realizing that two riders were missing. "Goddammit! What the shit!" he cried, dismayed. At the same instant, Fairhair and StraightLimbs cantered around the corner. They had been lost in discussion when far ahead they had heard the braying of panic-stricken horses and the voices of men crying out.

"Something's happened!" StraightLimbs had cried. "Hurry, we better go see!"

Now making the bend and seeing what was occurring, both Danes realized the peril. Fairhair unsheathed his sword while StraightLimbs grasped his ax, and without a word, each picked out a man in the bunch ahead and rode at him with weapon swinging. Fairhair caught his target across the ear with the full swing of his blade as the top half of the man's head sliced open horizontally, then flopped over sideways onto the opposite cheek, hanging only by threads of flesh and sinew. But as Fairhair swung his horse about, two other men dropped from the limbs above and wrestled him to the ground.

StraightLimbs, delivering a charging blow to the head, had also killed his man. Just as he buried the blade of his ax deep into the man's skull in passing, he lost grip on the handle. He tried to unsheathe his sword but five men were on him before his hand could free the sword from his belt. Instinctively, StaightLimbs abandoned the effort, and with his unrestrained hand, pulled a dagger from his tunic, plunging it into the throat of the man choking him. The assailant fell back, screaming in Gaelic. Still, StraightLimbs was soon overwhelmed and pulled from his horse. Others then joined the fray, forcing StraightLimbs' dagger from his hand and pinning him to the ground.

Fairhair, meanwhile, had also been subdued and was on his knees, arms held fast by men on each side. A tall man stood over him, raising his ax to deliver the death blow when one of the Scotsmen yelled, "No blood on the tunic, Aengus said! Use the flat side!"

The tall man complied. With the ax hovering over his shoulder, he turned the handle a half measure. Summoning his strength, he raised on his toes for leverage to smash his victim's head when Fairhair raised his head, gazing directly into his executioner's eyes.

Seeing Fairhair's face, the tall man gasped as the ax suddenly wobbled in his now tenuous grip. Stepping back in shock, the man rasped, "*You!* The one with long blond hair to your waist!"

Fairhair's eyes flared upon seeing the man's face. Then he, too, suddenly faltered, and his head dropped to his chest in discouragement.

"Courage, Fairhair!" StraightLimbs screamed, still pinned to the ground. "You'll not die alone! I'm with you!"

The tall man, still pale as a ghost, glanced over at StraightLimbs, whose long arms lay fully extended, pinned to the ground by several men. This sight seemed to undo the tall man even more than the sight of Fairhair, causing him to quake from head to toe as his face flushed purple.

StraightLimbs was about to exhort Fairhair once more and curse the man standing over him, but as he glared at the man, he himself turned ashen and silent.

"Come on, get on with it!" cried one of the men holding onto Fairhair. "We don't have all goddamn day! What the Hell's wrong with you?"

All the outlaws watching the tall man's collapse wondered the same thing. Only StraightLimbs and Fairhair understood. Both recognized the birthmark set upon the man's cheek, perfectly shaped in the form of a wolf's paw.

***

Having completed their bloody ruse of driving the wolves, Aengus' men gathered at Jack's shanty. Other than the casualties inflicted within Alf's group, each group remained fully intact. "A fine job!" purred Aengus, congratulating his men. "And Alf, they tell me you've had your revenge!"

Alf, his face and arms smeared with streaks of black, caked blood, shook his head. "No, I've only begun."

"But you're not even smiling, lad!" snorted Aengus. "Yet they say you disassembled those two alive, one slice at a time. My boys couldn't even watch, they said, for it made them ill!"

"I'll smile when the day's done. There's three more sitting in the castle, but I'll have them, too, before dark."

Aengus looked at Jack and cackled. "Aha, Jack-boy! By this night you'll finally have your DuLac on the end of a pole, too, eh?"

Jack nodded. "But we'll have to succeed at business first, so listen carefully. I want your bunch to start filtering into the rear of the village and wait as me and you lead the others up the hill. When the guards see us dressed in French garb, they'll assume the hunt's done and open the gate. And that, Aengus, will be the entire key to this whole thing."

Aengus smiled. "Yeah, getting in the goddamn gate is the trick. But my compliments, this is one Hell of a plan you've come up with!"

Jack continued. "I took fifty of DuLac's riders out with me at dawn, but I want seventy of your men going back in as we'll need all the manpower we can slip in. Have the extras toward the end of the file since they won't be dressed like Frenchmen." Turning to Alf, he said, "The moment we get past the gate-house, you'll bring the men hiding in the village up the hill. Speed is of the essence, here, Alf. I figure they've got about two hundred men-at-arms inside, and we have close to the same. But if we're quick, surprise will swing things in our favor."

"Oh, I'll be there," said Alf, clenching a fist.

"Aengus," Jack continued, "I want you to pick about ten good men and assign them to the Keep door as soon as we get in the gate. It's only locked after dark when DuLac secures himself for the night, so it'll be open now. But if the guards have time to bar it, we'll play Hell breaking through to get to DuLac. The Keep's also where he stores his wealth so, again, speed is important here, understand?"

Aengus grinned, giving Jack a wink of approval. "You've thought of everything, Captain, just like in the old days!"

"One more thing, Aengus. Have you told your men about my two conditions?"

"Yes, Jack-boy, very clearly. You want DuLac alive, and Lady Asta's not to be touched."

"Very well, then," Jack said, gazing about at Aengus' collection of warriors. "Let's get on with it."

Jack's file of disguised horsemen streamed toward the castle in ranks of two, and after clearing the village, began the ascent to the castle. From their lead position, Jack and Aengus heard a cry come from the gatehouse, followed by another cry, then saw movement along the ramparts.

"Dammit!" Aengus growled beneath his breath. "What's this? They seem *a* bit edgy up there."

"Easy, Aengus," Jack whispered. "Stay calm."

Several more shouts rang from the ramparts as four or five additional guards appeared above the gatehouse. Two of them pointed to the procession coming up the hill, and it appeared that a heated discussion had broken out amongst them.

"Goddammit!" Aengus muttered, "I smell fish here, Jack! They know something's up!"

"Easy now, big man," Jack said, holding his smile for the guards watching from the ramparts.

"The Hell you say!" Aengus exclaimed, just at the point of reining his horse and turning about to signal his men into retreat. But then the doors of the castle began to creak open. "Saints alive, they're opening the gates!" he sighed, glancing at Jack who only stared ahead.

Within moments they were inside the gates. Without even a signal, the riders fell upon every soldier they could get their hands upon as stone masons and laborers scattered. Taken by surprise, DuLac's men were struck with that paralytic disbelief that accompanies unforeseen disaster. Capitalizing on this hesitation, Aengus' men hacked and sliced away, taking out a good fifty men before their victims could react.

Crowbones, who had been sitting on the butcher's stump with ax in hand all day, moved swiftly. Grabbing his shield, he stormed one rider with his ax, decapitating him, then repeated his action on another. From the stable, Orla rushed out to join his brother, breaking into a furious war whoop.

But the raiders had the momentum and DuLac's forces were quickly driven back to the Keep, having lost a third of their troops within the first ten minutes of battle. Some of those surviving this first assault, sensing slaughter, began to run for the gate. A fortunate few commandeered riderless horses thrashing about in the melée and took flight toward the village, charging through Alf's warriors who were now surging up the hill toward the castle.

"Don't let those bastards escape!" Alf bellowed.

When the attack had opened, most of the Danish Guard were in their garrison behind the stables. Hearing the outbreak of cries and clashing of iron that could only signify battle, they knew the castle was under siege and swarmed out into the yard en masse with ax and sword raised for battle. Within minutes, though their numbers were limited, they managed to repulse the tide of Aengus' attack and create a bloody bottleneck.

Men from both sides furiously carved at each other as screams and moans of the wounded filled the yard. Aengus and his selected platoon, as instructed, immediately attacked the Keep door and quickly overwhelmed the handful of Frenchmen guarding it. Next, they charged into the Keep seeking DuLac and treasure.

Seeing them enter, Jack dismounted and followed. "I want him alive!" he screamed, dashing about the bottom floor, then up the steps. "Do you hear me Aengus?"

"Aye," Aengus hollered, "but he's nowhere to be seen!"

"Oh, he's here, Aengus! Hiding like the coward he is!"

In the yard, the vicious fight continued as more Frenchmen tried to break through the knotted ranks of battling raiders to flee out the gate. Seeing this, DuFresne cursed them while staving off several attackers to his front.

"For shame, you bastards!" he cried in outrage. "Come back, cowards, or you'll hang!"

By this time Alf had slashed his way into an opening and was searching about, hoping to locate the three remaining Danes he so desperately sought. "Orla!" he cried. "Where are you, you filthy bastard!"

As Alf cried out Orla's name, Crowbones stood just paces away extracting his ax blade from a Gael's ribs. Looking up, he spotted the Norseman's birthmark. "WolfPaw!" he gasped.

Simultaneously, Alf recognized Crowbones and went berserk with rage. "You!" he cried, pointing at Crowbones. "You goddamned butcher!"

Crowbones stood stone-still, appalled, as though he had just seen an apparition. In that instant, Alf brought his sword down in one mighty sweep, cleaving Crowbones' forearm clean from his elbow.

"Aie!!" Crowbones screamed, falling to his knees.

Alf fell upon him then, kicking him in the face. As Crowbones collapsed backward, he saw Alf's eyes burning with hatred, and also the broadsword raised above Alf's head, ready to drop like a deadly pendulum.

"Oh, vengeance is sweet!" he heard Alf snarl, feeling himself on the edge of blacking out from the horrific pain of his severed arm. "WolfPaw!" he moaned, fading. "Th-the last thing I see in this life!"

Alf, his face purple with vengeance, looked to the sky and screamed his father's name, then brought the sword down with all his strength onto Crowbones. A mighty clang ensued, then Alf felt his sword leave his grip as it went flying aside. Someone had appeared from nowhere and deflected Alf's intended deathblow.

Confused, Alf's arms dropped to his side and he looked about. "You!" he cried, recognizing his assailant. "The silent one!"

Guthroth's eyes flared, spotting the wolf print on Alf's face, but without hesitation he carried his swing through with cold precision, and sent Alf's decapitated head flying toward the Keep. Saying nothing, Guthroth sheathed his sword and dropped to his knees, grabbing the unconscious Crowbones. Despite men fighting furiously all about him, Guthroth took Crowbones' massive shoulders and began dragging him from the yard toward the garden shed. Managing to get him halfway through the door, Guthroth spotted Asta, Elder Heidi and Willy crouched behind tables inside the shed.

Asta cried out in surprise at first, but settled after recognizing Guthroth. Looking down, she caught sight of Crowbones, mutilated and bleeding profusely. "Oh my God in Heaven!" she gasped, rushing forward. "Get him inside and close the door, Guthroth!"

"H-hi-his arm—" Guthroth tried to explain.

"Asta, grab these herb sacks and stop his bleeding!" shouted Elder Heidi. "Quick or he's dead!"

Trembling, Asta complied, clumsily trying to wrap the severed stub of Crowbones' limb. "How can this be happening!" she cried, her heart shred to tatters by the sight of her beloved Crowbones dying on the floor of the shed.

"Gather your senses and save him!" ordered Elder Heidi. "We've got to stop the damned bleeding or he's done! My God, girl, have you never been under attack?"

"No!" Asta wailed, trying to collect herself.

"There's no time for blubbering, dammit!" Elder Heidi replied sharply. "Hold him still while I bind him!"

"Oh, my God," Asta gasped, unable to bear Crowbones' agony as he lay writhing on the ground. "Crowbones, don't die!"

"Pull yourself together, Asta," Elder Heidi scolded. "French blood's flowing in streams out there, and by day's end it'll be a new world for you, Dearie, one way or another! So be strong, girl."

Wrestling with the nub of Crowbones' arm as he continued to writhe about, Asta looked up at the old woman and said, "What are you saying, Heidi?"

"By the setting of the moon," Heidi said, her tone flat, "either DuLac and your Danes will be dead, or my son Jack will be dead."

"Jack?" asked Asta, confused. "He's your *son?*"

"Yes, dear, and this is all his doing. And no matter who carries the day, you'll suffer one way or the other. That's what men bring, even my boy Jack. And we women, we're left to bleed for their foolishness. God ordained it, and so it shall be!"

"Jack?" Asta repeated, unable to believe he could have anything to do with an assault on the castle or be involved in such bloodletting.

"Ha! Don't be so innocent, girl," Heidi sniffed, working Crowbones' bloody nub. "You sleep in bed each night with a man who's butchered Saxons by the thousands to get where he stands, women and children no less. Where's your shock at that? Jack suffers from boiling blood like any other man. He simply seeks justice today. Do you know what that is, Dearie, or has the fat French life washed it from your head?"

Stunned, wounded by Elder Heidi's blunt talk, Asta threw her arms about Crowbones' neck, but cast her eyes at Elder Heidi. "What are we to do?" she whispered.

"What women always do, my girl," muttered Heidi, "wait for the outcome and then live with it." Then her eyes softened. "If Jack kills DuLac, I'm sure many a Norman would love to have you as his mistress. But maybe you should know, Jack wants to take you away with him when this is done."

"What? How?"

"No time to think, Dearie. It'll be over quick. Either you stay here in misery or flee and take your chances. I had such a choice once when I was young, but fear froze my feet and I've suffered since. The choice has now come to me once more, but age isn't my friend so I'll stay yet again." Taking Asta by the shoulders, Elder Heidi embraced her. "But you, sweet girl, just for once in your cursed existence fluff those feathers and take to the air!"

Guthroth the Quiet was still at Crowbones' side and had heard the entire exchange between Heidi and Asta. Asta had forgotten he was there. When she happened to look down and see him, she saw him heave, as though fighting back emotion. "Guthroth?" she stammered.

His feelings would not allow him to speak. Instead, he pointed a finger to Elder Heidi, and gave a single nod of his head.

"Guthroth?" Asta repeated, raising her shoulders in question of this gesture.

Embarrassed, flushing red, Guthroth pointed to Elder Heidi again and gave an affirmative nod. Then he turned and rushed back out the door to rejoin the fight.

Orla had seen his brother go down, but was unable to cross the yard to assist him because of the wall of attackers coming at him. Placing all his might behind each swing of his ax, he turned it into a deadly pendulum, swinging it back and forth with merciless precision until the enemy before him began to back away. After much effort, two raiders managed to hold him at bay with the point of their extended lances. This momentary impasse gave Orla time to search the ground where his brother had fallen, but Crowbones was nowhere to be seen. "Ivar!" he howled. "Where are you, dammit?! Can you hear me?!"

Having gained their breath after this brief moment of respite, Orla's attackers began to move forward again. As several harried him, another managed to poke a lance between Orla's legs, hoping to trip him. Simultaneously, two others encircled the ferocious Dane just as the man with the lance between Orla's legs, gave a twist, causing Orla to lose balance. Feeling himself toppling, knowing his enemies would now make quick work of him, he swung out with his ax a final time, cleaving off one man's leg at the ankle. Then he erupted into a burst of Danish profanity and snarled, "Oh, I'll take you with me, you sniveling bastards!"

Orla expected to meet his end within the next instant, but DuFresne appeared from nowhere with a pack of Frenchmen, falling onto Orla's assailants so quickly that they tumbled like fallen timber. "Get up and live, you big oaf!" DuFresne shouted. "Get up, dammit, more are coming!"

Stunned by DuFresne's miraculous intervention, Orla gained his feet and joined DuFresne's side, crouching into a defensive stance with ax and shield at the ready. "I owe you, DuFresne!" he yelled, his nerves jangled at having just escaped death's grasp.

"Indeed, you owe me *twice* now! But where's your brother! We need his ax!"

But it was Guthroth that replied, charging to the line and taking a position beside Orla. "He-he-s been—he's d-down!" Guthroth stuttered.

Hearing this, Orla became enraged. "What! Dead? Speak up, man! Has he been killed?!"

Before Guthroth could answer, another wave of Gaels and Scots rushed forward, throwing themselves against DuFresne's line. At the same moment a final clutch of Danes who had been working behind the stable when the attack broke out streamed out whooping and shouting. They reinforced DuFresne and Orla's position, and their racket was so intimidating the enemy slowed its advance, then fell back. Seeing this, disheartened Frenchmen on the other side of the yard near the Keep gained courage and surged forward to join DuFresne's advance.

As this bloody struggle teetered back and forth, Aengus and the men within the Keep found DuLac's treasury, a hidden chamber concealed on the top floor. The hidey-hole was filled to the brim with gold chalices and crosses, gold and silver coins, bejeweled weaponry, precious gems, and scores of other priceless objects, most of which had been looted from Saxon churches and nobility during the Harrying. "Aha, Jack!" Aengus wheezed, issuing a crow of triumph. "We've found DuLac's cache!"

But Jack was little interested. "Where's DuLac?!" he screamed, rushing from hall to hall, chamber to chamber.

"We'll find him before it's over!" shouted Aengus. "But for now, help us gather loot!"

"To Hell with the goddamned loot!" Jack cried. "Help me find DuLac!"

But the eyes of Aengus and his men were now blinded by plunder and they abandoned Jack, filling their sacks with everything they could grab. Moments later they heard the stamp of boots clamoring up the stairs. "Alf's dead, Aengus!" a voice rang out. "Come quick! The battle has turned against us!"

"What?!" Aengus roared, signaling the others to continue hoarding the treasure. "Hurry it up, men! Then get downstairs and make a run for the gate! Don't pause for a goddamn minute until you're across the border! Come along, Jack, the tide's shifted! Besides, DuLac's not here. He must be in the yard!"

Hearing this, Jack followed Aengus down the stone stairs, sword and dagger at the ready. Running out the Keep door, they found themselves in the midst of a raging hand-to-hand fight to the death. Around them men from both sides were straggling about the ground, moaning and clutching at deep wounds while others lay trembling flat on the ground, their throats gurgling that final rattle of death signaling the end of life.

Despite this bedlam, Jack's eyes swept across the yard in search of the absent DuLac, but he was nowhere to be seen. Still, Jack ran here and there screaming DuLac's name until stumbling over a dying Frenchman. Looking down at the man, Jack saw him extend a limp, mutilated arm and heard him gasp with supplication. "W-wa-ter…" the man pleaded, his eyes glassy and spent.

Jack grabbed him by the shoulders, shaking him violently. "DuLac! Where is DuLac, by God?!"

The man stared at Jack with that vacant gaze of the dying, not comprehending. When Jack repeated himself, the man raised his bloody arm again, pointed to the gate, rasping, "A-at the quar-ry, w-with th-the st-one ma-sons…"

"H-he's not here at the castle?" Jack stammered in disbelief. The man did not reply, so Jack shook him again, becoming hysterical. "You mean to say he's miles away!" he screamed, suddenly realizing that this entire endeavor was for naught and his plan to murder DuLac was now dissolving before his very eyes.

"Y-yes," the man whispered hoarsely, "ch-checking on a new v-vein of rock they f-found at the quarry." Then the man's head dropped and he passed, his eyes frozen open.

"No! Not possible!" Jack wailed.

Above the clashing of iron and above the din of men shouting and cursing, from within the garden shed Asta recognized Jack's voice. Disregarding all peril, she ran to the door and out into the yard toward him. "Jack!" she bawled. "Oh, Jack, what have you unleashed?!"

Seeing her, Jack dropped his weapon and ran to her. "My God, all is lost!" he cried. Grabbing her hand and pulling at her, he shouted, "Come with me, Asta! Flee with me now!" Before she could respond, he began dragging her toward a loose horse that was rampaging about in panic and confusion. He grasped the flailing reins and pulled at the horse's snout, forcing the horse to settle. "Come with me, Asta!" he pleaded with desperate, imploring eyes, grabbing her and shoving her onto the saddle.

Asta's entire existence since the age of twelve had been one self-imposed, disciplined response after another. This had been her only means of survival in the face of ugly circumstances forced upon her year after year by others. Indeed, she had forced herself to mask emotions and never show her hand to others. But in this moment of madness now confronting her, she weighed Elder Heidi's words and remembered Guthroth's expression in the garden shed just moments earlier. Inexplicably, her heart throbbing, she decided that she would, this once, determine her own fate and follow the impulses of her heart. "I'll come!" she whispered hoarsely, her heart flushing wild with rebellion. "But be quick, Jack!"

Jack threw her a blank look, unable for a moment to absorb her rapid consent. Then he saw her smile at him, and felt her hand urge him onto the horse. "To Scotland, then!" he shouted, vaulting onto the saddle behind her.

Seeing this from a short distance, Orla thought the gamekeeper was abducting her. "Asta!" he bellowed, breaking through the ranks of the enemy standing before him with complete disregard for his own life.

"Stop!" cried DuFresne, still pressing his charge against the enemy. "Orla, have you gone mad!"

"O-Or-la! D-don-t st-stop h--her!" screamed another voice above the clanging of weapons. It was Guthroth, dropping his sword and taking a run at Orla. "L-let her g-go!"

"Guthroth!" shouted DuFresne, thinking both of the Danes had lost their senses.

As Orla rushed forward, he was struck on his left arm by the glancing blow of a Gael's sword. The blade cleanly sliced the upper meat of his limb but failed to slow him. He was then hammered across the head by a lance shaft, but it broke across his skull like a brittle branch. "I'm coming, Asta!" he cried, desperate to save the person he most revered in life, shoving men aside one after another.

"N-no, O-Orla!" bawled Guthroth, giving frantic chase.

Jack caught sight of Orla's hulking shape coming at them, as did Asta. It was more frightening than the rampage of a rousted bear slashing a swath through the forest. "No, Orla!" Asta cried, her eyes pleading for him to stop.

Jack kicked the horse in the flanks and jerked at the reins, turning him toward the gate to flee. Frightened, the horse jumped, then rose up angrily on hind legs, braying and throwing its head about with agitation. This action of the horse allowed Orla just enough time to reach out, grab Jack by the arm, and pull him down from the saddle. Even before Jack's frame touched the ground, Orla's ax made a single sweeping arc through the air, splitting Jack's skull into halves.

As Jack's body slumped into the dust, Orla felt a violent push from behind that sent him reeling against the horse's torso. It was Guthroth trying to stop him, but he was an instant too late. Orla, thinking Guthroth had only been trying to keep him from charging so perilously through the enemy, turned and embraced his friend. "Guthroth! Don't worry, I'm fine!" he yelled. "Just a little blood on the arm!"

Guthroth dropped his head as emotion flooded his face for Asta. Misinterpreting this, Orla patted Guthroth across the shoulders, convinced that Guthroth was, indeed, the best friend a man could ask for in life.

Asta was still atop the horse, her frame frozen in horror by what had just occurred. Her heart swelling to bursting, she stared down at Jack with abject dread and disbelief. Wilting then, she began to weep, her tears coming in long, unrestrained sobs. "Jack!" she screamed, feeling her entire body going slack. "Oh, God, Savior in Heaven! What have you done to me?!"

Orla saw this and concluded that her sudden display of delirium was the result of her terror at nearly being abducted by the treacherous gamekeeper. "No need to be afraid," Orla insisted, consoling her. "He can't hurt you now, Asta!"

From the window of the garden shed, Elder Heidi had witnessed everything, and so had Willy. Shedding no tears, Elder Heidi made the sign of the cross. "God you have taken two husbands from me through war," she whispered bitterly, "and now my fourth and final son. Shall you never forgive this old woman her sins?"

Willy, having watched his father struck dead, dashed from the shed straight toward his dead body in a rage at Orla. As he ran, he grasped an ax that was lying next to a corpse, preparing to bury it in Orla's huge back. Just before he struck, a Frenchman standing behind Orla swung out with his sword and took off the boy's head. Elder Heidi, still watching from the window, saw this, too. As young Willy's headless torso crumpled to the ground, she dropped to her knees, tears finally flowing from the hardened old Saxon woman's eyes.

Aengus's forces were by now fleeing the castle, with DuFresne's Frenchmen and Danes on their heels. Nonetheless, as Aengus fled through the forest, he was a happy outlaw because he had escaped the castle during the height of the battle and was now beating a trail back to Dumfries loaded with plunder. His only regret was the loss of his close friend and former captain, Jack Forest. He had hoped that on this day Jack would have his revenge on Desmond DuLac, despised villain of the Harrying.

As for the other men Aengus had lost, he cared little. *Misfits and brigands they are*, thought Aengus, content that there would now be only half as many hands to split DuLac's treasure. "Aye," Aengus sniggered as he crossed into Scotland, "it'll be a big time in Dumfries tonight for those of us who made it out today!"

***

Through the blur of distortion and misperception, war creates a fog that taints both truth and reality. In the case of Jack Forest's conspiracy against Desmond DuLac, truth became an especially murky quagmire of misconceptions that became known as the 'Gamekeeper's Revolt'. To begin, those few Frenchmen who had managed to commandeer horses and flee at the onset of the attack immediately headed to the quarry three miles away to alert and warn Desmond DuLac. Hearing their reports, DuLac fled south in terror, taking these men with him. He did not return until several days later upon receiving news that his forces in the castle had actually repelled the invasion and prevailed.

His first act on returning to his castle was to decorate those men who had fled on horseback, thereby deserting the battle, to warn him of danger. His second act was to hunt down and execute for cowardice those other Frenchmen who had fled the fight on foot, claiming they lacked honor and had violated their oath of fealty by not staying to defend the castle.

Following the revolt, Normans throughout England began to laud Desmond DuLac for now having crushed a second Saxon rebellion in his realm, even though neither attack had been a revolt by Saxons, but merely a plunder expedition by foreigners from across the Scottish border. DuLac had cowardly locked himself in the Keep during the first attack on his castle, and run away during the second. Lacking these details, Normans throughout England held DuLac up as a shining example of French and Norman courage. To honor him, he was decorated in a formal military ceremony in London which was presided over by none other than Prince William Rufus, son of William the Bastard of Normandy.

Yet another quirk occurred. Desmond DuLac decided to honor Orla for saving Lady Asta from being abducted by Jack Forest, the gamekeeper. During his speech dedicated to Orla's exemplary display of loyalty, DuLac proclaimed, "Oh, to think of the horrid existence and misery my poor wife would have had to endure had Orla not stopped that vile, lust-driven gamekeeper from dragging her off into the wild!" DuLac, of course, had no idea that Asta had intended at that final moment to flee from England with Jack Forest. Nor did anyone else save Elder Heidi and Guthroth the Quiet. These two, haunted by Asta's despair, maintained an inviolate silence about this secret which they would ultimately each take to their grave.

Elder Heidi, having now lost her last son and only grandson to God's hammer, concluded that God had all along intended to replace the lot of them with a single daughter—Lady Asta of the Danes. The two of them, subsequently, drew ever closer beneath the dark shroud of their shared desolation.

As for Asta, she developed a new understanding of the sensitive, often over-looked Guthroth, and he came to occupy a special place in her heart. Many failed to understand this turn, especially Orla and Crowbones. Another change also occurred in Asta, one that soon became evident to all who inhabited DuLacshire. Lady Asta, since the day of the Gamekeeper's Revolt, lost that glacial resolve that she had always worn like some irrefutable badge of honor. It seemed, for some queer reason, that she was now weak of spirit. Adding to this mystery, she next detached herself from nearly everything and everyone around her, acting as though she had somehow slipped into the realm of the dead. Even when healing the sick or in the presence of children, she rarely smiled or bantered with them as before. Many remarked, in fact, that she had disengaged herself from life, and was now spending most of her time alone, lost in private reflection in the garden shed or the chapel.

This change in Asta was ill received by Desmond DuLac. Grumbling and deprecating at first, he next began to badger and interrogate her about it. This hounding soon evolved into resentment and anger, which led him to seek mistresses amongst Saxon whores. Asta heard the rumors, but turned an indifferent ear to them. *Better that he rut around between some Saxon wench's thighs than my own* she thought, becoming increasingly repulsed by the very sight of him with each passing day.

Her private sorrow continued to grow as days turned to weeks, then into months. Watching, Elder Heidi grew concerned. "This melancholia is devouring you, Asta," she said one day. "You must breathe again! And pray tell, what is it you think about day after day sitting there alone in the garden shed?"

"My Jack," Asta replied, staring into space, "and what might have been. And my two sons, Guillaume and Tristan…and what might have been. But at least Jack is finally free of Desmond DuLac, and my dear boys, thank God, have never had to endure him. Though their absence breaks my heart, how overjoyed I am that they are tucked into the quiet safety of a monastery with the Black Monks of Cluny, never to be tainted by the poison of politics, or world affairs, or high nobles who plot and plunder and betray. My little Guillaume might survive it for he is tough as a bear cub, but my dear Tristan who loves God and learning so profoundly, he would never survive such a tempestuous arena as the politics of men!"

Chapter Thirty

Monastery Life Continues

After returning from Tuscany, Tristan and Guillaume resumed their schedules with their respective co-horts. Guillaume was not academically driven, but as a result of his summer with la Gran Contessa, he developed a newfound interest in his classes, especially Latin and Italian. This incurred something else. As Tristan had already mastered Italian, he was able to assist Guillaume, which gave them common ground and led to spending more time together again in the Dorter after hours.

Of all the boys who returned from their summer visit, it was LeBrun who seemed most eager to seek out Tristan. LeBrun had come across a secret, and believed that in this secret, he had uncovered Tristan's Achilles heel. "Ever heard of the Romani?" he asked Tristan on his first day back from Normandy.

Tristan looked at LeBrun, assessing his malevolent expression. To LeBrun's irritation, Tristan said nothing and walked away.

That next day LeBrun approached again. This time he cocked his head to the side and said, "Happen to know a Romani girl by the name of Mala?"

Tristan again said nothing, although inwardly his heart turned and he felt heat licking at his cheeks.

"Leave me alone, LeBrun," said Tristan, turning away.

Denied the reaction he anticipated, LeBrun scowled. Not giving up, that next evening while the other boys were out of the Dorter, he decided to go for the jugular. "Sure, you know a Romani girl named Mala!" he said.

Tristan looked at the freckled LeBrun, feeling the seeds of fury, but again chose to skirt the issue.

"You might like to know that she lives in our manor now, 'Smart Boy'," needled LeBrun. "And you know your big friend, Letellier? Well, seems his father employed the Romani on his manor...you know, the one your mother used to own? Anyway, it seems Papa Letellier has been poking some Romani crack." Running his tongue over his lips in a lurid gesture, LeBrun then said, "Yeah, he's been diddling Mala's mother and her aunt for quite some time now!"

Tristan had no idea what this meant, but as LeBrun rattled on, Tristan surmised it was something unspeakable.

"Yeah," LeBrun continued, "and that Mala's a pretty little thing, too. But I have some news, *Smart Boy*. Lord Letellier has now passed the Romani along to *my* father, and now he's poking Mala's mother and aunt. So again, do you know Mala or not?"

Mala's face flashed before Tristan, turning his stomach into knots. "I know her," he said slowly.

LeBrun grinned, seeing that Tristan had begun to tremble the least bit. "Too bad she's going to end up a whore like her mother, eh?"

Tristan remembered Peter the Hermit's constant use of this same word. Still not understanding its meaning, he remembered the Hermit had used it as a slur. Now, watching LeBrun's face, the wickedness of the word magnified.

"That's right," LeBrun continued, his voice heavy with malice. "And now my father has set his eyes on Mala. Aye, he'll be diddling *her*, too, before long...and so will I!" Then LeBrun began poking an index finger of one hand in and out of the circle he had formed with the index finger and thumb of the other hand. "Diddle! Diddle!" he exclaimed, his eyes wide with mockery.

Uncertain of the meaning of LeBrun's motion, Tristan knew it could not be good.

"That girl, Mala, she doesn't really like you, you know," LeBrun continued. "She thinks you're a little show-rooster, same as the rest of us think about you!"

Tristan could have cared less what LeBrun thought, but these stinging words about Mala were searing his sensibilities. He knew LeBrun was full of spite, but he felt a pang of anguish thinking that Mala might have said something, anything, about their friendship to LeBrun. And LeBrun had now twice called him 'Smart Boy', a moniker that only Mala knew. That, for some reason, opened the flood-gates. In a moment of feverish spontaneity, Tristan balled his fist and struck LeBrun in the mouth, then followed with a punch to the nose. LeBrun, his vision turning to stars, found himself reeling backward with blood streaming from his broken nose. Collapsing, he next felt himself being pummeled about the head, neck and chest.

This was followed by the sudden tramp of footsteps and voices of other boys appearing from nowhere, yelling and shouting. The one voice LeBrun heard above the others was that of Guillaume, who was now as big as himself. On entering the room, Guillaume saw Tristan and LeBrun grappling on the ground, and quickly understood LeBrun had once again bullied his brother. Unaware that Tristan was already giving the red-head a sound thrashing, Guillaume leaped into the fray and also began pounding LeBrun, screaming, "You'll never touch him again, you ugly red bastard!"

This was followed by a raspy voice down the hall accompanied by the clitter of a cane tip hastening toward the room. "Damnation, you rascals!" cried Placidus with alarm as he entered and clumsily tried to separate the tangle of boys thrashing about the floor.

"*Damnation, you rascals!*" mocked an anonymous falsetto voice from the crowd of on-looking boys.

This precise mimicry of Brother Placidus' voice created such an uproar of laughter that even old Placidus could not help but snicker as he tugged at flailing limbs and fists. "Dammit!" he chuckled, "I'll learn which of you weasels is mocking me one of these days!"

Letellier, Hébert and Scule watched until content that LeBrun had received a sufficient battering from the Saint-Germain brothers. They then joined Placidus' efforts, and the combatants were separated. LeBrun, wiping blood from his face, pointed to Tristan and cried, "He attacked me for no reason! Then his damned brother joined in!"

This forced grumbling amongst the other boys, directed at LeBrun. "Ha!" cried Scule, "*You're* the one whom starts all the trouble around here, you pig!"

"Yeah, jackass!" shouted Letellier.

Placidus tapped his cane against the floor. "Quiet now, boys, all of you! This appears to be a matter for your good friend and mine, Brother Allaire, eh? Looks like some of you will be visiting the Misericord so Fat François and Petit Paul can kiss your arses again!"

At this silence fell over the room and the boys looked at each other with dread. But LeBrun, still snuffling and swiping tears from his cheeks, shouted, "Yes! Brother Allaire'll take care of these Saint-Germain sons-of-a-traitor! They attacked me for no reason and need to be punished!"

"Hmm," said Placidus, rubbing at his chin. "No reason, LeBrun? Now that just doesn't sound like Tristan, nor our boy Guillaume, huh, boys?"

The other boys nodded in unison, looking hopefully at the old monk. "Maybe he'll have mercy and leave Brother Allaire out of this," Scule whispered to Letellier.

LeBrun stuck a finger at Placidus. "Oh, you'll report this to Brother Allaire, all right!" he said with insolence.

"And if you don't, I'll go directly there myself, you pitiful old relic!"

At this the other boys gasped. Any disrespect toward a Black Monk of even the lowest stature was purely anathema. Scule balled his fists and started to move toward LeBrun, but Letellier dragged him back.

"Really?" responded Placidus with unexpected calm, the faint trace of a smile creeping into a corner of his mouth. Tapping his cane against the floor in slow, deliberate fashion, he gazed directly into LeBrun's eyes and said, "*Cheese*-cloth." This mystified everyone, including LeBrun, but each boy stood motionless, intent on seeing what Placidus would do next. "Yes, Master LeBrun," Placidus continued with an accusatory nod, "did I ever relate to you the story about a boy who one day grabbed a *cheesecloth*? Aye, an interesting maneuver, especially when someone is *standing* on it."

This still made no sense to any of the boys listening, including Tristan. But LeBrun remembered the hog oil incident, and also knew where the old monk was headed. Saying nothing, he shot Placidus a pallid look, then hung his head.

"Very well then," clucked Placidus, "it appears the matter is settled and we can bypass Brother Allaire, eh?"

"*We can bypass Brother Allaire, eh?*" cried that anonymous, girlish voice from nowhere. This again precipitated an uproar of hilarity in the room, making everyone laugh until tears were streaming down all eyes except LeBrun's.

"Dammit," muttered old Placidus, grinning, "do I really sound that bad, lads?"

Two days later LeBrun was summoned into Abbot Hugh's chambers by Prior Odo, which caused a stir in the Dorter. Abbot Hugh rarely met with individual students. The mystery heightened when, upon his return to the Dorter from that meeting, LeBrun refused to answer questions despite being hounded for days by the other boys. Then, two weeks after the meeting with Abbot Hugh, LeBrun quietly packed his affairs and loaded onto a coach headed for Normandy. The boys assumed a family tragedy had occurred and LeBrun was only taking a short leave. But whenever they made inquiries, Brother Placidus and the other monks would simply shake their heads and say nothing.

For his part, Tristan did not miss his red-headed nemesis in the least. Yet, there was a part of him that worried intensely about LeBrun's close proximity to Mala in Normandy. Tristan still carried her ring in his pocket at all times, still harboring a secret hope that she might, as mentioned during her last visit, convince her mother to live in Burgundy—especially now that the Romani had apparently moved onto the LeBrun manor. Trying to chase this concern from his thoughts, Tristan began to refocus all his energy on his studies with Brother Loiseaux and the teacher-monks. Still, he found himself frequently thinking of Mala; dreaming that he might one day catch sight of her little box-wagon coming up the rise to Cluny.

***

After LeBrun's departure Tristan settled into his routine of studies and the Treasury Tower. As fall arrived, he discerned that Prior Odo's role had begun to shift into a new direction. Also, an increasing influx of correspondence was coming from Rome, most of it from Pope Gregory himself. Moreover, there came an increase in the flow of papal couriers arriving at Cluny, including the secretive Benedictine spies, Jurgen Handel and Dieter Muehler. On occasion he was privy to their conversations, but only rarely.

Tristan also began to take notice of large increases in military expenditures and distributions coming out of the Tower. Much of this was designated for the manufacture of armaments, the payment of troops, and the securing of mercenaries. One day as he was recording an unusually large amount of funds going to a certain duchy in Saxony, he asked Prior Odo, "This support that we send against King Heinrich, does it not disturb Abbot Hugh? I know the Abbot still holds great affection for him."

"He does," said Odo, "but it is often those who are close to us that hurt us the most. Abbot Hugh understands that even his own heart must not bar God's will, therefore he does what he must. There is only one way to fight a bear, and that is with another bear. Heinrich continues to send his armies into the field against our supporters in Germany and northern Italy, and continues to think he should be master of the Church, so we must continue to send armies against him. And war is costly. But then, think of the alternative, Tristan. Would you have a king control a pope?"

Tristan shook his head. "Certainly not, Prior." He went back to his figures then, but several minutes later he looked up at Odo and said, "Prior, I do not by any means wish to be inappropriate, but could you answer another question that has been bothering me for some time?"

"Of course," Odo replied, not looking up from his manuscript.

"What does it mean to diddle?" asked Tristan.

"What!" Odo cried, shocked.

"What does it mean to diddle?" Tristan repeated.

Odo put down his quill and stared at the boy. "Where on this earth did you hear such a thing?" he demanded with evident displeasure.

"LeBrun," said Tristan, sensing he had ventured into deep water. "H-he said that his father was diddling some women, then he made this motion with his hands." Tristan then meekly reconstructed as best he could the maneuver LeBrun had made that day with his finger and palm.

Odo watched with a scowl, rocking back and forth with disapproval. "Best you not ask about something like diddling, Tristan. God would not want you thinking about such things!"

Reading Odo's scowl, Tristan's cheeks reddened and his eyes dropped back to his work. But Odo, in studying the boy, could tell something else was bothering him still. "Tristan, something else on your mind?"

Tristan shook his head. "Of no importance, Prior Odo. I apologize for making you angry," he murmured, his voice trailing off as he buried his face so close to his work that it was touching the paper.

This picture of humility touched Odo. "I am not angry, Tristan, I was just taken by surprise. So what else is going on in that little head? Come along now, out with it."

Tristan looked up, setting his hands in his lap. "Very well then, with your permission I will ask. I was wondering, Prior, what exactly is a whore?"

"Mon Dieu!!" Odo exploded. "Was that LeBrun again!"

"Yes," Tristan stammered, "and Peter the Hermit!"

"The Hermit! Oh, alors, pas possible! Tristan, never ask me such questions again! And forget LeBrun, he'll not be returning. And if we are fortunate, neither will the Hermit!"

***

On January 1 of 1078 the monastic community of Cluny heralded New Year's Day with mass in the Abbey of Cluny. Tristan and Guillaume knelt together that morning with the other boys of the Dorter and their teacher-monks. Abbot Hugh was the mass celebrant. Launching into his homily, he said "A great tide of change is washing across the continent. Our Church has evolved from a once united and holy endeavor into two camps, the Eastern Byzantine Rite and the Roman Catholic Rite. And now, even the Roman Catholic Rite itself has broken into two camps!"

As Abbot Hugh preached, most of the boys of the younger Dorter, including Tristan, were paying little heed. Tristan's attention was focused on the diverse crowd sitting in the pews and standing shoulder to shoulder against the walls. Foreigners were in attendance, most of them pilgrims. One small group, dark of skin and wearing the dress of the Romani, caught Tristan's eye and he peered into their midst hoping to perhaps spot Mala. To his disappointment, she was not among them. During Mala's previous visit her clan was on its way back to Spain to bring more Romani north, and Tristan had hoped to see them again on the return leg of that journey. Sadly for Tristan, they had never shown up.

Tristan's eyes wandered back to his own pew, and he began to survey his Dorter mates. Several seats down Letellier was sneaking a finger into Hébert's ribs. They would both be leaving Cluny in several months to begin training in arms under their fathers. He would miss them, but not as deeply as would Guillaume. This saddened Tristan; he wished for his brother's happiness.

Tristan's next point of attention became Scule who was actually praying, eyes closed, lips moving. As Tristan surveyed his little friend's flat face and short, knobby limbs, he could not understand why God had bestowed on someone as fine as Scule such a horrendous shape. He also wondered how an inherently cruel world would react to a dwarf monk, if indeed, the Church even allowed Scule into the novitiate.

Looking over at Guillaume, he noticed how tall he had become. Now two inches taller than Tristan himself, his boyish frame was transforming into the muscular physique of a gladiator, though his face remained angelic like their mother's.

This turned his thoughts to Asta, whom he had not thought of in months. This shamed him a little, causing a sudden longing to see her again, if even for only an instant. This, in turn, gave rise to a moment of self pity, but it passed. In truth, despite being forced from the Saint-Germain family territory, he had landed onto a path of opportunity. He was receiving a high education within the splendor of Cluny, and he had met teacher-monks, Prior Odo, Abbot Hugh, la Gran Contessa, and even the Pope. Moreover, he had been exposed to the grand stage of world affairs.

I wonder if Mother would be proud to know that I have assisted the Holy Father, he wondered. *Nothing in this life would make me happier than to see her lift a brow of approval at me.*

Chapter Thirty-One

The Pendulum Swings

Late January saw the arrival of Tristan's twelfth birthday, and the onset of puberty. He began to notice changes in his body as the fuzz of his face began to develop seven or eight tiny, bristle-like protrusions attempting to turn to whiskers. The bigger change was his voice, causing him an embarrassing series of high-pitched cracks that would occur at unexpected times. This caused a bit of raillery in the Dorter, but fortunately, other boys were experiencing the same thing.

In February, Cluny received word that Pope Gregory had finally had his fill of King Heinrich's religious lackey, Archbishop Guibert of Ravenna. Pope Gregory excommunicated him. This enraged King Heinrich, as well as German royalists and clerics alike, but Gregory felt it necessary due to Guibert's ceaseless military threats against the papacy. Still, Gregory made no direct threats against Heinrich himself, and continued to remain silent on the matter of the German civil war.

By early June, when Guillaume turned ten, the cracking of Tristan's voice began to evolve into deeper, froggish tones. June also saw Letellier and Hébert packing for their departure from the monastery to rejoin their families and to establish positions within France's aristocracy. Depending on which overlord or king their fathers chose to support, the outcome could be glorious and filled with promise, or disastrous as with Roger de Saint-Germain.

Letellier and Hébert, fully aware that a Cluny education would carry great weight in the years to come, were thankful to the Black Monks, especially Brother Placidus who had so faithfully served as their Dorter Master. Accordingly, their families showered the old monk with expensive gifts, gold coins and jewelry, which he promptly turned over to the Treasury Tower. The two families also awarded exorbitant free-will alms to the Cluny monastery as a gesture of gratitude for raising and educating their sons.

Scule had also completed his schooling, but was not leaving the monastery because the Black Monks had consented to his entry into the Cluny Novitiate. His family bestowed even more gifts on the monastery than did the Letellier and Hébert families. Scule's doting mother was especially proud of Scule, fawning over her misshapen son as though he were about to be enthroned as the future pope. Her behavior was so maudlin and over-done that poor Scule could barely look his classmates in the eye.

Scule's father was a different story. Throughout the graduation visit, it was difficult to tell who embarrassed him more, his wife or his son. He had never taken to Scule. It was even reported that at the baptismal font, Scule's father had cursed God for saddling him with a dwarf. It was further reported that God responded by rewarding such blasphemy with six daughters over the next eight years. These younger sisters had also come to Cluny to celebrate Scule's entry into the Cluny Novitiate. They, like Scule's mother, fawned and pawed at him ceaselessly.

The graduation was formalized through the celebration of high mass in the Cluny Abbey. As Abbot Hugh conducted the service, all two hundred Cluny monks filled the cavernous cathedral with the reverberation of somber ritualized chants in the revered tradition of Schola Cantorum. Abbot Hugh delivered a stirring homily on the importance of education and God in the lives of young men, and shared kind words lauding each boy's efforts though he barely knew the boys' names.

After mass, all filed onto Abbey Square where a sumptuous outdoor feast of roasted pig, lamb, goat and calf awaited. The monks brought forward their finest wines and ales, as well as baskets of fresh fruit, vegetables, sausages, cheeses and breads. As at any occasion signifying a rite of final passage, the mood was jovial and conversation flowed freely, peppered with compliments and praise. Brother Placidus was the recipient of much of this praise, and was reveling in the appreciative words of students and parents alike. His face red with spirits and laughter, he raised his goblet and with emotion, cried out, "God bless these wonderful lads, each and every one!"

An instant later, a falsetto voice rang out in perfect mimicry, much like an echo, *"God bless these wonderful lads, each and every one!"*

The crowd fell silent as Placidus swung his head from left to right and back again, his hawkish eyes scanning the crowd. Then the voice came again, and the culprit stepped forward, beaming like the morning sun.

Gasping with disbelief, Placidus then burst into laughter. "Scule!! You rascal! And to think you're to be a monk!"

Scule waddled his short frame up to Placidus and threw his stubby arms around the old monk's waist, holding him in a tight embrace. "Thank you for everything, Brother Placidus!" he bawled, falling apart as large tears streamed down his fat cheeks in rivulets. "I will never be able to repay your kindness!"

This ignited a hearty round of applause from the crowd, and also caused Scule's mother and six sisters to charge forward in a stampede of unbridled sobbing and embracing. From a distance, Scule's father glumly shook his head in disgust as he reached for yet another cup of wine.

When the affair was done and the family caravans departed, Guillaume stood by the gate, watching as the wagons moved down the hill. The White Witch was standing there alongside the road, and though he could not hear her, he could tell she was haranguing and cursing each wagon as it passed.

"Why does she do that?" he asked Tristan, who was standing beside him.

"She has her reasons," Tristan replied.

Seeing Letellier waving at him from the bottom of the hill, Guillaume raised his own hand in a final farewell. "Do you suppose we'll ever see Letellier and Hébert again?" he asked.

"I don't know," said Tristan, "but I hope so. At least Scule will still be here."

"Yes, but he'll be moving into the dormitory above the Novitiate Cloister this evening, and he'll be praying all day. We'll probably never see him. But would you have ever guessed it was Scule who's been mimicking Brother Placidus all these years?"

"No, not ever," Tristan replied. "But you know, he was so good at it that he even made old Brother Placidus laugh at the end."

"Yeah. I think Placidus is going to miss the three of them, too, just like we are. I wish they weren't leaving, Tristan."

"I know, but you'll make different friends now. When we return from our visit to Auntie Mathilda in Tuscany, the new boys will be arriving."

"Yeah, I know," said Guillaume. "I guess we're the big boys in the Dorter now, huh?"

Chapter Thirty-Two

Tuscany Again

One week after the graduation ceremony, Tristan and Guillaume were on a coach bound for Tuscany. Tristan was content enough about returning to Italy for another summer sojourn, but Guillaume could barely contain his excitement at seeing la Gran Contessa again. After arriving, he was propelled into a rigorous program of weapons and riding with Master Morelli, and as well, resumed his chase of boar and stag with Auntie Matilda. He also, for the first time, began to take interest in the lively political discussions occurring nightly at the dinner meal amongst Matilda, Tristan and the incessant stream of noble guests and clerics.

Tristan's presence during these exchanges was at first a novelty because of his age, but it soon became apparent that he was far better schooled in European and Church history than nearly every adult at the table. Those listening began to take the boy very seriously and began to spread word throughout Italy about the boy prodigy. This could not have made la Gran Contessa more proud. "Ah, my boys," she crowed, "I have within my own house the very future of the continent! A grand intellectual and a great general!"

In late August, one week prior to returning to Cluny, Tristan and Guillaume were outside the gates of Canossa with Matilda as she gave final instructions to the wagon-master of a caravan delivering arms to the Saxon princes of Germany. From the gatehouse parapet, a voice rang out, followed by the deep knell of the alarm bell. "Rider coming hard!" shouted the look-out.

The Canossa fortress had been built as a defensive structure, so the approach to its gate had been made deliberately circuitous by design, and in places was quite perilous to make access difficult for the unwelcome. This did not impede in the least the horseman coming up the hill, who was riding full tilt. Within minutes the clatter of hooves drew near and the rider galloped up to the Countess. It was the papal agent, Jurgen Handel. "News from Germany, Countess!" he shouted.

Seeing that the horse was bathed in sweat and that Handel appeared troubled, Matilda approached. "What is it, Handel?"

"Heinrich!" Handel wheezed. "Ten days ago he met Rudolph, Duke of Swabia, on the fields of Melrichstadt in Franconia—and routed his armies!"

"Heinrich has defeated Rudolph?" said Matilda, stunned. "But just prior to repenting here at Canossa in January, Heinrich himself was in full rout by the Saxon princes!"

"The pendulum's shifted, Countess," said Handel. "Heinrich now chases Rudolph and the Saxon upstarts. More importantly, Heinrich has now declared war against you and Tuscany!"

Matilda nodded. "I see," she said, showing little trace of surprise at this last bit news. "To be expected, as I have been supplying papal forces and Saxon rebels against him." Pointing to the line of wagons behind her, she said, "I am dispatching this very caravan today to supply his Saxon enemies."

"You'd best hold it here for now, Countess," suggested Handel, shaking his head. "He's tramping through Saxony as I speak, and you wouldn't want Heinrich to intercept it. And something else, his archbishop, Guibert of

Ravenna, is insisting that after capturing Rudolph of Swabia, they should next invade Rome and eliminate Pope Gregory once and for all!"

"Blasphemy!" exclaimed Matilda. "Oh, that Guibert is such a horror! Pope Gregory excommunicated him, and instead of seeking forgiveness, Guibert spreads more fire!"

"He wishes to be pope, Countess," said Handel with disgust.

"Indeed," replied Mathilda, "but God will see him punished one day."

"Until then, you'd best mobilize and keep an eye to your borders."

"Well, war it will be, then," declared Mathilda. "My cousin against me, my cousin against the Pope, my cousin against God!" Turning to the boys, she said, "Guillaume, tend to his horse, and Tristan, see that Handel is fed while I speak to the wagon-master about a change of plans."

Tristan led Handel to the dining hall and instructed the servants to ready a full meal and prepare a room. Handel, meanwhile, took a seat at the table and began stamping road dust from his boot and trousers. Tristan watched him with interest while taking a seat across the table. There was something about Handel and the other agent, Muehler, that had intrigued him since that first winter encounter on the mountain pass. They seemed constantly on the move, passing secrets, delivering news. Their arrival always seemed surrounded by a sense of urgency, or couched in personal risk.

"Is something on your mind, lad?" asked Handel, noticing Tristan's stare.

"Yes," Tristan replied, his eyes alight with curiosity. "The work you do, Sir Handel, do you enjoy it?"

"I'm not a *sir,* I'm a monk, so you may call me *Brother* Handel."

"A monk?" asked Tristan, surprised. "I knew you worked for the Benedictines, but I had no idea you were actually a religious!"

"Yes, since sixteen. But what did you think I was then, just a messenger?"

"Well, in truth," he said gingerly, "I for a while now have suspected that you are a spy. And I was wondering if you enjoyed such work."

At this, Handel gave the boy a hard look. "We don't use that word. It's ugly. But you know, I've wondered about you also a time or two, lad. I've seen you with Abbot Hugh, with Grand Prior Odo, Countess Matilda, and even the Pope. I've also heard you have access to the Treasury Tower of Cluny, which is one of the most highly guarded structures in all Europe. How is it one so young knows the great figures of Europe and has such access to things even great nobles are denied. So just how is it you're so privy to such?"

"I don't really know," said Tristan. "I was of nobility, but shame fell upon our house. My mother remarried and abandoned my brother and me by sending us to Cluny. I have been somewhat fortunate, I suppose, but also unfortunate."

"Ha!" snorted Handel. "That's all of us in life, boy, especially in the beginning, so don't feel special! It's what happens at the end that counts. So tell, what do you hope to become in the end?"

"Well, I like to learn, and read," he began, drawing at each word as though uncertain of his own persona. "I am good at solving problems and keeping account of things, I suppose, thanks to Prior Odo. But mostly, I like to be of assistance...and of value. If I could make a change that created justice and fairness, I should wish to follow *that* path."

"Ha!" laughed Handel. "It's very simple then, boy. You wish to be a monk!"

"What?" Tristan said, rattled by the suggestion.

"Listen to yourself. Everything you just said tells me there's but one direction for you. Do you think noblemen accomplish the goals you cited? Or soldiers? No, nor merchants! The Church is calling you, lad, can't you see?"

"I love God, Brother Handel," Tristan replied, "but have no wish to spend my life on—"

Pressing, Handel said, "Well, spit it out."

"Not to sound ugly, Brother," Tristan shrugged, "but I have no wish to spend my life on my knees, nor do I wish to preach or lead a parish."

Handel sat back, shaking his head. "Do you think *I'm* interested in doing such things? No! But there are many directions for a monk. Some of them labor, some pray, some write, some do nothing but study. But then, some such as myself and Muehler find very unique areas of work. The Church is *vast*, boy, and has many needs. Me, I uphold the Church because it's more important than any man, any king, any empire. Mother Church is the keystone of civilization in these dark times, so what I do is valuable work, in the name of God."

"But what you do, does it not also involve war and killing?"

"Of course it does!" replied Handel. "But many things do that in the end: commerce, diplomacy, even conversion of heathens. But you know, lad, there's only one way to fight a bear, and that's—"

"With a bear!" Tristan exclaimed, completing Handel's sentence.

"Yes!" Handel cried, slapping his palm hard on the table. "Ha! I see you've been talking to Odo de Lagery, eh, lad? But in that vein, my line of work is to *unleash* the Church's bear. You know, to repel the charge of the enemy's bear. I *equalize* the fight, though at times things get dirty." A servant entered the dining hall, setting on the table a large tray of meats, fruits and wine. As Handel dove into this welcome fare, Countess Matilda and Guillaume arrived. "So then, lad," Handel concluded, his mouth full of food, "think about what I've said. Seems your course is set, huh?"

Chapter Thirty-Three

Upheaval

It was late evening when Tristan and Guillaume's coach returned from Tuscany and plodded up the hill to the Cluny monastery. The boys made their way to the empty Dorter, and not wishing to awaken Brother Placidus because of the late hour, they crept into bed.

"Our new Dorter mates will be arriving in a few days," whispered Guillaume. "Before we left, Brother Placidus said I was to take Letellier's spot as Dorter Acolyte this coming year."

"Yeah, because you're the toughest one in the Dorter with Letellier gone," Tristan replied, pleased for his brother. "Now go to sleep."

That next morning they sought Brother Placidus, but he was neither in his room nor anywhere within the Dorter. "I'll go check for him," said Tristan. "Maybe he can tell us who is coming and which cohort they have been assigned to."

As he crossed over to the covered walkway of the cloister courtyard, he met Brother Damien. "Well now," Damien smiled, "Back from Tuscany, eh?"

"Yes, Brother. I'm looking for Brother Placidus."

At this, Brother Damien stopped in his tracks, giving Tristan an odd look. "Placidus is no longer with us, Tristan," he said, losing his smile.

"Where did he go?" Tristan asked, confused.

"He has finally gone home."

"Home? But he *has* no home. He was abandoned here as a child. He—"

"Tristan," Brother Damien interrupted, "old Placidus has gone *home*...to the Father. His soul is risen, but his body lies in our cemetery now."

"Oh, no!" Tristan stammered. "But I just spoke to him before leaving, and... "

Brother Damien placed a hand on Tristan's shoulder, offering a squeeze of comfort. "He passed while you were away, lad. He was not feeling well, and in the end was ready to go."

"But what do you mean? He was so happy and healthy during graduation, laughing and carrying on!"

"Yes, but just two weeks after you left for Italy, he fell ill. We found him dead in his infirmary bed, but his hands were crossed over his chest in prayer, clasping his Bible. He was ready to go."

"I see," said Tristan as a large tear began to well in the corner of one eye. "He was a good monk. I wish I could have bade him farewell at least." Wiping his eye, he offered a weak smile. "And as you say, he is home now. I suppose I will go to the Treasury Tower, then, and let Prior Odo know that Guillame and I have returned." As he said this, Brother Damien's expression darkened, just as when Tristan had inquired about Placidus. "What is it, Brother?"

"Well, then," Damien said, pulling each word, "another development since your absence. The Treasury Tower is locked down for the moment."

"What did you say?" said Tristan, feeling the approach of something iniquitous.

"Yes, and Prior Odo is no longer with us either."

Nothing in this life could have jolted Tristan more than these words. Too dumb-struck to speak, he stood there looking at Brother Damien with a blank stare.

"I'm sorry, lad," continued Brother Damien, "I know you were very, very close to the Prior, but he has been moved."

"Moved?" said Tristan.

"Yes, to Ostia near Rome. He won't be coming back to Cluny."

"But... " Tristan stammered, as now tears came in streams. "He did not even let me know such a thing was going to happen! Could he not have sent word to Tuscany, at least, or sent a farewell?" A wave of sheer heartbreak swept over him then and he fell silent, staring bleakly at the ground, reminded of that desperate morning his mother had suddenly informed him that she would be leaving for England without him and Guillaume. This was followed by a wave of bitterness, and he turned and stalked away.

"Tristan!" called Brother Damien.

But Tristan did not hear due to the fury that was now consuming every muscle and fiber of his body. Blinded by the salt of his tears, he hastened to the Abbey and entered. Fuming, his angry gait swept him down the main knave and into the first row of pews where he flung himself onto his knees, crossed himself, and began to speak to God. But his words were neither devout nor prayerful. "Why have you done this to me again, Lord?" he shouted, his face twisting with angst. "Have I not already lost my mother, my home, the Danes? But now you take Brother Placidus and Prior Odo who took the place of everyone else in my life! Am I to be abandoned at every turn?"

As he shouted these last words, Tristan felt the grip of a hand grasping him, shaking him by the arm. Startled, he turned. It was Abbot Hugh.

"Oh, but *shame* lad," said Hugh, shaking his head sternly. His voice was elevated and his eyes grave, not so much in anger as with chastisement. "One does not talk to God in such a manner!"

Tristan froze, then shrank back apologetically. "I just learned that Prior Odo has left me," he stammered. A moment later he tearfully added, "I have been abandoned again, Abbot Hugh!"

Hugh nodded, unable to dispel a tug of empathy as the youngster before him shook and sobbed with sorrow. "There, there, now," he said, trying to offer solace, knowing well that Odo de Lagery meant everything in life to young Tristan. "Prior Odo did not abandon you," he said. "The truth is, I sent him away."

"You, Abbot?" Tristan said with confusion, wiping tears from his eyes. "But *why*?"

Closing his eyes, Abbot Hugh sighed heavily. "Because since Canossa, Pope Gregory's judgment has become erratic and questionable. He has faltered on this business between Heinrich and the Saxon revolt, letting it deteriorate. As you know, Pope Gregory at first promised to support the Saxon rebels, but his promise collapsed after Heinrich's penance at Canossa. He then promised Heinrich that he would work toward reconciling Heinrich with the Saxon princes, but has done nothing while they have since crowned Rudolph of Swabia as their new German king. Infallible as the Pope is, he needs guidance and direction."

"But what has that to do with Prior Odo?" snuffled Tristan.

"The Pope needs an anchor on this business with Heinrich. Unless Pope Gregory is steadied, he will swamp the Church. As Gregory remains in Limbo, blood flows in Germany, Catholic soldiers butcher each other and the civilian population suffers daily. The Pope needs strong counsel, therefore I determined that only Prior Odo can accomplish such a task. Thankfully, Pope Gregory agrees. Odo will refill the vacancy as Cardinal-Bishop of Ostia near Rome, but his true purpose will be to serve as Gregory's First Counsel. I shall miss him terribly here. I know that you will also. But God's call is greater than ours, and we must both accept that."

Tristan stood listening in silence, still tremoring with dejection, trying to absorb Abbot Hugh's words.

"I know this is a blow to you," Abbot Hugh continued, "but please know Odo was thinking of you on the day he departed, and voiced a final request."

"Yes, Abbot?"

"As we begin the process of selecting the new Grand Prior at Cluny, he asked that you continue in the Treasury Tower. You know enough to be of some assistance as we flounder through the transition. So then, what do you say?"

Drying his eyes, Tristan slowly nodded. "Yes, of course, Abbot Hugh," he replied. "I will do so...for the Church."

***

Five days later the new batch of younger students arrived at Cluny, sons of high French lords fortunate enough and wealthy enough to receive educational assignments at Cluny. In place of Brother Placidus, Abbot Hugh appointed a new Dorter Master in the person of Brother Xavier who had just completed his novitiate at Cluny. He was young and inexperienced with managing boys, as well as with managing anything else in life but prayer. Not knowing what to make of the unruly herd he inherited, he discovered that young Guillaume possessed a natural penchant for dealing with these rascals that far surpassed his own timid insecurities. As a result, he began to rely heavily on Guillaume as Dorter Acolyte. Guillaume relished this new role, while proving to be both even-handed and clever in meeting these responsibilities.

Abbot Hugh was slow in selecting Cluny's next Grand Prior, as there was nobody possessing near the ability of Odo de Lagery, and the significance of the position was vital not only to the Benedictines, but to all Christendom. Hugh's solution was to appoint several potential candidates to work as a temporary cooperative to carry out the duties of the Treasury Tower. In a move that seemed odd to outsiders but made perfect sense to those within Cluny,

Tristan was appointed to assist this committee as they became acquainted with the Treasury Tower. Tristan performed this task responsibly, but found little pleasure doing so in the absence of Odo de Lagery.

Chapter Thirty-Four

Fernando of Spain

While helping the new committee in the Treasury Tower, Tristan received an unexpected benefit. With the arrival of a new monk to Cluny, a certain Brother Fernando, Abbot Hugh gave Tristan permission to learn Arabic. Fernando, though not of the Benedictine order himself, had been a monk since eighteen in Spain where the Benedictines possessed vast estates, castles and monasteries. Abbot Hugh had happened to make his acquaintance during a visit there. Of special interest to Tristan was the fact that Brother Fernando had spent the entirety of his service dealing with the rising tide of Muslim power in Spain. He, therefore, spoke Arabic with fluency and was well versed in a culture that was entirely foreign to Tristan.

Though fascinated by the rather flamboyant Fernando, Tristan was not aware that Fernando had been temporarily removed from Spain by his superiors. Born and raised of noble Spanish stock, he early in life grabbed onto the entitlements of aristocracy, embracing the good life. By fifteen, he had developed a love of wine and women, and had become the ceaseless source of his mother's fears and frailties. As the fourth son, Fernando was forced by family into becoming a cleric, as were many late-born males of large noble families. Fernando fought this at first, but on realizing that many clerics had concubine, wealth and estates, he developed a newfound fervor for the Church and completed his novitiate at the Monasterio de San Juan de la Pena in Aragon.

His early years of monastic life were not productive spiritually, but did offer many opportunities for continued debauchery. As the Benedictines filtered Church reform south into Spain, he found it more and more difficult to satisfy his temporal cravings. His licentiousness, once ignored, now became less tolerable to superiors. After becoming entangled in a scandalous carnal affair with the wife of a high nobleman of Aragon, his abbot sent him to Cluny to spare his life from an enraged, cuckolded aristocrat.

Initially, Fernando resisted instructing Tristan in Arabic because he was neither a tutor, nor did he like children. Nonetheless, his objections evaporated on realizing the boy's insatiable curiosity and passion for learning. Being a lively man of Aragon, Fernando refused to restrict his lessons to grammar and syntax. He delved into Moorish foods, spices, dress and philosophy, which Tristan found compelling. Oddly, despite having been engaged in curbing Islam, Fernando much admired many aspects of Muslim culture. On the topic of God, despite his own questionable spiritual purity, Fernando possessed a fiery opposition to heathen religion. "The infidel Moors need to be pushed back to Africa from whence they came!" he insisted.

"You know," Tristan told him one day, "because of this conflict between King Heinrich and the Pope, they rarely speak about Islam here at Cluny. But I often hear my aunt in Italy, the Countess of Tuscany, claim Islam is infecting the world."

"La Gran Contessa Mathilda?" asked Fernando, surprised. "Oh yes, she has for years sent weapons and money to Spain to fight the Moors. But you say she's your *aunt*?"

"Well, not really. But in her kindness she informally adopted my brother and me."

"Oh, you are blessed! She understands the Islamic spiritual plague, and has even suggested Christians unite in a grand crusade to retake Jerusalem from them."

"A crusade?"

"Si!" replied Fernando. "Islam is a dark disease. If not stopped, will spell the end of Christendom!"

"No, surely Christianity is too great, too powerful!" exclaimed Tristan.

"The Hell you say!" snapped Fernando. "The Great Schism cut us clean in half, Roman Christians against Byzantine Christians. And now even our western half is fractured as King Heinrich and Pope Gregory fight, while from the south the Moors encroach, and from the east the Turks are pushing."

Tristan had never for one moment in his existence considered the collapse of Christendom. "It could not happen," he muttered. "We *must* not allow it to happ—"

"You, my boy," interrupted Fernando, "in your time will see the great clash between our world and Islam. The wheel has already loosened. It's a good thing, too, that you are now learning Arabic; your future may well lay there."

"Huh?"

"Look, the west has men-at-arms aplenty, but in this struggle we'll need strong, capable leaders. But intelligent, perceptive leadership is a rare commodity, and it seems God has for some reason armed you with such qualities, young as you are. I believe that—"

"Peter the Hermit," Tristan whispered to himself, trailing off into his own thoughts.

"Qué dijiste?" asked Fernando.

"I was just thinking of Peter the Hermit, a monk that I met."

"Si!" nodded Fernando. "We know of him in Spain, preaching from the back of a donkey. But what of him?"

"He told me once that I was dangerous and would sow the seeds of war. And now I hear your talk about me and war in the future."

"This man the Hermit, dicen que advina el futuro, eh?" said Fernando.

"Yes, I know many say he sees the future," said Tristan.

"Yes, so maybe he was right. Maybe he meant your destiny is to fight Islam. Perhaps you've been chosen by God to do so. You are an unusual creature, and from what I hear, your life in itself has been highly peculiar. It seems someone has been directing you from one height to the next. Only God works in such a manner."

"Oh, I am but a student here and cannot begin to guess where I shall end when schooling is done. If I refuse to become a monk, I have even feared ending as a beggar."

Fernando shook his head. "God has no such intentions, nor does he wish you to waste away behind monastery walls. I hardly think I'm the first to believe that something of God's design awaits you. But enough of this since it seems to make you apprehensive. My lesson today is to acquaint you with the Qur'an and arkan-al-islam, the Moslem Holy Book and the pillars of their faith. Though it's rubbish, it makes for interesting discussion."

***

Within a month of working with Brother Fernando, Tristan began to grasp the basics of Arabic. This spurred him into seeking every scrap of information he could uncover about Islam by scouring the vast Cluny library. Beginning with the birth of Muhammed in the year 570, Tristan traced the prophet's early history up to his first revelation delivered by the Archangel Gabriel in the year 610. Infuriated by his heralding of a new socio-religious order denying pagan deities and professing allegiance to only one God, the leaders of Mecca expelled him. Muhammed and his followers moved to Medina in 622 in an event known as the 'hijra' or emigration, which marks the beginning of the Muslim calendar. There, Muhammed established a foothold in Medina and over the following years continued to attract followers. Upon his death in 631, a series of four caliphs known as the Rightly Guided continued to spread the message of Islam with their armies and carried the new faith from the Arabian Peninsula to the shores of the Mediterranean and to the eastern reaches of Iran. From there they conquered Syria, Palestine, and Egypt from the Christian Byzantine Empire, and Iraq and Iran from the Persian Sasanian Empire. In these conquered regions, Islam fostered a political, religious and cultural commonwealth that morphed into a global empire.

Tristan's newly acquired obsession about Islamic history and culture became all encompassing, working as a salve of sorts that healed the wounds left by Prior Odo's abrupt departure. It also created certain confusion. Tristan accepted that Muhammed was the last in the line of Judeo-Christian prophets, rejecting paganism in favor of the one true God, all of which was similar to Christianity. But Muhammed was not Christian, and to not be Christian was anathema to Tristan, as it was to all Westerners in 1078. Consequently, the juxtaposition of so many binding similarities between the tenants of Christianity and Islam contrasted to so many divisive differences between the two became an issue that would confound and disturb Tristan for the remainder of his existence.

At the onset of these new studies, Tristan, like most Europeans, possessed an extremely vague understanding of who the Muslims were, assuming that Moors, Saracens and Turks constituted a single, united population. But as Tristan researched the profusion of Islam, he was able to ascertain the differences, learning that the term Moor actually referred to several historic populations of the Berber people inhabiting northern Africa. From there, the term also came to be used for all Muslims of Black African and Arab descent who invaded Spain. These African invaders then crossed the Pyrénées north into France but were violently defeated by the Frankish king, Charles Martel (Charles the

Hammer) in 732 at the Battle of Tours. Retreating south back into Spain, the Moors then became involved in a series of battles against Christian kings set on recapturing territory in Spain from the Moors during what became known as the 'Reconquista'.

Tristan further learned that the term Saracen actually originated in reference to nomads belonging to tribes of the Syrian and Arabian deserts. Saracen then became a general term used incorrectly by Christians to describe all Arabs and all Muslims. Discovering that Moors and Saracens were different people with different geography, he next learned that it was Turks who ruled Asia Minor and Syria east of the Byzantine Empire. Above all, he learned that bitter infighting and war existed amongst the varying sects of Islam despite adherence to a common faith, which was similar to the feuding between various factions of European Christians, such as the Byzantines and Catholics, or even between King Heinrich and Pope Gregory.

As Tristan delved deeper and deeper into the historical evolution and subsequent spread of Islam across the continents, nascent seeds of alarm began to take root in his conscience, and he began to sense that Islam was, indeed, a threat to both the Holy Church and Europe. Recalling the words of Nuri the Romani years before at the campfire along the Seine River, and linking it to the warnings of Peter the Hermit, Tristan began to believe Brother Fernando's dark predictions of a great collision between Christianity against Islam.

Chapter Thirty-Five

The Change

As Christmas passed and Cluny began the New Year, Tristan was elated to receive news that Prior Odo, now Cardinal-Bishop Odo, would be returning to Cluny for a brief visit in April. The wait seemed an intolerable test of perseverance, but April finally arrived as Tristan constantly pestered the guards daily about traffic in and out of the valley. On April 29th, a procession of coaches became visible from the gate-house as the monastery bells tolled the arrival of dignitaries. Tristan hurried through the open gate and stared in the distance as the procession traversed the valley and began its ascent to the monastery. Tristan met them at the top of the rise, running from coach to coach calling out, "Prior Odo! "Prior Odo!" He found his mentor in the third coach, and as Odo tried to exit, Tristan nearly bowled him over in an effort to grasp his hand and embrace him.

"Ho, there, Tristan!" Odo laughed. "Oh, but I've missed you, my boy! My Italian accountants are nearly incompetent!"

This pleased Tristan, who had not yet uttered the first greeting as he was still dancing about with excitement at finally being again in the presence of the man he revered most in life. Catching a breath, he began to spout his news of the last year in a garble of disconnected thoughts.

"Whoa!" Odo cried, "We have time. I am here to await emissaries of Duke Guiscard the Wily returning from Normandy, but they won't be arriving for several days yet."

"Guiscard the Wily?" asked Tristan. "Is he not the Norman lord who accused me of listening in on his conversations at Lord Franzio's manor some years ago? But I thought he had been excommunicated."

As Tristan said this, an older gentleman stepped from the coach. "Oh, no," the man said. "He has been put back in the graces of God by Pope Gregory!"

"Ha, thanks only to your negotiating skills," said Odo. "Tristan, this is Cardinal Desiderius, Abbot of Monte Cassino."

"Monte Cassino!" exclaimed Tristan. "Is that not the site of the very first Benedictine monastery founded by Saint Benedict of Nursia?"

"Yes, your history is correct!" replied the Cardinal, smiling. "So, you must the young man Cardinal Odo has spoken so much of. The Wonder of Cluny, eh?"

"Tristan, Cardinal Desiderius holds great sway in Lower Italy where Guiscard rules," said Odo, "and has been mending fences between Guiscard and the Vatican. But Desiderius is also a dear friend of Abbot Hugh and wanted to accompany me for a visit while I tend to my main purpose for returning, which is business concerning you."

As Odo said this, Tristan noticed a microscopic shift in his expression. *What's this?* he wondered.

"And Tristan," he continued, "I will be meeting with Abbot Hugh first thing in the morning and I want you to be there—just the three of us."

There it is again, thought Tristan, unsettled by something in Odo's glance. And his inflexion as he had said 'just the three of us', had the ring of formality.

As instructed, Tristan reported to the Abbot's quarters that next morning where he found Odo and Hugh huddled in conversation. "Ah, Tristan," said Abbot Hugh, waving him forward. "Be seated, Cardinal Odo and I have something important to share with you."

Tristan took a seat and glanced at Odo, finding there the countenance of a man filled with purpose. Unlike the day before, he now wore the impressive, scarlet finery of a Roman cardinal, and was barely recognizable. Sensing that something was about, Tristan grew uneasy.

Hands in his lap, Odo directed his gaze at the boy. "Have you thought of your mother lately, Tristan?" asked Odo.

The question surprised Tristan. Odo had mentioned meeting Asta on the day Orla delivered the boys to Cluny, but never once after that time. "Well..." replied Tristan, his cheeks coloring, "though it shames me, Prior Odo, I—"

"He's a *cardinal* now," interrupted Abbot Hugh. "Prior Odo no longer exists."

Tristan acknowledged the correction with a bow. "Yes, Abbot Hugh," he said, turning back to Odo, "I have not thought of her in a while now, yet I carry her in my heart always."

"And well you should," Odo nodded, pulling a folded parchment from within the folds of his cleric's sleeve, opening it. "Upon sending you to Cluny, your mother placed this letter in the trunk presented by the man who brought you here."

"A letter from my mother?" asked Tristan, his heartbeat rising. "But that was years ago."

"Yes, I have held this letter six years now. You were but seven when I opened it. Now you're already a young man of thirteen, an entirely different creature from the small, nervous boy who stood looking up at me in my office that day. I have read your mother's words a hundred times since then, and because of recent events, her letter brings me back to Cluny. I wish to read it to you, Tristan."

Tristan nodded, as in his mind a foggy image of his mother began to knit itself together.

"My Dear Prior," Odo read aloud, "I have determined that God placed you in my path that dreadful day of my husband's punishment at Rouen. I was there to witness his execution. I forget now what it was that brought you to the Norman capitol that week, but I thank you for your words of comfort that day. More importantly, I thank you for accepting my sons despite the ruin of our name and the confiscation of all that I possess. In marrying my husband's brother, I have brokered an agreement with him that may appear unseemly, but I have little now to barter with except my own life." Here Odo paused and looked at Tristan. "Little to barter with but my own life," he repeated, shaking his head with reflection. "Do you hear the desperation of her words, Tristan?"

Tristan's gaze was directed at the floor, but he nodded as with each word of the letter, Asta's shadowy features became more clear.

Odo continued reading. "I have managed to negotiate Desmond DuLac into presenting the Black Monks with the ample monetary contents of this trunk in order to pay for the boys' education at Cluny until they come of age. I say I managed to 'negotiate' because Desmond DuLac is a greedy man. From the very beginning, he refused my sons. Nor did he wish to part with a penny of this wealth. As a final part of my negotiations, I also insisted that he employ, shelter and provision my Danish Guard, a party of nearly ninety, counting wives and children. In exchange for these two demands, I abandoned my sons, which no Christian woman would ever do under normal circumstances. Still, I wish to salvage their future. In Rouen as I spoke to you of perhaps consenting to Desmond DuLac's conditions, you listened patiently without castigating me. You said that God would direct me, and you were right. He made me see, through prayer, that my life holds less value than the future of my two sons and ninety others of my second family. Therefore, I deliver my Tristan and my Guillaume to you in the hope that they shall be well-educated and well-raised.

You will receive no further correspondence from me, nor will I accept correspondence from Cluny. This sounds harsh, but is the final condition my husband has imposed. I also request that you never share this letter with anyone, including my sons. In closing, as a mother torn, speaking to a devout man of God, I now have one special request of you. Please, I beg you, under no circumstances, ever abandon my sons as I have. In God's name I pray, Lady Asta de Saint-Germain."

As Odo completed his reading, Tristan sat mute and still, lost in his own world of private devastation. He was so dumbfounded he could not move, nor could he find tears or even speak. He had these past years always thought she had abandoned him and Guillaume in order to marry into wealth so she could maintain her noble status. He had regarded her decision as a calculated business transaction. Tristan had never once considered that sending him and Guillaume away was the most devastating event of his mother's life.

"Tristan," said Abbot Hugh, "your mother placed herself on the altar of sacrifice for Guillaume and you, as well as for the Danes. Tu comprends ça bien, n'est-ce pas?"

Tristan, his eyes still directed at the floor, slowly shook his head yes.

"In now acquainting you with this letter, I have violated your mother's request about confidentiality," said Odo, "but God forgives me this trespass because in the end, my intention is to honor your mother's primary request, which is to never under any circumstances abandon you and Guillaume. I, therefore, have been working on a means of honoring her request. I would like you to return with me to Ostia."

Tristan looked up, stunned. He began to speak, but the wave of confusion washing over him tied his tongue. He tried again, but hesitated, then started again, and fell yet again into hesitation. Odo's proposal seemed simple at first, sending an initial shock of joy spiraling through Tristan.

But this was quickly followed by the onset of a dozen complications racing through his head.

Odo had already anticipated this. "I imagine you have certain concerns," he said, "so let me begin with your brother. I wish to take him with us, but in my communications with la Gran Contessa, she has inquired whether it might not be better for Guillaume to go to Tuscany."

"Tuscany?" asked Tristan.

"Yes. She and Guillaume share a special relationship which I believe you are aware of, and Mathilda wishes to take him in."

This proposal put Tristan in a greater state of discomposure than had the original suggestion of going to Ostia. "But Prio...Cardinal Odo! No! I could never just leave my—"

"Tristan, think of *him*, not yourself. He would have opportunities with Matilda that neither you nor I could ever hope to match."

"Discuss it with him," added Abbot Hugh, "but remember, you are his older brother, not his parent."

"Then, too," Odo continued, "I suppose you have concerns about your schooling. Yes, Cluny offers the highest form of scholae monasticae in all Europe, but I intend to establish a new cathedral school in Rome and have already recruited some of the finest academic minds on the continent to teach there. The school will specialize in languages, political history and diplomacy, your strong suits, perhaps even your future. Abbot Hugh informs me you are now studying Muslim culture and mastering Arabic. You can continue learning and perfecting that language in Rome. Also, I would like you to begin learning Persian, the language of the Turks." Leaning forward, Odo turned his palms toward Tristan, as making an offering. "So now, Tristan, how does this sound to you thus far?"

So much had been thrown at him so quickly that Tristan's head was aswirl. Despite feeling overwhelmed, the very possibility of being within the heart of Rome had already piqued Tristan's interest. His previous trips to Lord Franzio's and to Tuscany had opened the world to him, making him realize there were fabulous opportunities to learn and study beyond the walls of Cluny. Above all, he would again be at the side of the man he adored above all men on earth. Looking at Odo, he said, "It sounds frightening, Cardinal Odo, yet full of promise."

"Indeed," replied Odo, pleased. "In the end, Rome is a vast metropolitan center and will open new doors for you. I realize you have no wish to be a monk, but meeting new and important acquaintances can guide you to other professions. Of course, I will not force you or Guillaume either one to leave Cluny, but my offer solidifies your mother's heartfelt concern to secure a future for the two of you, even though that future was to be without her. As the big Dane said that day, you and Guillaume are the Lady Asta's prize possessions in life, and she delivered the two of you to me alone. I believe she would be pleased at the opportunities my offer affords you both."

"You have much to think about, Tristan," said Abbot Hugh. "Go to the cathedral, then, and pray over it. *Dieu te dirigera...*God will show the path."

***

Tristan gathered Guillaume from the Dorter and, without a word, led him into Cluny Abbey. Dipping his finger in the font of holy water just inside the main nave, he crossed himself and walked down the huge center aisle. Puzzled, Guillaume followed and took a position next to him in the front pew.

"What is it, Tristan?" he whispered. "Why are we here?"

"Do you see Jesus on the cross there?" Tristan whispered, pointing to the life-sized crucifix hung high behind the massive altar. "I want you to say a short prayer to Him asking guidance. Then I'm going to ask you a question."

Guillaume shrugged as Tristan closed his eyes and began praying. Guillaume followed suit. A few minutes later he opened his eyes and looked at his brother, who was already now looking at him.

"Guillaume, if I were to leave Cluny and go to Rome," said Tristan, "would you not wish to come with me?"

Guillaume blinked, surprised. Shaking his head, he said, "I wouldn't want to go to Rome, and I wouldn't want you to go either. Cluny is our home."

Tristan nodded. "Yes, this has *been* our home. But do you wish to become a monk?"

Guillaume shook his head no.

"If we stay here, we will probably end up as monks," said Tristan. "But very well, another question. If you were given the chance to live in Tuscany with Auntie Matilda, would you still choose to remain here?"

At this, Guillaume's eyes widened and he nudged closer to his brother. "Tuscany with Auntie Matilda is the only place I would ever choose over Cluny. But Tristan, *you* would be there with me and not in Rome, right?"

Tristan's face tightened and his shoulders raised a measure. "No," he whispered. "I would be in Rome with Cardinal Odo. But if you insist on staying here, I will stay also, Guillaume. This is all confusing to me, and I just learned of it all this morning. Cardinal Odo—"

"I choose Tuscany and Auntie Mathilda," interrupted Guillaume. "But you'd come visit me, wouldn't you, Tristan?"

"Of course. But perhaps you should think about it for a time. Cardinal Odo will be here for several days yet." Then Tristan pointed to the crucifix. "You *did* pray to Jesus, did you not?"

"I did, even though I had no idea what I was praying for," said Guillaume.

That next morning, Tristan and Guillaume spoke again about Odo's proposal. The more they spoke, the more excited each became, not only for self, but also for the other. Tristan then confirmed to Abbot Hugh and Cardinal Odo that he and Guillaume were ready to establish new roots in Italy.

"Excellent!" said Odo. "Say your farewells then over the next three or four days then and start packing. Then it's off to Italy we go."

Duke Guiscard's Norman emissaries arrived several days later. Cardinal Odo took them about the monastery describing operations and reviewing the vast farmlands belonging to the Black Monks. Tristan was assisting with this tour in the fields when he noticed two tiny box-wagons just entering the valley. They resembled Romani box-wagons; the sight of which stirred Tristan. Taking his leave from Cardinal Odo and the visitors, he moved toward them, wishing in his heart that this could somehow be Mala and Nuri passing through Cluny for some reason.

As the wagons approached, he thought he spotted two women sitting side-by-side in the first wagon, which caused his heart to soar. Shading his eyes and straining to get a closer look, he saw that one woman's face was covered by a scarf, but the other appeared elderly and stooped. Sagging with disappointment, Tristan recalled that Mala's mother was young and beautiful, so he turned to leave. At that instant the wagon's pace quickened and a young female voice rang out. "Tristan! Oh, my Tristan! Don't walk away!"

Recognizing the voice, he took off at a mad dash and intercepted the wagon on the road. Mala, her dark eyes aglitter, threw on the wagon brake and jumped from the seat, heaving herself onto Tristan in a wild embrace, kissing his neck and cheeks. "Still have my Moorish ring, Smart Boy?" she laughed.

"Yes!" Tristan was startled by Mala's greeting, as well as by her now incomprehensible beauty and shape. He had always thought her pretty, but the last time they were together she had been but twelve or so. Now she was about fifteen and had taken on the shape and fullness of a grown woman. Pulling the small ring from his pocket, he held it up, grinning. "But what are you *doing* here?" he asked, his voice as elevated as his heartbeat.

Mala stood back and admired Tristan a moment, then embraced him again, pressing the full breadth of her breasts and torso against him. "I have been thinking of *nothing* but you, Tristan, for weeks now, ever since we began our trip back to Spain!"

"Back to Spain?" asked Tristan. "But during your last trip there I thought you were bringing more of your family to France."

"Ah, too many things happened after returning from Spain. Our life became hard, and continues to be hard, Tristan." She pointed to the stooped woman in the wagon. "My mother, Nuri, she'll have no more of France. She wishes to go home and I'm taking her. She has become less afraid of the Muslims than of the French and Normans."

Tristan looked toward the wagon, appalled. The once beautiful Nuri now appeared aged and infirm; her face scarred nearly beyond recognition. "What happened?" Tristan said, unable to hide shock.

"She was violated, then her face cut to ribbons when she tried to defend herself," said Mala, her teeth clenching. "It was a boy you once knew here, that red-headed devil!"

"Who?" said Tristan, thinking a moment. Then he whispered, "LeBrun."

"Yes, that's the one," Mala said. "My mother and her sister worked for his father. The father took liberties with them both, which they accepted because he helped from time-to-time with food and money. But then the son came back from Cluny and thought he deserved the same privileges. When he was refused, he got angry and attacked my aunt, killing her, then carved up my mother's face!"

Tristan stood back, aghast. "Oh, LeBrun! He never was any good!"

"And does not deserve to live," said Mala. "That's why I killed him a month past," she stated, showing no emotion as she pointed to the dagger poking from her belt.

Tristan's jaw dropped. "You...?" he muttered, aghast.

"Yes, me, my mother and those in the other wagon fled Normandy and went to Paris then, but my mother wants no more of France. She insisted I take her back to Spain, which is where we're headed now." She reached into a slip-pocket then and held up a gold coin. "I have money now, so you won't have to ask your prior for favors on our behalf this time."

Tristan accompanied them up the hill and settled Mala and Nuri into the Guest Hall along with those in the second wagon. Cardinal Odo had requested that Tristan have dinner with Duke Guiscard's representatives and Cardinal Desiderius that night, but Tristan excused himself and met Mala outside the refectory as previously arranged. They spoke there a short while, then moved out to the steps of Cluny Abby where they had spent time together as during Mala's last visit to Cluny.

"I was afraid I would never see you again," said Tristan, still struck by this unexpected stroke of fortune.

Mala looked at him and smiled. "Just as last time, it was *my* decision to come by Cluny, because I knew you were here." Then she shook her head. "Nuri is nearly like a child now, helpless and afraid. She begged me for Spain again, so we're going there to reunite her with her other sister who refused to migrate north. But I've no heart for Spain, so I'll be returning to France."

Tristan pondered on this a moment, finding it incredible that Mala had taken charge of such a venture. He could not comprehend her ability to simply pick up and leave one place for another, nor could he grasp her independence and courage. But Mala's gypsy existence bore no resemblance to Tristan's sheltered confinement, so she thought little of the magnitude of her actions. In truth, she rather pitied Tristan's shackles, wondering how he could bear such a rigid existence within the walls of a monastery.

Still, she had recognized something phenomenal in Tristan since that first encounter along the river, and this attraction had only magnified with time. It was his intelligence and his sensitivity. Too, despite him being younger than she, he was so pleasant to look at, and was so sophisticated when matched against her fellow Romani, or even the other French and Norman boys she had met along the way.

They lingered on the cathedral steps until late into the night, sharing their respective experiences during the long separation and reveling in their adoration of each other. Tristan would have remained there until dawn, but just after midnight Mala stood and said, "Best I check on Nuri. She doesn't sleep well anymore and gets frightened."

With regret, Tristan returned to the Dorter and could think of nothing but Mala until finally he fell asleep dreaming of her. When he awoke, he hurried to the Guest Hall to fetch her again, spending the entire day together walking about the monastery and sitting on the Abby steps.

As dusk approached, Mala asked, "Tristan, do you never leave the walls of this place? Could we not go beyond the gate there and sit upon the hill?"

"Certainly," Tristan replied, although it was forbidden for students to venture outside the monastery gates at night. As they walked beyond the gate, he looked back, fearful of being noticed.

Mala led the way. Once beyond sight of the gate, she took a seat along the steep hillside, grasping Tristan's hand so that he was seated next to her. During this entire time Tristan could scarcely quell the pounding of his heart. Being in Mala's stunning presence was nearly more than its walls could bear.

"Did you think of me, Tristan, even though it's been so long since my last visit?" asked Mala, her tone coy but expectant.

"Yes," mumbled Tristan, "often...every time I looked at your ring, in fact. And I—"

Mala interrupted him with a soft kiss to his lips, pulling him back with her flat onto the grass as she gazed up at the moon's filtered glow. "I told you I'm coming back to France, you know," she said. Turning her head, she placed her palm flat against Tristan's chest and caressed him. This created a flutter that skittered the entire length of Tristan's torso. He closed his eyes, thinking that he had never felt such pleasure. Then, without a word, Mala pulled at his hand and slowly slipped it beneath her blouse, upon her bare breast. "Touch me, Tristan," she whispered, kneading his fingers about her nipple.

Feeling the tender flesh of Mala's full breast, and her taut nipple, Tristan felt the shock of fire searing through him; experienced a strain in his groin that made him feel as though he was drowning in sin. Yet, he was hopelessly intoxicated by the sensation caused by the tenderness of her flesh, and he felt his fingers begin to move about, plying her ample breast.

"I made up my mind on the way to Cluny," said Mala, gently moving her hand with Tristan's. "It would please me to be near you, so when I return from Spain I'm coming back to Cluny, just to be close to you."

These words jolted Tristan from the surreal reverie of Mala's flesh, causing him to immediately withdraw his hand from her. "Huh?" he said.

"Yes, I'll take a little job down in the village and I'll live in my wagon," she purred with contentment. "Just think, we could see each whenever we wish, then."

"But Mala," he said, confused, "I—I am— "

"You what?" laughed Mala, certain her words had left him speechless with anticipation.

Sitting up, Tristan stared at her, too distraught to offer a reply. Then, in a burst, the words tumbled from his mouth. "I am leaving Cluny for Rome tomorrow morning—with Cardinal Odo."

Failing to quite understand, Mala shrugged. "Oh, but you'll be coming back soon, huh?" she chortled.

"N-no," stuttered Tristan. "I am…moving to Rome… for good."

"No!" gasped Mala, refusing to believe what she had just heard. "No, impossible, Tristan!" She stared dumbly at the night sky a moment and began to say something, but her lips trembled so violently her words caught in her throat. Turning, she stared at him, dumbfounded. "But I've thought of nothing since fleeing Normandy but coming to live in Cluny! Just to be near *you*, Tristan!"

Tristan, at a complete loss for words, had no idea how to respond. Mala could come and go at this point in her life, apparently, but he could not. His life was anchored to Odo de Lagery and the Black Monks. "I have no choice," he stammered, looking at her helplessly. "I am but a boy, still. I have no means."

At this, Mala pushed her palms against the ground behind her and stood. "Tristan," she said with desperate, imploring eyes, "you could leave the monastery and come stay with me in the wagon, maybe find work in the fields, or in town even."

Tristan tried to envision the proposal a moment. But shocked, the image quickly fled as everything suddenly turned frightening. "No," he muttered, "Mala, I am but twelve and—"

"Amongst the Romani, boys must work at your age, Tristan!" Mala insisted, clasping her hands in frustration. "And so do most others, even in France. Besides, I'm fifteen now and there's nothing unusual about a girl my age taking up with someone, or even marrying! I love you, and think I always have! I thought you felt the same. Do you not love me in return, Tristan?"

"I…yes, I think so," stammered Tristan, "but what you suggest is impossible!"

"For *you* maybe," Mala said, tears washing down her cheeks, "but not for me!" Pawing at her face, swiping aside her tears, she crossed her arms and looked at him crossly, her eyes narrowing. "You're afraid, aren't you? Yes, that's it. Your entire life you've been cared for and sheltered! And now you cling to that prior monk like a frightened pup, knowing nothing else but to follow his shadow!"

"Mala, I—"

"Say no more, Smart Boy!" she said coldly, her lips quivering with hurt. "Best then that I get back to Nuri, and we'll be on our way!"

Before Tristan could stop her, or even say a word, she turned, entered the gate, and disappeared. Numb with confusion, Tristan sat there, quietly dissolving in a storm of sorrow. He had never understood what it was about Mala that had so enraptured him from the very beginning, nor did he understand why they seemed to encounter each other only at unexpected junctures, and for such brief moments. But he did not like it, and it was now beginning to hurt.

Tristan found no sleep that night. At first light, he slipped from the Dorter and ran to the Guest Hall in search of Mala, but the two box-wagons were gone, and so was Mala.

Hours later, Cardinal Odo's party began loading into their caravan for the journey to Italy. As the procession of coaches and wagons left the monastery and began their descent into the valley, Tristan was in an absolute haze, and could think of nothing but Mala.

Perhaps I'll see her again, he mourned, *if God wills it.*

As Odo's procession reached the bottom of the hill, unlike Tristan, Guillaume was filled with gaiety. He possessed not a single regret, and was already looking forward to Italy with burning optimism. "Look, Tristan," he said, pointing out of the coach he shared with his brother and Cardinal Odo, "it's the White Witch!"

"Be glad you are gone from this ungodly nursery of evil, you boys!" the woman cried, spotting Tristan and

Guillaume inside the coach. "Save yourself from the wickedness of God's so-called holy men! They're but peddlers of abuse and corruption!"

"Pay her no heed," said Odo, noticing that Guillaume appeared amused by her. Then, looking at Tristan, Odo noticed that Tristan appeared lost in a world of regret. "You'll not have to tolerate her again now that you are leaving Cluny, Tristan," Odo said.

But Tristan was not bothered by the woman. Still distressed over Mala, he peered out the window. "I pity her," he said, "and understand her anger. She has a dreadful story...and holds the Church responsible."

At this, Odo reached over and closed the lace curtain of the coach window. "Yes, there are those in the Church who are responsible for her sad tale," he said, "but not the Black Monks. We attempt to purify such abuses through the reform movement."

"But what of priests such as Bishop Villier of Saint-Germain-en-Laye who presides over the diocese where I once lived?" asked Tristan.

"Bishop Villier?" said Odo. "What do you know of Bishop Villier?"

"Only what Peter the Hermit told me," said Tristan, trying to shove thoughts of Mala aside. "I once thought the bishop to be a holy man, but the Hermit says he keeps women and sells them to others. Is that so?"

"I will simply say that the Holy Father recently delivered a ban of excommunication against Bishop Villier of Saint-Germain for such behavior, and many others like him. As for the White Witch, her folly is that she lumps all of us together with clerics such as Villier."

"Perhaps," mumbled Tristan. "Still, I understand her plight."

At this Odo smiled, marveling at the new, deep richness of Tristan's voice as well as his objectivity in assessing the woman ranting outside the coach. *Ah, Tristan is becoming a young man, a frightening young man.*

***

Along the way to Tuscany, Tristan had the opportunity to become better acquainted with Cardinal Desiderius, developing an immediate affection for him. He also became acquainted with the two emmisaries from Lower Italy who had joined Cardinals Odo and Desiderius at Cluny. They had been in Normandy making contact with Duke Guiscard the Wily's family, the noble Maison d'Hauteville. Their mission there had been a military recruiting effort of sorts during which they encouraged adventurous and dispossessed men-at-arms to join Guiscard's forces in Sicily and Lower Italy. The first man was Bernard LeRoux, a Norman born and bred. But it was the second man who captured Tristan's interest, a Muslim, which Tristan found surprising, who went by the name of Kareem al-Rashid. He dressed as a Norman, however, since traveling through France in Muslim garb invoked hostility.

During their first overnight stay at one of the Benedictine monasteries along the road to Tuscany, Tristan discovered that this man spoke French poorly, as he did Italian. Resorting to the year's worth of Arabic he had learned from Brother Fernando, Tristan asked him, "How is it that you fight alongside Robert Guiscard, a Christian Norman?"

Surprised the boy possessed even a cursory knowledge of Arabic, Kareem nodded with approval. "Guiscard invaded Sicily in 1061," Kareem responded, "surprising the troops of Emir Ibn al-Hawas. Guiscard then made an alliance with my master, Emir Ibn at-Timnah, enemy of Ibn al-Hawas. Guiscard and my master next marched their combined troops into central Sicily, fighting until 1072 when Palermo fell. Guiscard and my master have remained friends. I am my master's envoy amongst Guiscard's forces."

"You joined forces with Guiscard, a Christian?" asked Tristan, surprised.

"Because of bad blood amongst the Muslims of Sicily. My master's fight in Sicily was not about Allah, but about vengeance."

"And now you go to Rome with Guiscard's man to see the Pope?"

"Yes," nodded Kareem. "But a question. Your pope, he put Guiscard out of your religion somehow years ago?"

"Yes, he was excommunicated for attacking papal territory," explained Tristan.

"Ah yes, that is the word, 'excommunication'. But then your pope let Guiscard back into your God's church, and now seeks a military help from him against the German king, Heinrich."

"Ah," said Tristan, "so that explains why you and Sir LeRoux go to Rome with Cardinal Odo."

Kareem nodded. "Yes, LeRoux goes to explore terms. Me, I simply go because my master, the Emir, is curious about your pope. We wonder, whenever this pope of yours is not pleased with someone, he can deny them your God as he did to Duke Guiscard? Then reopen the doors to your God again whenever he likes?"

"Sir Kareem," Tristan replied, "there is much more to it than that!"

Upon reaching Tuscany, Odo accepted Matilda's offer to spend a week at Canossa before turning south to Rome. During this time Tristan worried about leaving Guillaume. On the other hand, Guillaume was in extremely high spirits, which gave Tristan great comfort.

Tristan engaged in several more conversations with the Muslim, Kareem, discussing differences between Muslim and Western culture. Kareem was impressed with Tristan's knowledge of Arabic history, as well as his curiosity about learning even more. Tristan enjoyed these exchanges, but was surprised when one afternoon Kareem remarked, "I have never met a Christian that knows so much about my people. They will use you against us one day."

"What do you mean, Sir Kareem?" said Tristan.

"There is talk in the shadows of a great war coming between the East and the West. I am sure this is not news to you, eh?"

"Well," Tristan responded, choosing his words, "I have heard certain things. And then, of course, there are the wars in Spain and the wars between the Turks and the Christian Byzantines to the east."

"Nothing but skirmishes," said Kareem. "No, I am speaking of a great war, and your knowledge of my people, our customs, and our faith could be valuable to your Christian generals one day."

"Well then," replied Tristan, "perhaps that is why you traveled to Normandy and Cluny, and now Tuscany and Rome, to be of value to your masters?"

At these words Kareem's dark face slipped into a smile. "Ah, you are as clever as they say," he said. "My emir and I have heard mention through Duke Guiscard of a boy from Cluny who is on familiar terms with the great figures of France and Italy. A boy with unnatural intelligence. You met Guiscard once, eh?"

"Yes," said Tristan, "he only spoke to me once, and that was in anger. He frightened me, but I was younger then."

"Ah, there is also talk in Italy about a boy who is more intelligent than the most educated of nobles and priests. *You* are that lad, eh?"

Tristan gave no reply.

That next day, two riders entered the Canossa gates. Tristan was delighted to again see the Bavarian agents, Dieter Muehler and Jurgen Handel. "Ho there, Tristan!" Handel cried upon dismounting. "I see you've grown another head taller since we last spoke!"

Tristan shook Handel's and Muehler's hands. "But what brings you here to Canossa?" he asked.

"We've just left Rome from briefing the Holy Father on the German wars," said Muehler.

"Aye, the stakes continue to rise," added Handel, "and it appears that if the Saxon princes can't contain Heinrich, he'll soon be heading south after Mathilda and the Pope. In any case, I'm headed somewhere south while Muehler's going another direction for other purposes."

The vagueness of Handel's last statement indicated a refusal to divulge destinations. "I see," said Tristan. "You should know then that Duke Robert Guiscard's man, Bernard LeRoux, is right here at Canossa as I speak. He's on his way to Rome with Cardinals Odo and Desiderius."

"Yes, we know, Pope Gregory summoned him," replied Muehler. "If Heinrich breaks free and attacks Rome from the north, Guiscard controls Sicily and Lower Italy and could reinforce Pope Gregory from the south. As Handel said, the situation's escalating."

"There is also a Moor here," Tristan said, "traveling with Guiscard's man, LeRoux."

"Ha! Is his name Kareem?" asked Handel.

Tristan nodded, noting that very little ever seemed to escape Handel.

"Keep an eye to him, lad," warned Handel, "he's a Muslim agent."

Three days later, the coaches lined up to leave Canossa. Giving his farewells to Guillaume, Tristan felt loss pulling at him as he looked into Guillaume's eyes a final time. Then, as the coaches slipped down the mountain trail leading away from Mathilda's fortress, Tristan saw Guillaume's figure atop the rise waving at him, and felt a wave of sadness wash through him. But Guillaume was smiling and laughing, engaged in pleasantries with la Gran Contessa.

Good for Guillaume, thought Tristan. *He does not hurt or think about things as I do. Nor does he suffer as much.*

Chapter Thirty-Six

Rome

Arriving in Rome, Cardinal Odo reported to Pope Gregory who over the next three days held a series of private meetings with LeRoux and Kareem. Tristan was not privy to the specifics of these encounters, but it was apparent that the Pope was anxious. As LeRoux and Kareem prepared to leave Rome on the fourth day, Pope Gregory appeared satisfied.

"May God watch over you during your final leg south," he told the two visitors as they left Rome, "and tell my dear Duke Robert that I send my personal blessings to him."

My dear Duke Robert, thought Tristan. *Is this how Pope Gregory now addresses a man he not long ago excommunicated for invading papal territory?*

Kareem, who was next to LeRoux, bowed to the Pope and Cardinal Odo while saying something in Arabic. Not understanding the Muslim's words, Gregory smiled awkwardly. This caught Tristan's attention, and he intervened. "He bids you farewell, Holiness."

Gregory nodded, but raised his shoulders with curiosity. "But so many words simply to say farewell?"

Tristan weighed the question a moment. "Holiness, his exact words were actually 'Salaam leium…Allahu akbar…la ilaha illa llah'. That means peace be with you, God is great, and there is no God but God."

"I see," said Gregory, a frown creeping over his face. "But does this man speak of our true Christian God, or does he speak of his Allah?"

"As a Muslim," said Tristan, "I suspect he speaks of Allah who he sees as the one true God."

Gregory's frown deepened and he scowled at Kareem who could by now detect the Pope's displeasure. "Is this not an affront?" asked Gregory. "Should a heathen give such an offensive, non-Christian blessing to the very Father of God's Holy Church?"

Tristan reddened, regretting that he had offered a translation. "I am certain, Holy Father," he replied, "that Kareem was simply being polite. He meant no offense."

"Very well, then," grunted Gregory, offering Kareem a false smile. Raising his hand, he made the sign of the cross over the Moor. "Peace be with you, and may God help you see the error of your beliefs before you stand in His final judgment."

As the coach pulled away and the Pope's entourage turned to leave, Odo pulled Tristan aside. "Well now," he said, "did you learn something just this moment?"

"Yes, Cardinal," said Tristan. "The Holy Father was more content *not* understanding Kareem's words than understanding Kareem's words. I was trying to light a candle, but darkness may have been more appropriate."

Odo placed his hand on Tristan's shoulder and nodded. "Sometimes simplicity out-trumps complexity, even the truth. Remember that lesson, for we are in Rome, and honesty can be costly. But enough of this serious business. We have been here nearly a week already and you have yet to see our parish of Ostia."

***

The ancient city of Ostia was located at the mouth of the Tiber River. In early antiquity it enjoyed a flourishing commerce, thriving in salt trade as a vital seaport on the western shores of Italy with immediate access to Rome which was nearby. Silting began to move the shoreline seaward, land-locking the city. Its commercial stature began to decline, and in the early 9th century Ostia was captured by the Saracens. In response, Pope Gregory IV turned an eastern section of the city into a fortified area dubbed Gregoriopolis. Years later, during the reign of Pope Leo IV, the Saracens were defeated and driven off the coast.

The position of Bishop of Ostia held high honor within the papal hierarchy. Since the year 336 A.D., it was the Bishop of Ostia who actually consecrated the popes after election by the College of Cardinals. Odo's appointment, therefore, held special significance. It also suddenly placed him in position for future consideration as a candidate for the papacy upon the need for succession. This fact did not escape Odo. Since he had never sought to acquire the position of pope, it was with certain trepidation that he had agreed to don the robe of Bishop-Cardinal of Ostia.

Tristan lost no time immersing himself in the vastness and bustling activity of Rome and its environs. He had presumed he would be working in an office behind closed doors with Odo as he had done at the Treasury Tower, but discovered that Odo's position as Bishop of Ostia was more titular than actual. Rather than minister to the parish of Ostia, a chore left for lesser priests, Odo's real purpose was to directly advise the Pope. This meant Odo spent much time in Rome, and little time in Ostia. It also meant that Tristan, as Odo's assistant, was spending his days in Rome, reporting to Ostia with Odo only for ceremonial purposes.

Odo's early responsibilities were heavily tied to Vatican diplomacy. Just as there existed division between Church and crown throughout Italy and Germany, there existed division within the close-quartered political network of Rome. Pope Gregory had developed enemies in Rome among those supporting King Heinrich. Also, many Roman aristocrats longed for the earlier days of debauchery and licentiousness, resenting the new morality espoused by Gregory. Fortunately, Cardinal Odo managed to make inroads amongst Gregory's opposition as he possessed a more reasonable tone than did the stubborn Gregory. Unlike the Pope, who sprang from rough peasant stock, Odo came from nobility, and was much more practiced in bartering and compromise.

Tristan immediately came under a new academic regimen, albeit irregular in terms of scheduling. In particular, Cardinal Odo pressed him to learn Persian. "The Turks now rule all of Asia Minor, but have since decades adopted the Persian culture and language," he told Tristan. "They will be a force to reckon with, so master their tongue!"

When not tending to his studies, Tristan accompanied Odo on diplomatic visits, soon becoming a familiar sight within the arena of Roman aristocracy. Just as these nobles appreciated the new Cardinal-Bishop of Ostia, they accepted his assistant, determining the boy was phenomenally capable and intelligent. They referred to him as 'that Cluny Lad', some even commenting that this young wonder was destined to become a cardinal himself, or perhaps even one day wear the Pope's tiara.

Tristan enjoyed his new diplomatic work within the great city; meeting new people and deciphering the political power structure of Rome, the very center of Christendom. Although he missed the formality of daily academic instruction, he now had access to the great libraries of Rome as well as to the great minds of Rome: politicians, philosophers, writers, orators and academics. Moreover, he was given the opportunity of working regularly with the two monks serving as Pope Gregory's Muslim interpreters, one fluent in Arabic and the other in Persian. With each passing week he felt himself growing intellectually, as well as socially.

Something else began to happen: adolescence. He began to feel changes in his body, and was also frequently forced into the company of females. The presence of girls and women had been a rarity at Cluny; Mala was the only girl he had ever really met. In Rome, females were everywhere, bold and outspoken.

Tristan began to suspect women and girls were taking notice of him, frequently catching them stealing a lingering glance, or messaging coy smiles. Although he failed to understand flirting, he found himself falling into the company of certain females requesting his presence. Invariably these females were much older than himself, causing him to wonder why such ladies would have any interest in spending time with him. Naively, he chalked it up to their interest in political, historical and spiritual issues, three topics on which he could provide sterling conversation.

The discovery of Tristan by Roman females did not go unnoticed by Cardinal Odo, which caused the cleric certain concern. He found himself intervening between Tristan's naivety and the connivances of bored female aristocratics. At these awkward moments, Odo would issue words of caution to his young liege. "Beware of that woman, Tristan," he would counsel, "she sets snares."

"Snares?" Tristan would inquire as Odo dragged him from one trap after another. "But how do you mean, Cardinal?"

"I will explain later," Odo would say. "But for now, do not let her catch you alone!"

But Odo never did explain later, so Tristan, still remembering that day he had asked Odo for the meaning of 'diddling', did not push for further explanation. Thus Tristan, beneath the watchful eyes of Odo, continued to dodge the advances of predatory females with a mix of innocence and blindness. Nonetheless, he did often think about every detail of that night on the monastery hillside with Mala, feeling a stir in his groin at such times. But then remembering how that night ended, he would fall into despair. He missed Mala terribly, and was now certain that he would never see her again.

Chapter Thirty-Seven

The Turks

I'm being sent on a mission to meet with Countess Mathilda in a few weeks," said Odo, one day after returning from the Vatican.

Delighted, Tristan replied, "Oh, perfect! I have not seen Guillaume in months."

"You shall not be accompanying me," Odo said. "Pope Gregory has requested that you remain behind to assist him as papal interpreter for an approaching visit by a Turkish delegation from the Holy Land."

"Me? But what of Brother Marco, his Persian interpreters?"

"On diplomatic missions in North Africa and Spain."

Not being able to see Guillaume disappointed Tristan, yet this twist of events now threw him into the realm of opportunity. Three days later, brimming with anticipation, he reported to the Vatican.

"Christian pilgrims had little to fear from the Fatimid Turks in the past," said Pope Gregory, "but reports are streaming in that the conquering Seljuq Turks, under the Sultan Malik-Shah, are victimizing Christian pilgrims on their way to Jerusalem. I've urged Malik-Shah to send envoys to Rome to discuss my growing concerns. They will be arriving soon. Tristan, your knowledge of Islam and the heathen culture might be helpful to my office during these transactions."

Honored, Tristan said, "I will humbly do my best, Holiness."

So it was that in late December of 1079, Odo departed for Tuscany, leaving Tristan in the care of Pope Gregory. Odo's mission, due to Heinrich's continued hostile actions in the north, was important in that the outcome of his talks with Mathilda might prove pivotal in helping Pope Gregory come to a decision about ending his neutrality in the war between Heinrich and Rudolph of Swabia. Odo's only reservation about the mission was leaving Tristan alone in Rome within the grasp of certain roving wives of noblemen. "Please keep an eye on our lad, Tristan," he said to Pope Gregory on departing for Tuscany.

The last thing on the Pope's mind was the well-being of a boy on the threshold of adolescence, especially in the face of the Heinrich problem and the threat of Muslim violence along the pilgrimage routes to Jerusalem. Pope Greogory was far more interested in Tristan's talents as a linguist than in preserving his adolescent virtue.

The Seljuq delegation arrived in January, just after Tristan's thirteenth birthday, at which time Tristan was summoned to assist the Papal Diplomatic Delegation. "You are to accompany Cardinals Graziano, Innocenzo and Crescenzio," instructed Pope Gregory, "as they negotiate with the heathens."

"Certainly, Holiness," Tristan replied, despite apprehensions already arising at the mention of these names. Tristan knew each of them, thinking them to be dour, inflexible clerics who held anything and everything Muslim with utter contempt. Cardinal Graziano was a zealous supporter of Gregory's austere reforms, dogmatic to the point of fanaticism. As for Cardinals Innocenzo and Crescenzio, their public display of piety aside, Tristan doubted their personal integrity, as well as their loyalty to the Holy Father. Tristan's suspicions would prove prophetic, as both would in the future slither into the camp of Heinrich.

Tristan knew that Pope Gregory was also of the same mind as the three cardinals, holding scorn for Muslims, so he offered a suggestion to the Pope. "Might it not be good to include Cardinal Desiderius of Monte Cassino in these talks, Holiness? After all, he is from Guiscard the Wily's southern territory, and Guiscard has Muslim allies. Cardinal Desiderius might have a better understanding of the Turks than the other cardinals."

"Oh, no, no!" Gregory snorted, put off by the suggestion. "Desiderius is much too moderate and soft on Islam. The Turks need to know we mean business!"

"Yes, of course, Holiness," Tristan replied.

The Seljuq delegation was large in number and quite impressive in terms of appearance, wealth and resources. Arriving by ship, they disembarked along the coast and made the short trek overland to Rome, setting camp along the banks of the Tiber River near Saint Peter's Basilica. This created a stir in Rome, drawing thousands of curious spectators who ogled the visitors from a distance, refusing to venture closer. No one was more curious than Tristan. Throughout his studies of Islam he had seen many pictorial representations of Moors, Saracens and Turks, but actually witnessing this culture first-hand was nearly more than his brain could absorb.

These Muslim foreigners now standing before him appeared overwhelming in their richly adorned, finely flowing fabrics, footwear and head-dressings. Their weapons seemed to glimmer even in the shade, as did the ornaments hanging about their ears and necks. Their dark skin seemed silken, especially the faces and hands of the heavily covered women moving about the camp as servants.

The master of this delegation was a tall, dark man who came to the fore as Tristan and the cardinals entered the Turkish camp. Tristan was struck by the man's thick but short and perfectly cropped beard, as well as by his meticulously groomed mustache. "I am Abdul Azim," the man said with a solemn, unsmiling expression in broken Italian, extending his hand to the elderly Cardinal Graziano who was the head of the Pope's delegation.

Cardinal Graziano shook his hand and mumbled something back in his limited Persian, of which Azim understood not a single word. Seeing this, Tristan stepped forward and shook the man's hand. "Abdul Azim, it means Servant of the Mighty, does it not?" he said in Persian.

Azim looked at Tristan, puzzled, and continued in broken Italian. "And you are?"

"I represent, with these other officials, the Holy Father of the Roman Catholic Church, sire," Tristan responded, again in Persian.

Seeing that the boy's mastery of Persian far surpassed his own ability in Italian, Azim switched lnguages. "You, a boy, represent Pope Gregory? He sent a *boy* to greet the delegation of the great Sultan Malik-Shah?"

"Please, sir, take no offense," bowed Tristan. "He sent three of his most powerful cardinals here, as you see, but he sent me along because I speak your language. Then, also, I have a great admiration for your culture and history."

Azim nodded as the stiffness of his posture loosened a degree. Perusing the gathering of cardinals in Tristan's company, he said, "These men with you, they don't appear especially happy to see us here in Rome."

"Sir Azim, it is not your presence that makes them look this way," said Tristan. "These men are solemn men of God and always carry this...grim look. Their faces never look happy, but they carry great joy in their hearts."

This made Azim laugh, as it did the Turks standing next to him. "Ha!" he cried. "You see things clearly, then bury them in honey!"

Tristan sighed with of relief, turned, and smiled politely at the Cardinals. "I beg your indulgence, but I should like to conduct this meeting in Persian as much as possible as a signal of respect and courtesy."

"You're doing fine, lad," grunted Cardinal Graziano, his expression remaining severe.

"Indeed, move forward," grumbled Innocenzo.

"Yes," said Crescenzio.

Tristan bowed and, from that point, commandeered the afternoon, requesting that Lord Azim give a tour of the camp. The Cardinals followed in an awkward file as they moved from one area to another, Azim providing explanation as the wide-eyed Tristan absorbed one wonder after the next. He was struck by the vibrant colors of the Turks' clothing and the sophistication of their equipment, as well as by the detailed artistry of their weapons and vessels. Everything within the camp seemed unusual, and Tristan's curiosity and wonder at things that seemed mundane to the visitors rather amused Lord Azim.

By afternoon's end, a cordial understanding had taken root between the two, kindled by cross-cultural curiosity and comparison. Azim's previous relationships with westerners had been restricted to fighting the Byzantines, which taught him to distrust Christians above all enemies. Though the Byzantine Christians had split from the Roman Christians, Azim viewed them with disdain as one and the same. Yet, in this boy, Azim thought he saw something unique and promising, and concluded that he might indeed be helpful in communicating with the Roman Pope.

As Tristan and the cardinals walked the camp, they came to an especially large, ornate tent. Curious, Tristan asked, "Sir Azim, what is this beautiful place, so richly adorned? Could we take a look inside?"

Azim looked at Tristan, his brow furrowing, then glanced at the Cardinals. "These holy men of your church," he said, "we're told they do not marry, or lay with women, yes?"

"Marry? Lay with women? Oh, certainly not!" cried Tristan. "They are men of the cloth and do not even *look* at women!"

"Hmm, so strange that men would choose to act in such a way!" said Azim, shaking his head. "But since they choose to deny themselves life's greatest pleasure, it is best I not let them enter this tent, for it is my harem."

"Harem?" asked Tristan.

Azim nodded. "It's where I keep my concubine during my travels."

"Concubine?" asked Tristan.

Azim thought a moment before continuing. "I have four wives, and many other women I keep for my pleasure, about thirty or so. Such women are my concubine. I don't travel with my wives, but I do bring a dozen of my favorite concubine along during my travels to satisfy my manly needs. Do you understand?"

"Certainly," nodded Tristan, although he was not at all sure what Azim meant by 'manly needs'.

"So, I don't think your holy men would understand such a thing, eh? No need to offend them."

Tristan agreed. "No, no need to offend them," he said. But looking at Azim, his eyebrows drew together. "But I would not be offended, Sir Azim, I assure you. So perhaps I could take a look another time when the cardinals are not along?"

"Yes, of course," nodded Azim. "I'll introduce you to my concubine. They might be pleased to see a fine boy such as you from the West."

***

Over the course of the next week, Pope Gregory held a series of meetings with the envoys of Sultan Malik Shah. As Gregory had anticipated, Tristan was useful during these communications, especially with Lord Abdul Azim who had taken a liking to the boy. Nonetheless, despite his outward efforts to be cordial and respectful, Gregory privately ascertained that his Muslim visitors were primitive and ungodly. Despite their extraordinary cleanliness and attention to personal hygiene, he decided they were dirty. In truth, it was simply their brown skin that had led him to this conclusion. But already possessing an irrefutable bias against them for being heathens, Gregory could not help but look upon them as inferior beings.

Tristan was shortly able to see through the Holy Father's false courtesy toward the visitors, creating in him a conflicting disappointment. He admired the Pope, looking to him as a beacon of Christian charity and hope. Yet now, before Tristan's very eyes, the Pope had closed his heart to his visitors because of their differences. Conversely, the more Tristan interacted with Lord Azim's delegation, the more Tristan began to wonder whether the God the Muslims worshipped might not in reality be the same God the Christians worshipped.

Tristan hoped the Pope's and the Cardinals' disdain for the Turks was not as evident to Azim as it was to himself. Such hopes were futile. Lord Azim saw through Gregory's charade as easily as Tristan. Regardless, Azim remained courteous in order to obey his master's instructions to listen, observe and agree to everything. This led Pope Gregory into incorrectly surmising that he was making impressive headway with the Turks. He was also incorrect in thinking that Azim's master was the Sultan Malik-Shah. In truth, Azim's real master was the Vizir Nizam al-Mulk who, despite perceptions in the West, actually held power over the Sultan Malik-Shah.

Interestingly, it was Tristan alone of the Vatican delegation who began to suspect such a possibility; not through direct communication with the Turkish delegates, but through observation and listening. At various points in camp and during negotiations in the city, he had overheard two names frequently mentioned by the Turks as they spoke amongst themselves. The first name was 'Vizir Nizam al-Mulk'. Each time this name was uttered, it seemed to carry more weight than the name of Sultan Malik-Shah, whom the Vatican believed to be the absolute

power east of Byzantium. Tristan began to suspect, therefore, that the Turks were playing a charade of their own,
though he kept this to himself. The second name Tristan
kept hearing was 'Mahmoud Malik'. Whenever this name
surfaced, anger and bitterness arose amongst the Turks.
This puzzled Tristan, and he wished to learn who this individual might be.

Two weeks after the Turks arrival in Rome, Pope
Gregory closed his negotiations, certain he had successfully
secured their solemn promise to police mistreatment of
Christian pilgrims traveling to and from Jerusalem. Despite
thinking these people inferior and ungodly, he, for some
reason, felt they would keep their word out of respect and
fear for the weight of the papacy.

*How could the Holy Father possibly believe them to
be lesser opponents than King Heinrich of Germany?* wondered Tristan. Yet, this is exactly what Gregory thought.

Anxious to return home, Lord Azim fell into a festive
mood as the talks closed. He had followed his master's instructions to the letter, had met the hierarchy of the Roman
Christians and had learned a great deal about the enemy.
Vizir Nizam al-Mulk would be pleased to hear his full report and gain information about the Roman power structure. Azim would tell him of western arrogance, overconfi-
dence and condescension, and conclude by sharing that of
all the Christians he encountered in Rome, there was but
one who deserved the tiniest measure of respect...a boy.

"Come with me, young one," he said to Tristan as he
and his diplomats made for their camp. "My delegation
leaves in the morning, but tonight we celebrate and you
shall be my guest!"

"Certainly! It would be a great honor," Tristan replied, falling in behind Azim and his entourage. Tristan had
little idea what to expect, but felt certain he was in good
company and that he now knew enough about Lord Azim's
people to conduct himself appropriately.

As they entered the Turkish camp, Tristan supposed that Azim's entourage would celebrate as European men did, becoming boisterous while overindulging in drink. To his surprise, there was no evidence of alcohol. Instead, veiled women came forth with trays of roasted mutton and goat accompanied by small baskets of dates, olives, pomegranates and figs. They also brought forth steaming pots of rice, a product Tristan had read about but never seen. For drink, the women brought forward spouted, beautifully crafted silver vessels from which steam emanated. Next they placed upon the table small, ornately gilded porcelain cups before each man as he sat upon his exquisitely carved Turkish stool. Fascinated, Tristan watched the women pour hot liquid into each cup after which the men slowly raised the cups to their mouths, taking slow, deliberate sips. He learned this was something called 'tea', which would one day become a favored drink of his own.

There also appeared tiny dishes that contained odd powders and seeds of different varieties. He watched as the men sprinkled various combinations of these substances onto their mutton and goat. "Spices," said Azim. "Pepper, saffron, cumin, cloves and ginger. Try them. You Christians know nothing about taste, and use only salt!"

Tristan picked at the different offerings before him, trying them all at least once. He drank the tea, tested the spices upon his meat, and enjoyed the sweetness of the dates and figs. The exotic meal introduced him to a new world of tastes and smells. "Interesting," he said to Azim. "I never knew such things existed."

"Perhaps you might one day come east then, maybe visit our territories. You would be welcome, Tristan, as my personal guest."

"I would enjoy that, Sir Azim," Tristan nodded. "It has always been my dream to see the Holy City of Jerusalem and the site of our Lord's crucifixion."

As the men ate, Tristan was struck by the low, respectful tones of the Turks as they spoke; their conversations often punctuated with comfortable periods of silence. Their discussions lacked the raucous interplay so characteristic of European nobility. Tristan rather admired this heightened sense of civility, which made him realize the Muslims were anything but the picture of primitive savages portrayed by Europeans.

"So, Lord Azim," said Tristan, "there is much confusion about the Muslims here in the West. They think you are all the same people sharing the same religion. And here in the West, many fear you are spreading everywhere and intend to take over the world."

"We are no different than you," said Azim. "Just as you have the northern people, the French, the Italians, the Germans, the Spaniards, we are equally divided. And we fight amongst ourselves, too, as you do. As far as spreading everywhere, we're also no different than you Christians. Your faith took root in what you call the Holy Land, then spread to the Romans who forced it north onto the Gauls and Germans, west onto the Celtic Isle, north onto the Nordics, and east into the Balkans, then back toward Jerusalem."

"Ah, you are versed in European history then?" said Tristan.

"Yes, I am a student of history."

"I have read your people, the Seljuks, are not at all related to the Saracens or Moors."

Azim laughed. "No, we are Turks. Our original people were of the Hsiung-nu tribes on the northern edge of the Gobi Desert and the Altai Mountains in central Asia. Over a period of centuries they moved west off the steppes, and in the 10th Century they embraced Islam, settling around Bukhara in Transoxania under their khan, Seljuk. Later, one branch moved to India, while the other struck west and entered military service under the Abbasid caliphs of Baghdad, the spiritual leaders of Islam. Our Turkish horsemen, known as gazis, eventually followed a Seljuk khan, Tugrul Bey, conquering Baghdad in 1055, stripping power from the Abbasid Saracens. We then made incursions into Anatolia, Armenia and other Byzantine territories which we now possess."

Tristan had never heard of many of these geographic names, but was fascinated by Azim's history lesson, quickly drawing analogies between the Turkish migrations and the movement of his own mother's people, the Danes who constantly roved, conquered territory, then assimilated into their new lands.

"Yes, you *are* much like the Europeans," agreed Tristan. Pausing, he weighed the wisdom of asking his next question. "Lord Azim," he said gingerly, "I have heard two names often mentioned in your camp, so I wonder if I might make an inquiry?"

"Two names?"

"Yes, the first is Vizir Nizam al-Mulk and—"

Azim dropped his cut of mutton, quietly placed both hands on the table, and fired a glance about the table. "My men spoke of the Vizir in your presence?"

Realizing he had poked a sore, Tristan said, "Not *openly*, sir, but simply amongst themselves."

"I see. And you just happened to be listening? Hmm, Little Brother, this makes me wonder then whether you are in actuality a spy."

Tristan remained calm. "Are you not a diplomat, Sir Azim?" he asked.

"Yes, of course."

"And are not all diplomats spies of one sort or another? I am simply like you, sir. I watch and listen."

Azim shrugged, gesturing to the men at the table. "Clever, this youngster, eh?"

The others smiled and shook their heads in agreement. "Best be careful, Azim," said one with a chuckle, "he has snared your ankle already. If you keep talking, it will be your entire leg!"

Azim turned back to Tristan. "The Vizir Nizam al-Mulk is my master. It is he who reigns over the Seljuq Empire. The Sultan Malik-Shah is quite content to serve as the figurehead. And we are quite content to let him be just that, for he lacks talent in both war and diplomacy."

"I see," said Tristan.

"And what was the other name?" asked Azim.

"Mahmoud Malik. I heard his name quite often, actually."

Azim's expression turned dark as the other men blenched, grumbling at hearing the name. "Ah, Mahmoud Malik," said Azim, stroking the point of his beard, "The Butcher of Medina, the most wicked and violent man in the Muslim world. He roves about with his horde of renegade gazis and preys on all he encounters, even our own people! We and many others have cried for his head, but Vizir Nizam al-Mulk defends him for unknown reasons. Mahmoud Malik is a pariah, a disgrace to all of Islam, bathing in the blood of the innocent! But no more about him, Little Brother. Tonight we celebrate and enjoy the stars above. And the smoke."

"The smoke?" asked Tristan.

"Yes, certainly," Azim replied, clapping his palms twice, as two of the women scurried toward the tents. When they returned, one was carrying a tray loaded with finely engraved silver pipes, small jewel-encrusted pouches of some sort, and lengths of tiny tubing. The other woman brought forth an exquisitely engraved gold and silver pot that Tristan initially mistook for a tea vessel. She connected the lengths of tubing to small openings that formed a ring below the top of the vessel, while her cohort distributed pipes to each individual sitting about the table. When she came to Tristan she hesitated, but Azim gave a gesture and she placed a pipe before him. Removing the top of the vessel, she revealed a concave inner lid that had been drilled with small holes. Then she opened one of the pouches and sprinkled its contents onto the concave inner lid.

Tristan, clueless as to what was transpiring, at first imagined the substance to be tiny chunks of bark. "Spice of some sort?" he asked.

"No, hashish," replied Azim. Accepting a lighting stick from the woman, he poked it down into the lid until the substance began to burn, at which point each of the men took up their respective pipes and inhaled deeply, drawing smoke from the lid through the vessel and through the tubing into their mouths. Shortly, each man closed his eyes and sat there in a meditative state for several moments before casting out a fine stream of smoke from their lips. "Go ahead, Little Brother," prompted Azim, "it's not difficult. It's how my tribesmen celebrate."

Tristan had never witnessed such a ritual, nor ever even imagined that men of any origin would willingly consume smoke. Nevertheless, as he was a guest amongst important foreign diplomats who had invited him into their camp, he picked up the pipe before him and guided it to his mouth, mimicking the action of the other men. Seconds later, he broke into a fitful bout of choking and coughing.

"Slowly," instructed Azim. "Here, have some tea to clear your throat, then try again."

The taste and smell of the smoke nauseated Tristan, and he had no wish to continue. But thinking it impertinent to reject a tribal custom, he carefully put the pipe back to his mouth and inhaled again, but more carefully. This time he coughed only half as much. Azim nodded with approval, which gave Tristan encouragement, causing him to make yet a third attempt at drawing smoke from the vessel.

Soon a peculiar sensation overcame him, forcing him to sit back, startled. The sensation seemed to emanate, for no reason, from his back, and quickly washed up over his shoulders, through his neck, then straight to his brain. This sent a flutter through his chest, which in turn made his entire body go limp. This unexpected wave of sensory overload then dissipated, but was then immediately followed by another, and another. He sat there as one seized by lethargy as wave after wave washed through and over him, until soon he felt as though his mind was somehow slipping into an ethereal state.

His consciousness began to drift from one place to another, and he began to take meticulous notice of things about the table that he had only slightly previously regarded. The food items began to take on a different appearance, and their aromas suddenly grew sharper and more pronounced, as did the colors of the Turks' clothing and all else about the camp. It was as though his own eyes had transcended previous capabilities and taken on telescopic qualities.

He sat there in a stupefied daze, entranced by everything around him. The hashish had also created in his head a fog, which seemed to, in turn, create a newfound calm that he had never experienced. Glazed, he started to stand, only to teeter back onto his stool. The men at the table seemed to pay him no mind, except the one sitting directly across from him. This man gave Tristan an odd look, shifting his eyes subtly to the other men, who returned the same furtive glance. Several men then chortled as Tristan tipped back on his stool.

Tristan absorbed their looks, smiling back meekly, embarrassed. Then, from nowhere and for no reason, he understood the silent exchanges that had just occurred. Thunderstruck, Tristan suddenly envisioned images of the Norsemen on the Seine River who had violated Nuri's people and captured their children to sell to the Arabs. Wild paranoia seized him then, followed by onset of hysteria. *I am at the complete mercy of these Turks' hospitality, just as the drunk Norsemen had been with Orla and the Danes just before the murderous ambush*, he realized with terror. The Norsemen had been incapacitated, therefore helpless, and now Tristan was himself rendered helpless by the narcotic effects of this substance he had been tricked into smoking. His eyes dilating, Tristan gripped the edges of his stool, his heavy-lidded eyes darting about for an escape route. *They have lured me into coming to their camp alone and mean to drag me into their wagons, bind and gag me, and will tomorrow cross overland to their ships to enslave me in the East!*

At that very moment, as though to confirm Tristan's horror, Azim stood and signaled for two other men to take Tristan by the arm and follow him toward the wagons. As they pulled him from the stool Tristan resisted and tried to cry out for help. Unable to find his voice, he ended by garbling a series of unintelligible sounds that the Turks found amusing.

Stumbling along in a semi-coma as the Turks laughed, swept forward by the power of the two men dragging him, Tristan thought of making a dash for the water's edge, reasoning that men from the desert would not dare enter the river. This plan quickly dissolved, though, as he realized that he, too, could not swim, and was equally terrified of deep water.

Oh, but I'm done now. I dropped my guard with these Turks, and now...I'm done!

Signaling his men, Azim stopped at the entrance of the ornately outfitted tent that Tristan had inquired about two weeks earlier. Finding Tristan's resistance upon being taken from the table odd, Azim raised a brow and said, "Little Brother, why do you protest so? Did you not say you might wish to see my harem?"

"Harem?" muttered Tristan, somehow finding his voice despite the wild palpitations pounding in his chest. "Y-you are not t-taking me to the wagons?"

"The wagons?" asked Azim, mystified. "To what purpose? But yes, certainly, if you wish to view the wagons, I'll gladly arrange it."

"N-no, that is not necessary," said Tristan, suddenly feeling the fool.

Azim nodded at the two men standing at the entrance, who bowed in return, pulling aside the tent flaps. Tristan had never in his life seen men as huge as these, and marveled as he passed. Nor had he ever seen black men except in paintings or illustrations, and these two behemoths outsized even Orla and Crowbones.

"Such mighty soldiers you have here at the entrance," mumbled Tristan to Azim, the haze of intoxication magnifying. "I have n-never seen such fierce looking men-at-arms as this."

"Not men-at arms," Azim replied, "they're eunuchs."

"Eunuchs?"

"Yes, slaves captured from Abyssinia as boys, at which time their testicles were removed. Then they were buried to their heads in burning sand to heal their wound. Most don't survive the ordeal, thus the ones who do are highly prized. These two have been with my family for years, have traveled everywhere with me, to guard my concubine."

As they entered the tent, Tristan was struck by the thick scent of burning incense and other richly perfumed aromas. Within, and all about, sat or stood young Turkish women, heavily covered but unveiled. Spotting Tristan, they quickly slipped veils from their necks up over their faces, and began whispering amongst themselves, looking toward Lord Azim with confusion.

Azim clapped his hands. "Come forward my lovelies," he instructed, "I've brought you a guest."

At this the women advanced toward Tristan in near wonderment, having never set eyes on such a fair and blond creature. They could not determine at first whether this guest was, in fact, a child or a young man. One curious woman slowly ran the back of her fingers down his cheek while another gently pulled at his thick sprawl of golden hair. Yet another held his cheeks, staring into his face with wonder, having never imagined such glacial grey eyes.

Tristan was mesmerized by their silken foreign complexion and the darkness of their almond eyes and raven hair. They reminded him of Mala. Gawking blankly into the exotic mystery of their veiled faces, he stood frozen as they fussed and cooed over him. Soon, all of them were running their hands over his face and neck, touching his hair and grasping at his fair hands to inspect them.

Azim approached. "Actually, Little Brother," he said, "it is usually forbidden for any man but the eunuchs to enter another man's harem. But these women, although some of my favorites, are my lowest ranking concubine and exist only for my pleasure. Therefore, this place is not forbidden as is my harem in Baghdad, where also I house my wives and raise my children until they come of age."

Still in a fog from the hashish, awed by the beauty of the fawning women surrounding him, Tristan simply nodded. But he felt something else also, something rising within him, stimulating him in a way that he knew was forbidden. He felt it in his groin, like a fire, not unlike what he had experienced that night with Mala on the hillside. He began to revel in it. *Perhaps,* he rationalized, *it was the hashish that was causing him not to retreat, or the fact that he was far away from Cardinal Odo.* But in his heart he knew that it was purely these women who were drawing him in, pawing at him, adoring him as though he were a foreign god of some unknown divinity.

So he did not choose to fight the sudden stirrings now consuming his loins. And when he felt their hands slip beneath his tunic and down into his trousers, he did not protest as he knew he should. Even when they led him to a palette of sumptuous bedding hidden behind a curtained corner of the tent and began to unclothe him, he complied. Seeing that several of the women began to remove their clothing, he next felt them embrace him and lead his trembling hands to their dark, protruding nipples, and between their soft thighs. Lost, so utterly consumed by the wonders opening before him, Tristan was not even aware that Lord Azim had left the tent, nor did he hear him say in departing, "Sleep well, Little Brother, for tonight you discover the Garden of Man's Delight. And do not worry, your Roman Church will still be there for you at dawn."

***

    That next morning, Tristan struggled to shake off his sleep, but fell back into the haze of the night several times before coming fully awake. The women had vanished and the tent was being stripped of its furnishings by an army of servants. Tristan sat up in the bedding, reared his head back in a long yawn, trying to reconstruct the events of the previous night.

    "So, how fares my honored guest?" Lord Azim laughed, standing at the entrance of the tent. "Now you know a bit about women, Little Brother, eh? But off you go now, unless you choose to follow me east! We're loading up and will depart shortly. But maybe I shall see you again in Asia Minor, eh?"

    Before Tristan could reply, Azim disappeared.

    Gathering himself, Tristan dressed and left the Turks' camp. Making a direct line for his quarters, he hoped to not encounter the cardinals or other members of the Holy Father's diplomatic entourage. He now clearly remembered events of the evening before, and was beginning to feel the crush of guilt, a guilt so profound, he feared any cleric he came upon would detect, somehow, what Tristan had done, which was to commit a grievous, unpardonable sin of the flesh.

    It was simple and withering. In one moment of carnal weakness he had cast aside years of religious training and piety—all that his mother, the teacher-nuns, Cardinal Odo and the Black Monks had taught him. *This sin will poison the remainder of my life*, he told himself bitterly, dropping into the precipice of remorse.

    By the time Cardinal Odo returned from Tuscany, Tristan's guilt had deepened and he could scarcely bear to look Cardinal Odo in the eyes. Odo, however, suspected nothing.

    "I am told you were quite valuable to the Holy Father in dealing with the Seljuqs," Odo commented.

Generally effusive on such topics, Tristan gave only a flicker of response. He did not wish to speak about the Turks.

"So what did you conclude about the Seljuq diplomat, Abdul Azim?" Odo inquired.

Tristan said nothing, because Abdul Azim had opened the gates of Hell and ushered him within.

Tristan remained tight-lipped about the entire Turkish affair for days, hoping to throw off any scent of indiscretion of that final night in the Turkish camp. But this action had exactly the opposite effect on Odo, who began to suspect something amiss, something involving the Turks. Tristan," he said one afternoon, "I notice, since my return, that you don't seem to be yourself. As clever as you are at masking malaise, the weight of something has you hobbled. Whatever it is, then, must be extremely serious."

As Odo said this, Tristan considered launching into immediate denial. Perceiving Odo's steady gaze, he instead began to feel ill.

"God has provided us the sacrament of confession, Tristan," Odo continued. "And if one repents, God forgives all trespasses. Best to cleanse the soul than to go about with filthy hands."

Tristan felt the reproach. Staring hard at the floor, he dumbly hoped a miracle might arrive. But in truth, Tristan had in his heart already surrendered. He knew that in a moment he would be confessing his mortal sin to Odo, and that the horror of Tristan's tale would turn the cardinal against him, perhaps forever. Still, Tristan turned, his heart heavy, his eyes beginning to water. Kneeling, words began to spill out one after another. "Bless me, Father, for I have sinned! I have committed a grievous offense against God and am heartily sorry! I beg His forgiveness, and yours!"

Tearfully, he then recounted the entire series of events that had unraveled on the final night of the Turks' visit, breaking down at certain points as he confessed. Finishing, he gazed up at Odo shamefully, waiting for the inevitable tongue lashing to be unleashed.

Odo was a tomb, saying nothing. After an interminable silence, he took a deep breath and shook his head. "You have forsaken all that we have taught you," he said. "Yet, you are neither yet a monk nor a priest, and probably will never choose to follow this path. You are but a boy who has been led into temptation by an agent of corruption in the guise of a Seljuk diplomat. But I see in your eyes genuine sorrow, and know that God will forgive you this trespass through penance, which I will soon administer."

At this, Tristan's head dropped onto his chest, and from his knees he collapsed flat onto the floor at Odo's feet. "Forgive me, Cardinal Odo!" he wept.

"But perhaps you should know," Odo continued quietly, "that I also in my youth once tasted forbidden fruit, just before donning my black robe."

Tristan grew still.

"It was my greatest moment of weakness and failure," Odo continued, his eyes taking on a reticent look. "But from shame and inner collapse, I found my purpose in life. Your tryst with the Turkish women, then, is neither fatal nor everlasting. But it is a threshold. You must now decide between morality or depravity, whether to move this direction or the other, whether to choose chastity until marriage or the pursuit of carnal pleasure as a sinner. And know this, my boy, I will not and cannot determine your path."

Odo withdrew his foot from Tristan's grasp then, and walked away.

Chapter Thirty-Eight

The Monk

As the first day of 1080 fell upon England, Lady Asta knelt alone before the altar of DuLacshire castle's reconstructed chapel. Though now just twenty-seven-years-of-age, she had taken on a frail, lethargic appearance that disguised her youth. Her once exquisitely brushed silver tresses had lost their shimmer, and she had abandoned the fragrant oils and salves that once graced her fair skin; had forfeited all vanity in exchange for personal reflection and prayer.

It was going on eight years now since she had sent her sons to Cluny. Though they had grown and changed, even should they happen to cross her path, she might not recognize them. In her heart, she still envisioned them as small boys, their childish, beautiful faces filled with innocence. *Those were happy days outside Saint-Germain-en-Laye,* she lamented. Thus, in her thought, she had begun to spend many of her private moments returning there, reliving scraps of events she could snatch from her failing memory. She longed so much for those days that she would now gladly surrender life itself in exchange for a single day of that past.

While it was true she still had Orla, Crowbones, Guthroth and Elder Heidi in her life, a pervasive emptiness had hollowed its way into her soul, carving deep chasms of regret that seemed insurmountable. Compounding this ach-

ing absence of her sons, the loss of Jack Forest also hounded her day by day. He, in fact, often showed up as the
ghostly phantom of her uneasy dreams. He sat there each
night, poised handsomely atop his harried mount, his eyes
aglimmer, calling her, then suddenly his forehead would
appear cleaved, his face streaming rivulets of blood. Yet,
with each gesture beckoning her forward, he seemed to
smile at her. "Flee with me, sweet Asta!" he urged. "Come
quickly, girl!" But just as she would throw herself upon his
horse, she would awaken.

She also thought of the handsome Fairhair, who
could never be taken seriously, providing constant amusement through his own narcissism and boasting bravado.
And there was the awkward StaightLimbs who had always
been so protective of her as a child. She missed his gangly,
comical mannerisms, even his predictable fits of anger on
being teased about his appearance by the other Danes.

All of them gone, like her father, she thought sadly as
she prayed in the chapel that first afternoon of 1080—
Guntar, Tristan, Guillaume, Jack, Fairhair, StraightLimbs.
Closing her eyes, she tried to recreate in her mind their faces, and reconstruct their voices. But just as she felt the images coming together, they would disappear, like Jack Forest in her dreams.

Closing her eyes, as to force them to reappear, she
heard the chapel door groan open as footsteps quietly entered, then paused. She turned about to look. A man was
standing there in a black robe—a monk. Bowing with deference, he quickly departed, as though he wished neither to
be spoken to nor recognized.

Several days later, Asta was in the chapel again and
the same thing happened. On yet a third occasion, the
strange monk entered, took a seat in the back of the chapel,
and appeared to be watching her. Curious, Asta stood, vacated the front pew, and made her way toward him. As she
approached, he crossed himself and hastily exited the chap-

el, closing the door behind him. By the time Asta reopened the door and peered out into the courtyard, he was gone.

That next day while assisting Elder Heidi with sick children in the village, Asta mentioned the odd encounters with the unknown monk to the old nurse. "Yes, yes," Elder Heidi mumbled, "I've seen him about the village these past few days. I spoke to him a good while yesterday, in fact. He's a member of the Black Monks, you know."

"A Benedictine?" said Asta with sudden interest.

"Yes, from the continent."

Asta immediately thought of her sons and Prior Odo de Lagery. "Did he mention the Cluny Monastery by chance?" asked Asta, her voice taking on the tone of a plea more than a question. "Was he from France?"

Elder Heidi shook her head. "No, Dearie. I even asked him about Cluny, thinking perhaps he might have come across your sons at some point. But no, I'm sorry. He's German, he said, and claimed he'd never been to Cluny."

Asta heaved with disappointment. "I wonder what he could be doing here."

"Ha! I wondered the same thing, so I asked him point blank, because at first I thought him a Scotch or Irish hooligan spying on the castle and the village while only posing as a monk. No, he's a monk alright, spoke Latin and was too well-versed in Church matters to be a hooligan."

"So what *is* he doing here?"

"Told me he was just traveling through, seeing the sights."

"*Here* of all places?" shrugged Asta. "The village is destitute and the castle unkempt!"

Elder Heidi thought a moment, then chuckled. "Aye, it does make little sense, eh? But he was nice enough, a talkative and curious type."

"Curious?"

"Yeah, seemed to ask a lot of questions."

"Questions?" shrugged Asta. "What kind of questions?"

"You know, about the village, the castle, about you and DuLac."

"Me and Desmond?"

"Well, not by name exactly, more like, 'Who's the lord and lady of castle? What are they like? Are they pious and devout?' But then, those aren't such odd questions, I suppose, coming from a cleric, huh?"

Asta scowled a bit and shook her head. "I twice got the sense he was watching me in the chapel. It happened yet a third time, and when I went to ask him about it, he took flight. Do you not find that a bit curious, Elder Heidi?"

"Ha," chortled Elder Heidi, "how many men have stared at you over the years, Dearie, or been frightened by you, my beauty? You may have set aside your hair brushes and fine garments, but you're still a flaming star in a dark sky. No, I don't find it strange that you frighten men, especially clerics. In any case, he's been all over the village and talked to a good number of people since arriving, so it's not like he's hiding or anything. And he's still about, I imagine, so see if you can find him. But I wouldn't fret, Dearie. You may just be imagining things, eh?"

Despite Elder Heidi's dismissive attitude, Asta's curiosity began to turn to suspicion. That next day, she walked the village, trying to seek out the monk so she could confront him, but he was nowhere to be found. By late afternoon she learned from the village smithy that the Black Monk had already left DuLacshire. "Yeah, I did some work on his saddle, so we ended up spending the afternoon together. He said he was returning to Italy."

"Italy?" asked Asta, puzzled. "But Elder Heidi said he was German."

"He is, but those damned Benedictines are like locusts, going everywhere. Wish I had such freedom as that!"

"I'm sorry I missed him," said Asta. Turning to leave, she added, "He didn't happen to mention his name, did he?"

"No, My Lady, but he did mention he has spent a good deal of time in Tuscany and in Rome. Does that mean anything to you?"

"No, I know nobody in Tuscany, nor anyone in Rome either, for that matter."

Chapter Thirty-Nine

King Heinrich

Mystified by the strange Black Monk who had appeared in DuLacshire, Asta continued to scour for information from villagers who had spoken to him. At the same time, on the continent, the vicious war between King Heinrich and the rebellious German princes took a turn. Heinrich's surging rampage came to an abrupt halt when he was decisively defeated by Rudolph of Swabia on January 27th near Muhlheim in Thuringia. Rudolph of Swabia regarded this victory as a divine decision cast by God Himself. Whether it was or was not is disputable, but this victory did reverberate up and down the Italian peninsula.

It was Brother Handel who delivered the news of Heinrich's defeat to Rome. "God has finally punished this usurper!" he exclaimed to Cardinal Odo and Pope Gregory in private papal chambers. "Heinrich's done!"

Pope Gregory was not convinced. "How many times have we thought this demon done?" he said, shaking his head. "He is like the trampled serpent that we think has been slain, but when we look down, he moves yet!"

Odo accepted the news with joy. "Holiness," he said, "you have remained silent too long on this German civil war. Rudolph and the Saxon princes have pleaded for your assistance and support, yet you have ignored their pleas. And now even without your help, Rudolph triumphs. The

418 - *Promise of the Black Monks/Hirsch*

time for neutrality is over. Harness this momentum and declare against Heinrich!"

Gregory closed his eyes, placing his palm to his chest, torn. "We will throw it open for discussion, Odo," he sighed. "Assemble the College of Cardinals."

If Odo was hoping for a unanimous vote of the Cardinals, he was sorely disappointed. Upon convening, the high clerics began to bicker amongst themselves over the advantages and disadvantages of declaring war against the German king. The more zealous supporters of Pope Gregory, such as Cardinal Graziano and Odo de Lagery, were convinced that Rudolph of Swabia's victory sounded the death knell for Heinrich's power on the continent. They ardently pressed Pope Gregory into abandoning his neutral stance and openly declaring for Rudolph.

"God has made this decision for us through Rudolph's sword!" cried the usually dispassionate old Cardinal Graziano. "Rudolph has taken this usurper to his knees, now let us *finish* him!"

Other Cardinals, such as Cardinals Innocenzo and Crescenzio, violently resisted siding with Rudolph of Swabia. "Let the Germans continue their butchery of each other in the north while Italy lives in peace!" exclaimed Cardinal Innocenzo.

"Amen!" agreed Cardinal Crescenzio. "There's nothing to gain here by declaring against Heinrich! How many times has he been crushed only to rise again? When he is actually in chains and every soldier of his is slain, *then* let us declare!"

This vociferous debate further confused the Pope, reminding him of the dispute at Canossa years before on whether or not to forgive Heinrich in the frozen courtyard. Odo sensed the Holy Father's confusion and could tell that the high level of emotions amongst the cardinals only exacerbated his frustration. With a masterful stroke of drama, then, he slowly strode to the center of the floor, raised a pointed finger to the ceiling, and began pacing in silent cir-

cles before the Pope. Odo's silent parade soon drew everyone's attention, forcing a hush over the hall.

Then Odo spoke, in a deliberately low voice which
made the cardinals strain to hear. "Holiness," he said, "you
extended the generous hand of charity to Heinrich at Nuremburg. He feigned penance, then resumed his same
wicked path. You extended this same generous hand to him
in the snow and ice of Canossa. After many tears and vows
of repentance, he again took to the same wicked path. How
many—"

"I object!" interrupted Cardinal Innocenzo. "At Canossa Pope Gregory promised Heinrich that he would heal
the wounds with the Saxon princes, but turned his back on
Heinrich instead!"

This created a buzz within the gathering, but Odo
raised his finger to the ceiling again, commanding silence.
"How many times do we let Heinrich lie to us? Will we
wait until he himself sits upon the papal throne? Holiness,
in God's name, cripple this usurper now who places himself above God and God's direct representative on the
earth!"

At this, all supporters of Gregory rose to their feet,
clapping and whistling in a raucous show of unity.
Innocenzo and Crescenzio looked at each other, disgusted,
then stormed out of the chambers. In actuality, their opposition to abandoning neutrality was based on fear of Heinrich's indomitable ability to resurrect himself, even after
personal and military defeats. Both also had many influen-
tial noblemen within their dioceses who despised the austere reforms of Gregory and secretly hoped that he might
one day be removed from the papacy in favor of a less rigid
leader of the Church. These particular noblemen carried
much authority within Rome, and felt that the threat of a
powerful Heinrich might temper Gregory's program of
Church reform.

As a result of the convocation of the College of Cardinals, Pope Gregory finally decided against Heinrich and

ended his long hesitation in taking sides in the German civil war. At the next Synod in Rome, he publicly invoked the aid of both Saint Peter and Saint Paul and announced a second, more severe excommunication ban against King Heinrich and his followers. This ban deprived Heinrich once again of his kingdoms of Germany and Italy, forbade any of the faithful to obey him as king, and awarded the crown of Germany, but not Italy, to Rudolph of Swabia. This edict was delivered by Gregory as both a prayer and a judgment in a tone mixed with cool reflection and religious fervor. It confirmed once and for all that as the direct representative of Peter and Paul, the Pope was clothed with supreme authority over the world as well as over the Church. In other words, all kings and political structures were declared subservient to the papacy.

Furious, King Heinrich himself then convened a council of German and Italian bishops at Brixen in the Tyrol of June 26, 1080, and once again declared that he was deposing Pope Gregory, this time on charges of avarice, ambition, simony, heresy and sorcery. Twenty-seven bishops and Cardinal Hugo Candidus signed this document with pomp and ceremony, then elected the excommunicated Archbishop Guibert of Ravenna as the new, legitimate pontiff under the name of Pope Clement III. In essence, Guibert of Ravenna had now been put forward as an anti-pope against Pope Gregory. In classic fashion, King Heinrich immediately declared Pope Gregory as the anti-pope and a 'False Monk'. Heinrich then acknowledged Guibert of Ravenna, now Pope Clement III, by genuflecting before him and vowing to visit Rome that next spring to receive the imperial crown of the Holy Roman Emperor from him.

The German civil war had already established itself as a bloody and merciless affair involving both military and civilian populations. But this simultaneous, double-deposing of emperor and pope now elevated the already visceral nature of this war and created a double civil war between rival popes and rival kings with accompanying horrors. Pope Gregory's military might included the Saxon princes, Countess Matilda of Northern Italy, and Papal forces, plus the potential threat of reinforcement from Normans of Lower Italy led by Duke Robert Guiscard the Wily who had recently signed an alliance with the Vatican.

Heinrich's base was made up of German royalists, Lombards from Upper Italy, German clergy he had appointed, clergymen from both Germany and Italy who opposed Gregory's austere reforms, and certain elements of nobility located in Rome itself. In addition, he enlisted much support from people who had previously supported Pope Gregory, but were now convinced that Gregory's second excommunication was not an act of faith, but a capricious grab for power.

Predictably, both Gregory and Heinrich invoked God's name in this struggle, painting the other as an enemy of God. Even further complicating this religious Gordian Knot was the fact that God's servants on earth, his clergymen, were vehemently trading charges of heresy, corruption, abuse of power and distortion of God's will. Both sides proclaimed righteousness.

As could only be expected, the hapless civilian population was trampled by the opposing armies as they moved back and forth across the landscape, and was terrorized by announcements and proclamations of eternal damnation by both bickering factions of the Catholic clergy.

***

Throughout the year of 1080, Brother Jurgen Handel continued to move between Germany and Italy, exchanging military intelligence and delivering messages to Cardinal Odo and Pope Gregory. Tristan had come to admire Handel's courage and panache, and was pleased to see him again in early November when he reported to the papal chambers as Tristan and Odo sat in conference with the Pope.

Tristan stood and extended his hand in a warm welcome. "Brother Handel, good to see you."

"Ah, Handel, come in!" smiled Odo.

Pope Gregory's reception was less enthusiastic. He simply gave a flap of the hand. Over time he had learned that the arrival of his papal agents often brought unwelcome news. "Well, *what now*, Handel?" the Pope grunted.

"Another victory for Rudolph of Swabia, Excellency, three weeks ago on October 15th near the banks of the Elster near Naumburg."

Odo and Gregory exchanged looks, then Gregory burst into a smile. "Praise Heaven!" he exclaimed.

But Tristan had been watching Handel's face, and saw no trace of elation in his expression. "Brother Handel, you do not appear pleased," he said.

Handel took a deep breath, then shook his head. "Rudolph of Swabia, h-he…"

"Come on, come on, Handel!" Gregory pressed, impatient with Handel's hesitancy.

"Rudolph," Handel continued, "he lost his right hand to an enemy soldier in the battle and—"

Gregory shrugged, interrupting. "His right hand? *That's it*? He merely lost a hand and that's got you turned on end?"

"Holiness," Handel continued, "after his right hand was severed, Rudolph was then mortally wounded by Godfrey of Bouillon."

"Mortally wounded?" whispered Odo.

"Yes, Cardinal. He died that same evening from Bouillon's wound. Hearing that Rudolph had been slain, a panic washed through the Saxon troops and they broke ranks. Their victory reversed itself into a rout, then a massacre. The rest of Germany now sees Rudolph's death as a judgment of God against the Saxon princes…and against you, Holiness. Mobs in the streets of Germany are now declaring *you* the anti-pope! They embrace Guibert de Ravenna as the legitimate pope and are calling you the Pretender, the False Monk!" Dropping to a knee, Handel crossed himself.

Odo and Gregory were stunned, as was Tristan. Silence filled the room. Gathering his calm, Odo said, "Handel, what about the Saxon princes? Can they regroup? Can Mathilda not reinforce them?"

"The Saxon princes are in total disarray and already feuding over succession to Rudolph," Handel replied.

"But what about Mathilda?" insisted Odo.

"Heinrich is now mobilizing south to cross the Alps back into Italy to attack Tuscany. We've already received word that the Lombards are preparing a hearty welcome for Heinrich and plan to reinforce his troops against Mathilda."

"Oh, those foul Lombards!" hissed Gregory. "How I curse my generosity, Odo. I twice had Heinrich in my grasp and, as a Christian, I forgave him twice!" Raising both palms and his eyes to the ceiling, he wailed, "Oh, Lord, I have done your labor faithfully! I have tried to cleanse the Church and tried to save its independence! So why have you saddled me with this pariah, Heinrich? Oh, why do you test me so mercilessly!?"

When Gregory finished his rant, Odo turned to Handel and once again asked about Mathilda. "Can she turn the tide, Handel?"

"Not likely, Cardinal. With the Lombard situation and all the people embracing Clement as the new pope, she is suddenly out-manned, out-numbered and out-armed."

This sent a shiver through Tristan, and he began to worry about his brother. "But Guillaume is in Tuscany with la Gran Contessa, what will become of him?"

"Don't worry," said Odo, "I will deliver word north to have him sent to us in Rome, Tristan. Mathilda would not for one moment tolerate his endangerment. Handel, mobilize what papal forces we can spare and go north to assist the Countess. Perhaps we can at least slow Heinrich's advance southward." Then, giving Handel a hard look, he lowered his voice so Gregory would not hear. "You do know, Handel, once he's done with Mathilda, he will be coming straight for Rome and Gregory."

Handel nodded. "Yes, Cardinal."

Tristan heard this exchange, and could not believe the Pope and the Great Church were under attack from a mere man. He thought back to Canossa, remembering Heinrich's frailty standing barefoot in the snow. He recalled the King's tearful pleas, then tears of joy as the Pope forgave him. Tristan simply could not imagine that any man could be so vile as to attack the Holy Father after twice being pardoned by him. *What form of insidious creature was this German king? Why did God not simply strike this serpent dead?*

***

Christmas of 1080 was glum within the papal community of Rome. Bad news continued to filter in as Heinrich's troops and the Lombards gained momentum against the reeling forces of la Gran Contessa. This shook Tristan's faith in the Church's future, yet he felt that, ultimately, God's intervention would still eventually quell the Heinrich threat.

As promised by Odo, Countess Mathilda sent Guillaume from the hotly contested region of Tuscany to the safety of Rome shortly after New Year's Day. As it happened, he actually arrived on Tristan's fifteenth birthday. Guillaume had continued to gain stature and muscle, and was unimaginably handsome though he was still half a year short of turning thirteen. He had also, under the tutelage of Mathilda, amassed an impressive knowledge of weaponry, warfare and horsemanship. That first night in their room, as Guillaume undressed and removed his first boot, Tristan watched him pull a dagger from it.

"You carry a weapon?" Tristan gasped.

"Yes, of course," replied Guillaume matter of factly. "Auntie insists on it in these dangerous times."

"Have you used it yet?" asked Tristan. "On a person, I mean?"

"No, but Auntie says we never know when danger will arise, or where, or from whom. When the time comes, I won't hesitate to use it."

This shocked Tristan, and he was about to comment, when Guillaume said, "Here, watch this." Guillaume placed the dagger on the back of his right hand, and before Tristan could blink, Guillaume had flipped his hand, grasped the dagger, made three or four parrying moves, then finished by rotating the dagger in a circular motion through his fingers in a startling display of dexterity and quickness. "You see," he said, "I'm well prepared. I begged to stay in Tuscany to fight the Germans with Auntie, but she refused."

Tristan marveled at Guillaume's courage, realizing how different their worlds had become since leaving Cluny. This thought was interrupted as Guillaume pulled from his bag a set of darning needles and a half-worked knitting piece.

Amused, Tristan snickered. "Ha! You *knit* now?"

"Laugh all you wish," sniffed Guillaume, "but this womanly art is useful for salvaging equipment and closing wounds. I may one day have to thread your skull together, Brother, and then we'll see who's laughing, huh?"

This drew Tristan's curiosity. "Guillaume, have you actually *sewn* flesh closed?"

"I have. I started on injured pigs and horses until mastering the art. Then Auntie sent me to one of her military infirmaries to assist with the wounds. I began with slash wounds, but later also helped the dismembered."

"My God! Did the blood not make you faint?"

"Blood doesn't bother me," replied Guillaume. "And though I've not yet spilled human blood through arms, I can't wait to enter battle. As I said, I wanted to fight in Tuscany, but Auntie insisted I come south. I told her I was as capable as any soldier in her army! She agreed, but said she must honor Odo's promise; that it was sacred and could not be violated. I'm not exactly sure what Odo's promise is all about, or who he made this promise to, but I think it's something about never abandoning you and me as we were once abandoned years ago. You know, by our mother."

Tristan had not thought of Asta in a long while, and the mention of her sent a pang through his heart. "The promise Cardinal Odo made," he said, "was to our mother, Guillaume."

"That makes no sense," replied Guillaume. "She *abandoned* us. How could she make someone else promise not to do the very thing she herself did? No. I think maybe the promise Odo made was to those men who took us to Cluny."

"Those men who took us to Cluny?" echoed Tristan, appalled. "Guillaume, you don't even remember their names, do you?"

Guillaume shook his head. "No, I was only four."

"There was Orla and Crowbones, Fairhair, Straight-Limbs and Guthroth the Quiet! God in Heaven, Guillaume, do you even remember *Mother*?"

Guillaume shook his head. "No, nor do I choose to. She left us, sent us away."

This angered Tristan and he rallied to Asta's defense. "It was more complicated than that, Guillaume! And you violate the commandments with such talk. You should respect our mother!"

Guillaume dropped his knitting and looked at Tristan, puzzled. "Why are you getting mad? And let me ask you a question then, since you bring the commandments into this. Do you respect our father? I don't think so! He was a traitor and a lout. Oh, and do you even remember *him*?"

This analogy only fueled Tristan's irritation. "There is a great difference between our mother and our father, Guillaume! She was trying to give us a future and an education. We have both now. We are fortunate, and all because of her! I'll explain it to you one day when you're mature enough to understand. Then you'll regret what you're saying now!"

Guillaume had had no intention of inflaming Tristan, especially over a topic for which he cared so little. Regretting this heated exchange, he was about to apologize, but Tristan had already turned his back to him and covered his head with a blanket. Guillaume sighed, set aside his knitting, and blew out the candle. As he lay his head down in the darkness, he closed his eyes, trying to envision his forgotten mother, for Tristan's sake. But probe and concentrate as he might, he could not recreate the first feature of her face.

Chapter Forty

Siege

Tristan could not remain angry at Guillaume for long, and the two reconnected. Guillaume avoided mentioning their mother, not wishing to inflame his brother's sensitivity on the topic, something Guillaume failed to comprehend.

For many in Rome, the war in the north seemed a distant thing yet. But alarm spread as word reached Rome in late March that Mathilda's resistance was nearly depleted. Then Jurgen Handel arrived in Rome with dismal news. "Heinrich has turned south and is headed for Rome!" he reported to Odo and Gregory. "And it appears that Mathilda's done!"

"My Lord!" cried Pope Gregory. "Has she been captured?"

"No, Excellency, but she's in constant flight for her life."

This sent Gregory into fits of apprehension. Odo tried to comfort him, knowing that Gregory loved no one on this earth more than la Gran Contessa. "Heinrich will not harm her," he said, taking Gregory by the shoulder. "They are, after all, cousins. Besides, she pleaded his case at Canossa. He may imprison her, but will not execute her. As for us, we must prepare!"

Odo took charge of defensive preparations within the Vatican, and also saw to it that Vatican treasures, artifacts and documents were packed and sent off for safekeeping. Some were sent south to Duke Guiscard the Wily in Lower Italy while others were shipped to Sicily, which was also under Guiscard's control. Yet others were shipped to Cluny. Odo then advised those cardinals who had been the most vocal opponents of Heinrich to evacuate Rome.

He also suggested that Pope Gregory consider seeking sanctuary in Lower Italy, but Gregory would not hear of it. "God does not flee," he shouted at Odo, "nor does his direct representative on this earth!"

On May 21st the Germans appeared on the horizon, their ranks bristling with armor and weaponry. Heinrich was riding at the head of these vast forces and ordered them to establish camp just outside the walls of Rome. In response, Roman forces hurriedly locked all gates to the city, blocking access in and out of Rome. Odo summoned the Papal Guard, reinforced defenses that surrounded St. Peter's Basilica, and gathered the papal community within the walls of the Vatican.

Heinrich's first act was to send an emissary into the city to demand that Pope Gregory open negotiations with him. Refusing, the iron-willed old pontiff held firm as a rock and prohibited any exchange of communication whatsoever between the Vatican and King Heinrich. "I am not afraid of the threats of the wicked," he snorted, "and would rather sacrifice my life than consent to evil!"

This infuriated Heinrich. "Does that old bastard never change?" he bellowed in red-faced frustration upon hearing Gregory's response. "He's as immovable as a goddamned dead mule!"

Heinrich's next inclination was to lay siege to the city, despite knowing that to storm it would be extremely difficult. Regardless, he quickly met opposition on this strategy from two sources. The first to object were his own generals. "We lack the manpower and the equipment to carry on a lengthy siege, Majesty," they warned. "Best that we withdraw, regroup and return next spring." Heinrich was displeased by such counsel, but was adept enough at war to know that his commanders were correct.

The second source of opposition to a siege came from within the city itself. The Roman citizenry was divided in this war between Heinrich and Gregory, even as it arrived at their very doorstep. Gregory held certain sway within the city, but the German king enjoyed much support there also. Heinrich's own supporters sent word imploring him not to lay siege to the city, as it would be devastating in terms of commerce and prosperity. "Surely you would not starve your own supporters!" they insisted.

Heinrich reciprocated by sending word back to his supporters to hurl open the city gates, thereby avoiding the calamity of a long siege and bringing a quick end to Pope Gregory's tyrannical reforms. His supporters refused, knowing that the hated Lombards who had swollen the German ranks would most probably sack the city.

Thus a stalemate ensued, which frustrated Heinrich into retiring to Upper Italy for the summer to regroup. This only served to convince Pope Gregory that he had done the right thing by refusing to negotiate with the German king. "You see, Odo," he crowed triumphantly, "God did not wish me to concede a single measure to the wicked Heinrich! And I did not, nor will I ever in the future!"

Chapter Forty-One

And Thus...the Heart

Upon Heinrich's departure to Upper Italy, Rome heaved a collective sigh of relief, praying that life would return to normal. A week later, Tristan was leaving Odo's office in the papal complex with an armful of scrolls to deliver when he spotted a familiar face coming his way. It was Dieter Muehler. "Good morning, Brother Muehler!" Tristan said. "Haven't seen you in nearly a year. Been traveling on behalf of the Holy Father?"

Muehler nodded. "You might say that, lad."

"And where has the road taken you, Brother?"

"Well, just here and there."

"Pax vobiscum," said Tristan, aware that such vague answers veiled covert activity, which also meant there was no point in probing.

Muehler entered the papal complex in search of Cardinal Odo, and soon found him surrounded by accountants and clerks within the conference chambers.

Seeing Muehler, Odo dismissed them and closed the door behind them. "So tell, how did you fare?"

"It was rather different from my usual assignments, Cardinal," said Muehler. Shrugging, his face contracted a bit and he said, "Cardinal, you sent me a great distance and had me take great strides right in the midst of this serious Heinrich mess for what seems to be a rather small affair."

Odo nodded. "A small affair, indeed, but an affair of the heart. And it is the heart, after all, Muehler, that led men like us into God's service, remember? Sadly, my rapid ascent within the Church has made me forget that, at times. So consider this task you undertook for me to be a penance of sorts for my own forgetfulness. What seems but a small affair to us has twisted and mangled the entire life of a decent, God-fearing woman."

"Well spoken, Cardinal," nodded Muehler, with retraction. "Aye, God's work doesn't always require a grand stage."

"So then, what did you learn?"

"I traveled first to Marcigny-sur-Loire in Burgundy," Muehler began. "There at the Benedictine Convent of Saint Pierre, I met with the Prioress Anjou and discussed your proposal and the required dowry as related to the subject of our concerns. Next, I proceeded to Paris and the court of King Philippe of France, meeting with Brother Dominicus of Saint Étienne Cathedral to review the history of Roger de Saint-Germain's plot against the Bastard. As suspected, King Philippe was up to his chin in the planning of it all. Actually, the entire plan originated with him and his ministers. Roger de Saint-Germain was but a pawn in the affair. The King promised him and the other conspirators land and position."

"So," said Odo, "when the Bastard uncovered the plot, King Philippe claimed innocence and sacrificed Roger de Saint-Germain and his accomplices?"

"Yes, Cardinal," said Muehler, "but Brother Dominicus added a twist to the story. It was Roger de Saint-Germain's own brother who actually betrayed him and chirped to the Bastard, along with Lord Letellier."

"His own brother? Desmond DuLac?"

Muehler nodded. "Yes."

"Well then, DuLac's hands are stained red in this affair, as are King Philippe's!"

"Yes, very much so. For the King to send his own pawn to the butcher block is heinous, but for DuLac to place his own brother's neck beneath the ax is even more ungodly. Anyway, I then rode to the Saint-Germain-en-Laye territory where the woman in question once lived with her two sons. I must report, the Lady Asta was loved by all to whom I spoke."

"I suspected as much," nodded Odo.

"From there I proceeded to Rouen. After presenting my papal documents, I dug up everything I could about the relationship between the Bastard and Guntar the Mace, Lady Asta's father. A strange thing, Lady Asta's father was like a brother to the Bastard, yet he also lost his neck to the Bastard."

"Oh, but the Bastard has no scruples for friend *or* foe. Pope Gregory once supported him, but this past year he wrote the Bastard and expressed his regrets at having done so. He accused the Bastard in writing of being a blood-monger."

"Eh, you say?" responded Muehler, surprised. "Well then, that explains the frigid welcome I received in his court upon presenting my papal pass. It also explains why the Normans were hunting down papal spies and sending them to the butcher's block. Fortunately, I was not suspected of spying since my papers identified me as a circutor simply auditing on our monasteries there. In any case, Normandy has become dangerous ground for our agents."

"Yes," agreed Odo, "because of the Bastard's fury at Pope Gregory. The Bastard does not wish to be reminded of his own evil doing, such as with the Harrying of the North in England or with Guntar the Mace and his daughter, Asta. The Bastard barely knew Asta, yet he crushed her life with a mere motion of his finger. He forced her to marry at age twelve, executed her father for opposing the marriage under the name of treason, later also executed her husband for treason, then denounced the Saint-Germain name and confiscated everything she had. Mere inconveniences to him, complete devastation for her. But go on, continue."

"While in Rouen, I also located Roger de Saint-Germain's jailer and spoke to him at length. He claimed that Roger de Saint-Germain was the foulest man he had ever encountered, and could not conceive that the beautiful woman visiting his dungeon each day would waste her prayers on such a worthless soul. After she left the dungeon each night, Saint-Germain would then tell the jailer perverted stories of her performing bestial sexual acts under threat of him injuring their two sons." At this Muehler spat on the floor. "God's justice, I'd say, the severing of that black soul's head."

"And what about the Bastard and Desmond DuLac, her second husband?" asked Odo.

"The Bastard loathes him as he would a boil on his neck, yet DuLac remains useful. Apparently, DuLac has been quite efficient at quelling Saxon revolts, both during the Harrying of the North and even recently. He appears to be as black-hearted as his brother was."

Odo shook his head. "These things you say are disturbing, Muehler. The young woman, Asta, is to be pitied."

"Aye, she's like one thrown from a storm-tossed ship, adrift and clinging to a spar in a black, raging sea, yet she still loves God and prays daily. Upon leaving the Bastard's court in Rouen, I crossed the Channel and made my way to western England just south of Scotland's frontier, and found the earldom of DuLacshire. Proceeding to the village now called DuLacville, I found there the lady of our investigation, in the chapel on her knees in devout prayer and reflection. It's there that she begins and ends each day. Just as in Saint-Germain-en-Laye, she is revered by the local people, even though they're Saxon and she's Norman, which is a hated race among the natives of that isle. But she claims to be a Dane, as do the men of her personal Guard, which has created some division in DuLac's castle, apparently."

"But Muehler, you are *certain* Lady Asta did not guess your intentions for being there?" asked Odo.

"No, Cardinal. We never spoke, so she suspects nothing."

Odo nodded, taking on the air of satisfaction. "Thank you for taking such efforts, Muehler. As I said, this mission is not about great events, but about small events. But in the eyes of God, small things may well outweigh the grand. In this case, I cannot think He would be pleased with the treatment of this woman at the hands of men."

Muehler agreed, then asked, "Is that all that you require of me, Cardinal?"

"Yes, yes. I could not possibly ask more."

Muehler stood to leave, but his face broke into puzzlement. "Somehow I feel you're not done with this England affair. Are you spinning a web, Cardinal?"

"Ah, clever, aren't you, Muehler?" smiled Odo. "Yes, I plan to help this woman."

"Very well then, Cardinal," said Muehler, "I should like to assist. The intrigue of the great stage has made me forget raising up the weak. Perhaps some personal penance of my own will rattle my memory a bit."

"God bless you," said Odo. "When the time comes, then, we will advance this cause together."

Chapter Forty-Two

The Battle for Rome

After abandoning Rome and reaching Upper Italy, Heinrich sent envoys to Emperor Alexius I Comnenos of the Eastern Byzantine Empire in Constantinople for the express purpose of forging a new alliance against Pope Gregory. The Byzantines had been resisting incursions from the Turks to their east, but had also been staving off attacks from Duke Guiscard the Wily on their western frontier along the Adriatic Sea. Guiscard, who now controlled Sicily and all of Lower Italy, had actually acquired much of this territory by conquering it from the Byzantines. While doing so, Guiscard had formed unholy alliances with Muslims, the Empire's most hated enemies. Emperor Alexius, therefore, saw the aggressive Norman as a dangerous threat to his Eastern Empire, and was eager to forge a treaty with the powerful King Heinrich. So eager, in fact, he sent the German king 360,000 pieces of gold so Heinrich would threaten Guiscard's realm of Lower Italy. After all, if Heinrich were to take Rome, it would be easy for him to continue south and take on Guiscard while he was stuck fighting the Byzantines.

In addition to developing this treaty with Emperor Alexius while in Upper Italy, Heinrich doubled his efforts against Mathilda by leading a campaign of devastation throughout Tuscany. Mathilda, capitalizing on mountainous terrain and defensive tactics, managed to avoid capture while continuing to harry Heinrich's forces.

Weary of chasing his elusive cousin, during Lent of 1082 Heinrich turned south again to attack Rome a second time. This time he arrived with more troops and adequate siege equipment, but was once more unable to actually take the city. Nor was he able to convince his supporters within the city to open the gates to his army, as their fear of Lombard pillaging had not subsided.

Cardinal Odo once again managed and organized the Vatican's defenses, and even though Heinrich's increase in men and equipment frightened the Roman citizenry, Odo felt confident that Heinrich could be held in check a second time.

Tristan, on the other hand, was not so sure. "Rome's military is so completely outnumbered...and so is the Holy Father's!" he said to Odo, gazing from the ramparts at the endless German and Lombard campfires sparking and flickering in the night.

"Yes," said Odo, "but we are behind the walls and they must come over the walls, which requires a ratio of five to one. Heinrich does not quite have the numbers, so rest easy, Tristan, and trust in God. But tell, how is Guillaume doing with all this?"

"He wanted to stay and fight alongside Auntie Mathilda but she would not allow it. He blames it on the promise you once made to our mother not to abandon us." Then a look of discouragement crossed his face. "I fear he does not even remember her, which disturbs me."

"Well now," Odo replied, "I suppose it *should*. Your mother is a fine person, and a prayerful woman. She lacked choices in life, you know, and the politics of the world overcame her. Powerful men sweep away the powerless like crumbs from a table, in a single calculated moment, to make yet more room for their gluttonous appetites. But your brother fails to understand these things yet, so be patient."

"I love my brother," sighed Tristan, "so I will be patient, as you recommend." Then he looked up at Odo and raised his shoulders. "My mother, do you suppose I will ever see her again, Cardinal Odo?"

The expression on Tristan's face as he said this touched Odo to the bone. In that single moment, Odo forgot the ring of German and Lombard campfires surrounding Rome, even though their reflection made Odo's eye's burn bright with glimmering embers. "I dare not guess at the moment," he said, "but even through the most violent tempest, God shines a light of hope. And it is hope, after all, that drags us forward through the darkness. So, Tristan, just as *you* hope, I, too, hope. *Alter ipse amicus*...a friend is another self. But having said that, everything is in God's hands."

***

As Heinrich's siege continued, he would send forays against the city's walls to probe for weaknesses, but these were summarily repelled by the Romans. And even though the German and Lombard dead left at the foot of the wall discouraged Heinrich's troops, they were of little significance to Heinrich. "Judas priest!" he would declare after each unsuccessful probe as the number of dead were reported to him. "If the goddamned Romans would open the gates, we could all just go home!"

Although many Romans continued to support Heinrich, reports of Lombard plundering and savagery in Tuscany had filtered into the city, strengthening Roman resolve to keep such disaster from entering their own gates. Still, Heinrich's siege was beginning to take effect and many Romans began to grumble amongst themselves that Pope Gregory should at least agree to open a dialogue with the German king. "If he weren't so stubborn," they complained, "then we could talk this out, Heinrich could be crowned Holy Roman Emperor, and the Germans and Lombards would go home!"

Odo became aware of these complaints as occasionally groups of noblemen or collections of city officials approached the Vatican walls requesting audience with him and the Pope. But the iron-willed, old Gregory stood firm on refusing to negotiate with Heinrich, and would fly into a rage exclaiming, "Heinrich is the devil, and Satan shall have no voice in the Church of Saint Peter!"

His concern growing, Odo gathered several papal agents, including Handel and Muehler, and had them slip into the Roman streets to feel the pulse of the general population.

"It's not good," reported Handel upon returning. "The citizens' anger at the Holy Father festers each day."

"Yes," agreed Muehler, "they claim Heinrich's reasonable because he doesn't attack the city in force, hoping bloodshed can be spared if only the Pope would compromise. They claim Heinrich has even sent for Abbot Hugh at Cluny to guarantee that a reasonable and acceptable agreement is ironed out. It's also said Abbot Hugh has sent for Cardinal Desiderius in Monte Cassino to meet him in Rome so they together can reason with the Holy Father."

"Abbot Hugh and Cardinal Desiderius?" Odo could not believe his ears.

"Yes," nodded Handel, "according to my sources, Hugh is already on his way, as is Desiderius."

"Oh, but it gets even more interesting," interjected Muehler. "Apparently, Heinrich has secretly agreed to arrest Guibert of Ravenna, who he himself crowned as the new pope to take the tiara from Gregory."

"Oh, Father in Heaven!" exclaimed Odo, yet more surprised. At this, Odo, sat down and clasped a palm about his forehead. "Oh, but this entire thing has become a crooked path!" Shifting his eyes to Handel and Muehler, he shook his head. "Still, surely both of you know Gregory will never compromise."

"The people in the streets are right, Cardinal," snapped Handel, weary of the Pope's stubbornness. "Gregory is unreasonable! Despite the thousands who have died during this ceaseless dispute, he continues to ride his own vanity and ego? Heinrich, at least, is willing to end this thing."

"Oh, but you insult the Holy Father!" Odo exclaimed, his face turning red as he pointed a finger at Handel. Turning to Muehler, he said, "And what do you say?"

Muehler rubbed his chin, looking Odo in the eye. "There's much to consider here, Cardinal. But was it not you who spoke of the grand stage not so long ago? About how the powerless become victims? You see, I've given thought to what you said, but you don't sound now like the same man who spoke those words to me that day."

"Well said," replied Odo, retreating a step. "I have become defensive, it appears…and frustrated, worn down over this mess."

"We're all frustrated, and have grown short-tempered," said Handel. "The same is occurring in Heinrich's camp, I'd imagine. Only Pope Gregory remains certain, but certainty isn't always right."

Odo could not sleep that night. It concerned him that doubt was beginning to bud even amongst the Pope's own agents. Yet, Odo recognized there were specks of truth in what Handel and Muehler had said.

As several more weeks progressed, visits by the politicians of Rome became more frequent and more intense. Then one day Odo heard a blare of trumpets emanating from Heinrich's camps.

"It's the wagon train from Cluny," reported Muehler. "Abbot Hugh has arrived!"

Hugh entered Heinrich's camp amidst clamorous fanfare as cries of joy and expectation arose from German and Lombard troops. "Hail, Abbot Hugh!" they shouted, clanging swords against shields and raising banners to the sky. "Hugh will untangle this knot!"

Heinrich was even more joyful. "Oh, my holy Godfather!" he declared, falling to his knees. "Thank God you've come. Only you can open Gregory's ears and bring peace after all these years of blood and steel!"

Over the next two days, Heinrich set out propositions to Hugh, explaining that he was more than willing to make major concessions if only Pope Gregory would crown him emperor within the graces of the Church. "I reserve the right to select my own bishops, as have all my ancestors and predecessors! And Gregory must renounce my excommunication!"

Three days later, Cardinal Desiderius arrived and met Abbot Hugh at Heinrich's camp. Later that afternoon they were both announced to the people of Rome and the gates were opened for their dual procession. Celebration broke out amongst the mobs as they thronged Hugh and Desiderius by the thousands. An hour later, the two high clerics were announced at the Vatican gate and allowed to enter.

Odo greeted them first. "Such a welcome sight, both of you!" he proclaimed before all. Then, taking them aside, he whispered, "I fear that Gregory has dug himself in and cannot extricate himself."

"Cannot, or *will* not?" asked Hugh. "Peace can be had. Heinrich gives much ground."

"But on the question of investiture?" asked Odo. "Does he give ground there?"

Hugh did not answer at first, but crossed himself instead. Taking Odo by the shoulder, he said, "No. On this one thing there may still be deadlock. But perhaps there is still room for common ground, at least, and both sides can save face."

Odo shook his head. "No, not on the issue of investiture. Gregory is a granite wall about the subject. I fear his disdain for Heinrich has turned to hate. And hate is a sharp shovel, one that has helped many a great man dig his own grave."

Desiderius shook his head. "That is not good news," he said. "Gregory is obstinate to begin with, but when he gets his blood up, he becomes impossible."

They spoke a while longer, and within the hour were presented to Gregory. "Ah, my dearest friends," sighed the old Pope on seeing Hugh and Desiderius. "Friendly faces at last! Come sit with me and shore up my banks lest they collapse in Heinrich's wicked currents!"

Exchanging small-talk, they began by catching up on each other's health and the on-going campaign in Spain against the Muslims. Hugh described the great cathedral rebuilding project he had begun in Cluny several years before, and Desiderius spoke of several projects going on at the Monastery of Monte Cassino where he served as Abbot. Never once was Heinrich mentioned.

That next day they met again, all three knowing that Heinrich would be the topic of the day. "You have gained much, Hildebrand," said Hugh gently, as though tiptoeing over a path strewn with jagged shards of glass. "The King begs your forgiveness, and vows to restore your position."

"*Restore my position?*" exclaimed Gregory, flushing purple. "Ha! I have never lost it, in the eyes of God. Only Heinrich thinks it has been taken, with his lackey, Guibert of Ravenna, now parading about as Pope Clement III!"

"But Heinrich will remove Guibert, Hildebrand," said Desiderius, "if only you give a little ground."

"*God* will remove Guibert!" Gregory retorted.

Seeing that Gregory's blood was rising, Hugh backed off, taking a different tactic. "The people of Germany and Italy, they beseech you to end this war. And our dear Mathilda, her life now hangs by a thread. What will become of her if an armistice is not soon declared?"

"Mathilda?" said Gregory. "Does she also abandon me now?"

"No, no, of course not," interjected Desiderius. "She remains faithful to you and fights on, but at a great cost. She has lost nearly everything, and cannot possibly hold out forever."

"God will snatch her from the devil's grasp!" exclaimed Gregory. "I have prayed on it."

Three hours later, Hugh and Desiderius left Gregory's chamber, both shaking their heads with frustration and fatigue. When they met Odo, they shrugged helplessly. "Oh, Odo!" lamented Hugh, "I fear that you were correct."

"Indeed," said Desiderius. "Every time Heinrich's name is mentioned, Gregory falls into his own hole. He refuses to budge!"

Still, the two high clerics did not give up. Hugh and Desiderius spent the next week shuttling back and forth between the Vatican and Heinrich's camp.

"Does he not see the folly of his own obstinacy?" fumed Heinrich. "Ha! I bet it's Cardinal Odo de Lagery who shores up the old goat's resolve! Yes, Gregory listens to the militant Odo!"

"No, you are mistaken," replied Hugh. "Cardinal Odo remains faithful to the Pope, but he has also done everything possible to steer Gregory towards a mutually acceptable solution short of abdicating on the issue of investment, as have Desiderius and myself."

"Yes," added Desiderius, "even Odo de Lagery sees that we must undo this deadlock."

But Heinrich refused to believe them because Guibert of Ravenna had already poisoned his mind against Odo. "Odo is the most dangerous man in Rome," he had warned the King. "He intends to wear the Pope's tiara one day, and knows it will never happen if we prevail! For this reason alone, he convinces Gregory to resist at all cost!"

By the end of another week, Abbot Hugh's and Desiderius' encounters with Pope Gregory had evolved into verbal duels, even shouting matches which could be heard by those outside the Pope's chambers. Odo overheard these heated exchanges, as did Tristan. Both found it difficult to believe that these faithful old friends had come to such an impasse, accusing each other of selfishness and pride. Gregory even went so far as to accuse the other two of playing the role of Judas.

"This fighting among our leaders of the Church," exclaimed Tristan, "it frightens me!"

"It frightens all of us," Odo replied grimly. "Indeed, it frightens the world."

***

In the end, the ever patient Hugh of Semur resigned himself to stark reality—Pope Gregory would rather perish than surrender even a crumb of fleeting victory to Heinrich. Cardinal Desiderius concluded the same. With profound regret, the two high clerics abandoned Rome.

As their caravans disappeared over the hills, two other men quietly made their way into the camp of Archbishop Guibert of Ravenna, now Pope Clement III, ushering the anti-pope into a private parley. Moments later, Guibert of Ravenna was collapsing into a blithering rage.

"Goddamn his twisted, bartering soul!" seethed Guibert. "I've stood by him through humiliation, penance and the edge of defeat! How could Heinrich do this to me?" Trembling with disbelief, he stared at the two men, playing their reported scenario in his head. Then, pacing back and forth, thinking perhaps to snatch a thread of hope, he said. "Dammit, you're both certain of this, then?"

"Aye," grunted the shorter man, a German henchman named Hans Marcus. "The King sent feelers to Cardinal Desiderius and Abbot Hugh of Semur offering to have you arrested and imprisoned in exchange for Pope Gregory rescinding his excommunication and recognizing Heinrich as Holy Roman Emperor." Looking over at his accomplice, a malicious Armenian known only as Vlad, Marcus said, "Tell him."

Vlad shrugged, offering a gaze that lacked all emotion, showing only limited interest. "It's true," he muttered, "as certain as I'm standing here, it's true. Should that old jackass Gregory ever show the slightest gesture of compromise, you're done." Baring his teeth the slightest bit, such that one could not tell whether he was about to smile or to show scorn, he added, "And then *you'll* shortly disappear into the belly of some forgotten prison to rot."

The Armenian's words cut Guibert with the precision of a razor, as did his gaze. The anti-pope knew Vlad was right. Guibert had known the impetuous, scheming Heinrich since the day of the Prince's birth, and realized early on that the child's only loyalty would be to himself.

"It's that goddamned Odo de Lagery," groused Guibert, more to himself than to Marcus and Vlad. "He knows Gregory's old and falling into poor health. Aye, Odo de Lagery is conspiring to seize the papal tiara, but knows I stand in the way."

"I heard nothing of Odo de Lagery in the mix," said Marcus. Motioning to Vlad, he asked, "Did you?"

"No," said Vlad, his thoughts wandering elsewhere.

"Competent as you are in matters of secrecy and violence," scowled Guibert, unconvinced, "neither of you understand the subtleties of courtly betrayal. Odo de Lagery's name may not have surfaced, but the man is clever and operates in the shadows. I tell you, his envious eyes are aimed at the papal throne, *my* throne, and his fingers are somewhere in Heinrich's ploy to trade me in. And oh, I'll have my revenge yet on that damned Benedictine!"

The impact of Hugh's and Desiderius' failure to move Gregory began to be felt throughout Rome within days of their departure. Anger at Gregory's obtuseness began to escalate as royalists marched in the streets, hailing Clement III as the true pope by regal appointment, many claiming that this was directed by God Himself. Even those who had been fiercely loyal to Gregory began to waver, weary of political turmoil, uncertainty and siege.

This, in turn, encouraged the anti-pope to openly voice accusations against Odo de Lagery. No longer containing his rants only within his own camp, Guibert began spreading rumors amongst the Lombards and Heinrich's troops, as well as to Heinrich himself. Moreover, knowing that his henchmen, Marcus and Vlad, had secret means of infiltrating Rome, he sent them into the city to spread subversion and discontent, targeting Odo de Lagery as the root of Pope Gregory's immovability.

Then, oddly, just as things were turning their darkest for Gregory and the Vatican community, word began to circulate throughout the city that Heinrich was once again withdrawing from Rome. Within days, the rumors proved true. Heinrich, who had always been prone to shifts of mood accompanied by unpredictability, gathered his army and slipped north. Jubilation spread amongst the streets of Rome like wildfire, with mobs even gathering at the walls of the Vatican shouting, "Glory be to Pope Gregory! Praise to Cardinal Odo of Ostia!"

But jubilation quickly vanished, just as unexpectedly as Heinrich had turned north. Months later, toward the end of 1082, his army appeared again, setting up siege for yet a third attempt to capture Rome. "Heinrich's back!" the mobs wailed. "He's as stubborn as Gregory, and it's us who'll pay the price for their damned vanity!"

As 1083 began, Odo looked out at Heinrich's vast forces from the walls of the Vatican one morning. The Cardinal sensed that Rome's resistance had run its course. *Rome is weary. In a matter of months, Heinrich will finally prevail*, he decided. Discouraged, he summoned Dieter Muehler and Jurgen Handel to his private chambers that evening.

"Handel," he said, "though the Holy Father does not accept it, Heinrich will soon breach the city, and when this happens, Heinrich will attack the Vatican itself. Time is running short for us, so I am sending you south to communicate directly with Duke Guiscard the Wily. Beg him to move his Norman troops to our defense."

Handel, his face etched with doubt, shook his head. "But Cardinal, Guiscard is in full campaign across the Adriatic in the Balkans against Emperor Alexius and the Byzantines. Simultaneously, he's also waging a war against rebel vassals who are strongholding in Greece. He can ill afford to abandon either campaign, not even for the Holy Father."

"I understand," said Odo, "yet we have established close ties with him since his excommunication was pardoned by Pope Gregory. We *know* he strongly favors the Pope over Heinrich, but he is not aware of the new alliance between Heinrich and Emperor Alexius. Once Heinrich takes Rome, he can then easily continue to move south against Guiscard's holdings in Lower Italy, while Guiscard is waging his campaigns across the Adriatic Sea. Guiscard will have much at stake when Heinrich takes Rome...and much to lose. I fear he may not see it coming."

Handel nodded. "True, Heinrich would find Guiscard's holdings in Lower Italy easy prey with Guiscard across the sea. Though Guiscard is heavily distracted at present, he'll be alarmed by the possibility of Heinrich invading his realm from the north."

Turning to Muehler, Odo said, "I have also finalized plans for that business over in England we discussed months ago. A courier is enroute to our Paris agent, Brother Dominicus, instructing him to proceed to north England and the Scottish border to make arrangements. This will take months, perhaps longer, but I need you to commandeer a vessel, slip out of Heinrich's blockade and sail west to France. You will hold at Cluny until Brother Dominicus sends word for you to come to Paris."

"But that'll be yet more time lost on top of the original delay, Cardinal," objected Muehler. "That's a long time to wait in Cluny with this Heinrich mess coming apart on us!"

"Yes, but we don't know what might happen to us here once Heinrich's army takes Rome. Should you get trapped here in Italy, we won't be able to carry out our mission in England. Just wait it out, Muehler, and when Brother Dominicus sends word, then put the wheel in motion. Leave Cluny, head to England, and present yourself to Lady Asta."

"Yes, Cardinal," replied Muehler. But uncertainity filled his expression and he said, "You know, we've never discussed the possibility of her rejecting your proposal. If she should refuse, what then?"

"We cannot, of course, force her hand, Muehler," shrugged Odo. "But either way there is no sense in you returning to Rome once Heinrich takes us over, so return to Cluny instead and await word of our fate."

"You sound as though all is lost," said Handel.

"The people are exhausted and afraid, turning against us by the score with each passing day, and Heinrich is beginning to smell victory at last. This poison between Gregory and Heinrich is so steeped in bitterness now that it has turned into a dance of death. It cannot, therefore, end well. We are soon done."

"Very well," said Handel, "I'll cross the Adriatic to warn Duke Guiscard. Let's just hope he sees the snare being set around him and chooses to return to Italy to help us."

"And when should I sail, Cardinal?" asked Muehler.

"As soon as you can find a ship," said Odo, moving to his desk and withdrawing a satchel. "Here," he said, handing it to Muehler, "my full instructions on how to proceed once you arrive in England. But beware of the Bastard. We've received word that his spies have captured and executed yet more of our Benedictine agents in Rouen. Be safe, then, and Godspeed."

As the two agents departed, Odo called the captain of the Papal Guard. Foreseeing an inevitable end to Gregory's reign as pope, and fearing a violent conflagration once Heinrich's troops broke into the city, Odo instructed him to begin provisioning the Castel Sant' Angelo for future occupancy by the papal community should the walls of the Vatican be breached.

The Castel Sant' Angelo was a stout and impregnable cylindrical fortress that stood just across from Saint Peter's Basilica. It had originally been constructed during Antiquity to serve as a giant mausoleum for Roman Emperor Hadrian and his wife.

As men scurried about following Odo's instructions, Odo grimly watched. Then, with resignation, he crossed himself. "So, " he said aloud to no one, "the end finally approaches. May God be merciful, then, in this hour of darkness."

Chapter Forty-Three

Assassination

In every empire, whether rising or rooted, there lies beneath the surface a dark underbelly of corrupt hooligans laboring on behalf of the power brokers beneath whose boot the empire exists. These men are fully lacking of morals, conscience or virtue. They live only to wreak havoc at the command of their masters. Hans Marcus and the man called Vlad were such men, working in the shadows under the employ of Archbishop Guibert of Ravenna.

Marcus was a habitual felon serving a life sentence in Munich until one day a high cleric showed up with documents freeing him under condition of employment to Archbishop Guibert. The Investiture War had broken out, and a need had arisen for henchmen adept in the streets who were amenable to committing violence, or even atrocities.

Vlad, on the other hand, was a cold-blooded murderer. After his capture and trial, he was scheduled for a visit to the gallows until the timely arrival of the same high cleric who had propositioned Hans Marcus. Vlad accepted the cleric's terms and was soon working beside Marcus, spying, intimidating royalist opponents, setting fires and crushing heads. The two also proved adept at planning and committing assassinations, leaving in their wake neither evidence nor suspicion. With time, they became Guibert's most reliable enforcers. So when Guibert marched his army south into Italy with king Heinrich, Marcus and Vlad followed.

Guibert had been enraged when the two hooligans uncovered King Heinrich's secret proposal to have him imprisoned if Pope Gregory would only give ground. Still, as hope springs eternal within the hearts of all men, part of him simply refused to believe the words of his two henchman. But now, as the siege lengthened, other sources seemed to verify Heinrich's offer of betrayal. Seething, Guibert still cast all blame on Odo de Lagery.

"It's the Cardinal-Bishop of Ostia, I tell you!" he railed after calling Marcus and Vlad to his tent late one night. "Christ alive! Something's got to happen to the man, or else I'm done!" His throat hoarse, Guibert settled, turning to Marcus and Vlad. "And that goddamned Heinrich, offering me up as a sacrifice! I stand here today only because of Gregory's obstinate will! But he is an old man and will soon depart this world. Oh, but Odo de Lagery stands in the wings, plotting to wear the papal tiara. Unlike Gregory, he is well-liked throughout the continent and could eventually mobilize Spain, France and Normandy, after which he would then come after me, perhaps even with Heinrich's blessing! Marcus, I need you and Vlad to root him out."

"Root him out?" asked Marcus, his forehead creasing with concern. "But he's behind the walls of the Vatican. It's one thing slipping in and out of the city, but the Vatican's like a damn fortress. It'd be impossible getting in, and even trickier yet getting out should the alarm be raised."

"There's a way," said Vlad, his voice dispassionate, his manner unperturbed.

"Huh?" said Marcus.

"There's a way," repeated Vlad, his tone remaining flat, "so no need to shit your pants, Marcus. Beneath the Castel Sant' Angelo lies a collapsed sewer. It's tight, but passable, and the Castel opens to the Vatican. We'll slip in at night disguised in Benedictine robes and find the cardinal." Pausing, he shot Guibert a look. "Of course, such dangerous duty calls for much higher reward."

"Yes," nodded Guibert, knowing that of the two, Vlad was the more wily and cold-blooded. "My future hangs in Odo de Lagery's palm unless I pull it from him. So let it be done then. Now go, and may God guide you!"

***

Within the Vatican, Odo was continuing the heavy provisioning of Castel Sant' Angelo. "What is this about?" inquired Tristan, pointing to carts of provisions passing through the Castel's gate.

"When the Germans come through the gates of Rome they will march straight to the Vatican, which is not as defensible as the Castel. The Castel has higher and thicker walls, and a single access point. When the time comes, we will make our final stand in the Castel."

Tristan passed this news on to Guillaume, who for some reason seemed to become inspired on hearing the words 'final stand'. "At last," he exclaimed, "we get to fight!"

Unlike Guillaume, Tristan faced this eventuality with trepidation. "I have never understood your naked courage, Guillame. Are you not afraid we could all die?"

"Of course I am, but to die for such a magnificent cause! Imagine the glory—dying in defense of the Holy Father and the Church against the unholy Germans and Lombards. Legends and heroes are made of such battles!"

Tristan shook his head, wondering what tripe Mathilda had drummed into his brother's head in Tuscany. "I will leave the fighting to you, then, Guillaume," he said. "As to me, I will pray when the Germans arrive."

Later that evening after a late communal dinner, Cardinal Odo assembled the entire papal community and led them through the rosary. All then offered their blessings to each other and retired for the evening.

Before going to bed, Tristan went to Odo's chamber, which was adjacent to his own and Guillaume's. "Do you think the end will be bloody, Cardinal?" he asked, his face contracting with concern. "And what do you suppose will become of the Holy Father?"

"Only God knows, Tristan," answered Odo. "Do I expect Heinrich to actually put an end to the Pope's life? No, most certainly not. There is an agreement amongst kings that they will not kill another king. Dukes, earls, yes, but not each other. And the Pope is like a king, far greater even. So no, the Holy Father may be imprisoned or exiled, but he will live."

"But Cardinal Odo, history has shown that many popes over just the past two centuries have been murdered. Pope John VIII was poisoned, and when he failed to die quickly enough, his head was smashed with hammers. Pope Benedict V was stabbed over a hundred times by a jealous husband, and Pope Boniface VI simply disappeared. Between the years 872 and 904, there were twenty-four different popes because so many met violent ends."

"Yes, but things have settled somewhat during the past century. Besides, despite King Heinrich's war against the Church, he has some decent qualities about him. He might be merciful despite the horrid blood between himself and Pope Gregory."

"And what about the rest of us?"

Odo looked at Tristan before responding, placing his hand softly on the boy's shoulder. "Should it come to battle upon the ramparts against the Germans, things could get bloody. We are far more expendable than the Pope, and victors often seek retribution especially against the lowly. Which is the very reason I plan to pray for mercy this very night to Saint Peter within the Basilica before retiring. Perhaps you and Guillaume would care to join me?"

So it was late on the tenth night of February, 1083, just weeks after Tristan's seventeenth birthday, Odo de Lagery was kneeling in the first pew between the two

Saint-Germain brothers within the Basilica of Saint Peter. Heads bent in, they failed to notice two intruders dressed as monks slipping into church, nor did they hear them come down the nave, one grasping a sword, the other a dagger.

Odo and the boys were jolted from their prayers as Hans Marcus, brandishing a sword, shouted, "Ho, there, Odo de Lagery! Prepare to meet your Maker!" Making a run, he burst into the tight pew space to get at the Cardinal.

Tristan, because of his position, was the first in Marcus' path. He was inadvertently blocking access to Odo, the target of Marcus' entry into the Basilica. Seeing the boy, Marcus raised his sword, thinking to quickly dispatch him, then go after the cardinal. In horror, Tristan glanced up and saw the glint of steel descending; knew in that instant that death was upon him. Without thinking, or even realizing, he cried out, "Mother!"

Tristan next thought he felt the blade slicing into his shoulder, but realized that the sensation was actually Odo's hand sweeping him aside. The crack of steel against oak then echoed throughout the cathedral as Marcus' sword missed Tristan, splitting the back of the pew into shards of kindling.

"Goddammit!" Marcus bellowed.

Shoving Tristan to the floor, while pushing Guillaume away in the other direction, Odo sprang to his feet and grabbed the intruder by the shoulders before the man could raise upright again. Odo then slammed the attacker's face into the back of the pew, breaking his nose, splitting it into a mash of blood and tissue. At that same moment Vlad appeared. Larger than Marcus, he raised his dagger and came after Odo, awkwardly struggling his way down the narrow pew space. But Marcus was blocking his path, writhing and flailing about in agony. This prevented Vlad from getting to Odo, but only for several seconds.

"Run, Guillaume!" Odo shouted, reaching down, shoving the still prostrate Tristan toward his brother. "Run for your life, Tristan!"

Reaching out with his long arms, Odo desperately attempted to hold Vlad's oncoming charge at bay as he struggled to get by his injured accomplice. Long-limbed as Odo was, his forearms became an easy target for Vlad's dagger, who easily sliced through the meat of Odo's forearms with three flicks of his double-edged weapon. Odo's wounds split open like pursed lips, slinging blood everywhere.

"R-Run boys!" he cried. "Call the guards!"

Marcus, continuing to buck and writhe in agony, was now blinded by the profusion of blood gushing from his splattered nose. Unable to see, he dropped his sword. Seeing this, still fending off Vlad, Odo reached down and grasped the dropped sword to defend himself. But Odo was not a man-at-arms, so the sword felt foreign in his hands; his movements with it clumsy.

Taking quick notice of Odo's ineptitude with the blade, Vlad laughed, his cackle filling the vast Basilica and reverberating from cavernous space to cavernous space. "You're dead you Goddamned Benedictine!" he screamed, finally managing to squeeze past the injured Marcus.

Odo was by now much weakened by the loss of blood hemorrhaging from his wounds. Feeling things going black, he sensed Vlad's dagger blade descending; knew at that moment that he would soon be drawing his final breath. Yet, in that final second, one thought after another streamed through his consciousness, flashing past like a constellation of livid sparks erupting one after the other in explosions of shock and horror:

So this is how I meet my end, he thought, the specter of death flashing before his eyes, *at the hands of assassins! But my work on this earth is not done! The boys, they must flee!*

The last thing he felt was the sharp blade slicing into his shoulder and through his flesh.

I feel the rapture. Almighty God, I commend myself to Thee...

At the very moment Odo's slack body began to drop, a shadow sprang over him from nowhere, hurling itself onto Vlad with the bold ferocity of the terrier attacking the bear. It was Guillaume, dagger drawn, eyes wild with blood. Vlad was still stooped, attempting to withdraw his dagger from Odo's body. Guillaume flung himself atop him, driving his own dagger down through the back of Vlad's neck with all his strength. Withdrawing the blade, he then quickly plunged it into Vlad's back again and again. Vlad howled at the first blow, then slumped dead onto the shattered pew seat as Guillaume continued to stab at this shoulders and spine.

"Guillaume!!" wailed Tristan, horrified. "My God, stop it! He's dead! He's dead!"

Hearing Tristan's cries, Guillaume looked up, as startled from a nightmare. Simultaneously, he realized the first assailant, still wiping blood from his face and eyes, was groping about for the sword Odo had dropped. Instinctively, Guillaume kicked at him and sent him reeling backward atop Odo's motionless frame as it lay upon the remains of the shattered pew. Finding himself flat on his back, Marcus' eyes rolled about, blinked, then stared up dumbly at Guillaume. Without hesitation, Guillaume flicked down in one swift arc of his dagger and sliced Marcus' throat clean through the neck-bone. Marcus sighed, gurgled blood, then slowly issued that final, mournful rattle of death as his soul passed from this life into darkness.

Tristan had fled the Basilica to alarm the guards. As they ran with them back into the cathedral, they found Odo de Lagery lying motionless within the pew space. The captain of the guard knelt, felt his pulse, then his temple…and found no sign of life. A grim look swept over him then, as he stood to address the others. "It is my sad duty to announce that Odo de Lagery, Cardinal-Bishop of Ostia is…dead," he said, trembling.

Hearing this pronouncement, many of the guards fell to their knees, crossing themselves, while others dropped their heads. Tristan and Guillaume, still numb from the trauma of the attack, stood there mutely, too overcome even to react.

A pall fell over the entire basilica, as sheer disbelief and denial swept through every individual within. Indeed, Odo de Lagery was larger than life. It was not possible that he had been taken from their midst, or from this life.

Suddenly, one of the guards shrank back. "H-his finger!" he shouted, trembling. "It moves!"

Huddling closer, everyone leaned forward to inspect Odo's body. Nothing occurred at first, but then a finger of one hand twitched the slightest bit. A moment later, two fingers of that same hand slowly curled.

"He lives!" shouted the captain. "Quick, gather him up!"

Even though Odo had shown this faint sign of movement, those attending him believed him mortally wounded and expected his death by dawn. Odo survived the night, but physicians indicated it was but a matter of time before he expired. Miraculously, he lasted through the day despite the severity of his wounds. As night approached, it began to appear that he might actually recover. "God's hand is in this," insisted Pope Gregory, "as no man could live after such an attack unless there was holy intervention!"

Odo himself remembered little of the attack. It was not until the end of a full week of convalescence that he learned it was young Guilaume who had saved his life by finishing off the assassins the night of the attack. "God bless you," he told the boy, his voice weak and thready, "you are fearless."

Deservedly so, Guillaume was proclaimed a hero by the entire papal community. Tristan, though he had been frightened by his brother's bloody actions in the basilica, could not have been more proud of Guillaume, and told him so time and again. But Guillaume had been profoundly affected by his actions, and fell into brooding. Though he had long looked forward to the day he would wage battle against evil, now that he had actually spilled blood, he was more appalled by it all than anticipated.

"Killing those men was easy enough at the time," he confided to Tristan, "but I now feel guilty about what I did."

"But you saved our lives!" objected Tristan. "It is Heaven's justice, Guillaume. They came to kill us within the sanctity of Saint Peter's Basilica, don't you see? It was God's anger that struck them down, and you were His instrument! You are a warrior for Christ, Guillaume. May evil forever fear you!"

Guillaume shook his head, unconvinced. "Listen to yourself, you sound like a monk."

But Tristan's words did manage to lift Guillaume with time, because Guillaume loved and admired his brother above everyone else in the world. Tristan was his blood, as well as his spiritual and intellectual ideal.

"Though you don't like to fight," Guillaume told him one day, "you in your own way are a warrior for Christ also, Brother. So we will stand together, you and me, the rest of our lives for righteousness. Agreed?"

Tristan looked at Guillaume, touched by these words. "Yes, Guillaume, agreed."

Chapter Forty-Four

Oh, Rome!

The siege of Rome by the Germans and Lombard continued for seven more months, creating hardship within the city for all. As summer approached, resolving that they could hold out no longer, the Roman leadership surrendered, opened the gates, and concluded a treaty with Heinrich. The Roman leaders also publicly announced that the quarrel between King Heinrich and Pope Gregory should be decided by a synod. In addition, to avoid retribution by Heinrich and the sacking of the city by Lombard troops, they secretly promised they would induce Pope Gregory to make a settlement. If Gregory refused, they promised to elect a new pope in his place.

Feeling victorious after so many years of bitter rivalry, Heinrich was now absolutely convinced the old pontiff would be forced to accept a compromise. In a gesture of reconciliation, Heinrich set aside his acrimony toward Pope Gregory and generously offered a peaceful settlement on the condition that Gregory would renounce his 1080 ban of excommunication against him, and also agree to crown him Holy Roman Emperor. Heinrich also confirmed that to save Gregory's honor and restore his legitimacy as pope, he would arrest Guibert of Ravenna.

Gregory, to the dismay of all, adamantly refused to discuss a single measure of compromise with his hated nemesis. From behind the walls of Castel Sant' Angelo, he then pronounced anew his anathema upon Heinrich and his followers, declaring yet a third excommunication of Heinrich. Adding salt to the wound, he called on the citizens of Rome to rise up and hurl Heinrich from their midst.

Dumbfounded upon learning Gregory's actions, Heinrich could not believe his ears. Becoming so enraged at being told this news, Heinrich had the messengers who delivered Gregory's refusals pummeled. "Has that old bastard *completely* lost his sanity?!" Heinrich fumed. "Does he wish to force me now to storm the Castel Sant' Angelo and actually drag him to the scaffold!?"

As agreed, despite Gregory's entrenchment in the Castel, the Romans attempted to assemble a synod of Gregory and Heinrich's respective clerics in hopes of forging a deal between King and Pope. The Romans soon discovered that Guibert had already set into motion efforts to prevent the attendance of Gregory's supporters. Then, just as it was becoming evident to the Romans that their synod effort was crumbling into failure, an improbable and confusing chain of events fell into place that would ultimately begin to spell doom for the city.

First, Heinrich received word that Countess Mathilda had revived a fierce counter offensive against his army in Tuscany. Despite his plans to storm the Castel Sant' Angelo, this news forced Heinrich and Guibert of Ravenna to vacate the city and return north to Tuscany to reinforce his retreating troops.

Next, learning that Heinrich had vacated the city, but fully suspecting that he would return, Pope Gregory remained locked within the safety of the Castel, thereby removing himself from visibility, spiritual leadership and political influence within Rome. This, in turn, caused the Roman people to fall away from any allegiance to him as pope. Many began to declare him deposed. Moreover, they decided that after Heinrich's return to the city, Guibert of Ravenna would be enthroned as the new pope.

And finally, news spread that Duke Guiscard the Wily and his troops had killed 6,000 of Emperor Alexius's forces at Durres across the Adriatic, and routed the Eastern Emperor's army. Furthermore, he had recently returned to Lower Italy and planned to march north to the rescue of Pope Gregory now that Heinrich was occupied in Tuscany. Panic spread like wild-fire; the Romans feared the Normans even more than the Lombards, especially since Guiscard employed Saracens as allies. In a move to protect themselves, the Romans sent envoys north to implore Heinrich to return and protect Rome from the savage violence of Robert Guiscard. Learning of this, Guiscard immediately shipped 30,000 pieces of gold to Rome to bribe the Roman leadership, thereby reconciling them with himself and Pope Gregory.

This worked splendidly, and the Roman leadership quickly changed their mind about wanting Heinrich to return. In the meanwhile, the Roman envoys who had previously left to implore Heinrich to return to Rome had by now arrived in Tuscany, convincing Heinrich to return to Rome, which he immediately did, arriving in spring of 1084.

Finding themselves now caught in the snare of their own indecision and greed, the Romans leaders were forced to open the gates of the city and hail Heinrich and Guibert as saviors. Heinrich immediately convened a synod of Gregory's opponents who took on the task of officially deposing and excommunicating Gregory while formally enthroning Guibert of Ravenna as Pope Clement III in the Cathedral of Saint Peter. Heinrich and his wife, Bertha, then received from Pope Clement the imperial crown of the Holy Roman Emperor in Saint Peter's Basilica on Easter Sunday, March 31, 1084. Interestingly, Pope Gregory and the entire papal community shut within the Castel Sant' Angelo were able to witness much of this from the ramparts of the Castel.

Nonetheless, unbeknownst to all, due to the chain of events that had already been set in place by Roman leadership, the future of Rome was about to take an utterly unexpected turn.

Chapter Forty-Five

Benedictine Agent, Dieter Muehler

Dieter Muehler, as instructed by Cardinal Odo, had slipped onto a ship and crossed the Tyrrhenian Sea between Corsica and Sardinia. Landing in Toulon, France, he made his way to Cluny where he was welcomed and given accommodations by Abbot Hugh who was aware of Cardinal Odo's secret mission. "Since you will be with us for a good while," said Hugh, "I will have you work in the Infirmary with Brother Damien."

Though Muehler was a Black Monk, he was dispirited by the prospect of being stuck in a monastery for such a length of time. He had grown accustomed to the road and did not relish confinement. Making the best of circumstances, he struck up a friendship with Brother Damien and soon became an asset to the infirmary. As couriers came and went from Rome, Muehler became increasingly concerned about the chaos consuming Rome. Finally, as days dragged into weeks and weeks dragged into months, a courier arrived from Paris with a message from, not Brother Dominicus as expected, but a certain Brother Thierry Petit-Jean. The message instructed him to depart for Paris, but this unanticipated switch of monks in the operation raised suspicion in Muehler's mind. Nonetheless, he began making preparations to depart Cluny.

It was late September when Muehler arrived in Paris and made contact with this Brother Petit-Jean, a Benedictine who worked directly for Cardinal Odo de Lagery, and had been under his clandestine direction since Odo's days as Grand Prior of Cluny. As directed by Petit-Jean's message, Muehler met him on the 28th of September in the fifth pew, west side of Saint Étienne Cathedral. After exchanging a series of questions and coded answers, the two monks next moved to a private office located behind the sacristy of the cathedral.

"Here," said Petit-Jean, a smallish man afflicted with a nervous tick. "These are your maps, additional identity documents, auditing journals and letters of introduction for your trip to DuLacshire." Petit-Jean then handed Muehler a burgeoning satchel.

"I was supposed to deal with Brother Dominicus," said Muehler. "Why is he not here?"

"He's no longer with us, Brother Muehler," replied Petit-Jean.

"Eh?"

"He's dead. His head was taken by the Normans in Rouen. Me, I'm simply a courier, but was instructed to take his place for this mission. I wasn't happy about it, yet I do as I'm told."

"But you've completed all the arrangements that Dominicus was supposed to make, then?" asked Muehler.

"Yes, it's all right there in the bag. When you're done with your business and leave DuLacshire, you'll go north to Scotland and cross over to Dumfries. I was there just last month making final arrangements and bartering with a Scotsman, a ruddy fellow by the name of Aengus MacLeod. He's a red-headed brute of a man, frightening to look at, actually. They say he's a legend in south Scotland, a well known rogue and pirate who hates the Normans and now leads raiding parties against them and the French. Anyway, he's perfect for your purposes. Once you leave DuLacshire, he'll see you safely out of England on a western passage by sea down and around to southern France, bypassing England and Normandy completely. It's a good plan because, if things go as I suspect, the Normans and the French will be hunting you down."

"Tell me more about Dominicus," said Muehler. "What happened?"

Petit-Jean shook his head and his nervous tick escalated. "As you know, the Bastard is now furious at Pope Gregory because he went on record accusing the Bastard of unquenchable thirst for human blood. The Bastard still allows Beneditine monasteries to operate and permits our couriers to pass, but at the first indication of anything other than religious business, the Bastard wants our necks on the block, especially for spying! Brother Dominicus got nabbed with secret documents on his body. As for me, I was ordered to complete his work in preparation for your arrival here in Paris. I've been shitting my pants since then because of what happened to Dominicus, especially since I've no idea how much information the Normans pulled from him. They're skilled in torture, you know. Anyway, I'm glad you've arrived and my part in this affair is done! By the way, because of Dominicus' fate, I recommend you avoid Normandy altogether and go to England via Les Pays de la Loire and Bretagne, then cross the Channel."

Muehler looked at Petit-Jean and shook his head. "No, that'd triple my distance and time. I'll take my chances. Besides, my documents are from Cluny and identify me as a Benedictine auditor. I'll be fine."

"Very well, then. Pax vobiscum," said Petit-Jean, crossing himself. "But keep an eye to the Bastard's agents once you cross into Normandy. He's got them everywhere, thick as flies, even here in Paris hidden in King Philippe's court!"

Muehler nodded, but was little detoured as he was highly seasoned in the art of secrecy and deception. Although he had neared the precipice a time or two, he had never once been exposed or captured.

Confidence comes with experience and is an asset in all trades. Nonetheless, Muehler's confidence did not serve him well on this particular day. As he departed Saint Étienne Cathedral, despite carefully perusing the passing crowds of pilgrims and visitors for suspicious individuals and lingering glances, he failed to notice the woman who had followed him across the bridge on his way to the cathedral, and was now following him again as he left.

***

Muehler's entry into Normandy was uneventful. Three days later he boarded a vessel to England without encountering any difficulties. During the crossing he happened to meet an engaging young French couple with two children who were, coincidentally, in the process of transitioning to an estate within twenty leagues of DuLacshire. It was rare that Muehler had occasion to speak to either women or children, so he rather enjoyed sharing casual conversation with the family, especially the personable young wife who introduced herself as Madame Marie Madeleine.

The woman was a doting mother, lavishing compliments on the intelligence and talents of her children. She also appeared to have a passing interest in the Benedictine order, stating that her two elder brothers were monks. "They're posted at the monastery of La Rochelle along the southwestern Atlantic coast of France," she said. "Sadly, I seldom see them anymore because their abbey constitution is very strict, so they're rarely allowed to travel or receive visitors." Then she launched into suppositions about her family's new life in England. As the ship docked, she said, "Oh, I've so much enjoyed speaking to you, Brother Muehler. By the way, my husband and I have commissioned a private driver. Since you're traveling our direction, we'd love to share our coach."

"I thank you for your generous offer," replied Muehler, "but I'm on a rather circuitous route and must stop at several of our monasteries to take an accounting of their resources for Abbot Hugh of Cluny."

"Abbot Hugh!" she exclaimed. "You know the celebrated Hugh of Semur?"

"Indeed," Muehler smiled. "But here, we are landed and I must be on my way. Best of luck to you and your family, Madame Madeleine, and may fortune smile on you."

"Yes," replied Madame Madeleine with a curtsy, "and may fortune smile on you also, Brother Muehler."

From the coast, Muehler proceeded to two different Benedictine sites, first Canterbury, then the Priory of Durham Cathedral, which was a cell of Cluny. This roundabout trek was to make it appear that he was truly on an auditor's circuit. And even though these stops devoured time, it was a necessary measure in light of the Bastard's recent edict against Benedictine spies.

Two weeks later, he finally crossed into DuLacshire on horseback, again without incident. Just before arriving in DuLacville itself, he dismounted at the edge of the forest with his satchel and began searching for a place to hide the satchel given to him by Brother Petit-Jean in Paris. After some effort he located a sunken hollow at the base of a huge oak, and stuffed the satchel within it. After covering the depression with leaves and brush, he mounted his horse and advanced into DuLacville.

It seemed a wretched place, and as he rode past the first conclave of huts and shanties, he could not help but notice that the villagers appeared more morose than during his previous visit. As he continued, he then caught sight of several villagers growing nervous at his advance. Casting furtive glances his way, they seemed to be averting his gaze. This aroused Muehler's instincts. *Something's about, they seem to be—*

At that very moment a squad of French soldiers appeared from behind shanties and rushed him. Seizing him, they threw him from his horse and roughly placed manacles about his wrists. "Ho, there, monk!" cried a voice, "I'm

Captain DuFresne and I arrest you in the name of Lord Desmond DuLac!"

Muehler struggled to free himself, but the efforts were useless. "I'm but a monk!" he protested. "I've done nothing! What's the charge?"

"Espionage!" hissed a voice from nowhere, as an attractive young woman stepped from the midst of the soldiers. It was Madame Marie Madeleine, transformed, now lacking all trace of the charm and gentleness she had played during the ship's crossing from Normandy. "I've been on your trail since Paris, monk! We learned from the spy Dominicus that someone would be coming to England from Cluny on a secret mission, and Cluny is the Pope's nest for reform and hostility to the Bastard. So now, what do you say, Muehler?"

"Cluny holds no hostility toward the Bastard," replied Muehler calmly. "Don't confuse Cluny's position with the Pope's on the topic of the Bastard."

"Bah! Cluny, the Pope!" snapped Madeleine. "Benedictines one and the same, everyone knows that! Now speak up or we'll take you up the hill where we've a fine collection of sharp instruments, monk!"

Muehler shook his head, offering only a vacant stare at his captors. "I'm a Benedictine auditor come from Cluny to carry out accounting duties in England," he said with conviction. "I carry no secret documents or hidden messages. Search me. And I harbor no enmity against the Bastard."

"Search him!" barked DuFresne, motioning to one of his men.

The soldier complied, stripping Muehler completely naked right in the road before the villagers who gawked at the proceedings with silent disgust. Their hatred of the French still simmered hotly beneath compliant deception.

"Nothing," said the soldier, glancing back at DuFresne.

"Check his robe, you fool!" cried Madeleine, her voice straining with contempt.

The soldier picked Muehler's robe from the ground, searched for hidden pockets, then looked at Madame Madeleine. "Nothing," he shrugged.

"I'll ask just once more," hissed Madeleine, her face contracting with agitation. "Have you anything to confess?"

"I'm a Benedictine auditor come from Cluny to carry out accounting duties in England," Muehler replied dryly.

"Be damned, then!" shouted Madeleine. "Play the fool if you insist, but I'll get at the truth before nightfall!" Pointing toward the hill, she said, "Take him to the Box, Captain, and notify DuLac!"

***

The 'Box' was a stone, block-shaped structure built into the south castle wall, which had served as a dungeon when the castle was engineered by the Saxons. It was a perfect square with walls barely taller than a man. In addition to multiple devices of torture and mutilation, it contained four jail cells, as well as four sets of shackles hung at the top of the wall, just high enough to dangle a victim without his feet touching the ground.

Muehler was dragged into the Box, shackled flat on his back atop a rack table, and questioned for half an hour by Madeleine and Desmond DuLac.

"We know your orders came from Rome," snapped Madeleine, "because Dominicus told us that much, Muehler. You're the Pope's man, then."

DuLac struck him across the face then with an iron poker. "We've learned also that you were right here in DuLacshire less than a year ago, and now you're back. What in Hell are you after, monk?"

Muehler groaned upon being struck across the face, but said nothing as Madeleine resumed her accusations. "We accepted that Domincus may not have known what your first mission entailed, Muehler, but when he said the same about this second trip, we burned his feet and spooned out his eyes. He then *still* claimed ignorance because he'd not yet received final instructions from Rome. Tell us, then, why are you here?"

"You're tied in with the Saxon rebels, aren't you, monk!" insisted DuLac. "The Pope sympathizes with them and has turned against the Bastard, charging him with cruelty and mass murder. Speak, you bastard!" Hearing no reply, DuLac struck him again across the face again with the poker.

"I'm a B-Benedictine m-monk," Muehler gasped, blood trickling from his forehead and the side of his eye socket. "I—"

"To Hell with you," snarled DuLac. Pointing to the jailer, he said, "Work him with the poker, but heat it up. And take your time burning sense out of him; let him suffer a bit, by God!"

That night, throughout the castle, screams could be heard piercing the darkness, coming in metered breaks, half an hour or so between sequences as the jailer intermittently applied the red-hot point of his poker to different parts of Muehler's body, beginning with his toes, and working up his ankles to his groin and face. The screams streamed down the hill also, into the huts as Saxons privately cursed their occupiers and pitied the poor Benedictine who had simply happened into the wrong village.

That next morning, the Box was silent except for the soft whimpering of the man being held captive. "He's a tough one," said DuLac to Madeleine as they left the castle with DuFresne and a platoon of soldiers to question the villagers. "The jailer still hasn't gotten a damn thing out of him though he worked the monk over all night long."

"Oh, he'll talk," replied Madeleine, "in time. Tonight have the jailer set the poker aside and start with the horse snips, one finger at a time, then the toes."

"Aye, you were right about him coming here to meet someone about a plot," said DuLac. "We'll get something out of the Saxon villagers; some of them must be involved, too!"

Lady Asta had heard the cries coming from the Box that previous night. Now as she made her way to the chapel to pray for his soul, she encountered Elder Heidi.

"Psst!" shooshed Elder Heidi, motioning Asta aside. "A strange thing, Dearie," she said in a low voice. "That man in the box they caught down in the village yesterday, he's a monk. The *same one* who was here a year ago. You were hoping maybe he had come from Cluny and might be able to share news of your boys, remember?"

Asta shrugged. "Yes, but he was from Bavaria and had never been to Cluny."

"Well then, another strange thing. As they were grilling him yesterday in the village, the monk claimed to be from Cluny. Now isn't that an odd twist that makes no sense, Dearie?"

"From Cluny?" exclaimed Asta, her heart stopping. "He said he was from Cluny?"

"Aye, claimed he was counting monasteries or some such thing."

"Oh, my Lord in Heaven!!" Asta whispered. "He will surely be able to tell me something of my sons, then!"

"Possibly," said Elder Heidi, spitting on the ground. "If your husband and that Norman bitch that's come to town don't kill him first."

Her heart suddenly pounding astray, Asta's mind raced from one wild thought to another. "Oh, God in Heaven, what to do?!"

"Go to the Box," gestured Elder Heidi. "Order the guards to allow you to enter. You are, after all, the Lady of the manor, Dearie."

"Yes, I'll do it!" Asta stammered.

She proceeded to the box, quickening her pace, "Allow me to pass," she demanded the guard.

"No, my Lady," one of the guards responded. "Lord DuLac said no one's to enter. Strict orders, I'm sorry."

Asta looked at the guard questioningly. Her face tightening, all trace of softness evaporated and her eyes grew frigid. "I will say it only once more, and if you refuse me, I will have your head on that block, yonder." Seeing Orla standing nearby, she added, "Do you know that big Dane there?"

The guard nodded, but said nothing.

"He's Orla Blood-Ax," Asta said, her voice dripping venom. "I will call him over in a moment, and he will lay you on the block himself, do you understand, soldier?"

The guard swallowed hard, glancing at his partner who was already moving aside. "Very well, as you command, my Lady," he said. "But I beg you, should Lord DuLac find out, plead my case?"

"Of course," she replied. Then she entered the Box, where she was not even questioned by the jailer. Having already heard what had transpired outside, he dismissed himself, leaving her alone with the victim.

Asta moved toward the monk, who presented a most horrid scene. He was stripped naked and shackled at the hands and feet to the rack, his body black with smoke, charred at a hundred points. Looking closer, she saw a trail of burn boils and blisters, some swollen to bursting while others had already erupted and were oozing puss onto the black smears speckling his body, this mix having turned to squid's ink. She gagged at the putrid smell of scorched flesh, feeling overcome by it all to the point of fleeing.

But the monk's lips began to move and she heard him mumble something. Stepping closer, she discerned that he was muttering a prayer in German, a language she knew.

Watching, her heart jumped. "Oh, Dear Lord in Heaven, have mercy on this poor man," she implored, crossing herself.

Muehler, barely conscious, heard this and slowly turned his head toward the voice. Recognizing her, his eyes gave a start and his body shuddered as he tried to raise up, only to be drawn back by his shackles. "L-Lady Asta…" he rasped painfully.

Asta drew back. "You *know* me?" she asked, startled.

'Yes. I have c-come for y-you, sweet lady."

"W-what did you say?" she stammered, confused even more.

He gazed at her, his cheeks and forehead purple with bruises, split open in gaping, swollen cuts that mutilated his entire face. Issuing the tiniest trace of a smile, he mumbled, "D-do you remember a m-monk named Odo de Lagery?"

"Yes, yes, of course!" Asta replied.

"He s-sent me a great distance with a p-pro-posal. And n-news of your sons."

At these words Asta's heart fluttered as an attack of palpitations erupted in her breast. "My sons?" she blurted, feeling faint.

"You s-sent your sons to Cluny y-years ago in the c-care of Odo de Lagery, b-but he was then appointed to Rome where he s-serves as chief counsel to Pope Gregory." Here Muehler licked his lips and coughed. "*W-water*," he gasped.

Asta ran to the water bucket hanging next to the hearth. When she returned, she sprinkled droplets over Muehler's crusted lips with her fingers. Next, she gently tipped the ladle and provided more. "R-Rome?" she stammered, her confusion deepening. "But my sons, are they in Cluny still?"

"N-no. Your youngest is in T-Tuscany, entrusted to la G-Gran Contessa Mathilda."

"What! The great countess of Tuscany? But how—"

"By the gr-grace of God alone, my Lady. And by the w-work of your older son's t-ties with Abbot Hugh, Odo de Lagery, la G-Gran Contessa, and the Pope."

At the mention of these names, Asta was struck dumb as her hands flew to her mouth.

"Your s-sons are fine," Muehler continued weakly. "Educated lads with great pr-promise. But they are n-not my purpose here in England. *You* are my p-purpose."

Asta nodded, though her mind remained a tumble of confusion.

Muehler paused, licking his parched lips. "W-water!" he muttered. Asta eased the ladle to his mouth again and he awkwardly slurped at it several times, then continued. "To begin, m-my Lady, d-do you still follow the word of God and remain as devout as the d-day you encountered Prior Odo de Lagery in Rouen on the day of your h-husband's execution?"

"Yes, most certainly so."

"And is it true that your m-marriage to Roger de Saint-Germain was f-forced upon you at age twelve as a p-political maneuver by the Bastard of Normandy? And that this m-marriage was officiated by the Bishop V-Villier of Saint-Germain-en-Laye?"

"Yes," Asta said, wondering how this monk could know such things. "The union was against my will and that of my father who was subsequently executed because of his objections. And yes, it was Bishop Villier who performed the ceremony."

"A-anulled!" rasped Muehler. "And is it true that after Roger de Saint-Germain's beheading, you m-married his brother, Desmond D-DuLac, to save your sons and y-your kinsmen in a ceremony officiated by the v-very same Bishop Villier who performed your first marriage?"

"Yes," Asta replied, "but—"

"Annulled! Th-that marriage also declared void because Bishop V-Villier of Saint-Germain-en-Laye was excommunicated several years ago from the Holy Church d-due to charges of immorality. Any consecrations or m-marriage vows he sanctified during his tenure as bishop have c-come under Papal Review...to include your own. Cardinal Odo de Lagery, with the approval of Pope Gr-

Gregory, declares that both of your marriages are dissolved!"

Asta looked at the monk, perplexed. "Is that possible?"

"Y-yes, I have the d-documents, h-hidden in a satchel at the bend just before the village, twenty-five paces south off the r-road in a hollow at the b-bottom of the biggest oak. And other p-papers for your…escape."

"Escape?" echoed Asta, barely a whisper.

Muehler motioned yes with his eyes, then closed them and sighed, feeling himself losing consciousness. Knowing his time was short, he struggled on. "I am t-told you hate DuLac."

"Yes, a foul, violent man. Repugnant and malicious!"

"Y-you are free to leave him now…w-with the Church's blessing."

Asta's eyes lit up, but only for an instant. Then she shrugged. "Yes, I see," she mumbled. "This is all very well and I am greatly indebted to Cardinal Odo for his efforts on my behalf, but I have nowhere to go, no means. And there is the Danish Guard. I cannot simply abandon them! They are one of the reasons I came here!"

Seeing that discouragement was sweeping Asta aside, Muehler said, "Cardinal Odo wishes to kn-know whether you would give your l-life to the Church…join the Brides of Christ."

"You mean," Asta whispered, "become a nun?"

"Yes, in B-Burgundy near Cluny…in the town of M-Marcigny-sur-Loire where sits the principal convent of the Cl-Cluny network. There are many women th-there, blessed by the Holy Spirit. Cardinal Odo has reserved a place f-for you there, and has himself provided the r-required dowry for entrance as a sister of m-means. He offers you respite from a life with DuLac. And you will b-be reunited with your sons, under certain l-limitations and circumstances."

Asta's mind was now awhirl! The thought of seeing her sons made her dizzy with joy, but then her thoughts circled back to the Danish Guard, and her shoulders dropped with resignation. "My kinsmen," she sighed. "I cannot leave them."

"This, t-too, is taken care of, my Lady, if th-they choose to follow you," mumbled Muehler. "Cardinal Odo has d-devised two plans, one for you to escape alone with the h-help of one of your men, and another if all your people w-wish to risk departure. If they do, the Cardinal h-has arranged employment f-for your Danish Guard in Tuscany under the banner of la Gran Contessa who seeks soldiers to f-fight the Germans."

Asta grew still, weighing everything the monk had thrown at her. A single brow furrowed over her eye, and Muehler thought he detected the trace of a smile, but then it vanished.

"There is much at stake here," she said. "Even though my husband has forsaken my bed for Saxon whores, he would rather see me dead than to see me leave of my own accord."

Muehler nodded. "This, also, the C-Cardinal foresaw, which is why he has chosen the M-Marcigny Convent in Burgundy. The Benedictines' Cluny territory is answerable to only the Holy F-Father himself, and by its original charter is fr-free of all secular laws and influence. Interference of any kind by all n-nobles, and even k-kings, is forbidden. It's the only such sanctuary in all of Europe. If you should decide to come, it is only a m-matter of arriving safely in Cluny or Marcigny. Once there, you can never be t-touched."

"Indeed," said Asta, looking at Muehler with a bitter shake of the head, "it is only a matter of arriving safely at Cluny or Marcigny with my kinsmen and all of their women and children—and Desmond DuLac in hot pursuit. It's *impossible*."

"It's all in m-my satchel, Lady Asta, under the b-big oak. The plans for y-you and all of your people. Be free, my L-Lady…be free!" Muehler sighed then, after which his breath began to pick up, forcing him to gasp. "The p-pain," he rasped. "I c-can take n-no more. H-have one of y-your men come in and end it for me, I b-beg you…I can t-take no more… "

"Oh, dear God no!" Asta cried, her heart breaking at watching the monk's unbearable suffering.

"*Please*, my Lady. Have m-mercy on me, now! C-call for one of your m-men… "

Horrified, Asta crossed herself, turned and fled from the box, her mind agog. Catching Elder Heidi in the yard, Asta ushered her into the garden shed and tried to describe her immediate encounter with the Bavarian monk. But the words spilled out in such a disjointed garble that Heidi was forced to grab Asta by the shoulders and throttle her. Startled, Asta recovered her senses and replayed her entire conversation with the monk.

When Asta finished, Elder Heidi raised her bent head and gazed into Asta's eyes. "A bride of Christ?" she said. "Can you live such an existence, Dearie?"

"Most certainly, Elder Heidi. When young, there was little on this earth that I hoped for but to serve God. That has not changed but for one thing now, I beg God that I may know of my sons! The vow of poverty does not frighten me for even with Roger de Saint-Germain's wealth, and now DuLac's, I have nothing. Nor does the vow of chastity disturb me for my appearance has been but a curse, attracting two men who sought merely to ply my flesh, then abuse me."

"You've already chosen, then, Dearie," sniffed Elder Heidi with displeasure. "I can tell it in your voice. But *think*, Asta, you're a young woman yet, and beautiful. There's still happiness out there for you, Dearie."

Asta placed her hand over the back of Elder Heidi's, searching her face for agreement. "And you, dear sweet nurse who has suffered so much during your lifetime, have you ever found this happiness you speak of, or has it continued to elude you all these years?"

"Ha, now you mock me," replied Elder Heidi. "I've found but a scrap of it here and there. Those moments could never stand up to the tears and suffering, or the trail of dead left in the wake of my years. There's no hope for me, Dearie. I didn't realize it before, but there never was. God cast my lot at conception, and it wasn't a good one. Who knows what he has yet in store for you in the end? But then, a nunnery is a safe place, protected from men. So if it's in your heart, go, I say. But what about DuLac? He won't stand for you walking out, you know."

"Yes, and therein lies the danger."

"Go speak to your men then, Dearie," said Elder Heidi. "The big ox and the one-armed bear that reads bones, and that quiet one who always watches over you. Their hearts belong to you. They'll help."

"But they have wives and children, some of them. They have much to lose."

"Ha! They've nothing but their own meager misery scrabbling about for the Mole! I've been watching your Danes, and they grow restless. The loss of honor soon becomes a boiling kettle, Dearie. Aye, they're ready for a change, so lead them. But do it now!"

Chapter Forty-Six

The Plan

Heeding Elder Heidi's counsel, Asta left the garden shed and assembled Orla, Crowbones and Guthroth in the stables, telling them about the monk and her conversation with Elder Heidi.

Seeing the grim look on Asta's face as she spoke, both Orla and Crowbones drew as quiet as the ever silent Guthroth who was standing beside them. Asta's frigid eyes lacked that dullness of late. In its place was that iron resolve of old. Guthroth noticed this, issuing a faint smile, sensing that something was about to drop.

"I am leaving this place," she declared, her voice cold and sure. Looking at Guthroth, she said. "Guthroth, can you help me flee and accompany me on horse when the time comes."

Guthroth nodded.

"Say that once more!?" said Orla, his mouth dropping.

"I am returning to France to join the Benedictine Sisterhood at Marcigny-sur-Loire in Burgundy."

Orla was stunned into silence, but Crowbones stepped forward. "You're to become a holy woman? A Roman nun?"

"A Benedictine nun," replied Asta without emotion.

Orla exchanged a swift glance with Crowbones, then flung himself onto a nearby stool, pushing his forehead into his palm. "A *nun?*" he sighed. "Oh, Odin's ass, Asta, not this! No, you're—"

"I wish to become a bride of Christ, and so it will be," interrupted Asta. "But I must ask, Orla, Crowbones, are you happy here? Have you ever been happy here?"

The brothers considered the question a moment. "No, of course we're not happy here," said Crowbones, waving his stub. "We're as miserable as you, Asta."

Asta sighed ruefully. "It's a funny thing, you know," she said, "but it was *me* that brought us all here. It was *my* plan, therefore *my* fault. I am the creator of this misery."

Guthroth moved closer, shaking his head. "N-no!" he stammered. "W-we had n-nowhere else to g-go! It's n-not y-your fault!"

"Ja," Orla sighed, "Guthroth's right. When Roger de Saint-Germain was executed, our goose was cooked. The Bastard wouldn't have us, nor would the King of France. You're not to blame."

"I would like *all* of you to come with Guthroth and me, Orla," said Asta, "but I fear putting you and your families at risk."

"Follow you to a nunnery?" exclaimed Orla.

"No," Asta scolded, "do not be ridiculous at such a serious time! Come away with me, then go to Italy where there is work for you and a home for your families."

"Eh?" said Crowbones. "Italy?"

"Yes," nodded Asta, "in the employ of Countess Mathilda of Tuscany. She will absorb the entire Danish Guard into her army and allow you to remain together as a single fighting contingent."

"And who exactly is she fighting?" asked Orla, his interest growing.

"King Heinrich, against whom she defends the Pope's position. I am told she pays well, and also provides well for families under her care."

"Well, this sounds grand," muttered Crowbones, "but what about DuLac? I don't imagine he'll be delighted with any of this, eh, Brother?"

"Hell no," snorted Orla, "he'd hang the lot of us for desertion, then our women and children for good measure."

"Not if we kill him first," said Crowbones, slicing his stub down through the air like a broad-ax.

Asta shook her head. "That would mobilize every Norman and Frenchman in England, and in the end, our Saxon villagers would also be blamed for DuLac's death. Retribution would be swift and merciless by the Bastard. Even if we made it to France, the French king might rally against us. We must escape England, by-pass Normandy, then slip through lower France until we reach the Benedictine territories of Cluny for sanctuary. From there, the Danish Guard can leave me at Marcigny-sur-Loire and go to Italy beneath the protection of the Countess."

"Wh-what about Du-Dufresne," Guthroth stuttered. "H-he is y-your friend, Orla. He m-might cooperate with us, eh?"

"He's my friend," said Orla, crossing his arms, "but how good of a friend? While it's true he despises DuLac nearly as much as we do, the Mole is his table, his shelter, and his coin. No, if we dare mention such a thing and he goes against us, we're done."

"Then we best go it on our own," said Asta. "But Orla, Crowbones, are you sure you wish to chance leaving? It would be safer to stay behind. As for Guthroth and me, we could hide and slip our way into Burgundy without risk to you and your families. DuLac would happily keep you in his employ and not seek retribution against the Danish Guard, if you are not involved in my escape. His fury would only be directed against Guthroth and me."

Orla shook his head. "No, I don't wish to remain here any longer, Asta." Looking at his brother, he said, "And you, Ivar, do you wish to stay?"

Crowbones shook his head. "Hell no."

"Very well then," said Asta, "let it begin now. Guthroth, coming from the east road there is a large oak on the south side, twenty-five paces from the bend itself, retrieve at its base a satchel concealed by the Bavarian monk. While awaiting your return the three of us will spread word amongst the other Danes and begin preparations to leave."

Guthroth nodded. "And wh-when w-will we be l-leaving, Asta?" he asked.

Asta looked at the ground, thinking, then raised her eyes to the three men she so dearly loved in life. "Tonight," she said.

***

Guthroth located Muehler's satchel beneath the oak and returned to the stables where Asta, Orla, and Crowbones joined him in examining the contents. They found papal documents related to Asta's annulment, a letter of introduction to a certain Aengus MacLeod in Scotland, a map to Dumfries, and yet more letters of introduction to Benedictine monasteries in France, as well as to the convent in Marcigny-sur-Loire.

Satisfied, they began to discuss several strategies for leaving DuLacshire en masse. As suggestions circulated, it became evident that actually getting out of the castle with the entire group was going to be a trick in itself, especially with DuLac and DuFresne present.

After more talk, it was Orla who finally came up with a feasible strategy. "The entire castle retires to their respective areas shortly after dark," he said. "What if we wait out the French, then barricade them in their own barrack? There's only one entrance, and that door is triple-timber constructed and reinforced throughout with iron bands and rods. It's impenetrable if we can just block it off."

"Ja," said Crowbones, "but what about the night guards who'll be outside?"

Orla thought a moment. "We'll overcome them, Ivar."

"Kill them?" asked Crowbones.

"No," said Orla. "We'll subdue them only. Once we snatch their weapons, they'll surrender. We can then go for the barrack entry and lock it down. Hell, they'll *never* be able to get out! That'll give us time to load up everyone and get out."

"Damn, sounds simple enough," said Crowbones, shaking his head. "Too simple, in fact. It might work, but I say we better think about this awhile." Shaking his head, he looked at Asta. "Ja, let's give this more time," he urged. "Tonight is too damned soon. We're just not ready."

Asta saw the logic in this, but resisted. "I intend to take the Bavarian monk with us," she said. "He'll not survive another night of torture."

Crowbones shook his head. "Not a good idea. It'll just draw more attention and slow us down."

"Ja, too risky," added Orla.

Guthroth interceded. "If A-Asta s-says we go tonight, th-then we go tonight! A-and if she s-says we take the m-monk, then we t-take the monk!"

"Yes, I'll not see him killed for trying to help us," said Asta. "If *he* stays, then *I* stay, and we forget all this!"

"Dammit, all right then," sighed Orla.

As afternoon arrived, the Danish Guard and their families quietly gathered their belongings, packing only the barest of essentials. The men gathered in huddles inside the stables and in their quarters, avoiding the notice of their French counterparts, reviewing the escape assignments given them by Asta and Orla. If the group was to succeed in crossing over to Scotland, the timing of every maneuver would be critical.

By late afternoon, Madame Madeleine, DuLac, and cadre of his troops returned from the village, dragging fifteen shackled villagers with them, mostly women and children.

"Take these filthy Saxons to the Box. Strap the four men to the wall," commanded DuLac. "We'll start loosening their tongues come dark, and they'll be chirping like magpies by midnight. We'll get to the bottom of this goddamned plot! And if they don't confess, the men can watch us hang their women and children from the ramparts in the morning!"

DuLac was especially expressive as he carried on this talk, because he had become rather enthralled with his guest, Marie Madeleine, the Norman spy. She was young and beautiful, and there was something alluring to DuLac about the clandestine role she played within the Bastard's court. He was working hard to impress her; perhaps thought with a little luck he might even bed her within the week. So even though the men being dragged into the castle had confessed nothing, ignorant of any plot, DuLac had put on a great show to Lady Madeleine of outsmarting 'lying, dim-witted Saxons'.

Dusk found all the laborers and servants within the castle trekking down the hill to the village as usual, and DuLac courting the young Lady Madeleine. "How about an evening outing on horseback through my woodlands, my Lady?" he suggested.

"In the dark?" Madeleine asked.

"Certainly, the moon's full and the woodlands are splendidly bathed by its pallid blue light," DuLac purred, too proud of his own words to see that she was little impressed.

"I'd be more interested in getting at the monk again, and the Saxon prisoners," she replied.

"Plenty of time for that, Madame. We'll get with the jailer upon our return. We'll just be a short while, you know. Come now, you're from the big city of Rouen, so you'll enjoy the pastoral beauty of my woodlands, especially beneath a full moon!"

"Very well," Madeleine sighed, guessing that DuLac would not relent until he got his way. "But just a short ride, then down to business again."

As they left the stables and rode out the gate just minutes after the sun dropped, Orla watched them from the ramparts. "Swine's head, Ivar," he said to Crowbones, "fortune smiles on us! DuLac's mind must be on plowing the Norman bitch's furrow tonight, so he'll be out of our hair!"

"Ja," grinned Crowbones, "and let's hope he plows it deep and long, Brother, so he'll be gone a good while, eh?"

Receiving news that her husband had unexpectedly left the castle, Asta decided it opportune to set the wheel in motion earlier than originally planned. Mounting the steps of the Keep, she went to the window of her private chamber facing the courtyard in her white finery and stood there, highly visible in the low light of the moon just peeking over the horizon. After a full minute at the window inspecting the courtyard below, she dropped a white lap blanket, as previously arranged, from her position high in the Keep. As it drifted down into the courtyard, Guthroth, Orla and Crowbones bolted into action from their position in the stables where they had been awaiting Asta's signal.

"Be careful now, Brother!" declared Crowbones.

"Ja, you, too, Ivar," said Orla, "especially with that last arm of yours!"

Orla's task was to attack the French guards who had not yet retired to their quarters for the evening. Since Asta had advanced the time table to capitalize on DuLac's absence and it was still early in the evening, there were more of DuLac's troops about than originally anticipated. Nevertheless, Orla whistled to eight Danes who had been stationed at various sites throughout the yard. Hearing Orla's signal, they withdrew swords and joined Orla. "Remember, subdue them only and convince them to surrender," he whispered to the Danes.

When cultural divisions exist between two peoples existing side-by-side, an uneasy truce develops in which differences continue to silently simmer beneath the surface. These differences can erupt upon the slightest provocation. In the case of the Danes and the French of DuLacshire, these differences were somewhat marginal. Although the Danes had kept to their traditions, they were still, in reality, Normans, and Normans had become very French. Yet, there still existed enough division to fan the flames of clannishness. When the Danes fell upon the French that night to subdue them, not to injure them, the phenomenon of simmering cultural differences reared its ugly head with a vengeance. Orla's plan went smoothly at first, but as more of the remaining Frenchman became aware that the Danes were laying hands upon their countrymen, they went into an immediate, unrestrained rage and pressed the attack against the Danes who were simply attempting to get them to lay down their arms. A vicious clash of steel quickly ensued, and though the Danes had hoped for a quick French surrender, blood quickly began to flow.

One of the Frenchmen fled toward the French barracks to raise the alarm and warn the others. "To arms! It's the Danes!" he cried. "We're betrayed! They're attacking us!"

Hearing this, the French within the barrack at first refused to believe what they had heard, especially Captain DuFresne. But as several soldiers ran to the door and witnessed what was occurring in the yard, they called to the others within the barrack. This precipitated into a wild stampede to arms.

Meanwhile, Crowbones had been given the task of blocking the huge reinforced door to the French barrack so bloodshed might be avoided. Motioning to ten other Danes awaiting in the stable, they grabbed up timbers and jacks they had amassed earlier. On signal, they rushed toward the barrack, hoping to barricade the door before the French could exit and threaten the flight from the castle. They made the thick, iron-reinforced door just as the French were attempting to exit, and a pushing match broke out as men from one side of the door heaved and shoved against the men on the other side.

"Push!" cried Crowbones, digging his shoulder into the door and rooting his feet into the ground for leverage. "*Push!*"

"Push, goddammit!" hollered the furious DuFresne from the other side of the door, now believing the Danes had maliciously plotted a deadly and deliberate massacre of his troops. "Orla, you bastard!" he howled, his blood boiling to bursting at the very thought that his friend, Orla, whom he had twice saved from death, could be involved in such treachery. "I'll kill you, you goddamned traitor!" he howled, nearly overcome with tears.

Hearing DuFresne's verbal rampage from the yard, Orla subdued the Frenchman standing before him by knocking him to the ground, but not killing him. Then he ran to the door to help the other Danes push against the French. "Dammit, DuFresne, withdraw I say!" he shouted. "Lay down your arms! We don't have to kill each other here!"

"Oh, you foul bastard!" screamed DuFresne, even more outraged upon hearing Orla on the other side of the door.

"Tell your men to lay down their arms, DuFresne!" Orla shouted. "This wasn't supposed to happen this way, dammit! Your men in the yard wouldn't surrender!"

But DuFresne only erupted into more profanity, cursing Orla and the Danes with every filthy word known to man.

"It's futile, he doesn't understand and he's not listening!" cried Crowbones, his body lathered in sweat from pushing against the French. "The French be damned, then, and DuFresne with them! It's a fight for life now!"

As this furious shoving match continued at the barracks door, and others fought it out in the yard, Asta descended the Keep, ran out into the yard and headed for the Box, where Guthroth had been instructed to meet her.

Dodging combatants as swords wildly hacked and clanged against each other, Asta reached the Box and ran through its opened door. Guthroth and three other Danes had already entered and had floored the jailer in a corner, jabbing at him with the points of their swords. "G-give m-me the k-keys!" Guthroth stammered.

"Mercy! Mercy!" the jailer cried, cowering into a fetal ball. Spying Asta, he held his arms out to her. "I b-beg you for my life, Lady Asta! I have a wife and six children!"

"Hold there, Guthroth!" she shouted, looking at the jailer, then glancing over to the cowering huddle of Saxon women and children who had also been taken prisoner. Then she went to the naked Muehler who still lay stretched upon the table, groaning in agony in a semi-lucid state of consciousness. Crossing herself, Asta gently stroked Muehler's forehead, and in an icy voice, said to the jailer, "Mercy? You plead for mercy after what you have wreaked on this man of God? Look at him, jailer!"

"Let us kill him!" fumed one of the Danes, his point pressing against the jailer's throat.

Asta possessed a Christian heart, but as she gazed down at the mutilated and suffering Muehler, her fury somehow surmounted an entire lifetime of adhering to God's charity, and as silence fell over the Box, she weighed the prospect of ordering Guthroth to gut the jailer.

But a nearly inaudible voice broke her thoughts. "L-let him live, Lady," the voice rasped. It was Muehler, fighting his agony, struggling to be heard. "L-let him live!"

"Back away, Danes!" Asta commanded. Looking at the jailer with disdain, clenching her teeth, she said, "Go to God, jailer, and beg forgiveness every day for the rest of your miserable existence. And find a new profession, or be damned!" Then she motioned to her men to unshackle Muehler and the four men who had not yet felt the burn of the jailer's poker. "Be quick!" she said. "We flee for Scotland within minutes!"

Hearing this, one of the villagers stepped forward, a small girl of perhaps seven. "T-take us with you, Lady Asta," she said, her voice more of a plea than a request. "Take us with you!"

The girl's mother stepped forward and chastised the girl, looking at Asta apologetically. "I beg your forgiveness, my Lady, she's but a child and—"

"Take us with you!" interrupted another voice. It was a woman, falling to her knees in tears. "Take us from this hell on earth!"

"Yes!" cried another woman. "Take us away from DuLac!"

Yet another woman advanced, pushing her two-year-old son before her. "This is my boy! We know you've lost two sons, but you can spare me mine, Lady! I beg you, let us follow you to Scotland!"

This sudden outpouring of emotion overwhelmed Asta, confusing her. These people were asking the impossible. "No," she mumbled, more to herself than to them. "From Scotland I go to France! There's no place for you there! I can't—"

"Let us follow you to Scotland only then, at least!" another woman pleaded. "Just get us out of England!"

"N-no!" stammered Asta. "I would if I could, but no, I—"

"T-take th-th-em," whispered Muehler in a slow and ghostly rasp that sent a shudder washing up Asta's spine. "They are G-God's flock."

"Oh!" Asta whimpered, lost.

Then her eyes fell on Guthroth, whose expression was as blank as her own, and she knew he would offer nothing. But one of the other Danes spoke out. "We must go quickly, my Lady, or we're lost! We've no time to deal with these Saxons!"

But Asta looked down at Muehler who was staring straight up at her, his eyes beseeching hers, and this turned her. "Guthroth, take these people to the wagons behind the chapel!" she shouted. "They're coming with us, so is any-one else in the village who chooses to flee. You other men, go down to the village and gather up those who want to leave. Tell them to gather wagons and horses! Be quick!"

Stunned, the other Danes gawked at Asta in disbelief, then looked to each other in the same manner.

"B-be gone, d-dammit!" barked Guthroth, breaking their hesitancy. "Did you not h-hear what she said!"

Chapter Forty-Seven

Flight

The struggle at the barrack entrance continued in a hopeless deadlock until more Danes, having subdued the remaining Frenchmen in the yard, rushed to join the effort. One of them finally managed to slip a timber into a diagonal position against the door itself. Orla and Crowbones shoved down on this timber and slowly forced the door completely shut. "Quick, get a jack in place!" Orla cried. "Then more timbers and more jacks!"

After much effort, the door was secured and the Danes stepped back, spent, as the French continued cursing them from the other side.

"They'll have a time breaking through with all that damned iron in the door," wheezed Crowbones, exhausted. "This'll hold them for most of the night while we move the horses and wagons north to Dumfries."

"Good work, Brother!" Orla huffed, close to collapse after his efforts at the door. Looking about the moon-lit yard at the corpses, he shook his head. "We didn't lose many, but the French! Dammit, what a shame, Ivar. If they just hadn't fought us!"

"Ja, and just listen to them in there still wanting to fight! Can you hear DuFresne raging? His is the loudest voice of all."

Orla nodded. Stepping to the door, he struck it loudly three times with his sword. "Ho, in there! DuFresne! Can you hear me?"

The shouting and cursing from within ceased, but a lone voice rang out. It was DuFresne. "Orla, you cowardly bastard!" he seethed with impotent fury "This is how you treat a friend, ambushing him and butchering his men? Oh, I curse the day we met! And I'll kill you yet when next we meet, you filthy traitor!"

Knowing there was no point in attempting to explain how things had fallen apart, or trying to describe the Danes' original intent to simply subdue the Frenchmen in the yard, Orla knocked on the door three times more, then shouted, "The Danes are leaving DuLacshire, all of us, DuFresne. Don't come after us, and don't force my hand. I don't wish to kill you, my friend, but I'll do what's required to save my kinsmen and our families! Do you understand, DuFresne?"

This only rankled DuFresne more. "Ha! You dare call me your friend?" he screamed. "I spit on your mother's grave, you goddamn snake! I'll have your balls in a cup and feed them to the vultures, you double-crossing vermin!"

"Hmm," said Crowbones dryly, "it appears you better keep a close eye to your balls, Brother. I don't believe DuFresne's kidding, huh?"

Discouraged, Orla stepped from the door as DuFresne continued his diatribe and the French resumed their futile attack on the door. A commotion arose then as Asta and Guthroth approached, followed by the Saxons who were litter-carrying the wounded monk. "What's this?" Orla asked, pointing to the Saxons.

Asta's reply was cold with certainty. "They are coming with us, Orla, and so is anyone else in the village who wishes to leave. I do not intend to barter this point with you, nor do I expect you to dispute it. Now gather your men and let's be on our way, your families are in the wagons waiting to depart."

There would be no way to adequately describe the shocked expression that came over Orla's face on hearing Asta's reply about the Saxons. Lost for words, he looked at her, sputtered, looked at Guthroth, sputtered. *"But—"*

"Shht!" hissed Guthroth, poking his finger at Orla with a scowl. "D-did you not h-hear what she said?"

Within the half hour the Danes' caravan was descending the hill and creaking its way through DuLacville, where groups of villagers stood waiting, waving and shouting. "Asta!" they cried. "God bless the Lady Asta! Asta's been sent by Heaven!"

As they moved through the village, Orla watched in dismay as some villagers piled onto the Danes' wagons, some gathered their own wagons, others jumped double atop Danish mounts, and yet others followed briskly on foot.

Someone shoved a small girl at him and cried, "Take my daughter! Her leg is injured and she can't walk!"

Before he could object, the tiny girl grabbed his belt and pressed her face against his back. "Thank you, sir," she said, "for saving me!"

By count, over half of the village population took flight that night, nearly three hundred and fifty Saxons in all, including nearly every single original inhabitant of DuLacville, including Elder Heidi, who rode in the lead wagon beside Asta. Those who remained in the village were mainly stonemasons and craftsmen who had come to DuLacshire seeking work with their families in tow. This group had no interest in leaving their work, nor did they have anything to fear from DuLac since he needed them and they, in turn, had not in any way betrayed or abandoned him.

Although the fleeing caravan moved in silence, under orders from Orla, the mood was infectiously optimistic, because hope draws the human spirit forward through even the most perilous of ordeals. Upon finally being able to at least anticipate liberation after a lengthy state of captivity, the human spirit swells with hope. In the case of Asta's caravan, it would have been difficult to determine who was more enthralled by it all, the Saxons or the Danes.

Asta's spirits were soaring, as were Elder Heidi's despite earlier refusals to consider ever leaving her home. Even Brother Muehler, who was only half conscious in the back of Asta's wagon, felt that he had been given a new beginning. The children, whether Dane or Saxon, were too excited to sleep, the women of each party chattered quietly with their friends, and each man, whether Saxon or Dane, felt that surge from within that builds on the thought of reclaiming independence and honor—even though not a one knew what the future held.

As the hours slipped by and the caravan crawled toward Scotland's frontier beneath the glow of a bright moon, a sense of relief and security began to settle in amongst the travelers. Even Orla, whose charge it was to get them all to Dumfries, began to grow less tense. Riding alongside Crowbones with the small girl still attached to his back, he nodded at his brother and smiled. "Hey, Ivar, it looks like we might make it, eh? I still feel bad about DuFresne though. He's a good man, that one. Poor soul, I bet he and his men are still trying to hack their way through that damn iron door!"

But the Danes had, in the viciousness of the fighting and the flurry of flight, dismissed DuLac and the Norman spy, Madeleine. As it happened, to DuLac's delight, he had indeed managed to get the lovely young spy to raise her skirt and part her legs while in the forest that night, which meant they ended up spending a good while absent. On returning, he was shocked to discover corpses strewn about the yard, and hearing DuFresne and his men furiously trying to break their way out of the barrack door. After much effort, with assistance from laborers scoured from the village, the timbers and jacks were disassembled and the troops, by now more inflamed than a swarm of rousted hornets, were released.

"Goddammit, come on, men!" DuFresne roared, vaulting onto his horse. "I want that bastard Orla's head as well as the whole bunch of them, by God! We'll catch them from behind, and if they cross the border, we'll go in after them!"

"Goddamn right!" cried DuLac, spurring angrily after him. "And that bitch of a wife of mine, I want her head on a lance!"

***

Although the Scotts were known to cross south into England to raid and pillage, it was a rare occurrence for the Normans or French to cross north into Scotland. Even so, the Scotts inhabiting the border lands kept a wary eye to the south, knowing that Norman incursions might appear at unexpected moments.

Accordingly, Aengus MacLeod of Dumfries kept a handful of scouts scattered along the border, and even leagues south into England. One of these scouts hidden north of DuLacville noticed something extraordinary occurring, spotting a full caravan in flight from DuLac's lands in the middle of the night. Knowing nothing of Aengus' previous secret meetings with Brother Petit-Jean of Paris, he still felt it his duty to inform Aengus immediately of the strange activity headed toward Dumfries. Springing into his saddle, he galloped across the border to Scotland.

Learning this news, Aengus smiled broadly and flipped the scout a gold piece. "Good news that is, lad!" he said. "That party's well overdue. Been waiting on them quite some time now, by God! We'll load' em on ships, get them out of our hair, then count our gold as it rains down upon us from the Benedictines. Now go round up the men and we'll meet the caravan at the border, then get them to the ships!" As the scout left, Aengus poured himself another goblet of ale, content that he was on the verge of one of the largest paydays of his career. Alone in the room, he lifted his goblet and raised a toast. "Ah, Jack Forest, here's to you! I miss you, Jackie-boy, and I'd give my right arm for you to be here with me now to share this upcoming bounty from Rome!"

Having forgotten DuLac, the Danish Guard had no idea that DuFresne and his men had been released from the French barrack and were charging north. Orla had anticipated that the French would be trapped for most of the night, thereby giving the caravan time to arrive safely at Dumfries. But just as dawn began to break and they arrived at Scotland's frontier, Guthroth galloped up from his position at rear guard. "Th-the Fr-French!" he sputtered. "They're h-here, coming up on us f-fast!"

"Dammit!" Orla exclaimed. "How's that possible?" He thought a moment, scanning the retreating caravan. "Spread the word, Guthroth, wagons forward and tell them to make a run for it! Men to the rear, even the Saxons! We're outnumbered and out-armed, but we'll have to hold the French back to buy time for the wagons!"

Word spread like wildfire; panic followed. Dreams of a new beginning vanished, replaced by fear of slaughter. Following Asta's lead, the wagons quickened their pace as the Danish Guard and Saxon men peeled to the rear to counteract the French onslaught. And it came quickly, like a rolling tide of fury hell-bent on sweeping all in its path aside, leave nothing in its wake.

DuFresne led the charge, cutting into the Danes' rear guard with the rage of a rabid beast, striking blindly everywhere. He was seeking Orla. DuLac was inflamed as well, but his sole target was Asta. Despite their rage, the French ran into ferocious resistance; the Danes knew that if they didn't hold, their families would perish, as did the Saxon men. Though poorly armed, some carrying nothing but shovels and pitchforks, the Saxons boldly followed the mounted Danes into the fray. As the Danes engaged with sword and ax on horseback against DuLac's cavalry, Saxons scurried behind on foot, grappling French cavaliers to the ground.

Orla and Guthroth hacked several attackers from their horses as the French washed into the Danish Guard. Crowbones, despite missing an arm, delivered one lethal blow after another by broadax with his good arm.

It wasn't enough.

"Fall back!" cried Orla. "Fall back!"

As Orla turned, flailing at a knight coming at him, DuFresne came crashing through the brush. Seeing Orla engaged against another, DuFresne raised his sword, and still riding full gallop, swept into him. Crowbones, seeing this, quickly dispatched the Frenchman he was dueling and reined his horse into DuFresne's charging mount. The two horses flew into each other in a collision of thundering flesh, and both Crowbones and DuFresne were flung from their mounts. Crowbones recovered first, but his missing arm threw him off balance, hampering him in maneuvering his sword into fighting position. As Crowbones teetered off balance, DuFresne fell upon him, pressing the attack. Despite his larger size, Crowbones found himself on the defensive as DuFresne hacked forward slinging his sword double-handed. Stumbling backward, he looked up, catching sight of DuFresne's sword rearing back to deliver the coup de grâce.

"Orla!" cried Crowbones, his brother being his last thought as he, with helpless abandon, faced imminent death.

From nowhere, Guthroth suddenly advanced at full gallop, aiming his mount directly at Dufresne, driving half a ton of charging horseflesh into him just as he was dropping his blade onto Crowbones. The rampaging horse razed DuFresne flat and trampled over him, its hooves cutting hard and deep. Not knowing what struck him, DuFresne lay motionless, flattened, his ribs crushed and his spine broken. Lying there on his back in a paralyzed heap, his eyes rolled about in their sockets like raw eggs cast into a bowl. When they grew still, DuFresne saw the face of Orla peering down at him.

Orla stared at DuFresne, torn, and knelt at his side. Though DuFresne could not move, he acknowledged Orla with his eyes. This sent a shudder of sorrow through the huge Dane, who felt his heart drop. "DuFresne," Orla murmured, his voice cracking with emotion, "it d-didn't have to be this way. I didn't betray you! You are m-my friend. I was just saving my people."

His body frozen, Dufresne gasped, struggling to speak. "Y-your p-peope...m-my people...we're all just p-people. Or-Orla...y-you were my b-best friend in this life...my *on-ly* friend." Dufresne's torso shivered then, and his throat slowly issued its last sound, the rasping rattle of death.

Orla began to heave, forgetting that war was raging all about him and that blood was effusing everywhere, that the Danes and Saxons were in full retreat and the French were already catching the trailing wagons of the caravan.

Someone struck his shoulder. It was Guthroth, his face bloodied, his eyes wild with the shock of war. "C-come on, O-Orla, or w-we are d-done!" he cried. "W-we-ve got to save Asta!"

* * *

Throughout history, the quest for freedom by some has meant death for others. As Asta began to realize what was falling around her, she felt her entire existence collapsing, as well as that of the other people she had impacted by her fateful decision to make a run for freedom. She fell into weeping then, even as she drove the horses forward and her wagon careened from one side of the road to the other. Her tears were promulgated first by Elder Heidi, the old nurse who would have stayed in DuLacville were it not for Asta's insistence. This weighed so heavily on Asta, she could scarcely even look over at this ancient woman she so loved, even though Elder Heidi appeared neither frightened nor discouraged, only compelled to push forward.

Asta wept also for Brother Muehler, who lay dying in the back of the wagon, his suffering now exacerbated by rollicking, bucking wagon wheels. Although she had extended the monk's life by another day or so, the monk had previously begged her for relief at the point of one of her own men's daggers. His suffering could have ended that day, yet she had prolonged it.

Then there were the Saxons. In one capricious decision she had allowed them to flee with her, in hopes of helping them. But now they were about to be slaughtered, along with her beloved Danish Guard and their families. Fairhair and StraightLimbs had already been lost, but now it would be Orla, Crowbones and gentle Guthroth. But throughout her emotion-charged self-flagellation, a single haunting thought wounded her more than others—her sons. Crushed, she feared they would never realize how dearly she loved them, nor would she ever know what would become of them. Realizing this, her tears burned hotly against her face, blinding her eyes.

Chapter Forty-Eight

Oh, Aengus!

Fate is a twisting, unpredictable proposition. Just as it cruelly disassembles the labor and dreams of one, it generously creates unforeseen bridges for another. And the latter is exactly what occurred as the morning sun cleared the horizon and the French troops fell upon the caravan in a clearing just across Scotland's border.

Aengus MacLeod had just arrived and positioned his men atop a rise at this location in anticipation of the caravan's arrival from England. From there, he intended to escort the escapees to awaiting ships near Dumfries. But now, as he peered into the open meadow below, he saw wagons charging forward with French cavalry in pursuit. At first he was perplexed by the sheer numbers of wagons and people, for he had originally been instructed that he would be ferrying only about eighty to France, but there were hundreds in this fleeing caravan. He was further confused by the presence of the attacking French. There had been no mention of violence from the French Benedictine monk, Petit-Jean, who had bartered with him months earlier.

Fearing that his payday might be slipping beyond his grasp right there before his very eyes, Aengus MacLeod issued the savage highland yell, and his mercenary band of cutthroats and marauders streamed down the slopes in a murderous tide of bristling blades, axes and hammers. The oncoming French were caught by complete surprise as the pendulum quickly took an unexpected track and the odds fled from their favor.

When Asta and the people in the wagons saw the Scotts coming, a clamor arose from their midst. Many began to cheer and whistle while yet others began to openly sob with joy. As Aengus and his men waded into the French, Orla, Crowbones and Guthroth were just emerging from the woods and brush in a desperate attempt to get to Asta for a final stand. "Odin's ass!" yelled Orla, seeing the Scotts, "What's *this*?"

"S-salvation," breathed Guthroth, falling exhausted at Orla's feet. Swiping blood from his forehead, he looked up at Orla and Crowbones. "We're s-saved!" he stuttered. "And m-maybe we sh-should take another l-look at Asta's G-God! I swear on this very d-day, I'm g-going to be baptized!"

***

Aengus quickly turned the tide of battle and the French fled in droves behind Desmond DuLac, who was the very first to leave the field. From the beginning of his retreat, throughout his flight back to DuLacville, he had only one thought on his mind, and that was a simmering fury directed at Asta. He would get back at her somehow, at some time, in some place, he vowed, even if it took the remainder of his life. Sweeping into the castle, he stormed into the Keep, swearing that his life would now have a new purpose, and that would be to destroy Asta the Dane, who had scorned and abandoned him.

Aengus, after routing the French, counseled with Asta and Orla, then led the caravan northeast. "I have two ships ready and waiting," he said when they arrived in Dumfries, "so you'll sail for France immediately."

"But these Saxons, what about them?" asked Asta.

Orla shook his head vigorously. "I said nothing before, just as you commanded, Asta, but now I'll not hold my tongue! We can no longer afford to worry about the Saxons. We got them to Scotland as they requested, but now we have to leave quickly. If DuLac shows back up, everything we've accomplished is undone!"

Aengus listened. Taking a deep swig of ale, he said, "I doubt DuLac'll be coming back north again, not even with Norman reinforcements. Especially when word goes out that you're no longer here in Scotland. As to the Saxons, they can settle here in Dumfries. I'm always looking for men to fill my ranks. Their families can stay, too, and help work the farms."

"Bless you, Lord Aengus," said Asta, clasping her fingers about his hands in a warm show of gratitude.

"*Lord* Aengus?" he chortled. "Ha, thank you, but I'm far from a lord, though my family once held titles further north." He gave Asta a queer look then, sitting back from the table. "You know, Lady Asta, this is a strange venture you've fallen into, but there's something I wish to know. Do you remember a man named Jack Forest by chance? He worked for your husband. But before that, he was the finest soldier and leader of men I ever encountered."

"Jack Forest?" said Asta, a shiver attacking her blood. "Yes, certainly, I remember Jack. He was a…gamekeeper." She fell quiet then and drew into herself.

Orla saw this, and sensed something had touched Asta upon hearing Jack's name. "Yes, I knew him as well," Orla interjected. "What about him? He betrayed us at the castle and attempted to kidnap Asta as we fought his treachery that day of the wolf hunt he devised! He was a no good bastard!"

"Betrayed you at the castle?" said Aengus, his face turning red. "Hmm, let's see here. Would that be like how you just now betrayed the French in the castle?"

This infuriated Orla and he sprang to his feet. "You don't know what happened or how it happened, Scotsman!

It wasn't supposed to happen that way, damn you! Say another word about it and I'll have your liver between your shoulders!"

"Ha!" retorted Aengus. "And you don't know a goddamn thing about Jack Forest or his assault on the castle that day, Dane!"

"Stop it, both of you!" implored Asta. "Orla, I'll not have you speak ill of Jack Forest. And Aengus, I'll not have you fighting Orla!" Settling, she gave Aengus a questioning look. "But why do you bring up Jack Forest?"

Aengus glared at Orla with resentment, but civilized his tone. "First I want you both to understand something, Jack attacked the castle because his people were butchered and slaughtered by invading Normans, with assistance from certain Frenchman like DuLac. Jack's family, land and honor were stripped from him. Now, Big Man, is there dishonor in righting wrongs such as that? No! And another thing, just so we clear the air. *I* was also there that day of the wolf hunt, and once before that. It was actually my men that attacked both times, once through the tunnel and once during the hunt."

"You?" hissed Orla, struggling to control himself.

"Yes!" Aengus replied. "With the very same men that just saved your ass!" He turned to Asta then. "A strange thing though, and I want to share it with you. It might mean something to you, it might not. As we were planning to attack the castle, Jack made us swear that whatever happened, you were not to be touched. He got angry about it and swore to kill any man who harmed you. Even me, his good friend who fought beside him for many years. There now, I don't understand his concern for you that day, or what it was all about, but I've got it off my chest now. I loved Jack Forest...he was my brother-in-arms."

Asta looked at Aengus, her eyes conveying profound gratitude, though Aengus couldn't fathom why. "That is good to know," said Asta quietly. "I am glad that you shared this with me." She wanted very much to say, *Yes, I loved Jack Forest also, Aengus! And we dreamed of a life away from DuLac and England...a quiet life of peace and simplicity!* But she kept these things to herself. Orla would not understand, nor would anyone else in this world except Elder Heidi, and Guthroth.

"Very well then," said Aengus, "let's get your people to the ships. You've a long journey ahead, and who knows what awaits you in France? Though the Bastard and King Philippe plot against each other ceaselessly, they also hold hands at times." Standing, he shook hands with Asta. "It's been my pleasure, dear lady. Good luck to you."

Chapter Forty-Nine

Guiscard the Wily, Norman Warlord

Despite having taken Rome, King Heinrich's hold on the city was a tenuous one. A good portion of the populace remained entrenched in the Gregorian camp, damning Heinrich's enthronement of Guibert of Ravenna as Pope Clement III as usurpation and sacrilege. Moreover, the King's action had created city-wide disruption of another sort, wrecking stability by dismantling the balance of power within Rome.

To begin, Heinrich unseated the greater portion of the Vatican hierarchy, powerful men who had for decades held authority and administered papal will. On seizing power, Heinrich and Clement initiated hundreds of purges involving priests, bishops, archbishops and cardinals, ousting the Gregorian faithful from office. This, ultimately, confused and agitated tens of thousands of parishioners throughout Rome who had supported these clerics and looked to them for spiritual guidance and salvation. Such purges were not restricted to the religious, experienced Gregorian politicians and city officials were also removed by the hundreds, thereby disrupting the flow of city service and administration. Adding to this chaos, an entire army of new hopefuls, both clerics and politicians, were jockeying for position in the new German regime while trying to establish their newfound authority in unfamiliar positions. This adversely affected massive numbers of parishes, laborers, craftsmen and merchants who suddenly found themselves falling from favor or losing work.

There had long been division in Rome between the King Heinrich's royalists and Pope Gregory's adherents, but now the tension between the two groups became more vociferous, manifesting itself daily in fisticuffs and street skirmishes.

As bitterness and acrimony continued to swell, Heinrich's opponents began to engage in conspiracy and talk of revolt. Then, too, there were the ambivalent of Rome who had agreed to Heinrich's entry into the city simply as a matter of practicality: a means to end ceaseless German sieges that had befallen the city, disrupting commerce and everyday life. Their indifference aside, many of them questioned the actual legitimacy of a puppet pope installed by a foreign king, and refused to accept German authority.

Aware of these liabilities, and thinking to out-wait the stubborn Gregory, Heinrich only half-heartedly laid siege to the Castel Sant' Angelo. Heinrich knew that once he actually captured the old pope, figuring out what to then do with him would become a delicate, if not a thorny issue. This passive approach, predictably, did little to settle the growing chaos dividing Rome. Two months later, in May of 1084, Heinrich exacerbated his position by unexpectedly pulling up stakes and vacating the city for Tuscany with his new pope. In departing, Heinrich installed his son in a Roman castle, instructing him, "I leave the siege of the Castel and Pope Gregory in your hands. Do not fail me!"

This abrupt departure raised the hopes of Gregorians throughout the city. Having received word that Countess Mathilda had rallied her troops in the north against the Germans and put them in retreat again, they foresaw a resurrection of their own political fortunes. "Aye, Heinrich's gone to reinforce his troops against la Gran Contessa," they claimed, "and now leaves the door open for us here in Rome!"

Meanwhile, Heinrich's royalists suffered a double blow on learning yet more ominous news. Word was filtering north that the dreaded Norman warlord, Duke Robert Guiscard the Wily, was now on his way to rescue Pope Gregory with a combined force of Normans, Apulians and Saracens equaling 30,000 footmen and six thousand horsemen. As this information circulated, a new instability emerged; emboldened Gregorians magnified their anti-German activities while Heinrich royalists were left to balance a potential Norman invasion. "Guiscard's the devil reincarnate," royalists whispered amongst themselves, "and his troops are rabid, pillaging beasts. Should they take the city, we are done!"

So it was that within several days of Heinrich's departure, a strange pall fell over the city, arriving in the form of ominous, rolling cloud-cover accompanied by scything rains. The storm intensified on the second day as jagged fingers of lightning ripped and crackled through the clouds shrouding the city, setting fire to a portion of Heinrich's palace and a German military barrack. The superstitious, interpreting this as a celestial omen, began filling the city's cathedrals. "God's wrath, come to punish the wicked!" they shivered, cowering as murderous thunder shook cathedral walls and flashes of bluish light exploded overhead.

By dawn of the third day the storm abated, but a strange mist was seen drifting in from the south. As it began to lift, from the city ramparts a solitary knight was spotted atop a distant hill, poised on a speckled war-horse. He sat there motionless for a long while, staring at the city walls, holding in place a tall black banner. Shortly, through the haze, another knight appeared at his side, then another, until soon the entire horizon was spilling with knights on horseback and men-at-arms on foot by the tens of thousands. The army of Duke Robert Guiscard the Wily had arrived.

As word spread, jubilant Gregorians filled the streets in celebration. "Pope Gregory is saved!" they cheered. "The rightful papacy is restored!"

At the other end of the spectrum, as the Norman army advanced, the more frightened royalists piled their carts and wagons with possessions and began heading for the northern gates. Others barricaded their doors and pulled Heinrich's banners from their balconies, angrily vowing to replace them once the Normans returned to Lower Italy.

Guiscard's vast army was comprised of three units, of which the lead component was Norman. Comprised of his own countrymen and most loyal troops, a good number of the commanders and captains were related to Guiscard by blood. As they entered Rome's southern gate, Guiscard rode in their midst, and was first greeted by those Roman politicians who had previously accepted his gift of gold. Next, he was thronged by cheering Gregorians throwing flowers and holding up crosses and holy objects. But as his entry into the city deepened, he encountered sullen onlookers glaring with contempt and voicing discontent. Several, well beyond reach, even dared make obscene gestures and hurl insults. As this hostile crowd thickened, they grew more agitated, bolstered by their own numbers and the growing bravado of the younger, less fearful men and boys in their midst.

Infuriated, Guiscard drew his sword, erupting into blasphemous profanity as his neck-flesh tightened, forcing dark veins to surface and pulse like tiny rivers gone amuck. Recognizing this reaction, the knight riding next to him reached over and said, "Hold there, Uncle. The crowd grows unruly and the streets are thick with enemies. Hold back, I beg you, at least until we reach Pope Gregory."

"Ah, this bastard population deserves no consideration," growled Guiscard, "but I hear you, Nephew." Clenching his teeth, he sheathed his sword and kicked his horse in the flanks.

The second component of Guiscard's army was comprised of Apulians, who were Italians. As they came into view of the royalist mob while Guiscard moved ahead, the whistling and yowling of derision increased. "Goddamned traitors!" the crowd shouted. "Norman lackies! You'll burn in hell for turning your back on Italy and fighting alongside Normans and Saracens!"

Refusing to fall into disarray, the Apulian captains ordered their men to hold fast. "Eyes forward!" they barked, even as fruit and vegetables began to be hurled their direction. "Hold your place, by damn!"

But the full fury of the royalists fell against the third component of Guiscard's force, the Saracens. Guiscard the Wily, having arrived in Italy from Normandy decades earlier, had initially served as a mercenary to Italian lords. As his power grew, he decided to attack and conquer Sicily, which lay beneath Muslim rule. In time, Guiscard learned of the bloody infighting and blood-feuds fracturing these various Saracen factions of Sicily. Slyly, he capitalized on this and managed to capture Sicily by forming an unholy alliance with Saracens who were in revolt against the reigning Muslim hierarchy. Since that lesson, he had come to rely on the services of Saracen allies and mercenaries.

As the Saracen component marched through the royalist gauntlet, the royalists abandoned fruit and vegetables and began hurling stones. Incensed, they could not fathom any Christian war lord recruiting heathens within his ranks, especially heathens of a dark and different race. Nor were they going to tolerate the presence of a Muslim military force marching through Rome, the very epicenter of Christianity itself. "Heathen bastards!" the mob screamed, hoarse with hatred and bile. "Go to Hell you black-skinned devils! There is no Allah! Only God!"

As the bombardment of stone and rock escalated, the Saracen captains sallied back and forth, forcing the surging mob aside with the massive weight of their mounts, knocking protesters to the ground or trampling them. Still, they kept their sabers in check and maintained order amongst their troops as best they could without sparking yet more violence.

After some effort, Guiscard's army reached the Castel Sant' Angelo where they encountered a contingent of German soldiers who had been left behind and instructed to offer resistance. Knowing that Heinrich's son had already fled the city, these men dropped their weapons and melted into the crowd.

"Let them go," grunted Guiscard, dismounting. Looking about, he stamped his boots against the pavement, dusting them, then stepped forward, standing cross-armed before the gates of the Castel. "I've come to restore you to your Blessed Throne, Holy Father!" he shouted. "You are saved!"

A burst of activity broke out atop the Castel ramparts, and soon the gates pursed open as Pope Gregory hurriedly met his Norman liberator, humbly embracing him. "Oh, Duke Robert, champion of the Church, savior of Rome!" he wept, freed from Heinrich's claws at last.

It was a joyful moment for those who had been so long confined in the Castel. As Tristan and Guillaume watched the Holy Father embrace Guiscard, Tristan was struck once again by Guiscard's fearsome presence. Just as at Lord Franzio's convocation, it was Guiscard's dark eyes that unnerved Tristan, darting first here, then there in unblinking glances that weighed and measured all standing before him. Also, there was that keen look about his nostrils, unique to stalking carnivores just before they strike. Even as Pope Gregory buried him in praiseful gestures and words of gratitude, Guiscard did not once look down at Gregory, but continued to look about as assessing the landscape for threats or booty.

"That man looks absolutely frightening," said Guillaume, watching Guiscard from a distance with his brother. "I hope I will one day strike such a pose as that!"

"No, I pray you never become *that*, Guillaume," Tristan whispered, unable to stave off a shiver as Guiscard's glance fell upon him. "No, there is something wicked and unearthly about him...and ungodly."

It would have behooved the Roman population to heed Tristan's assessment that day, because if God had ever created a man who savored violence and the taste of blood, it was Robert Guiscard of Normandy. He was the type of warrior who, when vastly outnumbered, sounded the charge, not the retreat. His utter disregard for mercy and forgiveness made him an even more fearsome opponent, one who pushed aside any thought of compassion or forgiveness.

As the old pope continued to hold Guiscard in a sobbing embrace, Guiscard shook his head with rancor. "This populace has crossed me, Gregory," he said, "and shown disrespect. I expected a more civil reception. How is it you have so many enemies here?"

"Ah, 'tis the way of things here," sighed Gregory, "and has been for a good while. Rome is a city divided. But were you not welcomed by our faithful?"

"Aye," grunted Guiscard, "at first, but it was short lived. Then we ran into Heinrich's people, and should they continue to show contempt, I'll set fire to them!"

That next day, Guiscard moved Gregory back into the Lateran Palace and issued postings throughout the city that the legitimate papacy had been restored. The postings also warned that any royalists demonstrating opposition would be severely punished. But this action served only to fuel an already simmering inferno. Having suffered no consequences from their demonstration against Guiscard on the day of his arrival, royalists took to the streets in droves despite Guiscard's sinister reputation, sparking a series of riots and protests that endured several days. King Heinrich had remained civil toward his Gregorian opponents, restraining his troops during protests against him. As a result, royalists assumed that Guiscard would reciprocate. That was a gross miscalculation. Robert Guiscard, unlike Heinrich, was born of black blood; men of such breed crucify reason and defy boundaries.

After a fourth day of mob-driven street confrontations, which grew into city-wide riots, Guiscard determined angrily that the entire city was in full rebellion, giving no more consideration to Gregorians than to royalists. Summoning his captains that next morning, he said, "Assemble your troops. I have something to say." By noon, Saint Peter's Square was bristling with Guiscard's entire military force as he stepped forward to address them. "This city has lost its way!" he declared. "They turned their backs on the true pope, welcoming in his place a heretical German king and a false pope, a sin of inexcusable dimension against God! Go then, I say." Raising his sword toward the Vatican gates, he waved it three times. "The city is yours!" he thundered to his troops. "And so are the people!"

Thus began a three day pillage and slaughter that eclipsed even the horrors the barbarians had committed centuries before when invading Rome. As Guiscard's horde streamed from the Vatican, they spread lizard-like onto the streets and boulevards, weapons drawn, blood on their brow. It was the Roman men who fell under the blade first. Hacking them in place, chasing them down the streets, cornering them in shops and stalls, Guiscard's troops showed no mercy, not even to those professing loyalty to Pope Gregory.

Murder itself did not suffice to satisfy the bloodlust, rather it required sheer brutality in the form of torture, mutilation and dismemberment. Those who were not murdered were maimed, their feet severed at the ankles or their arms cleaved at the elbow. Within hours, the streets were running scarlet as corpses of Roman men were piled one atop another, forming heaps of dead flesh and limbs. Women and children knelt in scattered huddles surrounding these bloody piles, praying and sobbing for lost husbands, fathers and brothers.

Their prayers went unheeded, and by dusk the rampaging troops began to go after the women. Throughout the night their screaming punctuated the blackness as lustful soldiers culled the elderly and unattractive from the ones who were pleasing in form. Those considered undesirable were butchered on the spot or mutilated, attention being given to slicing off breasts and carving genitalia. The others had their clothing ripped away and were held in place spread-legged as man after man after man took turns violating them. When satisfied the women could take no more, the assailants then propped their victims on their knees and gang raped them from behind as their comrades guffawed and applauded, making lurid bestial sounds, mimicking wild animals of every breed imaginable. As this ensued hour after hour, Saracen troops happened upon a Benedictine convent. Having no compunction about violating holy women of the Christian Church, the Muslim troops stormed the heavily reinforced gates and doors, and began dragging terrified nuns from their sleep. Stripping them bare and throwing them to the ground, the Saracens began mounting them, raping them violently, filling them with semen while beating them with merciless intent. In passing, a number of pillaging Apulian and Norman troops happened along. "Ho, there! What's this, by God!" they objected, shocked. "These are Brides of Christ, by damn, and untouchable!"

The Saracens neither understood nor cared. Laughing, they urged the Christian soldiers to join them. Looking about, seeing that they were far outnumbered, several of the Apulians and Normans noticed that a few of the younger nuns were well formed. "Ah, shit," grunted one of the Apulians, shedding his weapons and pulling down his trousers, "they're just women, after all!" Soon afterwards, his comrades followed suit.

As the rampage escalated into its second day without respite, children became the final victims of the troops.

Disregarding age and gender, aroused troops inflicted every form of atrocity imaginable upon the young, even skewering infants and heaving them down wells and into water cisterns. Amused by certain children pleading to be spared, the troops mocked and mimicked their supplication for life before dismembering or beheading them.

Finally, sated by blood and gore, Guiscard's men turned to defacing monuments, smashing public statues, and pillaging historical and religious artifacts. They especially sought cathedrals and rectories, finding them a bountiful source of gold, silver, precious gems, valuable manuscripts, and other forms of wealth. Any priests or monks standing in their path were summarily executed and their corpses flung aside. Then came the fires. Weary even of plundering, the troops set aflame anything they could ignite, including homes, palaces, market stalls, and public buildings. With consideration, they spared churches and cathedrals.

By the end of the third day, as Guiscard's spent troops straggled back to Saint Peter's Square, they left in their wake a scene of inconceivable destruction. Bodies were piled high as cord-wood amongst the smoldering shambles of what was once a magnificent city. Survivors had fled or remained in hidey-holes, leaving the streets devoid of all life and movement, and the once magnificent boulevards had become a wasteland of ash, rubble and ruin.

Such was the fury of Robert Guiscard the Wily, and such was the retribution he exacted when his black blood erupted to boiling. Yet, on that final night as his troops returned to the Vatican, Robert Guiscard reverently entered the Basilica of Saint Peter to pray and light a candle in honor of the Virgin Mary. "Blessed Mother of us all," he said with folded palms, "I have cleansed this city, and returned it to Your Son, our Lord."

Chapter Fifty

Gregory's End

By late afternoon of the day Guiscard unleashed his troops, Odo happened onto the Vatican ramparts with Tristan in tow. Hearing shouting and screaming below, Tristan peered over the ledge. "But what's that commotion down there, Cardinal?" he asked.

Joining Tristan at the wall, Odo gazed down at the streets. "It appears to be yet another riot by the royalists," he said, "and evidently Guiscard had dispatched some troops to restore order." But focusing more closely, shock filled his expression—no large mob had assembled, and there was no massive protest, only murdering soldiers wreaking havoc. "Come along, Tristan," he said with urgency, "we must find Pope Gregory. Guiscard has set his troops against the population!"

They found Pope Gregory in chapel, lost in prayer. Seeing alarm creasing Odo's face, Gregory stood. "Has something happened?" he said.

"God in Heaven," replied Odo, "Guiscard has gone mad and ordered an attack on the city!"

"N-no, that could not be," replied Gregory. "I just served him communion this morning. We knelt together praying for the restoration of peace."

"No, it's true," interjected Tristan. "Come to the ramparts! You will see!"

A short while later Gregory stood quaking atop the ramparts, his lips trembling somewhere between horror and prayer as he surveyed the massacre occurring in the streets. Crossing himself, he wailed, "No! This can't be! God help us! Come along, Odo, we must find Guiscard and end this!"

Hurrying from the ramparts, they discovered Guiscard in the Square conversing with one of his captains. Raising both hands, throwing them onto Guiscard's shoulders, Gregory cried, "Duke Robert! What have you done?!"

"Ah," muttered Guiscard calmly, "you refer to the actions of my troops, I suppose? It's a simple thing, really. The people of Rome, with much effort, have earned my wrath. My patience has run thin, so has their time."

"I implore you," begged Gregory, pulling Guiscard near. "Call your men back! God deplores such wanton violence. And for God's sake, man, much of Rome still supports us! That aside, even our enemies deserve life!"

"Yes," agreed Odo, stepping forward. "We have managed to co-exist for years despite the deep divisions. Even King Heinrich showed tolerance and restraint during his occupation of the city."

"I am not Heinrich," Guiscard replied coldly. "Let the goddamned city rot, and every Roman within it. To Hell with these people, Cardinal, they deserve no more time on this earth. First they denounce Gregory as pope, then defy me as overlord!"

Tristan, from his position beside Odo, settled his eyes on Guiscard. He knew there would be no mercy from Guiscard; that even men as powerful as Pope Gregory and Cardinal Odo would not be swaying the will of this devilish, iron-willed monster standing before them.

Catching Tristan's stare, Guiscard glared. "Have you something to say, boy?" he said.

Though he felt his knees buckle, Tristan stood firm. "Only that God is watching, Duke Guiscard. God is watching."

"Indeed," said Odo, scowling. "God *is* watching, and you shall be *damned* forever! And when this is over, I will solicit a proclamation of damnation on you with the College of Cardinals!"

"Aye, God watches," Guiscard said, a near smile forming at a corner of his mouth. "He's watching me do his labors." Then his expression turned. "Tread lightly, Cardinal, and step back. It's a short dance between where you stand and the graveyard."

"Oh, but God in Heaven!" Gregory exclaimed. "Robert, do you threaten a Cardinal of God? But—"

"I but threaten a *man*," said Guiscard. Turning, he spat. "Be on your way, all of you," he said tersely. "As God's instrument, I've set the wheel and I'll not stop turning it."

After three days of slaughter and pillaging, the streets of Rome fell silent. Slowly, survivors began to emerge and many who had fled the city returned, hearing that Guiscard's rampage had run its course. The casualties and damages were so high that no count was taken other than comparison to the murderous barbarian invasions of old. More disturbing yet was the fact that this rape of Rome was ordered by neither pagan nor heathen, but by a Norman Christian knight in the name of the true pope. Understandably, and as fate would have it, the victims of this horrific onslaught, upon dragging themselves from the ashes and burying the dead, blamed Pope Gregory.

Survivors cursed the Pope, calling for his death. Even former supporters turned against him, calling for the return of Heinrich and the anti-pope to save the city from the False Monk and his Norman henchman, Guiscard. Gregory was himself horrified by Guiscard's butchery and had spent days and nights on his knees, pleading for God to bring an end to the bloodletting. But to the people of Rome, the fact that Gregory was the root of Guiscard's arrival in Rome was unpardonable. Filled with hate, they washed their hands entirely of Gregory and declared him done.

This outcry was so pervasive that Gregory, swollen with remorse over Guiscard's butchery, determined that he should leave Rome, never to return. Under heavily armed escort from Guiscard's troops, Gregory's entourage packed and vacated the Vatican. As they slowly traversed the city and made their way to the gates of Rome, they were forced to now see first-hand the havoc wreaked by Guiscard's Normans, Apulians and Saracens.

All within the entourage were sickened as they passed through these ruins. It was a haunting, ghostly scene, similar to one's imagination of Hell itself. No one was more profoundly disturbed by it than Tristan. He could not keep himself from weeping as he stared in stunned silence at what man had done to fellow man, at what a Christian army led by a Christian general had done to the very center of Christendom itself.

And this was the moment Tristan first heard that haunting sound in his head, a sound that would follow him the remainder of his years—coming from nowhere, striking at traumatic, salient moments such as the one he now faced as he stared from the coach at this Hell on earth. The sound emanated from deep within the back of his brain, slight and slow, rhythmically cantered at first. It pulsed there a while, dimming his vision and forcing him to blink. Then it began to build and deepen in tone.

What is that sound? Tristan asked himself, becoming frightened.

It's a rumbling...twenty or thirty seconds apart...

A cathedral bell?

Indeed, it was the deep, rolling knell of a great cathedral bell, resonating like distant thunder, vibrating in his head, rattling his chest. It came again, just as he peered from the coach, seeing a pile of charred torsos lying in a heap, some missing heads, others missing limbs. Palming his ears, he closed his eyes and winced. When he opened them, the coach had moved down the avenue where stood two small children, bloodied, crying for their mother who lay at their feet, a dead infant clutched at her mutilated breast.

This sight precipitated another knell of the great cathedral bell, forcing him to shut his eyes and cover his ears again as the coach proceeded. When he opened his eyes again, he saw three dead women lying on their backs, stripped naked, legs splayed, their breasts cut away and their genitals mutilated. Again the bell thundered in his brain, and this time he finally cried out. "Oh, my God in Heaven!" he cried, tears streaming down his cheeks in rivulets. "This is not possible!"

"What is it?" asked Odo, startled by Tristan's outcry.

Tristan failed to hear him because the cathedral knell tolled yet again as the coach next came upon an area where the entire avenue was covered in blood, now curdled black. It stained the avenue block after block, as did the gray ash that had blown from the remains of what were once proud structures that made up living and business quarters. Scores of injured lay there, dragging themselves from one spot to the next, unable to walk or even stand, because their feet had been severed above the ankles.

"Where is God in all this?!" Tristan sobbed, slumping onto the seat of the coach, no longer able to bear the scenes unveiling themselves to him as the coach clattered forward.

"What is it, Tristan?" repeated Odo, concern rising.

But Tristan had collapsed into unconsciousness.

"It's the blood," said Guillaume quietly, answering in his brother's place. "And the horror. I am sickened by all this as are all, Cardinal, but Tristan's heart is different than ours. He's stronger in many ways, yet he has a weakness for the suffering of others."

Odo looked at Guillaume and nodded. "Indeed," he said, "you are precise in your words."

An hour later they were out of Rome and Tristan awakened. Sitting up, he looked out and found relief at being far from the city. "Oh, such violence Guiscard's men wreaked!" he muttered. "How could God allow such a thing?"

Odo placed his hand on Tristan's shoulder. "Such is war, Tristan," he said, "and God has nothing to do with it. War is Satan's labor, never forget that."

"B-but Guiscard is on *our* side, Cardinal Odo!" Tristan replied. "He fights for the Pope and the Church. But I-look at what he's done!"

"War is Satan's labor," Odo repeated. "Guiscard did this, yes, but it was all brought on by Heinrich and Guibert of Ravenna. Do not allow tears to distort what stands before you."

Hearing this, Guillaume looked at Odo. "Cardinal," he said, "this may be Satan's labor, but it was performed by Robert Guiscard, the Pope's man. I can't accept reasoning that blames this slaughter on anyone but those who committed it."

Tristan sat upright, taken aback by his brother's forthrightness. "Guillaume!" he said. "Enough."

"No," Guillaume replied, keeping his eye to Cardinal Odo, "not enough. I wish to know whether Cardinal Odo supports the actions of Robert Guiscard, because if he does, then I no longer wish to become a Christian soldier." Turning to Tristan, he said, "Do you not remember our vow, Brother? That we together would fight and stand forever for righteousness?"

"Enough!" Tristan insisted. "Show more respect to Cardinal Odo! He—"

"Guillaume is right," interrupted Odo, "and displays courage for standing firm. No, I abhor what Guiscard has done. It is shameful. But such is the way of war. You are young yet, boys, and will see much more blood in your time. Just never forget, at times war can be avoided, but at times it is the only way, as stated by Saint Augustine of Hippo. This is not a fight over territory, or gold, but a struggle for righteousness. This is the fight over saving the Church and its flock from the grips of a power hungry

German king who would use the Church to his own benefit! No single man is greater than man's faith, or greater than the Church itself. If it takes blood to save the Church, then so be it! Exitus acta probat…the outcome justifies the deed!"

Silence fell over the coach then as the two boys, in their own mind, wrestled with the words they had just heard, and Odo wrestled with the words he had just uttered. These were strong words for Odo de Lagery, and there was something so cryptic about them that they confounded and disturbed Odo himself.

Chapter Fifty-One

The Miracle of Monte Cassino

Gregory's departure from Rome was hailed through-out the city, yet gave rise to rumor and confusion. One story circulated that he had been taken south by Guiscard and abandoned, while another purported he was wandering about, lost and penniless. Yet another story claimed he was dead. Hearing these reports, the bewildered Countess Mathilda sent several parties south from Tuscany to search for the Holy Father, fearing that the ultimate calamity had befallen him.

In truth, after retiring from Rome with many cardinals and selected members of the papal community, Pope Gregory traveled eighty miles southeast to Monte Cassino. When Gregory's caravan arrived, it was Cardinal Desiderius of Monte Cassino who met him at the top of the mountain, waiting there at the gate with other monks of the monastery

"Oh, Gregory, woe is the Church!" Desiderius lamented to his old friend as he dismounted from his coach. "We heard the news about Guiscard's terrible destruction of Rome and anger at its people. But dear friend, how is your heart?"

"Weary, Desiderius, and broken," responded Gregory, his movements lethargic and quavering; testimony that age, trauma and infirmity had taken an irretrievable toll during recent years shut within the Castel Sant' Angelo. "I fear that I am finished."

Tristan heard this, and as he watched the Pope clumsily dawdle his way to the gate with Desiderius, he was struck at how feeble and defeated Gregory appeared compared to the man he first encountered that fierce winter in Canossa. Still, even as the old cleric struggled to move forward, Tristan realized that this man alone, though of humble origins, had stood against the most powerful emperor of all Europe for many years. This, in turn, gave meaning to Cardinal Odo's earlier words in the coach about war.

It dawned on Tristan, at that very moment, that this aged cleric, born Hildebrand of Sovana, son of a blacksmith, was a fearless Christian warrior who had taken on the corrupt clergy, the emperor and an entrenched royal system that had manipulated the use of God for centuries. Even though many of Gregory's efforts had evolved into perversions of themselves, even though he could be accused of brokering his own power and authority, a light dawned within Tristan. Truly, Gregory was an extraordinary hero of a man who had risked everything, even his own life, to defend the Church, which was the only institution where the poor, the uneducated, and the dispossessed masses of Europe could seek hope. And if it took war to carry on this fight, then so be it. If it took rivers of blood to save the world from the avarice and greed of the wicked, like King Heinrich, Guibert of Ravenna or Desmond DuLac, then so be it!

Thinking this, Tristan felt a low tremor rising in the back of his head, that same rumbling that had attacked him while escaping Rome. It was rising again, reverberating like the toll of a great bell slowly arcing upward, thundering its call from the mountain top where he stood down into the valleys and across the opposing peaks. Tristan felt suddenly overcome then, as he gazed out over the vast horizon, witnessing the wonder of God's majestic landscape. Standing there as in a trance, more revelations began to open to him, pouring in one after another.

His mother's beautiful form appeared to him, kneeling in prayer just as she had done a thousand times during his early childhood at Saint-Germain-en-Laye. Then he imagined the Danes: Orla, Crowbones and the others. An image of the beautiful Mala appeared, her dark eyes aglow and her raven hair streaming in the wind. She seemed so near, he reached out for her, but she dissolved, replaced by the White Witch, who was then replaced by King Heinrich, then Robert Guiscard, and finally by Pope Gregory, who in this vision was on his death bed, appearing haggard, barely clinging to life.

Gasping at this image of Pope Gregory, Tristan fell to his knees, gazing fervently skyward. "Oh, God in Heaven," he cried, "I beseech you! Do not let this battle for righteousness end with Gregory's death! Give rise to more champions of the cross like these other courageous men You have placed in my path to carry on this crusade against the evils and terrors of this world! I hear Your great bell thundering across the Heavens, Lord, therefore I know You are there! So hear me, Lord, do not allow the Church to sink into the chasm of kings and war lords seeking to rule Your domain! Help Your people and bring forth new shepherds to tend Your flock!"

Those standing near Tristan as this occurred were struck dumb by Tristan's actions. Then, as they stood there, a deep and wondrous rumble of thunder came from nowhere, shaking the entire top of the mount, sending out wave after wave of vibrations that unsettled all. Feeling them in their feet and in their chests, connecting its inexplicable arrival to Tristan's unworldly trance, their awareness of Tristan's actions heightened. Many soon perceived his trance God-sent, a celestial message of grace.

As they stood there gaping at him, more thunder ensued as Tristan then fell silent and still. Onlookers felt certain he would move shortly, so waited, but seconds turned into minutes, and the minutes themselves began to stretch until finally, Odo stepped forward.

As he reached down to shake him, Pope Gregory cried, "Do not touch him, he communes with the Lord! This is a sacred moment!" Dropping to his knees, the old pope shouted, "He is touched by the Holy Spirit!"

Hearing this, Cardinal Desiderius crossed himself, also falling to his knees, which in turn led others in Gregory's entourage to follow.

Rare, phenomenal occurrences escaping explanation have befallen mankind since the dawn of light. When confronted with such events, man has sought to seek answers within the realm of the 'supernatural'. Herein lies the wellspring of both superstition and miracles, and depending on the beliefs of the witnesses present, the unexplained then takes on one of two directions. If the witnesses are struck with terror, the event is declared witchcraft or bedevilment, and treated accordingly. However, if the people present are struck with awe and inspiration, the event is thought to be miraculous, hailed as a heavenly sign. Those standing atop the crest of Monte Cassino at the moment Tristan was seized with prayer, accompanied by an endless chorus of thunder from a clear sky, concluded that they had just born testimony to a miracle.

History is also filled to brimming with ruses devised by charlatans feeding on the ignorance and superstitions of the masses. But the individuals atop Monte Cassino that day did not belong to the ignorant masses. They were amongst the most educated, intelligent and enlightened men of their era. Within their midst stood Pope Gregory VII, Cardinal Desiderius, Cardinal Odo de Lagery, fifteen other Cardinals of the papal entourage, and nine monks of Monte Cassino. Nor was Tristan in any way a charlatan or trickster. What happened to him was a sudden and unanticipated attack of revelation, one so overwhelming that it physically and emotionally took control of his body. If this is the definition of being 'touched by the spirit', then that is precisely what occurred. As to the strange and ceaseless outbreak of wondrous thunder, only nature could provide an explanation.

But the miracle did not end there. Tristan remained motionless, other than his lips riffling in prayer, all that afternoon while the thunder continued. As the sun finally dropped down into the valley and darkness came, the thunder dissolved, but in its place a strange and distant rumbling rose far to the east. "From the direction of Jerusalem," those on the mount proclaimed. The faraway thunder was soon accompanied by an extraordinary display of distant lightning that fired the entire black horizon. This surreal display of nature continued throughout the night as Tristan continued to kneel motionlessly in place. Members of the papal entourage and monks of Monte Cassino stood upon the ramparts and outside the gate of Monte Cassino until dawn, struck with awe, whispering, at times, crossing themselves.

Finally, the dawn sun broke this stirring spell and Tristan arose, confused, lacking all idea of where he had been or what he had done.

Chapter Fifty-Two

Return to Cluny

After a brief respite at Monte Cassino with Cardinal Desiderius, Pope Gregory decided he would live out the remainder of his exile at Salerno along the southwestern coast of the Tyrrhenian Sea. He was a broken and bitter man at this point, and did not expect to live much longer. He let it be known and documented in writing that, upon his death, the College of Cardinals should select Cardinal Desiderius of Monte Cassino to succeed him as pope. In addition, he cited Cardinal-Bishop Odo of Ostia as the next in line. Furthermore, in writing, he absolved all of his enemies as well as all those who had turned against him or abandoned him—except 'the wicked King Heinrich' and that 'usurper of the Holy See, Guibert of Ravenna'.

Leaving Gregory at Salerno, Odo made the decision that he, Tristan and Guillaume would return to Cluny until such time as Rome might be reclaimed. At the same time, Guibert of Ravenna returned with his army to retake the Vatican in order to continue his role as Pope Clement III. King Heinrich did not accompany Guibert of Ravenna back to Rome, nor did he ever return to Rome again.

It was a forlorn and bedraggled caravan that showed up in Cluny a month later, and as it crawled up the rise to the monastery, the White Witch was on the side of the road waiting for them. "Oh, be damned you who enter these walls!" she cried. "The Black Monks are the army of Satan, and this monastery is their hatching nest!"

Abbot Hugh met them at the gates. As Odo stepped from the coach, Hugh could see that Odo carried the mantle of the defeated. "Come share wine and bread, my dear friend," he offered. "Such a long, tortuous trial for you since my unfruitful journey to Rome to negotiate a settlement, and God has tested you to the limit since then. We have heard about Guiscard's rape of Rome, and about the Holy Father's exile. A crushing blow for Benedictines and true followers of the Faith."

"Yes," sighed Odo, exhausted and spent, "but in prayer there is hope. Though we have lost the Vatican, and though the Cardinals are scattered throughout Italy and France, the Church stands, not in Rome, but in our hearts. Let us pray there will be recovery from all this and that one day we will once again minister from the Vatican. *Dum spiro, spero*...while I breathe I hope."...

Tristan and Guillaume then stepped from the coach, and Abbot Hugh greeted them warmly. "Look at you two," he exclaimed, "no longer boys but handsome, strapping young men! Heavens, Tristan, you must be about fifteen or sixteen now, eh?"

"Eighteen," Tristan said, his voice so deep and rich that Abbot Hugh was taken aback.

"And I'm about to turn sixteen, Abbot," grinned Guillaume.

"Indeed you are!" laughed Hugh, embracing both boys. "It seems just yesterday you came to us as small boys!"

Guillaume nodded and said, "Aye, and Tristan and I would like to look around if you don't mind, Abbot Hugh. Maybe go see the Dorter and the stables?"

"Certainly," Hugh said. "Oh, and Tristan, your friend Brother Fernando has returned to Spain, thank Heaven! He was becoming a handful down in the village, I'm afraid."

As the boys moved away, Hugh took Odo to his chambers and closed the door. "I received your message two weeks ago, Odo, about Tristan. It's a strange thing, I thought at first, and did not welcome your proposal."

"Oh?" said Odo. "I'm surprised. I imagined you would embrace it."

"I said at *first* I did not welcome it. I am still in reflection."

"And?"

Hugh sat down, crossing his arms. "To bypass the novitiate is highly unusual, Odo. After all, the Benedictine Order has long-established practices and rules."

"Ah," Odo smiled, "I didn't realize that!"

"Oh, but you mock me, Odo."

"Perhaps so, Hugh. But it is well known among every Benedictine who has ever graced the walls of Cluny that you, Hugh of Semur, were so graced by the Holy Spirit as a young sixteen-year-old that the recommendation was put forward that you forego completing the full year of novitiate and be declared a Black Monk. Or does my memory fail me?"

"Oh, you setter of snares!" Hugh chortled. "Yes, I was an exception to the rule, as have been only a handful of others through the centuries. But I knew from the beginning that I wanted to become a monk and serve God for the entirety of my existence. Such was not the case with our Tristan. He has always denied the Black Monks. Don't you think it wise, then, that he should spend a year preparing himself so as to be certain? Besides, just what brought on his sudden change of direction, anyway?"

"The Holy Spirit, Hugh, that's what," said Odo. "I witnessed it myself atop Monte Cassino with Cardinal Desiderius and Pope Gregory. Tristan was struck by the Holy Spirit after years of denying the Benedictine Order, and his call was further heralded by a mysterious chorus of thunder throughout that entire afternoon, then by distant thunder and lightning from the East all through the night.

But there's more to it than just that, Hugh. I have been with the boy since his arrival, watched him grow. And so have you. We have both seen his extraordinary gifts, and seen how he shows his love of God through his actions. He is blessed, Hugh, bathed in grace. You said it yourself years ago. Or have you forgotten?"

Hugh shook his head. "No, certainly not. And, yes, the lad is special and holds great promise."

"Holds great promise, Hugh? Oh, come now! We both know that there has *never* been anyone within these walls like our Tristan, so does everyone else. He now wishes, after all this time, after all his experiences, after all he has seen and all he has endured, to become a Black Monk. I am not asking for your permission, Hugh, it has already been given by his Holiness, Gregory, and agreed to by Cardinal Desiderius and myself."

"Well then," said Hugh, "why are we having this discussion, Odo?"

Odo exhaled, giving Hugh a look of affection. "Because I want your blessing, Hugh, and Tristan wants your blessing. He knows you bypassed your full novitiate, and feels unworthy of such an exclusion unless you, Abbot Hugh of Semur, approve."

"Eh?" Hugh said.

"Yes," Odo nodded. "He leaves it to you. But the rest of us feel that he, as you did, has earned the privilege of bypassing the regular novitiate and undergoing a special prayer ordeal, concluding with an open celebration of the mass to formalize his entry into the Order. There is little purpose in the novitiate for him, Hugh, he already knows everything that is taught during that year. He could teach it himself!"

Hugh sat there thinking back to his induction into the Benedictine Order. His initiation had, indeed, entailed a departure from established Benedictine practice. "Very well, then," he assented. "I have often wondered how it was that the boy came to us in the first place, and thought it fate. I have also wondered to what purpose God laid so many gifts at the boy's feet, hoping it was to serve the Church. In retrospect, that is exactly what he has been doing in one fashion or another since arriving here. And finally, I have often wondered what would become of Tristan, but in the back of my thoughts I suspected that he might one day become a Black Monk."

"I did not suspect it, but hoped for it," said Odo. "I prayed on it, in fact; have never ceased throughout these past eleven years, ever since he was burned by the hog oil and God brought him to my eye. And now, Hugh, *hoc erat in votis*…this is the very thing I prayed for."

* * *

Word spread quickly that there would be a special mass for a young man at the Benedictine monastery of Cluny, a young man who would be excused from the one year novitiate required of those joining the Benedictine Order. The last Cluny monk to be awarded such an exception was Abbot Hugh himself, so this announcement created a stir throughout Burgundy, and well beyond. Stories had been circulating for years now about a young boy prodigy within the monastery who had phenomenal abilities in language and academics, and these stories underwent a revival as the date of Tristan's induction approached. Many of the curious even came to the monastery itself, hoping simply to catch a glimpse of this young man who was so blessed.

This curiosity was not restricted, by any means, to the lower classes of the surrounding area or just the religious community. The nobility was equally interested, as there existed within their ranks a certain awe for the mystical and the spiritual. For the Church to make such an exception as this for one individual impressed them greatly. It was through their network that word of Tristan's ordination reached as far as Paris and Normandy.

Tristan was unaware that he had become the subject of such great interest, as he remained confined within the monastery walls. He took up temporary teaching with Brother Loiseaux and also assisted Brother Damien in the infirmary, though he had a weak stomach for blood and suffering. Guillaume volunteered in the stables for a time, but was determined to rejoin Countess Mathilda in Tuscany at the first opportunity that presented itself. He was now more than ready to don armor and assist her cause. Several weeks after his arrival in Cluny, he received good news from Tuscany. Due to Tristan's ordination into the Benedictine Order, Mathilda sent word to Cluny that she would be coming to attend the ceremony, then taking Guillaume back with her to Tuscany.

"She's coming for your ceremony, Tristan!" cried Guillaume, elated. "And she's written that after that, I'm returning to Italy to be knighted! At only sixteen, Brother, imagine that! A Golden Knight of Tuscany!"

Tristan was overjoyed for his brother, not because he was headed to war, but because knighthood had always been Guillaume's dream. Guillaume possessed a burning drive to become a chivalrous and powerful soldier of Christ, protecting the weak and righting the wrongs of this earth. He would, not through the cross, but through the sword, serve God.

Finally, two months after returning to Cluny, Tristan's ordination ordeal was formally commenced. During a solemn, private mass with only Black Monks from throughout southern France in attendance, Tristan was stripped before the altar of the majestic cathedral of Cluny monastery by Cardinal Odo de Lagery. "I shed you of these secular garments, Tristan de Saint-Germain," he proclaimed, "and replace them with this prayer robe of white linen that signifies your purification. Do you willing, therefore, don this robe?"

"Yes, in prayer, I do," Tristan replied, loud enough for all to hear.

"Do you willingly, therefore, present yourself to the Misericord of the Cluny Monastery for a period of three days and three nights of solitude?" Odo said.

"Yes, in prayer, I do," Tristan replied.

"Do you willingly, therefore, submit yourself to prayer and reflection for all that you have done in the past and all that you shall do in the future?"

"Yes, in prayer, I do."

"Do you willingly, during a three day period, agree to flagellate yourself with three strokes of the whip every three hours upon your bare back for the purpose of purifying your soul from past sins and misdeeds?"

"Yes, in prayer, I do."

Odo placed the prayer robe over Tristan's head, arranged it, then gazed upon him. "Go then, Tristan de Saint-Germain, into the Misericord and review your life—past, present and future. Examine your duty and your debt to God. Bare your soul to him within the solitude of the Misericord walls, and come out a follower of Christ!" This last statement Odo proclaimed more loudly than the rest. Five hundred Black Monks from throughout France, in response, began to chant in low and deep rhythmic tones, their voices vibrating from wall to wall and up through the celestial spaces of the cathedral. Then they fell silent and began filing out of the abbey, forming a procession to the Misericord. Arriving at the Misericord door, Tristan entered alone. As he walked to the altar and went to his knees, he heard the door close behind and the lock fall into place.

He looked about room, lit only by three candles, before beginning his prayers. It was bare except for the crucifix hanging behind upon the altar wall, and a vessel of water and three fresh loaves of bread sitting on the altar itself. There was one other article on the altar also, a scourge. On the floor beside his prayer position he saw an hour glass. He picked it up so the sand was in the upper half, then set it down and began to reflect. His first thought was the Misericord itself. He remembered that day he and his Dorter mates had been dragged into this place to face Brother Allaire. He pictured his brother, tiny then, stepping forward to confess breaking the chamber pot on LeBrun's head to keep Letellier and Hébert from being unjustly punished. As this nearly brought Tristan to tears, he shoved the thought aside.

In its place came an image of Scule, the dwarf, and Brother Placidus, now gone from this life. Then he thought of Orla and Crowbones, their hulking frames and dry humor, and FairHair, the handsome one, StraightLimbs, the awkward appearing one who was so tall and gangly, and Guthroth, who never spoke. He remembered that night they massacred the Norsemen. He also remembered the day they delivered him to Cluny, how terrified he was though he tried to appear calm. These thoughts were followed by memories of the scullery, his classes, the hog oil, LeBrun, and other things he had long ago set aside.

It was the face of Mala that weighed most heavily on his mind. He wondered where she might be at this very moment, desperately wishing that he could see her just once more before donning the black robe. *Mala, my very heart since my seventh year in this life,* he thought, his heart aching. Such a strong and beautiful soul, burdened at birth by trials and difficulties, her young heart broken so many times and in so many ways, even by himself. Oh, how he wished he could hold her just once more, and tell her how she had enriched him and lightened his own burdens.

When the final grains of sand within the hourglass attained the bottom half, he turned it, continuing to reflect on his life since leaving Saint-Germain-en-Laye—the trials, abandonment, the loneliness, the blood, the hopes and dreams.

On the third turn of the hourglass, he disrobed and proceeded to the altar to gather up the scourge. It was a simple device: a wooden handle with eight leather thongs attached. Taking the whip in his hand, he struck backwards over his right shoulder, whipping himself. The thongs stung, but he knew that the scourge did its work slowly, and would really begin to take its toll on his flesh by the second day. And on the third day, its thongs would deliver excruciating pain, and his back would be bleeding profusely. He delivered three strokes over his left shoulder, then three more over his right, then returned to his knees at the foot of the altar.

This is when he thought of Asta, that beautiful woman of the striking silver tresses hanging to her waist who had brought him into this life, set him on his path under the tutelage of her teacher-nuns. She had expected much, and also demanded much. He seemed to recall that she bore little patience with misbehavior or lack of courtesy or lack of consideration for others. It also seemed that she had given little to him and Guillaume in terms of affection. He began to pray for her then, and continued to think about her intermittently throughout that entire first day between prayer and the scourge.

He was older now, had experienced suffering, loss and disaster. He had witnessed the evil of men, unquenchable greed, the grab for power and the abuse of the poor. Knowing these things, he had begun to see his mother in a different light. She, too, had suffered, more so than him, even. He began to dissect her life, but it was difficult because he had not seen her since his seventh year; could not imagine how she was now, or even what she looked like. But of one thing he was certain, she would be proud to learn that her eldest son was to become a Benedictine, because if nothing else, Tristan knew that she was a devout and pious woman of the Church. Also, he was educated, as was Guillaume. So perhaps she had been correct in the very beginning, sending them away as she did. She had, as planned, secured for them a better future than the one they were headed for after the execution of Roger de Saint-Germain.

As Tristan reflected, prayed and scourged himself during those three days, pilgrims, visitors and invited guests began to arrive at Cluny in unprecedented droves to attend the special ordination ceremony of the heralded 'Cluny Wonder'. The guest halls of the monastery were quickly filled by families of the highest nobles in France, and even King Philippe sent a representative from his court. The religious of high rank appeared from all over France, from many different dioceses and monastic orders. There were so many, in fact, that Abbot Hugh was forced to place them within the quarters of the Black Monks and even within the Dorters with the students. The cardinals he crammed within his own quarters, and when Countess Mathilda arrived with her entourage, he turned over the Treasury Tower to her. Even King Heinrich, of all people, sent a delegation, out of deference to Abbot Hugh, his beloved godfather. Though the infirm Pope Gregory could not attend, he sent Cardinal Desiderius as his papal proxy.

Guests and visitors of less means were left to their own devices, many of them taking lodging within the town of Cluny, some even settling for stables and barns while others camped on the outskirts of town. This is where a small train of box-wagons from Paris settled in to await the ceremony. This group was not French, but a band of Romani gypsies led by a beautiful young woman of twenty-one named Mala. Word of her striking appearance and lithe dancing quickly spread throughout the town and valley to native residents and visitors alike, which led to ceaseless evening treks of curious spectators who came to the gypsy camp to watch her perform.

"She is the Sister of the Wonder!" some claimed.

"No, she's of a different race," disagreed others. "She was sent for by the White Witch of Cluny to bedevil and place a hex on him, but he overcame it!"

"Ah no," whispered others, "haven't you heard? She was his lover before God struck him with lightning!"

None of this was true. Mala had heard about this ceremony while in Paris. On learning that the monk-to-be was an eighteen-year-old prodigy from Cluny, she investigated further, suspecting that the novice in question was her own Tristan. Her suspicions confirmed, she immediately informed her musical troupe that they would be traveling south to Burgundy to attend an ordination.

She had never forgotten Tristan; had thought of him many, many times since over the passing years. In fact, after his departure to Rome, upon her return from Spain she had moved to Cluny, desperately believing he would return one day. Indeed, she had thought herself so in love with him that she could not live without him. After two years of working in a little shop, staring at the road coming into Cluny, she decided that he would never return. Crestfallen, she moved north to Paris. Yet, even now as she awaited the ordination, she still thought herself in love with him, as foolish at that might be. Regardless, she was driven to see him once more before he donned the black robe of the Benedictines. Besides, who knew what the future might hold? It was not uncommon for priests to 'wander'.

Chapter Fifty-Three

The Black Monk

Finally, the third day of Tristan's ordeal came to an end, just before midnight. The Misericord door was unlocked and Cardinals Odo and Desiderius entered. Tristan was administering his final three strikes of the scourge as they entered. As he set the scourge aside, Odo and Desiderius began to wash his naked body and remove the blood and broken skin from his back. They next laid salve over his wounds.

When they were done, Odo whispered, "It is time, Tristan. Are you ready?"

"Yes, Cardinal," Tristan replied, without turning.

"You are certain this is your chosen path, then?" asked Odo.

"Yes, Cardinal. No doubt remains. God has called and I am prepared." Then a strange moment occurred. Tristan slowly turned, his face flushing red, upon the verge of breaking. "I w-want to thank you, Prior Odo." he whispered. "I know you are a Cardinal now, but it was as Prior that you found me, taught me and saved me. I owe you everything."

A short silence followed as Odo looked at Tristan, their eyes sharing a profound communion of understanding and manly adoration. Odo nodded. "I owe you much also, Tristan. This is not the end, but the beginning. God has not brought us all this way for no purpose. There is much that awaits us both. We must raise up the Church, and raise it up we shall—together."

Odo motioned to another monk who stepped forward with a razor and snips. The monk began to form the Roman Catholic monk's tonsure, shaving a bald circle on the top of Tristan's crown and forming a single ring of short hair around this circle. Tristan, in silence, watched his golden locks fall aside, filtering softly to the ground as if to symbolically announce his renunciation of worldly fashion and esteem.

Another monk handed a black robe to Cardinal Desiderius. Desiderius placed the hooded garment over Tristan's head, pulled it down, and pressed it in place. "Very well" he said, "the procession awaits."

The high mass began at precisely midnight, to signify the end of one period and the beginning of another. As the army of five hundred Black Monks entered the cathedral in columns of four-by-four files led by Cardinal Odo and Cardinal Desiderius, they passed through a double formation of armed knights standing at attention, their swords held high in salute. Tristan was at the end of the monks' procession. And as he passed by the knights, he was surprised to see Guillaume standing there in this line, outfitted with a gleaming Tuscan helmet and vividly adorned hauberk knightly wear, holding his sword high.

"From Auntie Mathilda! My own uniform!" Guillaume whispered, winking.

The procession could barely make its way down the nave as people were thronged elbow to elbow in every direction, and those who had no seats had crowded together squeezing out every available space. Halfway down the nave, though his face and eyes were nearly covered by his hooded black garment, Tristan saw a disheveled man staring at him, his dark eyes agleam. It was Peter the Hermit, and as Tristan passed him, the Hermit gave a gesture and cried, "Help us reclaim Rome, lad! And take us to war against the Muslim horde!"

Upon nearing the altar to the mystical chants of hundreds of Black Monks, the cardinals bowed and moved to their places at the front of the cathedral. Marching behind them, the columns of monks peeled off in opposite directions, taking their places in reserved seats behind pews occupied by cardinals, archbishops and bishops from throughout France, Italy and Spain, all dressed in formal clerical attire that rivaled the finest garb worn even by the many high lords in attendance.

As Tristan himself came near the end of the nave, it was there in the first row of non-cleric attendees that he saw the beautiful Mala. It had been seven years since he had last seen her, but he recognized her immediately. She raised her face upward in an adoring nod of recognition, and smiled. But there was something hauntingly sad in that smile, just as there was something sad in the smile that Tristan returned to her. As he passed, she leaned forward, reaching toward him, and he heard her whisper ever so gently, "I love you, Smart Boy."

When he attained the altar, he went to his knees, crossed himself, and lay prostrate across the floor with arms outstretched, legs together. The mass began then, in the high form, meeting every hope and expectation of every visitor and guest in attendance. Cardinal Desiderius was the mass celebrant, as Pope Gregory's direct Papal proxy, but it was Cardinal Odo who delivered the homily, a stirring plea to follow the word of God, to restore integrity and unity to the Church, and to pray for the young novice prostrate before the altar.

"God has chosen this young soul from many, yet this young soul needs your intercession through prayer!" he said, exhorting the crowd to pray en masse. "God has given us many signs over the years that Tristan de Saint-Germain would rise from the multitudes and serve the Lord, our God, as a shining representative of the Benedictine Order of Cluny, as a shining example of what the Church stands for, as a shining beacon of hope and light and faith!" Odo spoke for nearly an hour, never losing the attention of a single individual within the cathedral. His words enthralled them, inspired them, and made them privately vow to more closely follow the original precepts of the true Faith.

Outside the cathedral, just as Cardinal Odo began this rousing homily, a procession of unannounced wagons began to gain the rise leading to the monastery. There were sixteen in all, accompanied by armed men on horseback. When they neared the gate, a large man and a slight woman clothed in a trailing white, hooded gown dismounted and approached the guards. The guards barred entry at first, thinking that it was the White Witch of Cluny come to disrupt the ceremony.

But the woman presented papers stamped by the seal of Cardinal Odo de Lagery. "We are on our way to the Benedictine convent at Marcigny-sur-Loire," she said, but we are weary and can go no further at this late hour. We were hoping the monastery might provide shelter for us. Then we will be on our way in the morning."

Struck by the woman's beauty, and the long silver tresses that fairly glimmered in the torchlight, the Guard stammered, "There is no room here, my Lady."

"Huh?" said the large man, impatience rising upon his face. "Did you not see that our documents hold the seal of Cardinal Odo de Lagery himself? He is a Cardinal of Rome, you lout, and it's he who sends us to Marcigny-sur-Loire! He was once a Prior here and ran this place, but now he's in Rome with your pope!"

"Rome?" said the guard, looking at his fellow guards. "No, sir, Cardinal Odo de Lagery, he is *here*."

"Here? Odin's ass, you imbecile!" the man replied. "He's in Rome with the Pope!"

"The Pope is no longer in Rome, but in exile at Salerno," insisted the guard, "and Cardinal Odo de Lagery is here in Cluny, celebrating a special mass for the young Wonder of Cluny, a lad by the name of Tristan de Saint-Germain."

At the mention of her son's name, Asta grasped at her heart, stunned. She stammered in disbelief, "D-did you say Tristan de Saint-Germain?" she cried. "Here?"

"Yes, my Lady," said the guard, pointing. "Right there within Cluny Abby."

"Oh, my *God*, Orla!" Asta wailed, collapsing. "Help me! I cannot stand!" Looking at the guard in desperation, she cried, "Is there another boy there? His brother? A boy named Guillaume?"

"Aye," the guard replied, "he's among the Tuscan Guards of la Gran Contessa Mathilda."

Orla reached down and steadied her, but even he was in shock and felt weak in the legs.

"My God, Orla!!" Asta screamed, beginning to weep. "Take me to them quickly, Orla!

Carry me if you must, but take me to them!!"

Orla turned and shouted back to Crowbones and Guthroth. "Boy's here, and so is the Mite! Come quickly, help me with Asta, she can barely stand!"

Of all relationships created and known within humanity, there is nothing as tender or profound or heart rendering as that of mother and child. It is perhaps the act of birth itself that gives rise to this inviolable bond, or perhaps the intense degree of apprehension and concern that women carry for their offspring. Whatever the explanation, Asta was so paralyzed with conflicting grief and joy that the Danes had to hoist her into their grip and drag her along, her feet not even touching the ground for most of the way. During this entire approach to the church, Asta was reduced to gasping, wailing and uttering completely incomprehensible attempts at making words.

The Danes had never seen her in such a state of blithering helplessness, so they themselves began to dissolve, knowing all that their beloved Asta had endured over the years. They knew her heart was flooding with inconsolable emotion as they neared the cathedral, and their own eyes became glazed, filling with emotion also.

"Hold on, Asta, we're almost there!" urged Orla, knowing that her many years of suffering and aching for her sons was now coming to a tipping point.

"Ja, Asta, you'll see them soon!" snuffled Crowbones, helping Orla move her along with his lone arm.

Following behind, Guthroth could say nothing. His heart was in his throat, and he could not manage to utter even a sound.

Within the cathedral, the high mass was nearing its end, and Tristan was instructed to rise. Cardinal Desiderius issued a final blessing. Taking him by the shoulders, he turned Tristan about to face those who had come to share this extraordinary celebration of his ordination into the Order of Cluny Benedictines.

"Go forward, then, Black Monk," proclaimed Cardinal Desiderius, "and perform God's work!"

At this, the procession of monks who had led Tristan into the mass reformed at the altar, led by Cardinals Odo and Desiderius, and began their march back down the crowded nave.

A commotion had broken out in the very rear of the cathedral, as Asta was dragged within by the Danes. The first person Asta saw was Guillaume, but she did not recognize him at first. Then, suddenly, despite his age, despite the uniform, and despite years of separation, she blinked several times and saw in his face the features of the little four-year-old child she had sent away.

"Oh, Guillaume!!" she shrieked, breaking loose from Guthroth and Crowbones and rushing forward. Stunned, Guillaume pushed her back at first. But then, despite not remembering her, despite his years of not even thinking about her, he somehow realized that the delirious woman throwing herself upon him was his mother, Asta.

At this shocking revelation, he unexpectedly dissolved, feeling his knees buckle. Dropping his sword, which had been held at his side in the at-ease position throughout the mass, he reached out with both arms.

"Mother?" he gasped, swept to tears. They threw themselves together in a tight, inseparable embrace, their eyes blinded by the salt of tears that had been so many years in the coming.

Such commotion would have agitated those nearby under most circumstances, but those in the rear of the cathedral witnessing this turmoil fell silent, knowing that something extraordinary had occurred. At the same time, the end of the monks' procession reached the back of the cathedral, and Tristan happened upon Asta and Guillaume. He looked in disbelief as his eyes met those of Asta. Blinking, then feeling as though suddenly thrown into a dream, he stopped mid-step and froze. Unable to breathe, he put out a hand, then the other, trying to call out, but he had no voice, which made him choke into weeping as his legs began to give, leaving him standing there quaking, about to fall.

Asta rushed to him, held him up, then buried him in her arms, kissing every feature of his face and neck she could find. "Tristan!" she wailed. "Oh dear God, it's you!!"

Tristan, still unable to speak, began to shake and tremble, and the tears poured so fast and hot he could no longer see. Finally, he was able to gain enough air that he muttered, "Mother! Mother!"

The Tuscan Guards were at this point unsure what to do about this sudden outbreak of bedlam, and were about to intervene when Odo returned from leading the procession out of the cathedral. Seeing what was occurring, he motioned to the guards to disperse, then herded Asta, Guillaume and Tristan to a side room in the rear of the cathedral so they could celebrate in private an end to a long and unnecessary separation; one contrived by powerful men who had sought to manipulate this family just as they manipulated all other things in their path that interfered with their ceaseless grab for power and authority.

And indeed, thought Odo de Lagery, *it was quite a collection who had broken this family, to include Roger de Saint-Germain, the Bastard, King Philippe of France, and Desmond DuLac. However, it was also power that had brought this family back together. The power of a Cardinal, the power of the papacy, and the power of God's hope.*

Conclusion

A Small Gathering for History

The high mass for Tristan's ordination had begun at midnight and ended by 2:00 AM, which is when Asta had entered the cathedral. Upon reuniting, Asta, Tristan and Guillaume spent an emotion-charged hour of sharing affection and exchanging news with Cardinal Odo, Orla, Crowbones and Guthroth present. Finally, Cardinal Odo led them outside out to the steps of Cluny Abby at approximately 3:00 AM. Nearly all of the four thousand visitors, pilgrims and guests attending the mass had retired for the night by then, but a handful of close acquaintances had remained by the steps of the abbey, awaiting Tristan.

Small, intimate gatherings of lingering acquaintances such as this happen frequently after a celebrated event. Yet, periodically, whether through chance or by design, such gatherings are a portal to the future. In this case, had a portrait been painted documenting the presence of these particular individuals, at this particular site, on this particular night, it would have become one of the most historically fascinating paintings of all time—of whom was present, what they were about to undertake and what stood before them.

Although this gathering was steeped in joy, appearing to be a moment of light and unity, it was in truth the first knell of future's dark wrath. Such is destiny, as thrust upon those who would dare hope to change the world by making it better in their own mind's eye, or their own image.

By way of explanation, let us begin with Cardinal Desiderius who stood speaking to Cardinal Odo that night. Desiderius had no idea that Pope Gregory would die within just ten months. On May 25 of 1085, the decrepit old pope would utter, "I have loved righteousness and hated inequity, therefore I die in exile." Then he would pass into the next life. The gentle Desiderius, as Pope Gregory's designated successor, would become embroiled in such unimaginable conflict and controversy that he would, despite his piety and faith in God, nearly cause the collapse of the Vatican, as well as the Gregorian-Benedictine reform movement itself. In the end, this struggle would have tragic consequences for him, and hasten his end.

This, in turn, brings us to Cardinal Odo de Lagery. Odo would one day be enthroned by the College of Cardinals as Pope Urban II, becoming one of the most dynamic and dominant pontiffs in the history of the Roman Catholic Church. As a man of Godly devotion and prayer, he would deliver one of the most stirring and passionate sermons in history at Clermont, France on November 27 of the year 1095, igniting through words alone one of the most devastating, divisive clashes of race, religion and culture known to man since the dawn of time. This war, despite Odo's holy intentions, would establish inconceivable levels of hatred, intolerance and butchery as Christianity and Islam collided in a bloody clash of annihilation over God and Allah that would extend over the next two centuries.

Also in attendance outside the Cluny Abbey that night was Peter the Hermit, known as KuKu Peter by many. He was destined to become one of the most charismatic and controversial preachers of all time. After hearing Odo's stirring plea for a Holy Crusade to reclaim Jerusalem, Peter would ride throughout France and Germany on his donkey preaching war against the Muslims. As 'told to him by God', he would arouse the spiritual fervor of fifty thousand paupers, convincing them to march to the Middle East to battle the Turks with staffs and pitchforks. This inconceivable expedition would become known as the Peasant's Crusade, and would culminate in an ending of unimaginable consequences.

Mathilda, warrior princess and Gran Contessa of Tuscany, stood upon the steps adoringly watching Guillaume in his Tuscan uniform and Tristan in his black robe. Blind in her allegiance to the Church and the papacy, she would continue to war against King Heinrich and Guibert of Ravenna on behalf of the Catholic faith. She was arguably the first modern woman in history, being educated, independent of spirit, and dependent on no man. Her wealth, military acumen and political influence would continue to straddle the entire continent of Europe until the day of her death.

And then, of course, there were the three Danes: Orla, Crowbones and Guthroth. As promised, they would enter the service of la Gran Contessa in Tuscany, at times placing King Heinrich's army on the run, at times fleeing from it. Although Orla and Crowbones both refused the water, Guthroth would be baptized in Tuscany and become a devout Christian. All three would fight in the First Holy Crusade under the command of Lord Guillaume de Saint-Germain, Royal Knight of the Tuscan Brigade, but none of the three would ever see Jerusalem, for fate would not allow it.

As for Guillaume, he would soon distinguish himself beneath Mathilda's banner in Tuscany against King Heinrich IV, and would within two years command an army of his own, in which Orla, Crowbones and Guthroth would serve. Remaining true to his boyhood vow, Guillaume would, upon embarking on the First Holy Crusade, become the shining ideal of Christian Knighthood, fearsome in battle, generous in peace, and devout in prayer.

Asta was literally aglow on this night outside the cathedral as she spoke to her sons, unable to keep from touching first one, then the other, as if fearing it was all a dream and she might suddenly awaken only to learn that she was back in England. This night was the single most joyous moment of her entire life. Shedding the controlled and frigid demeanor that she had carried since birth, she laughed, smiled, and simply could not restrain herself from showing affection and emotion. It was as if a dark shroud had been lifted from her soul and she had risen from the dead. In several days, she would depart for the convent at Marcigny-sur-Loire to become a Benedictine Sister, spending the remainder of her existence there, content in prayer and reflection, far from the threat of war, far from the hands of men. As a sister of means she would be allowed to receive visitors, and she would see her sons whenever circumstances allowed. She would become a shining example of what Benedictine Sisterhood embodied as she healed the sick, taught the ignorant and fed the poor.

Mala, the gypsy beauty, was also waiting outside the cathedral for Tristan. She, unlike Asta or Elder Heidi, would not spend her existence being victimized by men. Rather, she would set the rules, and in the end recreate herself through an impossible series of events that would spell hardship, tragedy and resurrection. But on this night, upon seeing Tristan exit the cathedral, she embraced him, kissed him violently on the lips, and said, "You know, Tristan, I think we might have fallen in love and traveled the world together, but now you wear the garb of a monk!" Neither Tristan nor Mala realized at that moment that some great wheel had long before set a common course for the two of them, and tethered them for life. Indeed, just as Tristan's destiny would be tied to Odo de Lagery for the remainder of his existence, so also would his heart be tied to Mala, despite the black robe. Of course, it would have been utterly impossible for either of them to imagine that night on the cathedral steps that war, circumstance, religion and politics would pull them apart as their future unfolded, or that these same elements would reunite them as well.

And finally, standing in the midst of this gathering on this propitious night was the gifted young prodigy himself,

Tristan de Saint-Germain, now ordained a Black Monk. If ever God placed on this earth a creature of sensitive and gifted spirit, it was Tristan. In the near future he would follow briefly in the footsteps of Dieter Muehler and Jurgen Handel, moving about clandestinely in the shadows, serving as a papal agent within the Benedictine Underground. But cast into a crisis of faith, torn between the Church and his feelings for Mala, he would be forced to save his soul, or save his heart. As he would struggle through this dilemma, unknown to all, it would actually be Tristan de Saint-Germain, serving as agent of Odo de Lagery, who would actually sow the seeds of the bloody two-century war that was to become known as the Crusades.

This, of course, forces one to wonder once again about KuKu Peter, his prophecies, and his discussions with God.

~*~*~

But, as concerns the specific details and the future of these people standing upon the steps of the Cluny Abbey on this particular night, and how they would begin to change the world...that is an entirely different story entitled: ***Hammer of God.***

Meet our Author
Robert E. Hirsch

Robert E. Hirsch was born in Korea (1949), but sent at age five, by his Korean/Buddhist mother, to his biological American father (an Army captain) in the United States at the end of the Korean War. Post-war Korea was a land of starvation, abject poverty, and political uncertainty, and children of mixed birth were socially shunned. He gained American citizenship at age twelve, having traveled extensively throughout the United States and Europe. In 1962, he was enrolled in a French lycée (grades 8-10), although he could not speak French in the beginning.

At age forty-five, through chance, he reunited with his mother after a separation of forty years, sharing many visits before her death in 2010. The turbulence and circumstances of his upbringing have greatly impacted his perceptions of race, nationality and culture, as well as the themes of his writing.

Since retiring as a public school superintendent (Ocean Springs, Mississippi, 2012), he has become involved in public speaking, educational consulting and writing. His debut novel, *Contrition*, was published in 2012 (JournalStone Publishing), and he is now completing book five (title to be announced) of the The Dark Ages Saga of Tristan de Saint-Germain: *Promise of the Black Monks*, *Hammer of God*, *A Horde of Fools*, and *God's Scarlet Fury*.

"We are each and every one, without exception, caught in sweeping currents of time and circumstance that far outweigh our feeble capacity to repel," says Hirsch, "thus the woe of the human condition, thus the subject of my writing: historical fiction that delves into the human heart and it's enduring struggle to... keep hope alive."

32562114R00310

Made in the USA
Middletown, DE
09 June 2016